I0760374

The Red Maiden

Mark of the Hunter Trilogy - Book Two

Morgan Gauthier

Never & Ever Publishing

The Red Maiden (2022)

Map by Gonzalo A. Mendiverry (IG: @gonzalom.art)

Cover and Character Artwork by Klára Dostrašilová (IG: @artzzofkae)

Edited by Ada Charlesworth

Dust Jacket and Naked Cover Formatting by Xyvah Okoye

www.midnighttidepublishing.com

Library of Congress Control Number:

ISBN (paperback) 978-1-7368282-5-0

ISBN (ebook) 978-1-7368282-6-7

THE RED MAIDEN

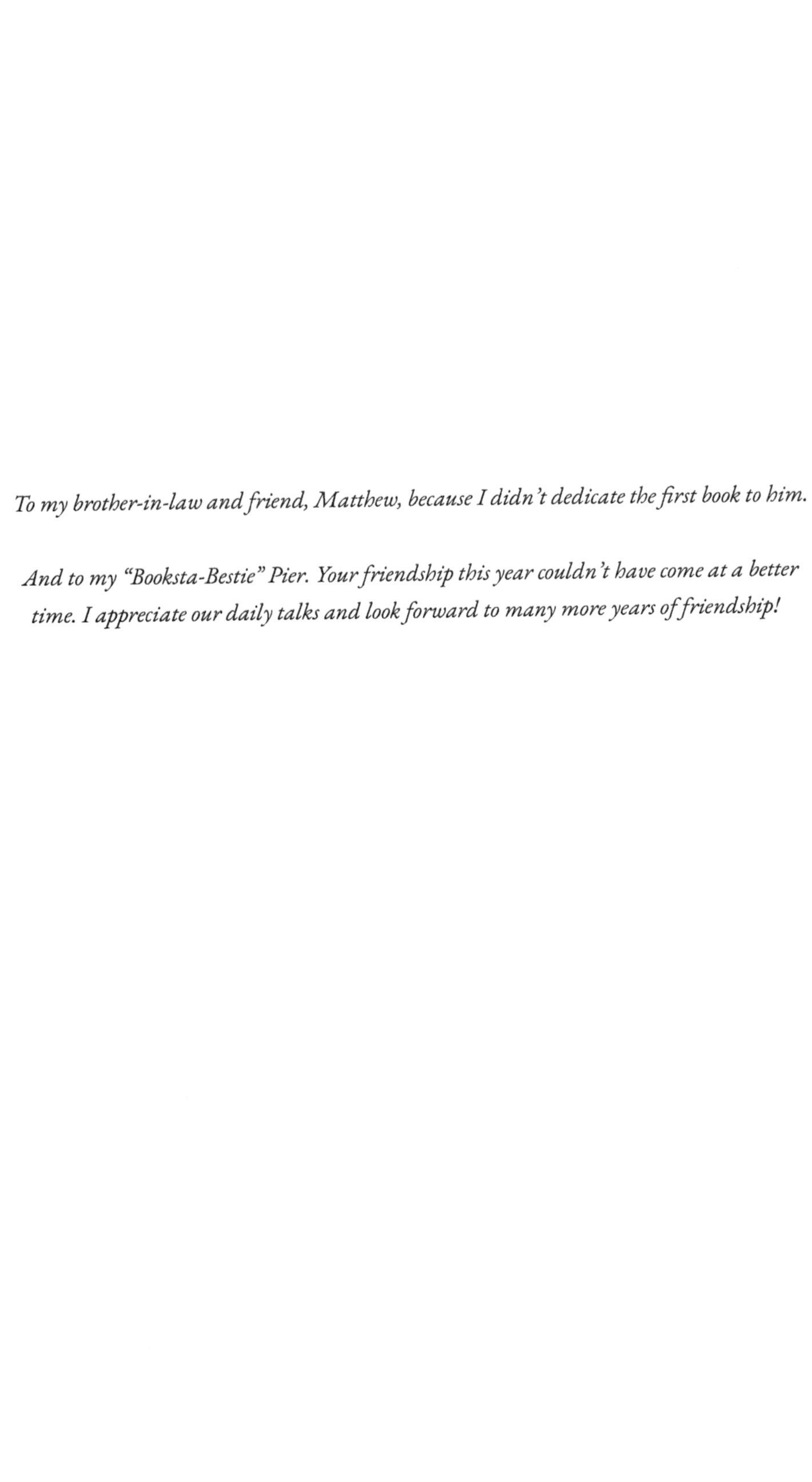

To my brother-in-law and friend, Matthew, because I didn't dedicate the first book to him.

And to my "Booksta-Bestie" Pier. Your friendship this year couldn't have come at a better time. I appreciate our daily talks and look forward to many more years of friendship!

ADALORE

N
NE
E
SE
S
W
W
NW

Taybourne Mountains
Northwind
Caelestis
Petram
Elisor
Black Forest
Oakenshire
Borg
Tree House Forest
Gomorrah
Bone Mountains
Sakurai
Forbidden Forest
The Hollow
Fennor
Valley Pass
The Sisters
Hidden Tavern
Port Daelon
Dead Man's Lands
Enchanted Swamp
Traders Bay
Jannat Sin
Caverns of the Undead
Isles of Myr
Pulau
Numbio

artzzofkae

Kae
artzzofkae

CHARACTERS

Northwind (North)
Niabi, Queen, Mistress of Shadows
Salome, Exiled Princess, The Hunter
Crispin, Exiled Prince
Gershom, Niabi's Second in Command
Pash, Commander of Shadows, Gershom's son
Ophir, Gershom's Brother, Pash's Uncle
Rollo, Niabi's Son, Prince (Deceased)

Borg (West)
Zophar, Crispin and Salome's Guardian

Elisor (Andrago)
Tala, Niabi's Most Trusted Advisor, Oldest Friend
Leoti, Tala's Daughter, Niabi's Daughter-in-Law
Dichali, Niabi's First Husband (Deceased)

Gomorrah
Matildys, Queen
Cyler, King
Thanos, Prince, Ranalda's Twin
Ranalda, Princess, Thanos' Twin
Thrak, Cannibal Soldiers

Sakurai (East)
Jinn, Prince and Heir to the Jade Throne
Kai, Ryoko Naga and Prince Jinn's Protection

Caelestis (Immortals)
Ethereals:
Harbona, Seer
Lavena, High Counselor

The Eldaar, King and Queen of the Immortals, Harbona's parents
Keeva, Lavena's Daughter (Demi)
Bellators:
Kayven, Leader of Immortal Warriors
Abba, Leader of Immortal Warriors

Numbio (South)
Osiris, King
Heru, Prince
Rayma, Royal Healer
Memucan, King's Advisor
Amunet, High Priestess

Isles of Myr
Nym, Queen, Grandmother of Niabi, Salome, and Crispin
Zara, Princess and Heir to Bronze Throne
Bilhah, Niabi, Crispin, and Salome's mother, Deceased
Damaris, Princess and Oracle of Myr
Mika, Princess and Red Maiden
Marina, Princess
Utara, Mika's Daughter
Seraphina, Qata Vishna, Rosalina's Twin
Rosalina, Qata Vishna, Seraphina's Twin

Pulau (Misfit Island)
Uri, The Pirate King
Nezreen, Shadow Wielder
Palma, Diviner

The Sisters (Blind Order)
Neempo, Sovereign
Penn, Master of Keepers
Balor, Master of Witnesses

Crew Members of the *Shadow of Death*

Haldane, The Captain

Rahab, The Stabby One

Corwin, The Quiet One

Phex, The Explosives One

Ondrej, The Giant One

Rafi, The Pint-Sized One

Leeondris, The Missing One

Members of the Order (Rebel Force)

Oden, Leader, formally known as Lord Maon

Nubis, Stormcrag

Ziggy, Call Girl from Borg

Makeda, Manages *The Whispering Fox* Tavern

Stormcrags (Mountain Men Tribe)

Cato, Scout

Torrin, Leader

Oifa, Torrin's Right Hand

Krazaks (Mountain Men Tribe)

Gerd, King of the City of Bones

Rune, Militia Leader

Hanzo, Rune's Right Hand, Archer

Orn, Giant Warrior

Other Characters

Adonijah, "The Wanderer"

Odelia, Enchantress of the Swamp

Vilora, The Old Witch of Endor

Diron, Captain of *The Golden Rose*

Anaktu, The Last Nephilim, Niabi's Iron Guard

Prologue

Niabi - 14 Years Ago

Niabi trudged through the snow; every breath she exhaled was icy and stung the back of her throat. Winter was upon them. She never liked the winter months. Her father used to blame her dislike for the cold on the Myridian blood in her. But that was not the only reason she despised it.

Antilles. Dichali.

Niabi tightly pulled her enormous black fur coat across her chest to shield her from the brisk and brutal winds that whipped through the Black Forest. There would be time to truly mourn her dead, but first, she had to amass her army.

Deep in the woods was a well-hidden encampment of exiled Northern soldiers loyal to Gershom, the disgraced former friend and commander of Issachar's army. Stripped of his distinguished titles and life of grandeur, Gershom embodied his House Sigil and was now only known as The Bear. She was going to meet with him whether he liked it or not.

Dressed head to toe in a black robe and fur coat, Niabi strutted through the camp and entered Gershom's tent with an air of confidence that did not go unnoticed by the men scattered around bonfires trying to keep warm. With Tala the Andrago and her Nephilim bodyguard following a step behind, she stood before the brute she had spent a year tracking down. Her eyes scanned the back of the tent and stopped when she saw Gershom sitting on a humble, some would even deem pathetic, wooden throne.

Ophir, Gershom's younger brother, stepped toward her with his hand extended to halt her approach. "Bow before His Lordship."

Anyone who came to visit The Bear would kneel before him, intimidated by the mere sight of him. But Niabi knew her place as Queen of the Andrago, born of both Northern and Myridian royal blood, and with a vicious glance in Ophir's direction, she refused to bend the knee.

Gershom's eyebrows raised and he leaned forward. "You do not kneel." It was not a question.

"I bow to no man." Niabi stood her ground, maintaining eye contact with him.

"You will bend the knee one way or another," Ophir snorted as he reached for his sword.

Before Tala could unsheathe his sword, Niabi had already exposed her twin daggers hidden up her sleeves and held one against Ophir's neck.

"I said," Niabi hissed, "I bend the knee to no man."

Gershom waved them to stand down. "Forgive my brother. He is as zealous as he is loyal."

Niabi's narrowed eyes darted from Ophir to Gershom. She retracted her knives and lifted her head up higher. She was not one to be threatened or challenged. That was now clear to everyone in the tent.

With Ophir safely by his side, Gershom sipped his wine and oscillated his gaze amongst the three newcomers with disgust. "You march into my camp with a Horse Lord, and this damned monstrosity," he pointed at Anaktu the Nephilim with his goblet, "and upon first meeting me, threaten my brother, and insult me."

"Surely, a man with your reputation is not so easily offended," she sneered. "If so, the Green-Eyed Raven has been told falsely about your abilities."

Gershom licked his dry lips and smirked. "I have heard about you. You're prettier than I imagined."

"Should I take that as a compliment?"

"Take it as you wish." He placed his empty cup down on the armrest of his chair and leaned back. Pressing his palms together, he raised his hands to touch his chin. "Tell me, Niabi, daughter of Issachar -"

"Niabi, Queen of the Andrago," she corrected.

"You deny your Northern birthright?"

"I deny the man who denied me."

Gershom motioned for Ophir to bring a chair for Niabi. She watched Ophir as he carefully placed the chair in front of her, but she did not sit.

"What do you want?" Gershom asked.

"I have come for your allegiance." Her eyes returned to The Bear.

"Allegiance for what?"

"To kill the King of the North, of course."

Gershom and Ophir exchanged a bewildered look.

"Word has reached me of your husband's untimely death -"

"You mean his assassination," she interrupted.

Gershom cleared his throat as Ophir refilled his cup. "I know more than most your hatred for Issachar..."

"But?"

"But to plot his murder, is suicide. It cannot be done. Not that it should not. It cannot."

Niabi flipped the bottom of her fur coat behind her and sat down in the chair Ophir had offered her moments before. She stared deeply into Gershom's eyes until he blinked. She pointed at the three scars on the side of his face.

"Those scars, ordered by him, were they not?"

Gershom rolled his shoulders back and tilted his neck to the side until it cracked loudly. "Yes."

"Your ancestors' land, your title, your wealth – stripped. Your family forced into exile, ordered by him?"

His eyes narrowed as he leaned toward her, hands resting firmly on his knees. "I am sure you will make your point quickly."

Niabi crossed one leg over the other, revealing her leather pants. "Does revenge not interest you?"

"I have my methods of repaying him."

She scoffed. "You burn his crops and pillage his outlying villages and for what? He does not lose sleep over such nuisances." She slowly leaned forward and whispered, "You are nothing more than an irritating fly and eventually, he will crush you as such. We both know this." She watched him squirm in his seat. "Everyone fears something. Let's be what they fear."

Gershom laughed and straightened up in his seat. "Issachar does not fear me, nor your Andrago." He once again flashed a disgusted glance Tala's way.

"Maybe not," she shrugged. "But he does fear me - the daughter and rightful heir he tried to silence."

Gershom's face brightened at the realization of what she really wanted. "You don't just mean to kill him. You want the White Throne."

"And I will have it. Even if I have to burn his entire kingdom to the ground to get it."

"You would have us battle the North?" Gershom offered her a drink.

"Men go to battle." She refused the drink. "Women wage war."

Gershom sipped his wine in silence. "If I should join you – what is in it for me?"

"Pledge your allegiance to me and I will give you what Issachar wouldn't."

"Which is?"

"Second of Northwind." She knew by the look on his face she had won him over. "More wealth, power, and splendor than you can imagine."

Gershom's lips curled. "How do I know I can trust you?"

Niabi stood, grabbed the cup he had offered her before, and downed the wine. "I do not trust you. But the enemy of my enemy is worthy of my friendship."

"All this because he denied you?"

"My reasons are my own." She set the goblet down. "Are you with me or not?"

Gershom stood and stared down at her with a twisted grin. "Ironic, is it not, how you look so much like your mother, yet your father's words flow from your lips."

Niabi's eyes narrowed, and her nostrils flared. Her fingertips flirted with the blades hidden up her sleeves. She glared at him. "Careful. Unlike my father, I am not afraid to wear your blood like war paint."

He smiled. "And that is why you may very well survive." He lifted his cup. "To the Queen of the North."

Chapter One

Crispin

Crispin opened his eyes and looked around the dark hovel. The last thing he could remember was being rushed down the River of Lost Souls. From that moment on, his memory was foggy.

He touched the loose long-sleeved white shirt that rested on his chest and realized he was not wearing his own clothes. He ripped the blanket off and sure enough, an oversized pair of brown pants had replaced his.

A fire was crackling near the bed he rose from. The entire house was one small room. There were no windows and only one wooden door to allow entrance and departure. As he paced around the foreign space trying to find a clue as to whose house he was in, he noticed freshly lit incense burning on a tiny wooden table in the center of the room. He spotted his clothes on a chair in the corner and eagerly put them back on, deciding it would probably be best for him to sneak out of the hovel before the owner returned. As he reached for the latch, a woman abruptly entered carrying a basket filled with freshly baked bread, fruit, and cheese.

Crispin had never seen anyone quite like her before and could not help but stare. Her brown complexion was flawless. Long, plum hair draped the right side of her body, while the left side of her head was clean-shaven, showcasing nearly a dozen ear piercings. Shorter than him by a foot, the petite fortune teller with haunting dark eyes and exposed midriff wore a stunning teal-blue robe adorned embellished with gold jewels. Her bare and dainty feet were adorned with toe rings and anklets.

The prince was clearly taken aback by her foreign beauty, but she did not seem to mind, as if she knew his thoughts were innocent.

"I see you have recovered." Even her accent was unlike any he had heard before. "You must be hungry. Come, sit, eat." She placed the basket of goods on a large, patterned rug surrounded by plush and colorful pillows as she sat cross legged in front of him. "Come."

Crispin did as he was told, confident that if he were in danger, she would not have taken the time to nurse him back to health. She extended a piece of bread to him, which he gratefully accepted.

"Who are you?" he asked.

"You are more concerned with who I am, rather than where you are? Interesting." Her eyes, outlined in smudged black kohl, danced as she continued eating the grapes that overflowed from her basket.

"Of course, I want to know where I am," he retorted, mouth full of food. "I suppose I was more curious as to why you helped me."

She glanced up at him. "You were in need of help, so I helped."

Such a simple answer. "What is your name?"

"Why do you wish to know?" She fiddled with her nose ring.

"So, I know who I am thanking."

"Why must you know me to thank me?"

Her questions frustrated him. "Listen, I am just looking for some answers. The last thing I remember, I was in the River of... I was in a river -"

"The River of Lost Souls." She knew more than Crispin gave her credit.

"Is that where you found me?"

"You found me."

"What?" Crispin raked fingers down the side of his face, more confused than ever.

"Your body floated to our shores, so I brought you inside before the others could find you."

"The others?"

She lowered her voice to a barely audible level. "You are in Pulau."

If he was not concerned before, he was now. Pulau was a cluster of small islands inhabited by bloodthirsty pirates, greedy gypsies, fortune tellers and halflings. Known as 'Misfit Island' to most Adalorians, Mainlanders stayed far from the wild, over-crowded kingdom

"Who are you?" Crispin asked again cautiously, wishing he had looked for his weapons sooner.

She pointed to the fireplace mantle where he caught sight of the handle of his sword resting inside a blanket. "My name is Palma," she revealed, sensing his anxiety. "I had a vision you would be coming. That is why I found you before the patrol did."

Crispin leaned back and arched one of his eyebrows. "You aren't going to turn me in?"

"If that were my intent," she nibbled on a slice of cheese, "I would have done so."

Her answer was acceptable. "How do I get off this island? I need to get back to my company."

"There is but one way, Crispin, son of Issachar, and that is by finding the Shadow of Death."

His breathing quickened. "How do you know my name?"

Palma smiled and brought out a folded up wanted poster from underneath one of her pillows. "I am not the only one who knows your name."

"Tell me what I need to do."

"I will take you to *The Dancing Lady* by the western docks. There you will find your way to the captain of the fastest ship in Adalore. He will help you escape Pulau if you agree to his terms."

"How will I get there unnoticed?" He scratched the fresh stubble along his jawline. "You said it yourself, there are other people looking for me."

"Put this on." Palma tossed a dark, hooded cloak to him. "If you keep your head down, no one will pay you any mind."

Crispin held the cloak but hesitated before putting it on. "What do you get for helping me escape?"

"I have already told you," she smiled, "you were in need of help, so I helped."

"The money on my head has no appeal to you?" He folded his arms over his chest, skepticism in his eyes. "I highly doubt you would risk your life sheltering me just for the satisfaction of helping someone in need."

Palma's eyes shifted toward the floor. "You are right, Prince Crispin, there is something I desire."

"What is your price?"

"There are whispers that you wish to take back your father's throne." Her toes tapped the floor. "If that is so, when you become King of the North, I ask that you allow me and my parents to live in the White City."

His eyes widened. That was not what he expected her to ask for. "You wish to live in Northwind?"

"My parents are growing old and are quite ill." She grabbed his hand. "I ask for a new life for us; a safe place where I can care for my family without fear."

Crispin's gaze softened and he gently squeezed her hand. "I wish I could give you more than just my word but -"

"You word is all I need." She patted his hand with a new-found hope. "Put the cloak on and we will be on our way."

As soon as Crispin's face was hidden, the duo made their way through the narrow, winding wooden streets. Pulau was composed of several small islands that had numerous canals running through the kingdom. The city looked as if the cliff-like terrain had fused with old wooden ships. The old-world structures were connected by ladders, suspended bridges, and ramps. Had Palma not been guiding him, he never would have found *The Dancing Lady*.

"Keep your head down," she whispered as four patrolmen turned the corner.

They were not at all what he expected. Not one of them resembled a soldier. One was skinny to a frightening degree with a hook nose while the other three sported tremendous beer bellies. Crispin could have sworn one of them was cross-eyed and wondered how he was able to even walk straight.

"*Those* are patrolmen?" he scoffed, clearly unimpressed.

"They might not look like much, but even rats bite." She motioned for him to keep quiet.

They passed the squad without prompting a second glance as they made their way through the humid city. *The Dancing Lady* was heard before it was seen. Dozens of tipsy sailors with semi-attractive, disheveled women hanging on their arms, were carrying on outside the tavern's signature red door. Loud piano music played daily, spurring the bar wenches to dance on the tables, making it popular amongst pirates.

Palma stopped abruptly. "This is where I leave you."

"Leave me?" Crispin whipped around; eyes wide. "What do you mean? You aren't coming inside with me?"

"I will no longer be of use to you, my lord." She leaned in as if to kiss his cheek and whispered, "Keep to yourself and find the Shadow of Death."

He wrapped his arm around her. "I swear your kindness will never be forgotten."

With a nod and one last smile, Palma disappeared into the bustling street, leaving him to continue his journey solo.

Crispin pushed his way into the crowded bar and sat on a stool at an abandoned table. While ensuring his hood was low enough over his face, he observed the pirates rustling about. Sitting quietly, he went unnoticed until the plump tavern owner came over to him.

"Kin I get ye anythin', sailor?" His chubby cheeks were flushed, and beads of sweat dripped down the back of his hairy neck.

Feeling compelled to blend in with the locals, he nodded, and in a muffled voice said, "Aye, a pint of ale."

"Comin' right up." The balding barkeep waddled away with a tray full of empty cups.

Crispin exhaled a sigh of relief but was still unsure of how he would find what or who the Shadow of Death was.

Suddenly, the pirates crowding the door parted, allowing three newcomers to enter without having to push their way in. The two men were accompanied by a woman wearing pinstripe trousers. As they walked up to the bar, three drunks gave up their stools.

The pirate on the woman's left was of average height with eyes as blue as the sea. The sides of his head were shaved. A strip of auburn, shoulder-length hair ran down the center of his head. Two thick strands of hair rested on either side of his black eyebrows and his chiseled face was framed with very little facial hair. Two silver cuff earrings graced his right ear and a hollow, circular pendant rested upon his hairless chest. Although he was consumed in a cloud of smoke from his reefer, Crispin could tell that under his navy, knee-length coat, he was heavily armed.

The pirate on the right had broad shoulders, wavy, black, chin=length hair which was mostly covered by a beige and red bandana. His cheeks, collarbone, and both arms were tattooed in the ancient runes of Pulau. The beastly seafarer was muscular from head to toe and carried at least six different types of knives in his leather belt.

The woman's brown complexion was as beautiful as Palma's. Her short, slick-back hair was icy blue, but her eyebrows were black. Her athletic arms were adorned with several gold pieces her crew most likely plundered. Unlike her heavily armed companions, she only carried a gold and ruby encrusted dagger which was tucked in her belt. By the way she carried herself, Crispin could tell she was more dangerous than her male counterparts.

Crispin watched the trio as an intoxicated sailor boldly, or stupidly depending on how one looked at it, marched up to the three newcomers. Puffing out his unimpressive chest, the drunk pirate leaned in and smiled at the female mariner.

"Lemme buy ye a drink," he burped.

The woman did not bother to look in his direction. "I have a drink."

"C'mon," he persisted. "Lemme treat ye."

She sipped her ale. "Get away from me."

"No need to be 'ostile," he turned toward his three mates and chuckled. "It's just one drink, milady." He bowed in exaggerated fashion.

She set her tin mug down. "I'll give you to the count of three to leave."

"And if I'm still 'ere at three?" He clicked his tongue at her with a wink.

"Stick around to find out."

The drunk laughed. "Ye got spunk, lass. I like that in me women."

"She told you to leave her alone," the blue-eyed pirate barked, a glint of violent mischief in his eyes. "Or do you not understand basic tongue?"

"Phex," the bandana wearing pirate said in a warning tone.

"Corwin," Phex hissed in response, eyes narrowed.

"A pretty lass like 'er wouldn't 'urt a nice fella like me." The drunk ignored the hot-headed pirate and placed his hand on the female's lower back.

"One."

"Uh oh! She's countin'," he smirked at his giggling buddies.

"Rahab." Corwin shook his head.

"Two."

"I suggest you leave," Phex warned him one last time.

"I ain't goin' nowhere."

"Three." In one swift motion, Rahab turned, pushed the drunk sailor away from her, unsheathed her dagger and stabbed him in the upper thigh.

"Ah!" he screamed. "Ye stabbed me!"

Rahab ripped her knife from his leg and wiped the blood on his pants. "You're lucky I didn't take your hand for putting your greasy fingers on me." She eyed his friends. "Get him out of my sight before I lose my temper."

As if nothing had happened, the trio turned their focus back to their drinks as the injured sailor was dragged out of the tavern leaving a trail of blood behind him. The music resumed and the rosy cheeked bartender hustled back to Crispin with a sticky goblet of ale.

"Who are they?" Crispin tilted his head toward the three buccaneers.

The bartender knew who Crispin was referring to and reluctantly whispered, "Corwin is the big one, and from what I hear, owns over a hundred knives from all over Adalore.

Phex, is the one smoking; some say he has a crazed mind, inventing all sorts of unholy things. And the woman is Rahab. That's a black-hearted pirate if I ever saw one."

"It seems like everyone in here is afraid of them," Crispin said, still watching the three pirates from afar.

"Ye must not be from 'round here," the barkeep sighed, his arms beginning to shake from the weight of his tray. "They're crew members of the *Shadow of Death*. Not to be messed with, they are. Dangerous bunch."

"Did you say the Shadow of Death?" Crispin hid his excitement and kept his voice low.

"Aye, fastest ship in Pulau. Stay as far from them as ye can. No telling what they might do to ye for sport." Afraid they might catch him gossiping, he rushed back to his bar to tend to his other patrons.

Crispin took a sip of the warm ale and nearly spit it out. Pushing it away, he knew he wouldn't be finishing it.

He found where he needed to go, but was it really the only way to get out of Pulau? While mulling over his options, the trio stood up and left the tavern. He had to make a decision: either follow them like Palma had instructed or find his own way off the island. He rolled his eyes and sighed. He was going to trust Palma. Hopefully, he did not find himself on the other side of the female pirate's blade.

Crispin slapped a coin on the table and tailed them from a safe distance as they walked down the ramps to the main harbor where their ship was docked.

From the exterior, the *Shadow of Death* was everything the name led you to believe. It was a black wooden ship with gold trim and skeletons mounted on the bowsprit. The black sails sported their emblem of a murderous mermaid etched in gold, ensuring once you saw them coming, you would know exactly who was chasing you.

He watched Phex, Corwin, and Rahab board the sleek ship and with a deep breath, he walked up the ramp. When he stepped foot on the main deck, the pirates he had followed were nowhere to be seen.

"What is your business here, stranger?" A voice boomed; catching him off guard. "Or have you lost your way?"

Crispin turned toward the odd voice and saw a halfling standing there. His straw-like, snow white hair was pulled back into a stubby ponytail. His moustache and beard ended in perfect triangular points which accentuated his round, sun-burned nose.

"I asked you a question," the pirate growled.

"I came to request an audience with your captain." Crispin's shoulders tightened. He lowered his head to make sure his face was shadowed in the safety of his hood.

"That can be arranged." The short pirate smirked as he motioned another crew member forward. "Ondrej, watch him. He wants to see the captain."

Ondrej was at least six-foot-eight, dark skinned, and had exceptionally long dreads all pulled into a bun atop his head. His bulky biceps were bigger than Crispin's thigh. The mere sight of him struck fear into the hearts of most men.

Crispin wondered if he made a mistake by boarding the *Shadow of Death*.

A few agonizing minutes later, the captain, followed by the halfling and the trio from the tavern, marched down the steps from the officers' quarters.

"Rafi tells me you're looking for the captain."

"Is that you?" Crispin asked, trying to keep all the pirates' names straight.

"I'm Captain Haldane," he nodded. "But by the looks of you," the captain sneered, "you're on the wrong ship."

"Is this the *Shadow of Death*?" Crispin asked, hood still covering most of his face.

"Aye," Haldane nodded, "that it is."

"Then I am on the right ship."

Haldane's raspy laugh echoed across the deck. "Do you know who we are, boy?"

"Pirates?" Crispin was confused by the question.

The captain roared in delight at his ignorance. "Pirates? We're not just pirates, lad! We're the Masters of the Seas; feared by Mainlanders and seafarers alike." He looked Crispin up and down. "If a job is what you seek, we don't need ye. If you wish anything more of us, look elsewhere."

"But -"

Haldane's narrow eyes flashed. "You're lucky, boy, that I'm letting you walk off my ship intact. Now get off before I throw you off." His shaggy blonde hair blew in the wind as he turned to head back to his quarters.

"I need your help," Crispin shouted.

"Did you not hear what I said, lad? Pirates aren't in the business of helping."

"I was told that you would help me if I agreed to your terms." Crispin took a step forward and stammered, "Perhaps... perhaps there is something you need that I can help you with?"

Haldane grinned, exposing three gold teeth. "I like you."

"So, you will help me off the island?"

"No." Haldane motioned Rahab forward. "Show the boy off my ship."

"Gladly." Her smooth-as-honey voice hypnotized Crispin for a moment as she glided toward him with every intention of throwing him overboard.

In a last-ditch effort to get Haldane's attention, Crispin grabbed Rahab, unsheathed the ruby encrusted knife from her hip, and held it against her throat.

"Don't move or I'll kill her!" Crispin stared intently at the green-eyed pirate. Testing his bluff, Haldane stepped forward only to stop as soon as Crispin pressed the knife into Rahab's neck, drawing blood. "I said, don't move."

"You've made a grave mistake, stranger." Haldane growled as he held his hand out to stop any other crew member from advancing.

"I need to get off this island," Crispin demanded through gritted teeth, "and you are going to take me where I need to go."

Haldane placed his hands on his hips. "And tell me why I would take orders from a faceless man on my own ship?"

Crispin yanked the hood off. "I am Crispin of Northwind; if you help me, I will see to it you are handsomely rewarded."

Haldane recognized the rogue prince the North was hunting. "You have my attention."

"You're hurting me," Rahab mumbled.

"Quiet, Rahab!" Haldane spat. "What is it that you want from me, Crispin of Northwind?"

"I was separated from my company and must rejoin them."

"Say I do what you ask." The captain stroked his scraggly beard with a smirk. "What's in it for me?"

"Enough gold for you to retire," Crispin promised.

"How do I know you're good for it?" Haldane tilted his head. "There is a hefty price on your head. Why not just take Queen Niabi's gold?"

"Do you actually believe she would pay such a sum? What would prevent her from executing you on the spot?" Crispin raised a good point. "I am good for the money; you will just have to trust me."

"Trust you?" Haldane cackled. "We trust no one, that is why we survive."

"Yet you will put your faith blindly in a black hearted queen?"

"Better a rich queen than an exiled prince."

"Palma was a fool for sending me here," Crispin muttered under his breath in frustration.

"Did you say Palma?" Rahab seemed surprised, rattled even, hearing Palma's name.

"Palma sent you here?" The captain's voice softened and if Crispin read his face correctly, he would have sworn Haldane's eyes were filled with longing.

"She told me you would help me, if I agreed to your terms." Crispin was cautious. He did not want to endanger Palma's life unwittingly.

"Well," Haldane hesitated, "that changes everything."

"How do you know her?" Crispin's eyes narrowed.

"Let Rahab go, and I'll answer your questions."

"No," he twisted Rahab's arm, "tell me how you know her."

"Twist my arm again and I'll rip your balls off," Rahab hissed in his ear.

"I'll tell you what you want to know," Haldane raised his hands and motioned for him to lower the weapon. "Just don't hurt her."

Crispin was taken aback by the captain's plea for Rahab's safety, so he loosened his grip. "How do you know Palma?"

The pirate took a deep breath. "She is my wife."

"Your wife?" The prince nearly choked.

Rahab seized her opportunity to escape his loosened grasp. She swept Crispin's legs out from under him and pinned him to the ground, her knee digging into his chest.

"Stop!" Haldane shouted. "None of you will lay another finger on him." The seafarer waved for Rahab to get off him, then helped Crispin to his feet. "Come. We have much to talk about."

Crispin extended Rahab's dagger to her as she stood up. "I believe this is yours."

She snatched it from him with a snarl. "Touch me again and I'll slit your throat."

Haldane led Crispin to a set of stairs. They could go up or they could go down. Instead of going up in the direction the group had descended when coming to meet the prince, they went down. They walked through a wood paneled hallway past the crew's bunks and the infirmary until they reached an arched opening where Haldane motioned for Crispin to follow him inside.

"Take a seat," Haldane tossed his hat on a long mahogany table. The sunlight streaming through the portholes lit the dining room. The scullery was just across the hall and Crispin could smell salted meat and a stew brewing.

Crispin obediently sat in a small chair opposite the middle-aged captain. After pouring himself a drink from the wooden wet bar, the pirate eyed the prince with great sadness.

"How is she?" he whispered.

"To be honest, Captain, I only recently met your wife and spent very little time with -"

"Did she look well?" Haldane pressed.

Crispin nodded. "She appeared well to me."

"Palma and I have been separated for several years now. She didn't approve of my choices..." The captain stared at his glass and tilted it back and forth to watch the liquid inside dance. "I'm not the man she deserves. Most days, I regret choosing the sea over her. Today, is one of those days."

"Perhaps you should tell her that," Crispin suggested.

"Aye, perhaps." Haldane snapped out of his depression, running his ringed fingers through his scraggly blonde beard. "But first, I will do as she promised I would. I owe her that."

"So, you will help me?"

The pirate downed the rum and poured himself another. He offered a second filled glass to Crispin. "Under one condition."

"What is your price?" Crispin accepted the glass.

"She is a clever diviner; she knew we needed to meet." Haldane shot the second serving and set the glass upside down on the wooden table. "My price is one rescued life for another."

"I'm afraid I don't understand."

"The *Shadow of Death* has never been boarded by an enemy, except for one time many years ago. I was a new captain, foolish and brash, and because of me stubbornness, we were overrun by the finest vessel from Borg. The commander of that ship was a young, fresh-faced boy who was under strict instructions to capture our ship and bring me to his king to be tried for me crimes against the West. To me surprise, he didn't arrest me – he befriended me and decided to let us go." Haldane leaned back in his chair. "He claimed his king had wronged his family and he had no intention of obeying any more of his commands. We abandoned his crew in rowboats, sunk his ship, and he joined us. After a few years learning our ways, he became more than just another pirate, he became family."

"What happened to him?" Crispin shot his drink and coughed; the rum burned his throat.

"He left. Unfinished business. Now word has reached my ears that he has been imprisoned, but by whom I am not entirely sure. Some say the Westerners finally caught up to him, others claim Gershom of Northwind had him imprisoned for attempting to assassinate him. No one knows for sure. That is where you come in, my new friend."

Haldane's smile made Crispin uneasy. "I will get you out of Pulau, but before I return you to your companions, I need you to help us find Leeondris. I owe him."

"A pirate with a heart," Crispin chuckled, more nervous than anything. "Not at all what I expected."

"Even pirates live by a code, Prince." Haldane extended his ring filled hand to him. "Now, do we have a deal?"

Crispin realized he did not have much of a choice if he wished to make it off 'Misfit Island' in one piece, so he shook the pirate's hand. "We have a deal."

Chapter Two

Salome

To the Sea, to the Sea,
The Sea is calling me.
Her mighty waves, her shapeshift ways,
The Sea is calling me.
All hail our Queen, she set us free,
Yet the Sea still calls for me.
When I breathe my last, send me to Death,
The Sea has called for me.

Salome did not have many memories of her mother, Bilhah, but the one memory she remembered vividly was on the nights she could not sleep; her mother would climb into her bed, caress her head, and sing her Myridian lullabies. As they sailed to the Isles of Myr, Salome found herself becoming more anxious. The only way to calm her ever-racing mind was to sing to herself, like she did growing up in the Tree House Forest. During her brief moments of peace, she felt as if her mother was still with her.

Every story Bilhah told her children about her homeland awakened a desire in Salome to one day visit the Isles of Myr. Maybe she could even learn to fight like the Qata Vishna. In Northwind, women were not permitted to learn about weaponry or politics, nor were they allowed to join the king's army. But the Isles of Myr was different.

It was known to the Mainlanders as 'The Woman's Kingdom'. Myridians were ruled by women. Their borders were protected by female warriors. Women owned and operated all businesses and if there was trading to be done, it was to be done with a woman. Property was deeded to females only and passed down to the firstborn female heir.

What of the men? was always the question kings of other Adalorian kingdoms would demand to know.

And according to the Myridians, the answer was simple: Men were good for breeding and not much else.

After Malachi the First established the Kingdom of Myr, he appointed a king who stripped women of every basic dignity a human could have. They were treated as property – bought, sold, and traded. Being forced into servitude, raped, or beaten to within an inch of their last breath was common.

But one woman, named Arsinoe, stood up to the first and last King of the Isles of Myr.

Women outnumbered men three to one and in an act of defiance, they joined Arsinoe and waged war against the self-proclaimed stronger sex. For seven days and seven nights, the newly banded female warriors burned the tyrannical king's castle to the ground, sparing the king himself for their queen's blade. Queen Arsinoe beheaded the oppressor who persecuted them and established a new reign. A better reign.

After the war, men were free to choose to bend the knee to the queen or face the executioner's blade where Death could gladly have them.

For nearly a thousand years, women had ruled the Isles of Myr and the Adalorian rulers respected and feared angering the Qata Vishna.

Originally, five islands comprised the Isles of Myr, but Vilora sunk Endor, so only four remained. Single Myridian men were kept on Bullmar, while married couples raised their children on Antrope. The third isle, Delta , was used explicitly for training unmarried women for the Qata Vishna. And of course, the fourth and main island was Capitol, where all business and governing matters were conducted.

That was all Salome could recall her mother telling her. The small room on *The Golden Rose* started to feel cramped. She inhaled deeply and exhaled rhythmically. She was used to being around men. Now she felt as if she was being sent into the lion's den and she wasn't sure if she was going to walk out unscathed.

She twisted her brother, Lykos's, Myridian ring around her right index finger and closed her eyes.

"To the Sea, to the Sea, the Sea is calling me..."

The quick rap on the door startled her.

She cleared her throat. "Come in."

Adonijah entered, eyes heavy. He had not slept much due to seasickness. He and water were clearly not compatible.

"Still not feeling well?" She could not help but feel sorry for him.

He shook his head and slowly laid on the second cot, placing a damp cloth over his eyes. "I am already dreading the journey back to the Mainland. If I were not committed to you, I would consider staying."

Committed to you. The phrase gave her goosebumps. Salome knelt at his bedside with a feline grin. "I don't think you'd like to stay in the Isles of Myr forever."

"Oh," he mumbled. "Why is that?"

"Because." Salome plopped an elbow on the bed and rested her chin in her hand. "The Isles of Myr doesn't look favorably on *your* kind."

Adonijah lifted the towel exposing one eye. "And by my kind, you mean... handsome?"

She rolled her eyes. "Male."

"Ah, yes." His eyes twinkled of mischief. "I've heard all of that before."

"But?"

With great effort, Adonijah turned to his side and supported himself on his elbow. "I'm sure I can change their minds."

Salome laughed softly. "Is that so?"

"What?" He flashed a wry smile. "You don't think my charm will win them over?"

"And what charm would that be?"

"The same charm that won you over."

Adonijah's smile had not worked on her before, but this time it sent a sudden sensation of warmth through her body. Her lips parted as if she had a witty rebuttal, but nothing came out.

His eyes softened as he rested his hand on top of hers. "I'll take your silence as a good thing."

"Adonijah, I -"

Harbona burst through the door with excitement smeared across his face. "We are approaching the Isles of Myr -" He stopped when he saw how close they were. "Am I interrupting something?"

Adonijah cleared his throat and rubbed the nape of his neck.

"No, Harbona." Salome stood and wiped her hands down her pants. "We were just talking."

Harbona's eyes shifted back and forth between them. If he had something to say, he kept it to himself. He motioned for them to follow him. "You should come upstairs, approaching the Isles of Myr is not a sight to miss." He turned to head back to the upper deck.

"Maybe I should stay here," Adonijah said softly, his eyes meeting hers. "I'll see it when I see it."

"Are you sure? We can help you." She motioned for him to get up.

"He's gone." He nodded his head toward the door.

Salome whipped around and sure enough, Harbona was gone. "Then I can help you."

"If it's all the same to you, Princess," he rested his back against the wall, "I'd prefer to be down here."

"Please."

He was taken aback. "Please?"

She closed her eyes and pinched the bridge of her nose. "I could use some company."

"Harbona is -"

She cut him off. "Please."

That was not a word she used too often, and she had used it twice in the span of seconds. Her hesitation of using the word was not because she lacked manners, but because she was used to doing things for herself, by herself. She found herself in a world she was uncomfortable in. A world that had seemingly forgotten all about her. And now, she knew she needed support. Needed help. Needed a friend. Maybe even something m ore.

She blinked rapidly, realizing she had been staring at him. Longing for him. But then she noticed he was looking at her differently too. His eyes. So mysterious and yet so telling at the same time. His lips, his arms. Her eyes scanned down to his slightly opened shirt. His chest, his ...

"So, what do you say?" she asked, shaking those thoughts free from her mind.

Adonijah inhaled; his tight lips curved into a smile. "You think I'm handsome?"

Salome's eyes widened and her heart raced. "What?"

"Earlier, when you said 'Myr doesn't look favorably on my kind' and I said, 'by my kind you mean handsome?'" He cocked his head to the side. "You didn't deny it."

Salome had never been in this position before. She was rarely lost for words. She stammered, hoping she could string together even the feeblest of sentences. But all she managed to say was, "Maybe I didn't want to hurt your feelings."

The sides of his eyes crinkled when he smiled. "Thank you for sparing my feelings."

"You're welcome." She crossed her arms across her chest, shifting her weight. She cleared her throat, "So, will you...?"

"Go with you?" Adonijah planted his feet on the ground and stood up. "How could I not?"

The warm southern sea air enveloped her as she made her way to the upper deck. Crystal clear blue water crashed against the side of the ship, rocking it gently. Salome turned back to look at Adonijah, expecting him to be leaning over the railing ready to barf, but he stood tall with his mouth agape. Her eyes glanced in the direction he was looking and landed on the bustling capitol city of Myr.

Salome's eyes scanned from the white sandy beaches of the shoreline up the coastal cliffs where the ancient city was built. Cypress trees lined the stone streets that spidered through the kingdom. Tales of her mother's homeland painted Myr to be beautiful, but that was severely understated. There was truly no architectural rival in all Ten Kingdoms of Adalore.

Wine, spices, and bronze were in high demand from the Myridians. One of the few memories she had of her father was his thorough enjoyment of Myridian wine. She was allowed a sip as a child and had held on to the bold taste hoping one day, she would have a glass to herself.

The castle was built at the top of the cliff overlooking the sea and other small islands belonging to the queen. The rest of the city was built into the side of the same cliff. With the sun beginning to set, the Alhambra stone glowed red, and Salome finally understood why the castle was called the Scarlet Citadel.

"Are you alright?" Adonijah asked.

Salome inhaled deeply, stifling a cry. "My mother used to describe her homeland to us, and I always wanted to visit when I was old enough. I just wish she were here with me."

Adonijah rested his hand on top of hers after she gripped the railing. He did not need to say anything – she could feel his compassion the moment his hand touched hers and she breathed easier.

As the ship neared the harbor, she saw a royal committee waiting on horseback for their arrival.

Salome glanced at Harbona who joined them. "A royal convoy?"

Harbona smiled. "They knew to be expecting us."

"Who are they?" Salome's gaze returned to the bronze armored soldiers with Myridian blue and green banners wafting in the sea breeze; the Myridian sigil of the octopus etched into each with gold thread.

Harbona motioned to the woman positioned at the front of the pack. "That is your cousin, Princess Mika."

"Her armor is different than the others."

Salome was right. In fact, Mika was the only warrior in Myr who did not don bronze armor. Hers was red.

"They call her the Red Maiden."

"Why?"

"Since the reign of Arsinoe the First," Harbona explained as he lit his pipe, "there has always been a Red Maiden. She is the fiercest of the Qata Vishna – unbeaten in combat."

"Is she the Red Maiden until she dies?" Cato joined them. Now clean of the clay and blue paint that was caked on his body, and now dressed in traditional Mainlander clothes, he looked like an entirely different person.

"Traditionally." Harbona nodded at him and exhaled a puff of smoke.

Adonijah's interest was piqued. "What does that mean?"

"There is a Red Maiden that still lives but does not don the red armor." Harbona shifted his weight, as if he didn't want to say more.

"Who?" Salome asked.

Trumpets blasted as the ship docked.

"A story for another time." Harbona extinguished his pipe.

Harbona trotted down the ramp with Cato beside him, the Stormcrag's short, cropped, white hair gleaming in the sunlight. It appeared the Seer had taken quite a liking to Cato and spent most of the voyage catching up on the feud between the two Mountain Men clans. Salome, too, found Cato's people extremely interesting, and also terrifying. Hopefully, they wouldn't be running into the Mountain Men anytime soon.

"Salome?" Adonijah stood behind her, waiting for her to follow Harbona, but she was frozen in place.

"What if she doesn't like me?" Salome whispered.

"Who?"

"The queen."

"Why would she not like you?" Adonijah circled in front of her and lowered his head to meet her eyes. "You're her kin."

"Blood is fickle that way."

Adonijah reached out and squeezed her hand gently. "She will like you."

"You really think so?" Salome steadied her rapid breathing, maintaining eye contact with him.

He nodded. "Once she accepts you for the stubborn pain in the ass you are, she will love you."

She swatted at his arm and laughed. "You're horrible."

"Someone has to keep you humble," he shrugged with a grin.

"And you're an expert on being humble?" She rolled her eyes and planted her feet on the ramp to join Harbona and Cato at the bottom.

Adonijah followed closely behind her and whispered so only she could hear, "I am not just an expert on being humble."

"And what else are you supposed to be good at?" she teased.

"Apart from being an excellent swordsman?"

"Sure," she agreed sarcastically, "apart from that."

"I suppose if I'm as humble as I say I am, I'll have to let you tell me."

"I hope you also excel in patience," she snorted, "because that doesn't seem very likely."

"We will see." Adonijah flashed his mischievous smile. "We will see."

The four Mainlanders found themselves standing before a host of seven warriors on horseback. Up close, they were much taller than they had looked from the safety and distance of the ship. The craftmanship, detail, and feminine fit of their bronze armor was both impressive and enviable. Their helmets framed their olive and brown faces, and it was then Salome realized each of their head gear had different designs etched into it: flowers, sea creatures, landscapes, prayers, and tales of Myridian history.

The Red Maiden slid down the side of her armored white horse and greeted Harbona with a warm smile. "It's been a long time since you've visited our shores, Seer. It is good to see you."

"We thank you for your hospitality, Your Highness." Harbona bowed, then extended his arm to his companions. "This is Cato, Adonijah, and Salome of Northwind."

The Red Maiden's eyes rested on Salome. Green eyes. Myridian royalty were known for their green eyes and Salome had always wanted them. She suddenly became extremely aware of her two different color eyes and diverted her gaze from Mika's.

Mika tilted her head, "Welcome home, Cousin."

Home.

Such a simple word, but the concept seemed foreign to her. She had been forced to escape Northwind when she was five years old. She had been forced to escape the Tree House Forest just a couple of weeks ago. Was she going to be forced to flee from this new home too?

Harbona cleared his throat when Salome did not respond.

"Oh uh," Salome bowed her head. "It is good to be... home."

"Come." Mika remounted her steed. "You are expected at the Scarlet Citadel."

As soon as their horses had disembarked *The Golden Rose*, and they bid Diron and his crew goodbye for the time being, they joined the royal convoy weaving through the city streets. The path to the palace at the top of the seaside cliff zig zagged uphill from one side of the village back to the other side until it reached the peak. The breeze was much cooler up top, and the view was more spectacular than Salome could have imagined.

The Mainlanders were escorted inside the Scarlet Citadel. Salome thought the façade of the castle was breathtaking, but once inside, she was rendered speechless by the architecture. She stopped and turned in a full circle to admire the intricate lace-like carvings in the walls, archways, and columns made of stucco. The floors were a mixture of smooth stone and colorful mosaic tiles. The indoor-outdoor living aspect was what stuck out to her the most. She had never seen anything like it. In Northwind, the White Keep was a solid fortress with designated entrances and exits, even those leading to the impressive gardens. But here, she could not tell which rooms were considered indoor versus outdoor. The ceilings were either open to see the clear blue sky or were covered with mahogany wood with notches etched into it so light still streaked through to the floor.

How did mother give all this up for Northwind?

It was a haven. Every window boasted a dreamy view of the sea or of the Paraiso Gardens: a wonder of the known world. What she would give to wake up to a view like this every morning. Maybe she could. She shook her head, rattling that thought free. She was there for a reason and then she would leave for the next phase of the journey. She closed her eyes and listened to the waves crashing along the shoreline, the trickling of the countless fountains in and outside of the palace, the laughter of Myridian children running through the city streets... peace. It was the peace she craved. The type of life she longed for. The life she would most likely be denied.

As they continued to make their way through the palace, she noticed a small group of foreign dignitaries, consisting of mostly men, that looked like they were from the Eastern Lands. Their fine silk robes, their black hair, and their alabaster skin spared from the sun's scorn. She had never seen citizens of Sakurai before and found them to be not only a fascinating people, but beautiful as well. In fact, the man leading the entourage was dangerously attractive.

As if her thoughts had pierced through his head, he turned to meet her gaze, and flashed a handsome smile her direction. Her eyes darted to the floor, and she tried to regain her composure.

"Is everything alright?" Adonijah whispered after hearing her gasp.

She blushed, "Everything is fine."

He shot a glance down the hall and chuckled, "Have you not seen Easterners before?"

She shook her head, internally muttering every curse word she knew because Adonijah had caught her staring. "No. What do you suppose they're doing here?"

Adonijah shrugged. "Trade, diplomatic mission, marriage proposal... Who really knows with them?"

"Curious."

"What is?"

"They're mostly men. I only saw one woman with them."

"They aren't like Myridians, Princess. Women don't run things in Sakurai."

"We're here." Mika interrupted their conversation.

They had reached double bronze doors at the end of the hall. Mika took her helmet off once they reached the doors and saluted the guards who stood watch.

Mika extended her hand which halted the men from advancing. "Men are not allowed in the Inner Depths."

Salome looked at Harbona, slightly panicked. Harbona nodded his head reassuringly; his kind eyes motioned her to follow Mika.

"Wait here." Mika instructed the three men and escorted Salome inside.

Salome silently followed Mika through the bronze doors, and she found herself walking down a long colonnade hallway. Neither side of the passageway had walls. It was open to the queen's private gardens filled with red carnations, pomegranate flowers, bluebells, and gazanias lining the graveled pathway. Cypress and olive trees shaded the stone patios and ornate bronze statues and billowing fountains. The breezeway was about a hundred feet in length, with red roses creeping up the colonnades, and led to a second pair of female warriors guarding another set of double bronze doors. These doors were different than all the other doors in the palace. Carved into them was the Myridian Sigil of a giant octopus with its tentacles crushing a ship.

The doors opened without Mika breaking stride. In the center of the Inner Depths was a rectangular pool of clear, still water with water lilies floating on top. In the reflection, Salome could see a woman seated on a throne which was set on a dais a few feet off the ground. Salome's, eyes rose from the water to the royal, but realized the woman before her couldn't be her grandmother. Although older, she was not old enough to be the queen.

"So," Zara's voice echoed, "you are the daughter of Issachar of Northwind." Although her foreign accent sounded melodic, her expression was chilly.

"And the daughter of Bilhah, daughter of Nym, Queen of the Isles of Myr." Salome responded, meeting Zara's menacing glare.

The room was quiet. Zara stared at the Mainlander, who looked very much like a Myridian, deep in thought before an odd smile stretched across her face. "You favor her."

"Thank you." Salome knew she was referring to her mother. She bowed slightly, not familiar with the traditional customs she was supposed to adhere to. "Forgive me, but I was under the impression I was going to see my grandmother."

Zara stood and descended the steps to get a closer look at Salome. "The Queen is indisposed. I am Princess Zara. Your mother was my younger sister."

Salome had noticed the similarities between Zara and her mother as soon as she entered the room. Long, dark hair, olive skin, green eyes, and their thick Myridian accents. The only difference was her mother's face was soft, kind, and gentle; Zara's face was hard, defined, and burdened.

"Tell me," Zara stood a foot in front of her. "Where have you been all these years?"

"My brother, Crispin, and I have been living in the Tree House Forest in the Western Lands."

"Instead of coming here?" Zara frowned. "Why?"

"It's where Zophar took us."

"And Zophar is...?"

"Our guardian."

Zara shook her head and looked her niece up and down. "He took you to live amongst boorish peasants instead of your own kin."

Salome could feel Zara's judgment oozing with each word she spoke. "How else would we have been safe?"

"The Myridians would have protected you. You bleed our blood." Zara's nose tipped upwards.

"And if my sister would have discovered you were harboring us and demanded you give us up, what would you have done?" Salome snorted indignantly. "I may have been a child when we escaped Northwind, but I am no fool. Northwind's fleet could overrun Myr without a problem."

"To attack the Isles of Myr would be foolish." Zara's eyes narrowed, her voice a bit higher in tone than it had been before. "Niabi would not dare bring war to our shores."

"Perhaps, you underestimate her."

"And perhaps," Zara clasped her arms behind her back, "like your mother, your tongue will land you in trouble."

Salome shrugged. "I'm used to trouble."

Zara smiled, which took Salome by surprise. "You were born in Northwind, but you are Myridian through and through." She motioned Mika to step forward. "Mika will see to it you have the finest rooms and robes while you stay with us."

"What of my companions?"

"You speak of the *men*?" Zara crinkled her nose.

"Yes."

Zara turned and made her way back toward the throne. "Naturally, they will stay in Bullmar, the male side of Myr.

"I would request they stay with me."

"Request denied." Zara's head nearly whipped off her neck when she turned to look at Salome. "Men are not allowed in our halls."

Salome stepped forward. "Unless they are foreign aides or dignitaries which permits them to stay in the Hall of Ambassadors."

Zara was clearly caught off guard by her niece's knowledge. "How do you know of the Hall of Ambassadors?" She shot her daughter, Mika, a cold look but was met with a shake of her head, denying any part in Salome's request.

"So," Salome chimed in, "they can stay in the Hall of Ambassadors?"

Zara growled, eyes still on Mika, "See to it her companions are accommodated." Her eyes floated down to Salome. "Rest, Niece. We will meet again soon."

Their first meeting was over. Mika led Salome back through the bronze doors they had entered. Once the doors were closed behind them, Mika finally spoke.

"How did you know of the Hall of Ambassadors?" she whispered.

"I saw men from the Eastern Lands head to a separate hall of the palace. By the look of their robes, I assumed they were ambassadors and were an exception to the rules. In Northwind, we had a Hall of Ambassadors, so I took a gamble you had one too."

Mika chuckled. "Very clever. My mother will be irritated the rest of the day that you outwitted her."

Salome blushed, "Your mother?"

Mika nodded, "Princess Zara is my mother."

"I hope I haven't offended you -"

"Sometimes she needs to be reminded she is not the smartest woman in the room." Marina interjected.

Marina was Mika's younger sister and was on her way into the throne room when she met them in the breezeway.

Mika side eyed her sister. "Salome, this is my sister, Marina."

"It is nice to meet you, Cousin." Salome bowed her head to pay respect.

"Tell me," Marina ignored her pleasantries. "The man in your company -"

"You will have to be more specific, Marina," Mika interrupted her with a snort. "There are many men in Salome's company."

Marina brushed off her sister's comment. "The handsome one with a pipe and leather gloves. What's his story?"

Salome's blood boiled and her cheeks instantly flushed. Upon first meeting Marina, Salome could tell she didn't like her a bit, and it wasn't just because of Marina's interest in Adonijah. The way her cousin carried herself, the smugness of her head tilt, the mischief in her eyes – a girl trapped in a grown woman's body. She desperately wanted to tell Marina to stay away from him, but Mika kindly beat her to it.

"He's young even for you, Marina."

Marina huffed and crinkled her nose. "I'll have you know, if I wanted him, I'd have him."

"Perhaps, you overestimate yourself, Cousin," Salome steadied her voice. "Unlike Myridian men, Mainlanders are aware of their options."

Mika stifled a laugh. Marina's eyes narrowed. If she had a weapon in her hands, she might have challenged Salome, but Marina was not the warring type.

Marina composed herself and flashed a disingenuous smile. "Enjoy your stay in Myr. With any luck, our paths won't need to cross again." Marina stormed past them; her hands balled into fists.

Salome's gaze went from Marina's back to Mika's awaiting eyes.

"It seems I've been here a few hours and already I've offended both your mother and your sister."

"If you are about to issue an apology, don't." Mika clicked her tongue. "Marina deserved every word. And believe me, it's good for her." They pressed onward back to where her companions were waiting for her. "Now, out of curiosity, what is the mercenary to you?"

Salome was caught off guard by Mika's question and her knowledge of Adonijah's profession.

"Don't look so surprised." Mika smiled, "I've been to the Mainland before and have seen my fair share of sell-swords. So, what is he to you?"

Salome's cheeks flushed. "A hired sword." Even she did not believe the words that just spewed out of her mouth.

"Surely he is more than that." Mika kept her gaze fixed on the bronze doors ahead of them, nodding to the guards on this side of the breezeway to open them. "I saw the way you looked at him when you arrived to our shores."

Salome's breathing quickened and the tiny hairs on her arms rose. *What was Adonijah to her?* He might have started off as a sell-sword in the tavern but now he seemed to be more. He had to be more. The way she felt around him, the way he looked at her. But that didn't matter. She couldn't be distracted by him. She had a job to do and even he couldn't come before that.

The doors opened at the end of the hall and her eyes immediately met Adonijah's as he leaned against the wall smoking his pipe.

She felt a tingle surge through her body and for that moment, she wished she could read his thoughts. Mika was right. They had a connection. There was no use in denying it. But she was unsure if he felt the same way.

Mika cleared her throat, snapping Salome from her racing thoughts. "I see." Mika turned her focus to her young cousin.

"See what?" Salome refused to look Mika in the eye, afraid she would see right through her.

"Do you know if he feels the same for you?"

Salome shook her head. "Maybe it's better that way."

Once they reached the others, Mika motioned her arm down the hall to their left. "I have been instructed by Her Highness Princess Zara to show you to your rooms in the Hall of Ambassadors." Mika stated matter of fact. "Follow me."

Harbona's eyes darted to Salome, and he smiled. "Now, how did you manage that?" he whispered as they trailed behind the others.

"It's a gamble Crispin would have taken." She smiled.

Harbona nodded with a grin. "Good girl."

Salome hadn't thought about Crispin in a few days. She tried not to. But remembering his risky antics tugged at the corners of her mouth. She muttered a prayer for him under her breath and put him out of her mind. If she kept thinking of him, she would certainly break down in tears.

Mika swept her arms toward two doors on either side of the hall from each other and announced, "These will be your rooms for as long as you stay with us. You three," she spoke to the men, "will share these quarters." She pointed to the room on her left. "And this room," she looked to her right, "will be for you, Cousin. If you should need anything, do not hesitate to ask. Your ladies in waiting will make sure you have everything you need while here in Myr."

Harbona stepped forward and bowed, crossing his right arm across his chest. "You have been most generous. We thank you."

Mika nodded, "Get some rest." She walked back down the hall and once she turned the corner, Salome opened the door to her room.

Her mouth dropped once she saw her private balcony's view of the water. Clear sky, blue seas, and nothing but the horizon in the far distance. She teared up; it was the view she had dreamt of for years. And the room itself was massive.

This is bigger than our entire treehouse, she thought to herself.

White linen draperies, thick rugs, pillows of all shapes and sizes scattered around the room. It screamed luxury. Luxury was something she was not accustomed to anymore. She walked into the adjoining room and sank in the enormous bed, big enough for four people to sleep in comfortably, and exhaled a sigh of relief. She would definitely get a good night's sleep tonight.

There was a knock on her bedroom door.

"Come in." She pushed herself up from the bed to see who entered.

"I see you haven't wasted any time getting comfortable." Adonijah opened the door and peaked inside.

"Is this not the most beautiful sight you've ever laid eyes on?" She squealed in girlish delight and jumped up from the massive bed.

"One of them." He smiled and followed her as she ran past him to the balcony attached to her living and dining area.

"You have to see this view."

Adonijah joined her, but instead of admiring the view, his eyes were glued to her. "It's beautiful."

Salome closed her eyes and soaked in the sun beaming down on them, the sea breeze gently whipping the loose strands of hair around her face, the scent of salt and native flowers enveloping her. She was home. *Home*. She prayed she was home.

"Did you tell them?" Adonijah's voice snapped her back to reality.

"Tell them what?" she asked, looking over at him.

Adonijah rested his arms on the railing next to her. "About your eye."

Salome shook her head and frowned. "It didn't come up."

"Are you afraid of telling them?"

"No." She hesitated. "Maybe."

"Do you think they'll support -"

"You're asking a lot of questions," she interrupted him. Just when she finally had a moment of peace, she was dragged back to reality, back to the issue of who she was: the Hunter.

Adonijah straightened up from the railing. "Apologies, Princess. I'll be across the hall if you need anything."

He stepped inside, but she grabbed his arm. "I'm sorry," she said, "I know you mean no harm."

"You're right," he said softly. "I was asking a lot of questions; you have enough on your mind."

"I promise, you aren't what is upsetting me." Her eyes met his and she could see nothing but kindness in the brown eyes that looked back at her.

"I know." Adonijah scratched his jawline and shifted his weight. "As long as you are alright."

"I will be."

They stared at each other in silence until Adonijah said, "I should let you rest. It's been a long day." He turned to leave.

"Adonijah."

He spun around to face her. "What?" he whispered, standing close to her.

"Why did you come with us?"

"What do you mean?"

"I've been trying to figure it out since we met you at the tavern." Salome rubbed her hands together, squaring her shoulders to his. "Harbona didn't offer you any money, but you came with us anyway. Why?"

"You really want to know?" Adonijah's eyes floated from her mismatched eyes to her lips.

"Yes," she breathed softly.

Adonijah's hand glided up to her face and he gently tucked loose strands of hair behind her ear. "Outside the tavern, when I realized you were the girl who bested me in The Hollow, I couldn't come up with one good reason not to follow you wherever you went."

"Why?" she whispered, her eyes shifting toward his lips, inching closer to him.

"Because, I -"

A knock on the door halted their advance. Neither of them moved. Their faces were inches from one another. Salome's heart fluttered, she wanted him to kiss her. How she wished whoever was on the other side of the door would go away. But she would not have such luck. A second round of knocking was more deliberate.

"It might be important." Adonijah had not taken his eyes off her, though she had turned toward the door.

"It might be," she grumbled. She was resisting every urge to grab his face and slam her lips against his.

"Salome?"

"Yes?"

Adonijah started to lean closer to kiss her but stopped when a third round of knocking, followed by a gruff female voice on the other side, echoed through her chamber.

"Your Majesty, Her Royal Highness, Princess Zara, requests an audience with you. I have come to escort you."

Adonijah glanced from the door back to Salome. His hand slid from her cheek down her arm and grazed her fingertips. "You should go."

By the tone in his voice, Salome could sense his longing, and his disappointment. She nodded in agreement, although she was inwardly cursing her Aunt Zara. She reluctantly walked to her chamber doors and opened them to find two Myridian guards waiting for her.

"Your Highness." They saluted and started marching down the hall.

Salome could feel his eyes on her. She looked back at him before disappearing around the corner and saw desire in his eyes.

This had better be important, she grumbled to herself.

Odelia was right. The way Adonijah looked at her could get her into trouble.

Chapter Three

Vilora

Released from her shackles and given a spacious room in the White Keep with a view of the Tayborne Mountains, Vilora once again felt like royalty. For decades, she had scrimped, scrounged, and survived with only one motivation: revenge. She had been denied the life of luxury and power she was born to have by those closest to her and she swore the night she destroyed Endor, she would make them all pay.

Now a member of the queen's small council, she was able to move about the White Keep grounds as she pleased. Every morning, she would walk the royal gardens, inhaling the sweet floral and cold sea air. Vilora knew she had not earned Niabi's complete trust, but being in the queen's good graces was enough, for now.

Soon her sister's heart would be hers. A crooked smile spread across her weathered face. With Nym dead, there would only be two people left on her list.

"Any word from Myr?" Vilora poked her head in the queen's office.

Niabi did not look up from her daily correspondence. "Nothing yet."

"Do you think -"

"My orders will be obeyed?" Niabi's eyes shot up viciously. "Without question."

Vilora gave an exaggerated bow. "Forgive me, my Queen. Of course, your orders will be obeyed."

Niabi did not respond but continued to scribble with her quill. Vilora quietly walked around the room, even stopping to enjoy the queen's balcony view. Half of the view was the sea, and the other half was the Tayborne mountains. Equal parts Northern and Myridian. One land, one sea. It made sense to Vilora. Perhaps that's exactly the reason Niabi used these chambers. They weren't the chambers her father had used when he was king. Those had been sealed off and deemed off limits to everyone, including Niabi. It was as if Issachar's ghost would pop up one day to claim what was once his bedroom.

"Is there anything else?" Niabi growled impatiently.

Vilora turned to face her, arms secured behind her back. "What news of your siblings?"

Niabi took her signet ring off and stamped it into hot red wax to seal the envelopes. "My brother was last seen in Numbio, and my sister was headed to the Enchanted Swamp. We believe she was on her way to Port Daelon."

"They've split up?"

"It would appear so." Niabi reclined in her chair and crossed one leg over the other. "Clever really."

Vilora rubbed her chin, deep in thought.

"What thoughts are racing through that dusty mind of yours, Vilora?" Niabi sipped her goblet of wine with a smirk.

"Dusty mind?" Vilora snorted, furrowing her brow.

"The way you scrunch your face when you are lost in your thoughts makes it appear as if you're in pain." Niabi threw her head back and laughed. "So, what is it that plagues you, Auntie?"

Vilora did not care for the sarcastic way she said "Auntie", but knew better than to argue with the one woman who could track her down wherever she tried to hide and imprison her until she whittled down to nothing but bone and ash.

"You said your sister was seen going to the Enchanted Swamp?"

"Most Adalorians are quite superstitious." Niabi shrugged nonchalantly. "They would not have to worry about being followed on their way to Port Daelon."

"They?"

Niabi stared at the bottom of her empty glass. "She is in the company of a sell-sword and an Immortal Seer."

Vilora's eyes widened. "Harbona is with her?"

Niabi glanced up at her, her curiosity piqued. "You know Harbona?"

"It was a lifetime ago." Vilora tried to brush past her relationship with the Immortal but by the menacing glare plastered on Niabi's face, she knew she would not be so lucky. "I knew Odelia as well."

"Who is Odelia?" Niabi's left eyebrow arched.

"The Enchantress of the Swamp, of course."

Niabi leaned forward, surprise etched across her face. "She's real?"

"Very much so, my Queen." Vilora flashed a bitter smile. "And very powerful last I knew."

"You think Harbona took Salome to see her?" Now it was Niabi who sported an ugly thinking face.

"I would be shocked if he didn't." Vilora made herself comfortable on the velvet lounge in the center of the room, stretching her short legs as far as they could go and wiggling her toes in her sandals. "Harbona and Odelia are... close."

Niabi grimaced at Vilora's exposed toes on her furniture. "How close?"

"They are very much *committed* to one another."

"You sound bitter, Vilora." Niabi diverted her eyes from the old woman's feet to the peaceful view from her balcony. "I think there's more you aren't saying."

Vilora reached over to the end table and snatched a few grapes, popping them in her mouth one at a time. "I was fifteen when my mother, upon consulting with my father," she said "father" with great distaste, "summoned Harbona to seek his counsel on what could be done for me." She frowned, smacking the small fruit loudly. "My mother was weak. She *actually* loved my father; sought out his advice, she even wanted to spend time with him. It's no wonder she died well before her hair turned white. An embarrassment," she growled.

Niabi cleared her throat, demanding Vilora's attention. "If I cared to know about your mother, I would have asked."

"Apologies, my Queen." Vilora bowed again in an exaggerated fashion. "You wanted to know more about Harbona and Odelia. Well, Harbona did come to the Isles of Myr to meet with my parents. And upon meeting me, he suggested I journey with him to the Enchanted Swamp to consult Odelia. He convinced my parents that if I really wanted to change, Odelia's magic could draw my power like a poison."

"I am assuming it did not work."

Vilora shrugged and wiped the juice from her hands on her skirt, catching Niabi's disapproving eye. "I did not think anything was wrong with me. But I do remember travelling with Harbona. He was the first person who did not fear me, didn't avoid me."

Niabi stopped pouring herself another glass of Myridian wine and lightly chuckled. "You fell in love with him."

"I should have known better." Vilora leapt from her seat and paced the room, braiding her wild white hair. "Men are a weakness."

"And Odelia? Does she share your sentiments?"

Vilora flashed a hateful glare at the mention of her name. "She did her best to help me."

"Yet you hate her."

"Is it that obvious?" The witch caught herself and turned her frown into a sinister grin. "I caught them kissing – the way he looked at her – he never looked at me that way."

Vilora did not appreciate the look in Niabi's eyes. *Pity.* She despised being pitied.

"Is that when you returned home?"

Vilora nodded. "As soon as I returned, I was sent to Endor. Locked in the Tower of the Goddesses for two years. I was alone. Forgotten by everyone – abandoned by my own kin." She tossed her braid toward her back. "I swore one day, I would make them all pay. When my power was strong enough, I destroyed that pitiful island, sank it with everyone in it." Vilora poured herself a glass of wine and dropped in the seat across from Niabi. "Not a day goes by that I regret my actions. If I could do it again," her eyes raged, "I would not h esitate."

They sipped their wine in silence for a few minutes before Niabi asked, "What of this Enchantress? What magic does she possess that would aide my sister?"

"Nothing." Vilora downed what remained in her cup and set it down. "Unless used in battle."

Niabi leaned forward. "She is a weapon?"

Vilora tore a chunk of bread from the freshly baked loaf sitting with the afternoon spread and bit into it. "Rumor has it, she can control earthly elements."

Niabi pushed a cloth napkin across the table toward the witch. "Meaning...?"

"She can draw from the energy of the earth. She can summon earthquakes. Open the ground and swallow men, if not whole cities, if she feels so inclined."

Niabi tsked and waved her hand in the air. "Nonsense."

"How else could I have sunk Endor?"

The question clearly confused Niabi.

"During one of our cleansing sessions, I felt Odelia's power surge through me. I attempted to harness it, to keep some for myself."

"And it worked?" Niabi nearly screamed in shock.

"How did you know where to send your Nephilim to find me?"

Niabi raised her left dress sleeve, revealing her darkened arm. "My blood."

"Transferred power." Vilora corrected.

"Do you mean I could...?"

"Summon fire like I do?" Vilora nodded, using her sleeve to clean the crumbs from her mouth. "Yes. Have you never tried?"

Niabi stared at her arm as if she'd never seen one before. "No."

Vilora extended her hand toward the queen. "May I?"

Niabi allowed her to touch her arm and examine it.

Vilora hummed as she caressed the darkness that had spread up toward Niabi's bicep. "Unused power will consume you."

"If I use my power, my arm will heal?"

"No, my Queen. But the darkness will spread no further."

"Do you still possess Odelia's magic?"

The witch shook her head. "Sadly, I do not. The little bit of her magic that I managed to harvest, I used to destroy Endor. My magic transferred to you through blood. It is now part of you, whether you like it or not."

Niabi had that ugly thinking face again and Vilora guessed correctly what her next question would be.

"Could you drain Odelia of all her power?"

"Transference is possible if she were physically before me. But why -"

"Teach me to use my power." Niabi shoved her arm into her aunt's hands.

"That is the beauty, my Queen. All you need to do is envision how you want to use fire, and it will happen."

"Could it really be that simple?" Niabi mumbled to herself. She closed her eyes, pondered, and extended her left hand.

"Visualize it," Vilora whispered.

Niabi's eyes shot open, and a small flame appeared hovering over her hand. A smile stretched across her pleasantly surprised face. She wiggled her fingers, playing with the fire. "It doesn't feel hot."

"Flame cannot burn flame." Vilora was very pleased Niabi had so quickly embraced her power. "You are now fire."

Niabi looked at the logs in her fireplace, flicked the flame in her hand toward the hearth, and the wood ignited. She laughed in wicked delight.

Vilora smiled. "You learn quickly."

Niabi's joy vanished, and a serious expression overtook her. "Keep this between us." She marched to her desk, scribbled on a piece of paper, and sealed it with her sigil.

"As you wish, my Queen."

"Guard!" Nubis entered the queen's chamber and accepted the envelope she extended. "Take this to the Pit of Shadows and have my men set out immediately."

He bowed and left.

"You mean to have your Shadows capture the Enchantress?"

"Yes. We need her on our side."

"And if she won't cooperate?"

Niabi's eyes narrowed. "Then we will kill her after she has been drained of every drop of magic."

Vilora grinned. *Another name she could cross off her list.*

Chapter Four

Zophar

It took four days to sift through the dark cavern to find their fallen brothers and burn their bodies. All but one: Crispin. Zophar had not eaten and had barely slept since Crispin slipped beyond his reach, claimed by the River of Lost Souls. He could still see the fear in Crispin's eyes as he let go of the rock he desperately clung to before being washed away.

Rayma told Zophar Crispin's death wasn't his fault and Heru did his best to stay positive and reminded Zophar that Crispin could have survived. But all Zophar could think about was how he was going to break the news to Salome. He had failed. Her brother was... gone.

He dragged the match he had been gnawing on across his chest and lit his long stem pipe. The first time Crispin saw him light a match that way, his jaw dropped. He thought Zophar was magical. He was six at the time, so Zophar cheerfully played along.

"I can teach you, if you like," Zophar smiled at the wide-eyed prince.

"Really?" Crispin nearly jumped out of his seat.

"Aye." Zophar nodded.

Crispin hesitated, a frown replaced the smile on his face. "Can you teach me how to kill?"

Zophar bit down on his pipe. "Why do you want me to teach you to kill?"

Zophar already knew the answer. They had only been in the Tree House Forest for a month after escaping the Green-Eyed Raven's invasion of Northwind. The battle was fresh and the wounds they bore would take a long time to heal; if they ever did.

"So, I can go back home." Crispin's teary eyes met Zophar's.

Those words haunted him.

The next day, he put weapons in the hands of two children, who without training, would more than likely die by the sword, or worse, if they were ever found by their enemies. He trained them. At first, the idea was for them to be able to defend themselves, if needed, but after several years, it turned into molding them into proper soldiers. And he knew one day, his soldiers would become generals. Northwind would be theirs' for the taking.

The rushing waters of the River of Lost Souls brought him back. Back to this lonely nightmare. The boy who could have been king, could have made it home, was gone. And Zophar never told him how much he loved him. Not just as his prince – not just as his pupil – but as a son.

Zophar had lost both of his sons, years before he met Crispin, and felt he had been given another chance to be there in a fatherly way. But he failed. Again.

The worst part of losing Crispin the way he did was he would never be able to say goodbye. He would not be sending him to the Almighty with a proper burial. The Caverns of the Undead seemed a little bit brighter with Crispin leading them. Now, it was exactly as it appeared: cold, dark, and lonely.

Zophar glanced over to the center of their encampment and spotted Heru and Rayma in what appeared to be a heated discussion. Of course, every conversation with Rayma seemed to end up that way. If by the grace of the Almighty they made it out of the caverns alive and reunited with Salome, he had a feeling the two, strongly opinionated women wouldn't get along.

The Westerner pulled himself up from the gravelly embankment and hobbled toward Heru and Rayma. Getting older brought about its benefits and challenges. In growing older, he gained wisdom and experience. But growing older also gifted him with crow's feet and bad knees. It was his right knee that seemed to flare up every so often and would cause him to limp around like a cripple. After seeing battle for the first time in over a decade, his knees were screaming.

Crispin was always the first to make a snarky remark about him shuffling around their tree house and Zophar would click his teeth in response.

"Another day older," Crispin would laugh.

"Another day wiser," Zophar would counter.

Zophar joined Heru and Rayma, muttering Western curses at his uncooperative knees. "What seems to be the trouble, Prince Heru?"

Heru broke his intense glare at Rayma and softened his brow. "Trouble, Zophar?"

"By your expression," Zophar frowned, "you seemed upset."

Heru's eyes shifted to Rayma and back to the burly Westerner. "Rayma and I were discussing what our next course of action will be."

"And what *is* our next move?"

Before Rayma could answer Zophar's question, Heru said, "We are going to honor our allegiance. We will make our way through the caverns and continue to Oakenshire to meet up with Princess Salome."

Rayma frowned; arms folded across her chest. "We should return to Numbio. We do not know what else lingers in the darkness. What if we are captured? What if we wander into their hive? What if we never make it out at all?"

"As I have already said," Heru's voice was steady, but his irritation was not hidden. "Your concerns are valid, but my decision is final."

"With all due respect, my Prince," Rayma popped her hip and spoke through gritted teeth. "Prince Crispin is...gone." She avoided looking at Zophar. "Your duty is to protect the Numbio -"

"I know my duty, Rayma," Heru barked. "My word does not become void because Crispin is gone. As long as Salome lives, so does our allegiance. Crispin -"

"Is dead!" Her voiced echoed through the cavern, drawing the attention of the Numbio warriors around camp. "Why do we continue to fight a dead man's war?"

The finality of her words pierced Zophar's heart. For as strong as he was, he found it hard to hide the tears that welled in his graying blue eyes.

Heru was fuming but took a moment before speaking, knowing his soldiers' eyes and ears were now fixed on him. "Forgive Rayma's wicked tongue and lack of honor, Zophar." He glared at her while he addressed Zophar. "She does not speak for the Numbio."

Rayma opened her mouth to spit her rebuttal, but instead, pursed her lips, bowed, and walked away.

"Forgive me, Prince Heru," Zophar whispered, "but she has a valid point."

Heru focused on Zophar once he ensured his men were no longer watching or listening to their conversation. "Thank you for your honesty, but the Numbio made a promise – a commitment to our Northern brethren – and we intend to honor that allegiance."

"But Crispin is..." Zophar did not have the strength or courage to finish that statement.

Heru rested his hand on Zophar's broad shoulder. "Northern law states a female heir can rule the North, yes?"

"Aye."

"Then Salome will sit on the White Throne. I will make sure of it." He patted Zophar's back and motioned to the tents being torn down. "I have already given the order to pack up and to move onward. I suggest you ready yourself, Captain." Heru sighed and rubbed the back of his neck. "I will depend on you to help me lead my warriors out of this darkness."

Zophar crossed his arm across his chest. "I will serve as needed."

After the caravan had packed their belongings onto the only cart that hadn't been destroyed by the sandstorm and run in with the Wagura, they moved as quietly as they could through the snaking cavern tunnels. They were not eager nor prepared to face another swarm of Wagura. But the further they travelled, the darker it seemed to become. The Numbio were not accustomed to darkness. Living in the Sand Lands, they were used to sunny days, warm weather, and cloudless skies. Down in these caverns, it was not only pitch-black darkness, but also damp and cold. The faster they found a way out and back to the surface, the better.

Zophar walked silently by Midnight, his black stallion, and strummed his nose to ease both of their nerves. Crispin's chestnut horse, Freya, trotted alongside them. *She knows*, Zophar thought, noticing the mare's downcast head and slow gait. He was cautious to reach his hand out to pet her. She was known to be a biter, except with Crispin.

When the time had come for Crispin and Salome to have horses of their own, Zophar took them to a farm north of Gomorrah where they picked their mounts. Salome was immediately drawn to her white mare, Snow, and from that moment on, they were inseparable. But Crispin's eye caught sight of Freya.

"She's not worth the trouble." The farmer snorted and spat on the ground. He pulled the waistband of his trousers away from his belly to give himself a little breathing room. "That one is stubborn as hell."

Crispin smiled. "I want her."

The farmer furrowed his brow and shook his head. "I'm telling you, son, she is the worst horse you could pick. She bites anyone who approaches her. Watch." He walked toward the mare with wildness in her skittish brown eyes, stretched his hand toward her and was instantly met with the click of her teeth. "Told you." The farmer shrugged. "She's not worth it. Best to forget about her."

Crispin gently stepped up to the horse, maintaining eye contact with her, and holding his hands up by his eyes to show he meant her no harm. She stomped a hoof as a warning, but Crispin steadily pressed onward. He smiled. "You are beautiful."

"The horse doesn't understand these things." The farmer's hands flailed around with each word he spoke. He turned to Zophar and Salome who were behind him. "Is the boy crazy? The Almighty gave him ears, yet he does not listen."

Salome stifled a chuckle. Zophar kept his gaze fixed on Crispin.

"My name is Crispin," he slowly lowered his hand in front of her nose. "If it's alright with you, I'd like to take you home with me."

Her eyes shifted but she did not attempt to bite.

"I promise to take care of you. To treat you with respect. To protect you." Crispin gambled with his fingers and rested them on top of the white snip of her snout. "I know what it feels like to be forgotten."

"She does not bite him?" The farmer scratched his protruding belly, clearly taken aback by the horse's unexpected demeanor.

Crispin placed his forehead against hers and stroked her neck. "Let's go home, Freya."

"The boy," the farmer clapped his hands together with a wide set grin, "he is magic."

Zophar knew Freya needed comfort. Mustering every bit of courage left in his weary body, he exhaled, squeezed his eyes shut, then plunged his hand toward Freya's neck and stroked her mane. His eyes popped open when he realized all five of his fingers were still intact and that Freya had accepted his small offering of kindness.

"I miss him too," Zophar whispered in her ear.

"You are good with animals." Rayma startled him with a low whisper.

"Not normally."

"She misses her master."

"Aye," he nodded and patted Freya again. "She does."

Rayma was quiet for a moment then said, "Forgive me, Zophar. My outburst before... I was... I just want my people..."

"There is no need to apologize," he saved her from stumbling over her words. "I, too, was once in a position to advise my king." Her eyes met the ground. "You and Prince Heru are close, I gather?"

"I serve the Royal Family," she huffed, rattled by the insinuation.

"Of course," Zophar cleared his throat. "I meant no offense."

They walked their horses in silence until Rayma couldn't help but ask, "Did he say anything about me?"

"No," Zophar shook his head and brushed his bushy red beard with his sausage thick fingers. "But I am not blind, milady. I see how you two interact with each other." His smile quickly faded. "You two remind me of another couple I once knew."

"May I ask who?"

"My best friend, Lykos..."

"That name sounds familiar," she picked up when he trailed off.

"He was Crispin's oldest brother. When he met Lavena, everything changed."

"What do you mean, everything changed?" Her eyes widened. "Changed in a good way or ... changed in a bad way?"

Zophar smiled fondly thinking of his friends. It seemed like a lifetime ago when he wandered the halls of the White Keep with Lykos and Lavena.

"King Issachar instructed Lykos to meet the new ambassador from Caelestis at the Harbor and escort them to the White Keep -"

"Caelestis?" Rayma interrupted him with a childlike grin. "The Immortals?"

Zophar nodded, "Aye."

"You've seen them? Up close? Do they really glow?" She rattled off her questions without taking a breath.

Zophar remembered when he first saw an Immortal. It was Harbona. But he didn't have the Immortal glow. He lost his aura when he was banished from his homeland.

"The Immortals have an aura," Zophar recounted how Harbona explained it years ago. "It is a glow of sorts. But they don't light up a dark room by any means."

"Was she on the ship?" she asked, more interested in the romance than the aura. Zophar realized then, beyond the tough exterior and serious expression that was always plastered on her face, she was a romantic at heart.

Zophar smiled. "Aye, she was. Lykos' heart was not interested in the political games the royals and their ambassadors played to his father's dismay. But King Issachar insisted if he was going to be king after him, he would have to learn to play the game of politics. Lykos dragged me with him anytime his father sent him on a mission, especially when it was a boring assignment. Meeting the new ambassador was one of those boring assignments, but we waited as the Immortals white ship docked. We fully expected to see another male elder disembark, but we were both shocked when Lavena led her entourage down the r amp."

"She must have been beautiful."

"Lykos was speechless, which was a feat in itself," Zophar chuckled. "Lavena seemed to float toward us. I still remember she was wearing a white robe and hood, her long platinum blonde hair cascading in front of her, and her gray eyes fixated on Lykos. They saw one another and just knew they had found the one they had spent a lifetime searching for." Zophar cleared his throat and sipped from his water canteen.

"What happened after that?" Rayma pushed him to finish the story.

"After meeting on the docks, they spent every minute they could secretly steal with one another."

"Secretly?" Rayma furrowed her brow. "Why secretly?"

"King Issachar was determined to marry Lykos to a woman of his choosing, to further the strength and power of Northwind. If I remember correctly, Lykos was supposed to marry Princess Anka of Sakurai."

"And Lavena?" Rayma looked at the ground.

"When Issachar discovered their love for one another, he ordered Lavena to return to Caelestis. He would never allow her to be the next Queen of Northwind."

"Well," she tried to wait for him to finish, but he was taking too long. "What happened to them?"

Zophar's voice cracked, "Uh, they..."

"Oh."

"Niabi invaded Northwind the night Lavena's ship set sail. Lykos made sure she was on the boat before the city was overrun. Before he ... died."

"What happened to Lavena?"

"I haven't seen her since."

Zophar didn't realize when he first started telling her about Lykos and Lavena, that it would be so traumatic for him. He felt like he was reliving every moment. He saw their smiling faces. He saw their love grow in secret, with him being their only help and confidant. He saw them on the dock the first day they met, and he saw them on the dock the night they parted.

"The point of the story is," Zophar forced himself to continue, "when Lavena and Lykos met, everything changed for the better."

Rayma bit her lip and looked ahead of them at Heru. "Better."

Zophar noticed who she was staring at nodded his head. "I pray your story does not end the way theirs did."

"Me too." She glanced back at Zophar. "Thank you."

"For what?"

"Sharing their story with me," she smiled. It was an odd sight for Zophar to see her smile. It wasn't something she did often. At least, around him. "Do you think you'll ever see Lavena again?"

"The Almighty willing, I might."

An eerie and unfamiliar sound echoed through the cavern and sent shivers up Zophar's spine.

"What was that?" Zophar stopped, his eyes scanning the darkness.

The group halted when Heru lifted his hand in the air. They stood in silence and listened.

Was that...breathing? A raspy, heavy growl?

Heru motioned one of the Numbio armed with a firelit torch in one hand and a sword in the other, to step toward the noise in the darkness. The soldier obediently did so with trepidation. Everyone held their breath, hoping it would turn out to be nothing but their wild and weary imagination. As the warrior made his way up the rocky incline, he stretched his torch forward and was met by the growling, jagged rows of blood-stained teeth of a Wagura. The beast howled a deep, guttural sound.

Fear struck Zophar like a knife to the heart when he heard more Wagura echo the battle cry. They had walked into a trap. They were surrounded.

"To arms! To arms!" Heru commanded, unsheathing his own sword.

Swords clashed as the Numbio and Wagura once again faced off. Before the Wagura launched their assault near Zophar's location, he grabbed Rayma's hand and pushed her under their only cart.

"You must stay hidden."

Rayma started to protest, "But -"

"Rayma," he interrupted forcefully. "No matter what happens to us, do not come out until this is over. You must get out of these caverns."

"Zophar -"

Long, bony fingers came into view, grabbed Zophar's shoulder, and dragged him deep into the darkness.

Chapter Five

Nubis

Nubis sat in the circular office beneath *The Whispering Fox* waiting for the other members to arrive for their meeting. Ziggy normally beat all of them to these sit downs, but she was still missing. His heart ached at the thought of her being caught and tortured for being a spy. Gershom was known for his cruelty – Ziggy was not the first working girl to be in his bed and not seen again. Whenever Ziggy was with The Bear, Nubis didn't sleep.

When he first arrived to serve Oden, she was the first person to welcome him. She showed him around the city when she wasn't working, and they became fast friends. He was often homesick for the Stormcrag way of life but being in Ziggy's company was calming.

He knew from the beginning Ziggy was working her way to being Gershom's call girl, but he didn't realize how much it would sting when Oden helped secure her place in his bed. Not only was it dangerous, but she was with a man other than him.

Of course, he and Ziggy weren't romantically involved, but to him, there was no one that could compare to her. She was feisty, fearless, and her smile warmed the very depths of his soul.

His eyes kept glimpsing the entrance, hoping to see her fiery red curls bounce as she pranced in and sank into her favorite red velvet, high back chair.

Nubis heard footsteps coming down the stairs from the tavern and he stood, expecting to see her, but it was just Makeda. His smile faded and he sank into his seat, a simple wooden chair that no one else wanted.

"Don't look too pleased to see me," Makeda teased and dropped into a plush leather chair large enough for two people to share. She sat cross-legged and pulled her hip long braids to one side of her body.

"I'm sorry," Nubis cleared his throat, "I was just expecting..."

"A bubbly red head?" She flashed a pearly white grin.

He smiled, crinkling the corners of his hazel eyes. "Is it that obvious?"

"Absolutely," she nodded. "But as far as I know, she doesn't know how you feel."

"And Oden?"

"Oden knows everything, Nubis." She arched her eyebrows.

Makeda was right about Oden. He did seem to have the answers to every question. And if he didn't, he would find out. Knowledge was power. At least, that's what Oden always rambled on about as he formulated plans and planted the members of the Order in positions to learn what he needed to know to further the rebellion.

As if summoned by the mere mention of his name, Oden marched into the room with Ziggy following closely behind. Nubis exhaled a sigh of relief and allowed himself to relax in his seat.

Oden pulled his leather chair from behind his desk and sat down. Papers, maps, and empty glasses were strewn across the table. As organized as Oden's mind was, his workspace was the exact opposite. Without Makeda running the tavern upstairs, Oden's cover would have been blown years ago.

Although only four of them sat in the room for the meeting, there were a couple other members in the Order, but Makeda, Ziggy, and Nubis weren't privy to knowing who they were. All Oden would tell them was that they were in positions of power, and they would reveal themselves when the time was right.

"Brothers," Oden called the meeting to order. "I have just returned from consulting with the Sovereign of The Sisters, and I now know what we must do to further our agenda. To find the Hunter, we must find Issachar's children."

"And how do we do that?" Nubis crossed his muscular arms across his enormous chest.

"By going where they would go." Oden laid a map of Adalore in front of them. "If I were them. I would go where I knew I had kin."

Ziggy leaned forward and pointed, "The Isles of Myr."

"Precisely." Oden flashed an impish grin. "I have already sent word to our brothers to be on the lookout for Crispin or Salome."

"Are these the phantom brothers who are in positions of power?" Nubis ran fingers across his dark beard.

"They may not be here in person," Oden shot him a glance, "but they are doing their part in our fight."

"Forgive me, Oden," Ziggy cut through the tension with her sweet voice, "but do we have brothers in Myr?"

"We have brothers scattered all across Adalore." Oden didn't answer the question. "We also have brothers who will have a good chance of finding one, if not both of Issachar's children. We are a step closer to the Hunter. A step closer to ending this stain in our history." Oden placed his elbows on the tabletop and splayed his fingers together in front of his face. "Now, what news, brothers?"

Ziggy started. "The queen had me brought to her in the dungeons."

Nubis' heart nearly climbed out of his throat. "What?"

"What business?" Oden remained focused.

"She wants me to relay information to her about Gershom since I have access to him."

"She wants you to spy on him?" Nubis rubbed the back of his head, trying to hide his anxiety.

"What a blessed day!" Oden clapped his hands together and leaned back in his seat with a smile. "Good work, Ziggy."

"You don't think this is too risky?" Nubis cut in. "She is already jeopardizing her life by spying on Gershom for us. Now she is supposed to spy on Niabi and for her?"

"No risk, no victory," Oden said.

"That is your response?" Nubis scooted to the edge of his seat, his hands firmly placed on his knees. "At any moment, one of us could be found out and be executed or worse, tortured to death, and you don't seem to care."

"Everyone in this room knew the risks of joining the Order." Oden's tone remained calm, though his eyes burned with fury.

"We all owed you a life debt and came to serve you -"

"Do you not believe in our cause, Nubis?" Oden shot.

"Of course, I do," Nubis huffed. "But I don't see the point in us risking our lives more than we ought."

"Perhaps you care too much for Ziggy and it clouds your mind, Nubis." Oden glanced at the blushing red head.

"Better to care too much than not at all," Nubis countered.

Oden slammed his hands on the desk and jumped to his feet. "Is that a challenge to my leadership?"

Ziggy reached over and rested her scarred hand on Nubis' arm. "No, Oden, it's not."

"Good." Oden growled, still eyeing Nubis. "What other business?" He slowly sat back down.

Ziggy squeezed Nubis' arm reminding him he was the next to give report. "The queen has made some sort of deal with the Old Witch of Endor and has dispatched her Shadows to track down some enchantress."

Makeda perked up at the mention of an enchantress. "Which enchantress?"

Nubis shrugged. "The swamps, I think."

"Why?" she pressed.

"For her magic."

Oden narrowed his eyes at his assistant. "Is this of personal interest to you, Makeda?"

She shrank back in her seat which struck Nubis as odd. Makeda was not one to shy away from expressing her opinion.

"I was just curious about what the queen would need her for," Makeda answered.

"The Old Witch of Endor isn't real, is she?" Ziggy asked with an audible gulp. "I thought she was just a character in sad ballads."

Nubis shook his head. "She is the one the queen met in the dungeons – the one she sent her Nephilim to find. She now sits on the queen's small council."

"Which begs the question, why?" Oden rubbed his chin.

"I heard the queen refer to the witch as Vilora, her aunt."

"Her aunt?" Ziggy spat, shooting him a sideways glance.

Nubis shifted in his seat. "And that's not all, I'm afraid."

"How much worse can it get?" Ziggy rubbed her forehead so hard Nubis thought she would scrape her freckles clean off her face.

Nubis cleared his throat and resisted the urge to reach for Ziggy's hand to comfort her. "It seems the queen somehow... has powers."

Oden leaned over his desk. "Powers? What do you mean powers?"

"Fire."

"What?" Oden's eyes widened.

"She can conjure fire," Nubis explained.

"How is that possible?" Ziggy interjected.

"Somehow the witch's power is in the queen's blood. She didn't know she even possessed it, until today."

"Did you see her use fire?" Oden walked around his desk and sat on the edge closest to Nubis.

"No, but I could hear them discussing it on the other side of her door."

"That's why the witch wants the Enchantress of the Swamp," Makeda finally spoke again, twirling one of her braids nervously in her fingers.

Oden's attention was now fully directed toward her. "Share."

"They intend to drain the enchantress of her power and harvest it for themselves," Makeda explained.

"Harvesting powers?" Ziggy brought her legs to her chest. "How is that even possible?"

"Powers can be transferred to another through blood. A small dose of transference means you have a little bit of their power. Drain all their blood..."

"You harvest all of their power," Oden finished Makeda's sentence.

"But Niabi didn't take the witch's blood. Did she?" Ziggy posed the question to Nubis, who knew about as much as they did.

"I am not sure," he tapped his feet on the floor. "But if I heard them correctly, the queen's left arm is where she possesses power. They have a history. Maybe the witch gave her some power years ago."

"We must keep our eyes and ears open." Oden paced in front of his desk as the others watched him carefully. "If Niabi gains powerful magic..."

"We might need a different strategy to defeat her." Ziggy rolled her shoulders back and sighed.

"We will deal with that in due time," Oden said.

"We should send a word of warning to the Enchantress of the Swamp that a company of Shadows is headed her way," Makeda placed her feet on the floor and rested her elbows on her knees.

"And why would we do that?" Oden stood in front of her, arms clasped behind his back.

"Like I said," Makeda glanced up at him, "to warn her."

"No one knows where to find her. No one knows if she's actually real," Oden countered.

"The witch seems confident she's real." Makeda gritted her teeth.

Nubis stared at her. She was acting very odd tonight. What could be setting her off?

"Then let them chase fairy stories. We keep our focus on the queen and her witch." Oden had made his decision and started walking toward his private quarters.

Makeda jumped up, "Oden -"

"That is my decision." Oden snapped back. "Be watchful for the night is long and a storm is coming." He disappeared into his room, ending their meeting.

Nubis and Ziggy stood at the same time, and he looked down at her. He saw panic in her eyes, but she averted her gaze.

"Are you alright?" Nubis rubbed her petite shoulder with his massive hand.

The anxiety that riddled her face a moment ago was gone. She was very good at hiding her fears and emotions. She would have to be, in order to be the great spy that she was.

"Oh, Nubis, I'll be alright. I always am." She smiled up at him and gently patted his hand.

"You know how I feel about you being with him."

"I know," she stroked his cheek. "But he means nothing to me. He's just the assignment."

"If you weren't involved with him, would you ..."

What was he doing? He thought to himself. He couldn't ask a working girl if she would give up her livelihood to live a nomadic life with him. She was a city girl, used to the finer things in life. Those luxuries she enjoyed were paid for by her clients. He had nothing to offer her. He was a Stormcrag. And once the rebellion was successful in dethroning Niabi and Gershom from the kingdom, he was confident he would return to his people in the Bone Mountains.

But what if he asked her to join him? Would she say yes?

"Would I what?" Ziggy's melodic voice cut through his thoughts.

"What?"

"You said, if I weren't involved with him, would I, and then you stopped. What were you going to say?"

Those blue eyes of hers. So alive. If she would but utter the word, he would give up everything he ever wanted just to make her happy. Just to have *her*.

"If you weren't involved with him, would you..." he took a deep breath, "would you leave the profession?"

That wasn't what he wanted to ask her. He wanted to ask if she would be with him instead, but of course, he couldn't brave the question. Couldn't brave the rejection.

She smiled warmly at him, as if she knew that wasn't what he intended to ask her, but sweetly answered, "No. I'm marked and once a girl has been marked, there's no respectable man who would want her to be the mother of his children."

The mark she was referring to was the tiny black rose tattooed above her heart. It forever branded working girls and she was right, respectable men wouldn't marry a woman like her, but they didn't have a problem sleeping with them in secret.

"A respectable man wouldn't let something as simple as a mark keep him from treating you right."

Ziggy wrapped her arms around Nubis' waist and rested the side of her face against his chest. "Oh, Nubis, you are one of the good ones."

He squeezed her as tightly as he dared, "Ziggy, I ..."

"Yes, Nubis?"

"I..." He looked up and scanned the room. Makeda had vanished. Where had she gone? She was acting so strangely. He hoped she was alright, but he knew not to ask Makeda questions. She would say the same thing to everyone who tried to get to know her. *What's my business is my business.*

"Nubis?"

Nubis glanced down at the beautiful, freckled face that stared back up at him. "Promise me you will be careful when you're around Gershom."

She patted his chest. "Don't worry about me, handsome. I've got my back."

Although her words sounded confident, her eyes told him an entirely different story. She released him from their embrace.

"I should get going." She scrunched her curls in her dainty fingers.

"Let me guess," Nubis pressed his hands into his pockets, "you don't need me to walk with you."

"Goodnight, Nubis," she stood on her tip toes and pecked him quickly on the cheek. She wrapped her silky, green shawl over her shoulders, an expensive gift from one of her clients no doubt and slipped out the door. She was so light on her feet; he didn't even hear her walk up the stairs.

He touched the spot where she had kissed him. He would continue to do everything in his power to protect her and in due time, he would save her from this city filled with cruel men.

Chapter Six

Salome

Salome's mind was racing as she followed the two guards down the corridors that led back to the Inner Depths where she first met her Aunt Zara. She didn't expect to see her aunt again so soon and couldn't help but wonder why she had been summoned.

I bet its Marina's fault, she thought to herself; her cousin's smug face flashed before her eyes.

The expression of utter disgust was evident on her face, and it did not go unnoticed by the soldiers posted outside the bronze doors that opened to the Inner Depths. There was no need to walk over the threshold with a sour look, so she relaxed her grimace.

Her aunt sat on the throne and was gripping the armrests tightly. Zara's eyes were as equally calm as they were wild. By her side, still dressed in red armor, was her daughter, Mika, who whispered something in her mother's ear.

Flat disks suspended around the intimate room hosted flames that lit the space. The first time Salome had been inside the windowless throne room, she failed to notice the five statues intricately carved into the walls. Her eyes bounced from one statue to the next, taking in their beauty. Each was carved in the likeness of the same woman, the only feature distinguishing one from the other was the type of bird perched on her shoulders.

She was amazed she knew who they were. Being in Myr somehow helped jog her memory of everything her mother had taught her about her homeland. These women were the Five Virtues. Wisdom was the first statue to her left, an owl on her right shoulder. Next came Strength with her eagle. Dead center was Love with her dove. Swinging around the right side of the circular room was Honor and her crane. Last, directly to Salome's right, was Rebirth with her dark eyed raven.

"Salome."

It sounded like the statues whispered her name. But that was impossible. She squinted her eyes, watching them closely.

"We've been waiting for you."

Their mouths did not move but she knew they were talking to her. How was that possible?

We've been waiting for you. What did that even mean?

Zara cleared the back of her throat, returning Salome to the present situation at hand. She tore her eyes from the Virtues and bowed before her aunt.

"I hope you find your accommodations satisfying, Niece."

"Most generous," Salome nodded, "but I assume that's not the reason you called me here tonight."

"How very intuitive of you." Zara extended her hand to her daughter, Mika, and grabbed two papers from her. "Actually," Zara held the wanted posters of Salome and Crispin up for her to see, "I summoned you here to see if you could explain this."

Salome froze. Tight-lipped, she exhaled slowly. There was no telling how much Zara knew about the posters, about the trouble she had escaped in the Mainland, but there was no reason to hide it. The Myrdians were a well-informed people. It would only be a matter of time before her truths would be public knowledge.

Salome shrugged, trying her best to appear nonchalant. "At least it's a flattering rendering."

"You don't deny this is you?" Zara's eyebrow arched.

"That would be a waste of my time and yours. Clearly, that is me." Salome admitted, relaxing her shoulders. It felt good telling the truth. Now to see what the truth would cost h er.

"You are wanted for murdering Shadows of Nor -"

"Shadows who tore through our community and slit a ten-year-old boy's throat," Salome interrupted with a snarl.

"And why would the Shadows terrorize your peasant community?"

"They were looking for m… for someone."

"Who were they looking for?" Zara leaned forward; her attention piqued.

Salome took a deep breath. Harbona didn't instruct her not to tell her aunt who she really was, but it was still a title she didn't quite believe. When Adonijah figured it out, she felt cornered, trapped, vulnerable. Now she had a choice. She could tell Zara about her mark and the real reason the Shadows were in her village, or she could lie. But if Zara were anything like her mother, Bilhah, she would not fall for the deceit.

"Who were they looking for?" Zara repeated herself.

Moment of truth. "They were looking for... me."

"And your brother."

"Not Crispin." Salome raised her head high, her fingers intertwined in front of her. "Just me."

"I don't understand." Zara handed the wanted posters back to Mika. "Why just you? Crispin is Issachar's last living son."

"They weren't looking for Issachar's children. They were looking for..." Panic began to set in. She felt her heart beating faster and her breath quickening. She remembered being a child running around the Royal Gardens with her brothers, Mosgalath, Elias, and Crispin. She remembered them making fun of her eye. They thought something was wrong with her; that she might be cursed.

As if she was sent to save Salome from drowning in her own anxiety, Damaris stepped forward from the shadows. "Tell them, Salome."

Salome spun her head toward Damaris. "Who are you?"

"I am Damaris, the Oracle of Myr." She bowed her head.

"You're my mother's youngest sister." Salome put the pieces together.

Damaris smiled and the corners of her green eyes crinkled. "You are safe here, Salome, tell them who you are."

Salome couldn't stop staring at her Aunt Damaris. Her mind was running wild. She felt like prey and wished Damaris could hear her thoughts. "*I don't think I can.*"

Damaris tilted her head and responded to Salome's thoughts with her own. "*It is time you are honest about who you are.*"

"*Wait!*" Salome's eyes widened. "*You know what I'm thinking?*"

Damaris stared at her intently. "*Yes.*"

"*How?*"

Zara cleared her throat startling Salome. Her Aunt Zara's nostrils flared, clearly irritated by the wait.

"*It's alright, Salome.*" Damaris' thoughts sliced through her own. "*Tell them who you are.*"

"*What if they don't believe me?*"

"*It is not them you need to be honest with. It is yourself.*" Damaris reached for Salome's fingers and gently squeezed them. Her green eyes were kind, like Bilhah's.

Zara impatiently tapped her long fingers on the cypress armrests of the throne. "Well?" She finally had Salome's attention. "Why were the Shadows only looking for you?"

Salome turned to Damaris who nodded reassuringly. She took a deep breath and admitted, "They were looking for the Hunter."

"The Hunter?" Zara spat, her brows knitted together.

"Yes."

Zara's eyes narrowed, "Are you saying that you are the Hunter?"

Now was her moment to be honest with herself. To admit what she still didn't quite believe. "I am the Hunter."

"There has never been a female Hunter." Zara crossed one leg over the other and lifted her chin.

"Until now," Salome squared her shoulders to Zara's throne.

"Adalore has not seen a Hunter in over two hundred years." Zara waved her hand dismissively.

"I suppose it was time for one." Damaris clasped her hands behind her back, drawing her older sister's wrathful eye.

"And how do we know she is who she says she is?" Zara asked what most sane people would. Salome knew her question was valid and yet, she felt the sting of her unbelief.

"I knew as soon as she entered the room, she was the Hunter, Zara." Damaris' voice was gentle and seemed to soothe her sister.

"It is well known every Hunter bears the sacred mark... do you?" Zara motioned for Salome to prove herself.

Salome indignantly pointed to her left eye. The one thing she spent years hiding was now what she had to showcase, if she wanted anyone to believe she was the Hunter. "See for yourself."

Zara motioned with her head for Damaris to confirm. Damaris placed her hands on Salome's cheeks and stared into her eyes. It was certainly uncomfortable, but seeing the warm smile stretch across Damaris' face once she saw the mark, was worth it.

"We've been waiting for you," Damaris said, the golden, tentacle crown weaved through her black hair sparkled under the flame disks suspended in the room.

Salome's eyes widened. That was what the Virtues had said when she first entered the room. Damaris winked and tilted her head back toward Zara who had stood from her seated position, grabbed her spear, and marched down the steps to be at eye level with them.

"With this new information, your bounty should be higher."

Salome left most of her weapons in her quarters, but she still had a knife strapped to her thigh and a small dagger hidden in her boot. With her fingers twitching in anticipation of an attack, she was prepared to defend herself.

Zara stopped a foot shy of Salome, handed her spear to Mika, and smirked as she ripped the wanted posters in half. "It is a shame no one will be collecting it. You will need protection."

Salome breathed a sigh of relief, the tension leaving her battle-ready shoulders. "I have protection."

Zara shook her head, displeased. "Do not rely on men, Salome. Rely on yourself. You must learn to be the greatest weapon and your strongest protector. Your training begins tomorrow."

"Training?" Salome snorted, hands on her hips. "Training for what?"

"To become a Qata Vishna," Zara stated, matter of fact. "What other training could there be?" She retrieved her spear from Mika and tapped the tiled floor, the echo silenced everyone. "Mika will meet you at the docks at sun-up. It is time to embrace your destiny."

Chapter Seven

Rayma

Rayma hid underneath the cart like Zophar instructed. Terrified, and in total darkness, she lost all track of time. She commanded her body to crawl to search for a torch, but her body disobeyed. It felt like she was paralyzed; her limbs were numb from the cold, damp cavern ground and the darkness was so thick, she felt she could taste it.

As frozen and lifeless as her body was, her mind had been racing since their company was attacked by the Wagura.

I warned them.

I warned them.

They refused to listen.

I warned them.

Why did they not listen?

I warned them.

This isn't my fault.

I warned them.

The first time she had heard about the Caverns of the Undead and its horrifying inhabitants, she was no more than seven years old.

Bast was the only man to escape the Wagura. When he tried to warn the Numbio of the horrors of the caverns, everyone made fun of him, called him names, and refused to pay him any mind. Her people dubbed him "The Madman". But to her, he was just *Papa*.

When he returned from the caverns, she did not recognize him. He had been gone for almost a year; she and her family believed he had died with his troop who disappeared in the desert. She was ashamed to admit she was frightened of him. His unkempt hair, his matted beard, his shifting eyes, the scars along his arms and legs. But nothing scared her more than the night terrors. He would scream, convulse, sweat, and fight anyone that attempted to touch him.

She and her brother, Inaros, avoided him. Their mother did her best to bring him back to the living. She fought to heal his mind and to mend his body, but it was a hopeless endeavor. Bast was gone. To save her children from being branded untouchable and unwedable, she divorced Bast and put him out of the house they had built together.

How could Rayma ever become the best healer in Numbio with a madman for a father?

How could Inaros find a suitable wife from a good family if he came from an unworthy one?

Rayma was ten when her papa's body was found in a deserted alley – his neck broken. Suicide? Murder? A mercy killing? She would never know – she never wanted to know.

A month after Rayma celebrated her eleventh name day, her mother died.

"Broken heart," the Healer had said.

Broken for a long time in Rayma's estimation. Her mother crumbled the day they thought Bast had died in the desert. But putting Bast out of their lives to save their children's reputation – she never recovered. Rayma was convinced her mother's grief for losing her husband in more ways than one, was what took her in the end.

Had their parents not left them a small inheritance, Rayma and Inaros would have been out on the street, begging for a meal and place to sleep. But as luck would have it, or misfortune depending on who you asked, Rayma and her older brother Inaros were taken in by a man of means when their funds ran out. He sent Rayma to the best apothecary school when she was twelve and had Inaros learn politics, diplomacy, and business with him.

For the first couple of years, everything was great. They were well-fed, housed, clothed in the finest linens, and were receiving the finest educations money could buy. But once they were comfortable, things changed. In the beginning, they were told to refer to the man who saved them as Uncle, but that turned into Master overnight.

The Master never beat them. But the kindness he had shown them had run dry, and they were now expected to do his bidding, to pay off their debt to him.

But late one night, Inaros shook her awake and said they had to leave. He had stolen something from their Master. He said the Master was evil. That he had to be stopped before it was too late.

But Rayma was too afraid to move – too afraid to speak. Inaros looked crazed, just like their father. Inaros tried clawing her out of bed, but she dug her fingers into the sheets and refused to believe they were in any danger.

"Please, Rayma, please."

Those were the last words she heard him say before he leapt from her window and made a run for it – a small black book tucked under his arm.

Even after her brother had been gone for several minutes, she still clung to her sheets in a stunned stupor. That was how Lord Memucan found her when his guards kicked in her bedroom door.

"Where is he, girl?" Memucan smacked her across the face, drawing blood.

"I...I..."

"I...I..." he mimicked, furiously shaking her by her shoulders. "Where is your brother? He stole from me, and he will be punished."

"Please don't punish him, Master!" she wailed, clutching his robes.

He patted her head gently, the first kind physical gesture he had shown her in quite some time. "Tell me, child, where is he?"

"You must promise me that you won't harm him." She wiped the blood that trickled from her mouth.

"I swear I will not inflict harm to the boy."

She pointed a shaky finger at the window, "He jumped."

"I want him alive." Memucan instructed the guards. "You have done well, Rayma. As long as you obey my commands, your brother will be returned to you when the time is right."

She had obeyed Memucan's commands for four years. Now eighteen, she was the youngest Royal Healer in Numbio's history. That was partially in thanks to Memucan, and partially to her own skills and training.

When Memucan noticed Heru had taken an interest in her, his new command was for her to get close to him. Very close.

"If I do this, will you finally return Inaros to me?"

"Of course, child, of course." Memucan nodded, hobbling around her apothecary room in the palace. "And in a show of good faith, here is a letter from him." He placed the tattered, rolled up paper on the wooden table.

She lunged for it and soaked in every word. "Rayma, we will see each other again soon. Inaros."

"It's short today," she frowned, flipping the paper to see the backside.

"Is that ungratefulness I detect in your voice?"

"No, Master -"

"I would hate for Inaros' letters to stop finding their way to you." He planted his cane in front of him, balancing himself. "Get close to our prince."

"Then?"

"Then," he hissed, "I will inform you of your next task."

She and Heru had secretly been seeing each other for eight months. She had obeyed – she just didn't expect to fall in love with Heru. His compassion, his patience, his bravery – the way he held her...

A howl echoed in the caverns throttling her back to her reality. Her nightmare. She had allowed herself, allowed her fear, to paralyze her. If she didn't get out from underneath the cart – Heru, Zophar, the Numbio – they would all die. She was their only hope of survival whether she wanted to believe it or not.

Take the first step. Just take one.

She forced herself to crawl forward, dragging her belly across the ground, tapping her fingers in front of her to guide her in the darkness.

One step. Just one step.

She was out from under the cart and felt around for the wooden torches in a box inside the cart. The box was empty, except for one.

One more step, Rayma.

Rayma tip-toed around the wooden cart, fighting the thought that a Wagura could strike at any moment. Her breathing quickened as their terrifying images flashed before her. Her heart raced; her feet stopped. She clutched her chest; she was frozen again.

Heru needs me.

The Numbio need me.

Almighty, give me strength.

Just one more step.

She inhaled and exhaled rhythmically.

One more step. Just one more step.

She fumbled through a cloth bag filled with flints and used it to light her torch. It worked. She wiped sweat from her forehead with her sleeve and looked around at what remained of the battlefield.

She gasped and lunged back seeing several dead faces, Numbio and Wagura, staring back at her. She picked up a knife from a fallen Numbio warrior and tied it to her robes.

As she danced around the bodies, she caught a glint of a blade and recognized Heru's sword. Green blood stained it. She picked it up and kept a tight grip around the hilt.

Rayma listened for any sound to indicate which way she should go to find her company. She strained to hear anything and caught the faintest sound of... drums?

She marched cautiously to the mouth of a tunnel and followed it. Patting the bag filled with her healing supplies strapped across her chest, she followed the narrow passageway. The noise grew louder with every step she took. After ten minutes of steady walking, she saw an opening at the end of a tunnel and shadows along the cavern wall. Flames from a bonfire projected the shadows making them look much larger than they actually were. She crouched and crawled to the opening.

Rayma's jaw dropped when she saw hundreds of Wagura dancing, beating drums, feasting, and fighting around a large bonfire. She scanned what appeared to be their city and looked for any signs of her company. She spied hovels made of mud and human remains, then she spotted the cages formed with the bones of fallen warriors enclosing the Numbio. Their horses were housed behind a bone fence. But she didn't see Heru or Zophar.

Panicked, she kept searching the encampment from her hiding spot above them, when her eyes finally rested upon Heru and Zophar. Keeping the commanders in a separate cage from their troops, she had to admit, was a smart move.

In front of the bonfire sat the largest hovel with a platform jutting out from it. She saw a throne made of some sort of material. She squinted her eyes and realized it had been formed with human flesh. Rayma shuddered at the thought of how cruel their leader must be, to use the torn skin of human victims to upholster a throne.

As if on cue, the Queen of the Wagura floated out of her hovel. She looked nothing like her hordes of demonic soldiers. She glowed – a bright, almost hypnotizing white.

The queen wore a long, black robe that made her look as if she were seven feet tall. The darkness of the robe clashed with the brightness of her illuminated pale skin. When standing, her six-inch-long fingers fell just past her knees. She was bone thin with a sunken face that Rayma was frightened to look at. Her eyes were solid white, as was her waist long hair. Her tresses floated around her. The crown on her head was forged of crystal, just like the dagger that dangled from her hip.

"My pets," Pyke's high-pitched voice sounded as if two women were speaking in unison. "After the sacrifice, we will feast on their flesh, build with their bones, and quench our thirst with their blood!"

The Wagura howled as one, which sent shivers up Rayma's spine. But as monstrous as the creatures were, their queen was oddly beautiful.

Pyke. That's what her father had called her. Pyke, the Demon Queen. She looked like a levitating spirit, but she was a physical being – meaning, she too bled. Her father had seen it – had seen her bleed – so, if she could bleed, she could be killed.

"*Defeat the queen. Defeat Pyke. She can be killed. Defeat the Demon Queen.*" Her father would chant those words daily.

Once when Rayma had garnered enough courage, she asked how the queen could be killed.

"The dagger. Her dagger. It forged her," Bast said, *"and it can kill her."*

"How do you know this?" She asked, but he didn't answer her question. He started screaming, convulsing on the floor, and her mother pushed her out of the room before she could see anything else.

Rayma took a deep breath before she slithered down from her hiding spot and slowly sneaked through the camp, careful to avoid any Wagura not dancing by the fire.

Pyke disappeared into her hovel. Rayma didn't know how much time she had before the sacrifice, so she had to be quick. She scurried toward the cage where Heru and Zophar sat with their heads down.

"Psst," she whispered as loud as she dared, but they couldn't hear her over the drums.

She picked up a little rock and then thought better than to throw it. She had never been an accurate shot. Rayma dropped the stone and poked her head around the hovel she was crouched behind and when she saw the coast was clear, she sprinted to the cage and ducked behind the bars before a Wagura noticed her.

"Psst." This time, Heru and Zophar looked up.

"Rayma?" Heru jumped to his feet, but Rayma held a hand up to stop him.

"Don't draw attention to us," she warned, her eyes darting around.

"What are you doing?" Heru asked, slowly sitting back down.

"I told you to escape." Zophar fussed, arms crossed over his chest, eyeing her like a disappointed father.

"I couldn't leave you behind." Rayma meant the collective you, but her gaze was fixed on Heru. "I know what I need to do. You just need to be ready should I fail. Here." She pushed Heru's sword in between the bones used as bars. "If you should need it."

"What are you talking about?" Heru furrowed his brow.

"I need to kill the queen."

"You what?" Zophar puffed.

"Kill the queen? You have never wielded a weapon in your life!" Heru was clearly not a fan of her plan.

"Would you prefer to die an excruciating death instead, Your Majesty?" She knew by addressing him formally it would sting and by the flash of surprise on his face, she was right. "If I kill the queen, the hive will not have a life source – their existence is tied to her survival."

"How do you know this?" Zophar looked just as confused as Heru.

"Trust me," was all she managed to blurt out, hiding her shaky hands before they noticed.

Heru and Zophar turned to one another, then Heru nodded.

"Rayma," he pleaded, "be careful."

She couldn't afford to stare into his hazel eyes a second longer or she would lose the little bit of reckless boldness she had mustered. Rayma once again made sure there weren't any Wagura nearby and bolted hovel to hovel, working her way to Pyke.

Rayma was grateful the celebration of capturing the Numbio made the Wagura lax in their patrolling duties. Pyke's hovel wasn't guarded, so she slipped inside the curtains draped in front of the opening, undetected.

Now that she was inside, she began to question how she was supposed to lift the crystal dagger from Pyke herself and use it to kill her. But she didn't have to worry long – the queen was sitting on a throne, twin to the one on the platform, weeping.

"Are you here to kill me?" Pyke's gaze was on the crystal dagger on her lap.

Rayma stepped forward. "And if I am?"

Pyke's solid white eyes shot up. "You will need this." She offered the crystal dagger with both hands to the healer. "Take it. Please."

Rayma was stunned and was unsure if she should reach for it. "You want me to kill you?"

"Please, free me from this misery." Tears flowed from Pyke's eyes but seeped back into her skin, leaving no trace of emotion.

"Free you?" Rayma still hadn't taken the blade, fearing it to be a trap. "You are the queen -"

"I made a deal with the Grim – and this was the price I had to pay." She patted herself. "To become this... monstrosity."

"What did you ask the Grim for?"

"To be with the man I loved. He was dying but I begged the Grim not to deliver him to Death, to spare us. I asked him for time." Pyke's voices echoed through the hovel. "The Grim said he would let us live together peacefully for ten years, but when he returned, he would take us both."

"What happened?"

"The Grim kept his word. Ten beautiful years later, he returned to claim both of our souls. Though he delivered my love to Death, he kept me for a darker purpose – to replace the last Queen of the Wagura who had paid her debt."

Rayma took a minute to let the queen's story set in. "If I kill you...?"

"Then I can be reunited with my love in Death's arms."

"Why hasn't anyone else agreed to this?" Rayma was skeptical. "You have slaughtered hundreds, if not thousands, of men over your years as the queen."

"Because only a mortal woman can kill me." She exhaled deeply. "This is the Grim's cruel game, knowing women do not venture through the Caverns of the Undead. But you can set me free."

"What happens to me if I kill you?"

"Have you ever made a deal with the Grim?" Pyke stood and was much taller than Rayma originally assumed.

"No," Rayma stepped back instinctually.

"Then you can finally put an end to the Wagura – you can set our indebted souls free." She extended the knife. "Take it. Free us. Free me."

Rayma eyed the crystal dagger – she knew what she needed to do, but wasn't sure she could bring herself to do the deed. She swore an oath to heal, to protect, to save – not kill.

"I..." Rayma's bottom lip quivered, "I can't do it."

"Oh please, you must." Pyke floated toward her and pushed the dagger into her hands. "If you don't, I will have no choice but to kill all of your companions. To kill you. Please, don't let me do it."

"You don't have to -"

"I do not have a choice." Pyke whimpered and just for a brief moment, Rayma saw the human trapped inside the creature.

Rayma accepted the knife with trembling hands. "Where do I... put it?"

Pyke tapped her chest. "Run it straight through what is left of my heart."

Rayma pressed the tip of the blade to Pyke's chest. She had come to kill the Demon Queen but now that she stood face to face with the monster, she couldn't help but pity and even understand her. Rayma had spent the years repaying a debt to Memucan, yearning for her own freedom. There were days she even wished for Death to come for her; for someone to end her misery.

But she had also sworn an oath to heal and not harm. Could she really live with herself if she killed Pyke? Could she live with herself if she didn't and watched Heru and the Numbio die?

She had come to kill the Demon Queen.

She was going to set the Demon Queen free.

Tears slipped down Rayma's cheeks. "I'm sorry." She plunged the knife deep into Pyke's breast.

Pyke gurgled and her light began to fade. Rayma held her as she died, her own heart breaking as she kept repeating, "I'm sorry," to the queen.

Pyke grabbed Rayma's hand tightly and managed to say, "Thank you," before she turned into dust, leaving behind the crystal dagger and a key that had been tied around her neck.

Rayma stared at what remained of the queen – she had never taken a life before and the guilt that burdened her was almost unbearable. But she knew the Numbio needed her. Heru needed her. As she rose, she snatched the key – perhaps it opened the cage doors – and after wiping the dagger clean with her robe, she holstered it, claiming it as hers.

She inched toward the opening of the hovel, expecting to see the Wagura still celebrating, but instead, with their queen – their life source – gone, their strength began to fade. There was no more dancing. No more drums beating. But there was the sight of Wagura soldiers clawing for their weapons, grasping their chests in agonizing pain.

Rayma ran to the cages and used the key to free her companions.

"Rayma!" Heru scooped her up in her arms and she inhaled deeply, stifling the tears she desperately wanted to shed, now that she was safe in his arms.

Safe? Not quite.

Rayma reluctantly pulled away from him. "I killed their queen. They will be at their weakest."

Heru was surprised but nodded and ordered the men to kill the Wagura. To leave none of them alive. The Numbio armed themselves with whatever weapons they could get their hands on and battled the Wagura.

Heru ushered Rayma away from the fighting. He caressed her face and kissed her forehead gently. "I don't want to leave you..."

"Go," she pressed her hand against his chest, feeling his heart racing.

Heru clutched his sword tightly and reluctantly turned toward the raging battle. "Rayma." She met his gaze, her exhaustion kicking in. "I owe you my life." He slipped beyond her sight.

Rayma could hear the clashing of swords and the wails of Wagura dying as she leaned her head back against the hovel Heru had hidden her behind. She could smell the Wagura's bitter green blood. Her heart was pounding in her chest – her head spinning. She kept seeing the image of Pyke's dagger in her chest, how she turned to dust in her grasp.

But it wasn't Pyke's eyes giving her an icky feeling.

Rayma's eyes shot open, and her head turned to the side. There, gawking at her, was Bantu, hiding from participating in the fight. He wasn't frightened. He stared at her with a blackmailing smirk.

Kill the prince. That was Memucan's last command – the final task that would free her brother.

Bantu looked in both directions before scrambling over to her, kneeling inches in front of her. "You don't look well, Rayma." His slippery voice enveloped her like a malevolent embrace.

"Get away from me."

"I'm sure you're especially glad to see I survived this whole ordeal." His hands trailed up her arm to her neck.

"Don't touch me." She pushed him away and he smacked her across her face with his enormous hand.

"Who do you think you are to give me orders?" Bantu hissed in her ear; his fingers tightening around her throat. "Who are you going to tell? The prince? The Westerner?" He hummed. "I'll do whatever I want to do to you," his free hand slipped underneath her skirt, "and you won't say a thing about it."

His lustful smirk disappeared as a grunt escaped his parched lips. Bantu's eyes darted from Rayma to his stomach.

"May Death deny you rest," she hissed and ripped the crystal dagger out of his body, pushing him away from her. She watched as he thrashed in a pool of his own blood and felt no urge to heal him.

Rayma had killed twice in a span of minutes and was frightened that killing Bantu didn't draw guilt or remorse from her. She enjoyed that kill. And honestly, if given the chance, she would not hesitate to do it again.

Heavy footsteps approached. Her eyes sliced through the air and rested on Zophar. Truly grateful to see the burly Westerner rather than a grotesque Wagura, she exhaled a sigh of relief. A tear slipped down her cheek as she leaned her head against the wall. Zophar tapped his foot against Bantu's lifeless body.

"He...I..." she stuttered, unsure of how to explain what she had done.

Zophar crouched in front of her and whispered, "Are you alright?"

Her bloodshot eyes scanned his face, and she realized his question was genuine. She nodded.

Spying the blood on the crystal dagger, Zophar took the weapon from her hands and wiped it clean against his pant leg. "No one needs to know what happened here."

It was a statement.

Rayma couldn't resist throwing her arms around his neck and the tears she had fought before now flowed. She wept as he returned the embrace and only let her go when she was ready.

Zophar extended the crystal dagger back to her. "Yours, I believe."

Rayma shook her head. "I can't take it."

"You are its rightful owner now." Zophar insisted. "And if needed, now I know you can defend yourself."

"I'm a healer. I shouldn't -"

"Kill?" he interrupted. "I taught Salome to value life. And that included her own." He placed the knife in her palm. "Value your life as you save everyone else's, Healer."

She wrapped her fingers around the hilt. *Value your life.* She met his gaze. She was prepared to do just that.

Chapter Eight

Matildys

Matildys glided across the black marble floors of the Black Tower with a sinister smile that could stop a heart from beating. Unlike her husband, her mind was filled with plans, with strategies, all with one goal – one purpose – to be sole ruler of Gomorrah.

She had been poisoning Cyler's food for nearly a year and took her already sickly husband and turned him into a useless invalid. Matildys had considered slitting his pale throat while he slept, but that would draw too much attention to who murdered the king. No, slow but steady, even if the brute was taking too long to die. No one would even suspect the dutiful wife, the loyal sister – she would be free of him, but not fit enough to rule the Gomorrians. Not with her son, Thanos, alive and well.

She didn't hate Thanos by any means, but she had no love for him either. Like King Cyler, Thanos was second born but because they were born male, they were named heir to the throne. Matildys was robbed of her crown – she would not allow the same fate for her daughter, Ranalda. In truth, Ranalda was mentally weak and Thanos was wicked but stupid, a true Gomorrian. But cruelty could be taught. Ranalda still had a chance to be a strong ruler, a mighty Gomorrian.

But there was still Thanos to contend with.

Matildys' eyebrows arched – a wicked glint in her icy blue eyes.

She could get rid of both Cyler and Thanos with one swipe of her blade. She would slit Cyler's throat, as she had wished to do for years, and use one of Thanos' daggers to do the deed. Thanos would be found guilty of assassinating the king and would be executed. It was perfect. The queen closed her eyes and exhaled a satisfied breath. Gomorrah would finally be hers.

"Mother?"

Matildys opened her eyes and turned to see her daughter standing in the hall.

"Stand up straight, Ranalda," Matildys clucked her tongue and swatted her bony fingers in the air. "You don't want an unsightly hump like your father."

Ranalda pulled her shoulders back, tipping her head upward. "Yes, Mother."

The queen tapped Ranalda's square jawline with the tips of her fingers. "That's better. What do you need?"

Ranalda's gaze faltered, not daring to look her mother in the eye. "The Thrak have returned from their hunt -"

"Tell me you look forlorn because they brought that bitch back to our mighty city dead and not alive as I instructed."

"Uh..." Ranalda cleared her throat, "not exactly."

"Ranalda, dear," Matildys cooed, "you look positively ill. What is it?"

"The Thrak didn't reach Port Daelon in time. The woman – Salome – was already on board a ship."

"Where are these Thrak now?"

"In the throne room awaiting your orders."

Matildys wrapped her arm around her daughter's shoulders and led her back down the corridor to the throne room. "My dear, it is time you handed down your first judgment."

Ranalda shook her head, "Shouldn't Thanos -"

Matildys dug her fingernails into Ranalda's upper arm causing her to wince. "If you want to rule Gomorrah," she hissed in her daughter's ear, "forget about Thanos."

"Yes, Mother," she cleared her throat as Matildys eased her grip.

"Soon, we will be free of our oppressors." Matildys spoke without looking at anyone in particular, her gaze fixed on the black wooden doors of the throne room. "Now is the time to take your place at the table."

The guards opened the double doors and the women walked through the awaiting Thrak to their thrones. Once they were seated, Matildys turned to Ranalda and tilted her head, indicating it was time to speak.

Ranalda gulped audibly but managed to say, "Thrak 47314, you and your company were charged with finding the peasant known as Salome, who is guilty of crimes against the crown. You have returned empty-handed. Why?"

The Thrak's soulless black eyes fluttered around the room. "The criminal had boarded a boat set for the Isles of Myr before we could apprehend her."

"So," Ranalda sat up straighter, mirroring her mother's posture, "you have failed your mission."

Thrak 47314 swayed side to side and sucked in a frightened breath. "We can still capture her, Princess. We know where she was headed."

"You propose to travel to the Isles of Myr?" Ranalda couldn't hide her surprise. She side-eyed her mother, searching for guidance but didn't receive any. She turned back to the Thrak commander, tilted her nose up, and lowered her voice. "Thrak 47314, you failed your mission, and you know the penalty for -"

"Go to Port Daelon and commandeer a vessel," Matildys interrupted, an idea sparked in her mind. "Sail to the Isles of Myr and bring me that girl, *alive*."

Thrak 47314 and Ranalda both breathed a sigh of relief. He bowed low spurring his band of thirteen men to do the same.

"But," Matildys continued, eyes narrowed, voice cold, "if you should fail the crown again, you know what the penalty will be."

The Thrak nodded with a grunt and snapped his finger in the air, summoning the pardoned company to follow him. They left before the queen had a chance to change her vicious mind.

"You...you let them live?" Ranalda croaked as soon as the doors closed behind them. "That is not the Gommorian way."

Matildys slithered from her throne, "No," she wiped strands of loose hair from Ranalda's face and tucked them behind her ears. "It is not the Gomorrian way, but do you remember what I told you when I first dispatched the Thrak to find this woman?"

Ranalda nodded, "Revenge before riches."

"Very good." Matildys flicked her index finger, beckoning Ranalda to follow her to the balcony behind the four thrones that overlooked the courtyard. "The same principle applies. They failed, yes, but how much harder will they push to complete this mission given this rare second chance?"

"You think their fear will motivate them?"

"The Thrak always fear – success or not." Matildys watched as the company of Thrak she'd shown mercy to saddle their horses and galloped out of the courtyard. "It is their hope of survival."

Ranalda shuddered at Matildys' tone. "You mean to execute them even if they bring that woman back, don't you?"

Matildys flashed a cruel grin. "How perceptive of you, Ranalda."

"But you said -"

"I never promised they would *not* die. They failed. What is the penalty for failure?"

"Death."

"And Death they shall receive." Matildys snaked her arm around her daughter's. "Now, off with you. There are some matters I need to tend to."

"I could help you -"

Matildys tapped Ranalda's arm and pecked her forehead with a rare kiss. "These are things I must do alone."

Ranalda's cheeks flushed. "Of course, Mother." She broke free from her mother's grasp and bowed.

Matildys watched her daughter disappear down the hallway. The sun was setting so she had to act quickly if she as to be successful in setting her plan into motion.

She turned on her heel and glided toward Thanos' quarters. Her son was especially careless when it came to his weaponry, leaving knives, maces, and ceremonial swords scattered around his chambers instead of locking them away in the armory or fastened on his person.

As she rounded the curved hall in the circular tower, she hastened her gait, and slipped into Thanos' unguarded room.

"Fool of a son," she murmured.

Thanos claimed he had no privacy when the Thrak were stationed outside his chambers at night, so he banned them.

His own undoing, she thought.

Matildys scanned her son's messy quarters and rolled her eyes in irritation. At least he wouldn't notice one of his knives missing. Until it was far too late.

She swiped the knife with a bone infused handle. "How poetic," she smiled. It was a well-known fact this dagger belonged to Thanos. It was given to him by his father for his Name Day the previous year. Forged with the ground bones of traitorous Mountain M en.

"For the future King of Gomorrah," Cyler had chimed, his chest puffed out like a peacock.

The next day, Matildys began to kill her husband. Slowly.

Hearing footsteps outside the door, she backed against the wall nearest the entrance, clutching the blade to her breast. She held her breath as the footsteps rounded past the room and continued down the hall. She exhaled.

Pity, she thought to herself. *I would have loved to have gotten in one for practice.*

Her gaze settled on the dagger in her hand. Matildys reached for the handle and pried the door open, slipping out unnoticed.

One step closer.

With the dagger securely hidden inside her billowing sleeves, she scurried to the chamber she shared with her husband. She waved her free hand sideways signaling to the two Thrak guards to open the doors.

Night was Maltidys' favorite time. She especially liked when the light of the full moon streamed through the windows, lighting up the black marble floors in the bedroom. She entered and heard Cyler, groaning like a wounded animal in bed.

"Matildys?" he wheezed, his weary eyes finding her in the dimly lit room.

"Yes, my love," she stepped forward, a wicked sweetness in her voice.

"You are early."

He wasn't wrong. Matildys couldn't stand the thought of being alone with Cyler for a minute longer than necessary, so she would occupy her time until he'd passed out.

"It's been a busy day," she sat at her vanity, carefully sliding the knife into a drawer, and began brushing her long blonde tresses. "Not to worry, my love, you just close your eyes and rest. Do not let my presence disturb you."

The king pushed himself up to a seated position with great difficulty and leaned his hunched back against the headboard. "It's been a long time since we've had some alone time, my sweet." He licked his dry lips, drawing a reproachful glare from Matildys.

Attempting to hide her disgust with the innuendo of having undesired incestuous relations, she let out a flirtatious chuckle and said, "You seem to have more vigor than I do these days, my love."

"Come, sit with me." Cyler patted her side of the bed with a lustful smirk.

"Perhaps another -""Now!" He might have been sickly and growing frailer by the day, but his tone was nothing short of menacing.

"Of course," she set the hairbrush down in the drawer and eyed the dagger. She had not intended to kill him that evening – but the thought of him touching her again made her retch. She snatched the knife, once again hiding it in her wide sleeve, and headed to his side of the bed.

"What are you doing?" He watched her approach with both excitement and suspicion. She roughly grabbed his hair and forced his head up to look at her. "Feeling feisty tonight, I see," he grinned, his appetite for her was obvious by his skinny chest rising and falling rapidly. "Do what you want to me."

"I intend to," she whispered coldly.

"Matildys?" A spark of realization ignited too late.

"I am no longer your slave."

"Matil -"

She sliced the blade across his warm, pale throat. It was bloody, but it was over quickly. She watched as the life drained from his eyes; she had killed many times before, but this was personal, intimate – and it was the most satisfying.

Releasing her grasp of his head, she let him fall back on the bed and went to work setting the scene. First, she dropped the knife where she stood. She changed into her nightgown, threw her bloodied gown into the roaring fireplace, and ensured the balcony door was wide open before climbing into bed next to her dead husband – her younger brother. She splashed some of Cyler's blood on her hands and nightgown. She held his limp hand in hers and took a deep breath.

It was time to finish this.

Matildys released a blood curdling scream so high pitched it could have been heard throughout the entire city. The two Thrak stationed outside her room rushed inside, spears ready to strike. Tears streamed down her cheeks as she held Cyler and wailed, "Our king has been murdered!" She pointed to the balcony. "He escaped."

One of the Thrak beelined to the balcony while the second knelt by Cyler's bedside and picked up the knife with fresh blood dripping from the tip.

"Do you recognize this, my Queen?" He held it up for her to see.

She gasped and slapped her fingers over her mouth, smearing blood across her face. "It cannot be!"

"My Queen?" Thrak 82419 stood up.

"That dagger belongs to my son, Thanos." She sucked in a breath, "He murdered his own father."

Thrak 26317 stepped inside from the balcony. "He got away, but we'll find him."

"We'll send the collectors to fetch his body, my Queen," Thrak 82419 began to follow his companion to the door. "Should we send for a healer?"

"I am not injured," she waved them off, tears pouring down her cheeks. "Find him," she rasped. "Find my son before he escapes."

They bowed and scurried out to the arriving Thrak, instructing them to close the gates and find the prince. As soon as the doors slammed shut, she stood up and walked back to her vanity, picked up her brush, and finished combing her hair. The deed was done. She smiled at the sight of her husband's dead body in the reflection of the mirror and at the sight of his blood smeared across her face. She was finally free.

Chapter Nine

Crispin

Crispin had been on a ship once before when he was younger. He and his older brothers, Lykos, Mosgalath, and Elias, joined their father to examine Northwind's armada. It was purely ceremonial. They never left the harbor, but Crispin wished they had.

He was Issachar and Bilhah's fifth child – nowhere near threatened to be named heir to the throne – so he was determined to spend his days sailing the seas as an admiral in Northwind's navy.

He breathed in the salty sea air, his hair wafting in the breeze. A smile spread across his face, not caring a lick that the blazing sun was beating down on the deck mercilessly. For the first time in years, he felt at home, which was odd considering he didn't know the first thing about sailing.

Crispin scanned the ship's deck, taking in the motley crew of the *Shadow of Death*. Thieves, swindlers, drunks, gamblers, and murderers. Not his first choice of company, but at least they were on the same side. For now.

Captain Haldane was the sensible one.

Rahab was the stabby one.

Phex was the explosives one.

Corwin was the quiet one.

Ondrej was the giant one.

Rafi was the pint-size one.

Leeondris was the missing one.

Crispin shook his head. *A motley crew indeed*, he thought to himself. Salome would be fascinated by them. He wished she were there. He felt so alone. In truth, he had never been on his own before. What a strange, empowering, yet vulnerable feeling.

"Mainlander!"

Crispin glanced over his shoulder and saw Rafi waving him forward. He approached quickly since the halfling seemed to be in a hurry.

"The captain wants to see you in his quarters."

Crispin waited for Rafi to show him the way to the captain's quarters, but the pirate clearly had no intention of helping.

"Uh," Crispin cleared his throat and pointed up the steps, "I'm assuming it's that way."

"Maybe," Rafi stroked his pointy white beard with a mischievous grin, "maybe not."

"I'll show you the way to the captain's quarters," Ondrej's deep voice boomed behind him causing him to jump.

Crispin swung around, his face at direct level with the giant's bare chest. He never heard Ondrej come up behind him. He wasn't sure if he was more impressed someone, other than Korah – may his soul rest in peace – had managed to sneak up on him, or terrified that he had been caught unaware, like prey.

Crispin followed the enormous pirate up the creaky steps. Ondrej took three steps at a time while Crispin had to sprint just to keep up pace.

"You'll have to forgive Rafi." Ondrej ducked as he entered the hall leading to the back of the ship. "He doesn't take kindly to Mainlanders."

"And you?"

Ondrej shrugged. "I distrust everyone equally."

"Even your crew?"

Ondrej suddenly stopped and Crispin ran into him. "Especially the crew." He pointed at the wooden door at the end of the hall. "Go ahead, Mainlander. Keep your wits about you if you care to survive." He flashed a toothy smile and retreated the way they had come.

What an odd fellow. Crispin rubbed his temples. He faced the door and raised his fist to knock, but stopped, because he heard an angry voice on the other side. Knowing he shouldn't eavesdrop didn't deter him from placing his ear against the door.

"This is madness, Captain," Rahab spat. "We should turn him in, collect the bounty, and be done with it."

"Now, now, Rahab," Haldane's smooth as honey voice sounded, unbothered by her ranting. "You want us to get Leeondris back, don't you?"

"You know I do, but -"

"Then this is the only way," he interrupted. "You think those blind bastards at The Sisters will help pirates? No," Haldane set his glass down on his desk with a *clank.* "But they'll at least give the Prince of Northwind a chance to explain himself without turning him away at the gates."

"And once we find Leeondris, we turn the Mainlander over to the Shadows."

"I gave the boy my word. He helps us find our companion; I'll return him to his." Haldane's voice softened, "I owe Palma."

Rahab growled, "Fine. For Palma. But let it be on record that Rahab Montu was against helping this Mainlander."

"It is so noted." Haldane chuckled.

"What's so funny?" Rahab huffed as she leaned against Haldane's desk.

"You can come in now, Your Highness."

Crispin moved away from the door, unsure if he should really enter or not. Clearly Haldane already knew he had been eavesdropping. Crispin felt like he was about to be scolded by a parent for misbehaving. He drew his shoulders back, straightening up as tall as his six-foot frame could go, and pushed the door wide open.

"Would you care for some rum?" Haldane shoved the bottle across the table toward him. "It's a good year," he winked.

"No, thanks." Crispin sat down at the table, sliding the bottle back.

"You were eavesdropping?" Rahab hovered over him; arms crossed over her chest.

"I didn't want to interrupt," Crispin shrugged and flashed a smile up at her.

She lunged toward him, stabbing her ruby encrusted dagger between his fingers resting on the tabletop. He didn't flinch, although he was screaming on the inside.

"Very scary," Crispin purred.

"Enough," Haldane raised a hand in the air. "Sit down, Rahab."

"But -"

Haldane kicked a chair out. "I said, have a seat."

Reluctantly, with her eyes still pinned on Crispin, she uprooted her knife from the table and sank into the wooden chair, kicking her feet up on the desk.

"Now that we're all getting along," Haldane side-eyed Rahab until she planted her feet back on the floor, "we can get down to business." He cleared his throat and threw back a shot of rum. "We've set a course for The Sisters, where we'll have you," he set his gaze on Crispin, "arrange an audience with the Sovereign Neempo. "

Crispin leaned forward, wiggling all his fingers before placing his hands to his chin. "And why would the Sovereign agree to meet with me?"

"You're the Prince of Northwind, are you not?" Rahab picked at her fingernails with her knife.

"I am," he ignored her flicking the dirt from under her nails in his direction. "But again, why go to The Sisters at all? Is that where your friend is?"

"We need access to their Hall of Records," Haldane said.

"You want to see if they have your friend's location on file." Crispin finally understood. "Ok," he nodded, scratching his sprouting facial hair. "I meet with him, find out where your friend is being held, we rescue him, then you take me wherever I need you to take me." His eyes rested on Rahab as he finished that last part.

"First of all," Rahab squared her shoulders to Crispin's, "you won't be meeting with the Sovereign alone. I'll be going with you."

"Rahab -"

"Someone should keep an eye on him, Captain," Rahab interrupted Haldane's protest.

"What's the second thing?" Crispin asked.

"What?" Rahab cocked her head to the side, confused.

"You said, 'first of all', like there was more to follow." Crispin stretched out his legs and reclined in his seat. "Was there something else you needed to say?"

Rahab looked gob smacked. Then angry.

"I'll go out on a limb here and say, no," Crispin's mouth curved, "there was nothing more you were going to say."

Haldane tried to mask his laugh as a cough. Rahab glared at the captain then at the Mainlander, fire in her eyes.

"Are we done here?" She stood up, holstering her weapon.

Haldane cleared his throat, "Aye, we're done."

"Good." She swiped her leather tricorne from the coat rack and plopped it on her head as she stomped to the door.

"Going so soon?" Crispin said sarcastically as he flashed an exaggerated sad face.

"If I don't, I'll gut you like a fish."

"You could try."

"Tread lightly, Mainlander," she hissed, her hands clasped both his armrests as she leaned closer to his face. "There is quite a bit of sea before we get to The Sisters. I would hate for you to fall overboard."

Crispin smiled, "You would miss me."

"I'd recover." Rahab straightened and walked to the door, slamming it behind her.

Crispin's gaze was fixed on the door until Haldane cleared his throat. "She won't really, you know," Crispin made a slit-my-throat motion.

"There's a good chance she might," Haldane nodded. "But there's an equal chance of her warming up to you."

Crispin flashed a boyish grin, "I'll grow on her."

"Let us hope so, my new friend." Haldane took one more shot, this time wincing with the burn down his esophagus. "I would hate to lose out on so much money on account of your untimely death."

"Me too."

Haldane waved him out. "Off you go, lad. Have my First Mate give you a rundown of the rigging."

Crispin stood from his seat. "Who would that be? Corwin?"

"No." The captain flashed a childish smile exposing his three gold teeth.

"Let me guess." Crispin looked Heavenward with a sigh.

"You'd be right." Haldane slapped his knee with a chuckle. "And a good First Mate she is."

Crispin made his way to the door, not looking forward to dealing with that woman again, but ready to make the most of it, seeing as he was stuck on a ship in the middle of the Obsidian Sea. He closed the captain's door and turned to walk down the hall to the deck when Rahab stepped into view, blocking his path.

"Miss me already?" Crispin strutted closer with a grin.

"Hardly." Rahab's arms were crossed over her chest. "I wanted to talk to you privately."

"How exciting." Crispin wiggled his eyebrows. "It just so happens the captain wanted me to talk to you, too."

Rahab moved forward meeting him in the middle of the corridor. In a flash she aimed her knee toward his crotch, but he anticipated the childish move and grabbed her knee, shaking his head with a tsk.

"Not nice."

"Wasn't supposed to be," she balanced on one leg while he held her right knee firmly.

"And not fair either," he released her and watched her stumble back a step.

"What can I say," she shrugged. "I'm a pirate. How did you know I'd try that?"

"I have a sister and have been on the receiving end of that move plenty of times."

Rahab smiled, "I see." She slithered up to the side of his face, grazing his ear with her lips, and whispered, "Did she ever use this move on you?" She swiftly swept his leg out from under him. Slamming him to the floor, she mounted him, and pressed a knife to his throat.

"Oddly enough," Crispin grunted from the fall. "Yes." He smirked. "But I don't seem to mind it when you do it."

"Don't do that," she crinkled her nose.

"Do what?"

"Enjoy yourself."

"If you're not enjoying yourself, you're living wrong." Crispin placed his hands on the side of her hips. "You seem to be comfortable since you're still sitting on me."

Rahab slapped his hands off her hips. "Let's get one thing straight, Mainlander," she growled, nostrils flared. "If you get cocky enough to try to lay a finger on me again, I will slit your throat."

"Before you even realize it," he propped himself up on his elbows once she stood, "you'll find yourself wanting me to touch you again."

"I doubt th -"

Rahab was abruptly slammed against the wall. Something had struck the side of the black ship. Rahab tumbled and landed on top of Crispin. Nose to nose, they could feel each other breathing.

"See," Crispin smirked. "I'm growing on you already."

"Shut up." She pressed on his chest to push herself to her feet and stumbled toward the main deck where the crew was yelling out attack orders.

Haldane's door flew open with a bang. He placed his hands on either side of the hallway, steadying himself as he stomped through the narrow corridor. He grabbed Crispin by the arm and hoisted him to his feet. "You alright, lad?"

Crispin nodded. "What was that?" He followed the captain onto the deck. As soon as Crispin emerged from the hallway his question was answered.

An unearthly high-pitched screech rendered him nearly incapable of hearing. He slapped his hands over his ears and squinted through the ice-cold water stabbing his face, finding the crew fighting off enormous tentacles wrapping around the hull of the ship.

"What the hell is that?" Crispin yelled to Haldane, who was drenched from head to toe already.

Haldane whipped around, his eyes sparkling with reckless abandon. "That there is Kubantu."

Kubantu. Crispin had heard tales of the sea monster but chalked it up to sailors' drunken exaggerations. But now, in the middle of the Obsidian Sea, the fabled creature was trying to tear the ship apart and drag them to their watery graves.

Crispin counted seven – no, eight – tentacles. When Kubantu rose out of the sea, Crispin saw its dark scaly torso. The human-like creature opened its mouth revealing long, razor-sharp teeth and a split tongue. His snaky eyes searched for prey, hissing loudly when he spotted them scrambling on deck. He lifted his scaly arms and fiercely dug its black fingernails into the ship.

Crispin tore his eyes from the monstrous creature and slid down the polished, wooden railing, and landed on the deck with a loud thud. He unsheathed his sword, and hacked into one of Kubantu's tentacles, extracting a ghastly howl from the beast as it released its hold on the ship.

Its eyes found Crispin.

Damn.

Crispin tumbled forward, avoiding an incoming blow from another tentacle. He heard the wood of the hull starting to split. If they didn't kill this thing quickly, no one would survive. The prince took cover behind the tallest mast where Phex was fiddling with a weird metal sphere.

"What's that?" Crispin pointed at the ball covered with spikes.

Phex's grin was truly menacing and sent chills down Crispin's spine. "A gift for the hungry beast." He twisted the halves together and the spiky ball began to tick. "Heads up!" Phex shouted before tossing the sphere over his head and toward the monster.

The blast rattled the ship. Kubantu squealed. Haldane cursed as he fought at the helm to keep the ship as steady as he could.

Crispin poked his head around the mast and saw a couple of Kubantu's tentacles hemorrhaging from the explosion. Crispin turned to Phex, but the pirate was gone.

Crispin watched as Haldane continued to hold them steady and was amazed at how Corwin used every knife on his person to stab close-by tentacles. Rafi and Ondrej quickly repaired and plugged any holes in the ship to ensure the beast's assault didn't sink them. Phex sprinted across the deck and lobbed more spheres at the sea monster, cackling with each throw and glorious explosion.

"*You'll* sink us before *it* does, you bloody fool!" Rafi spared a moment to fuss at Phex as he slammed his hammer down on the piece of wood he nailed to the deck.

"Better to go out with a bang, then be taken by force." Phex danced around the halfling with a grin so wide, Crispin thought for sure his face would split.

"Off with you, crazy bastard!" Rafi shook his hammer at Phex and went back to his repairs.

Everyone was accounted for except Rahab. Crispin looked all over the deck and didn't see her. He stood up and circled the mast slowly, not wanting to attract Kubantu's serpentine eyes. But as he looked up at the monster, he realized its soulless eyes were already preoccupied.

Rahab launched a harpoon toward the creature, but he caught it and let out a thunderous laugh. She took a step back when he hissed, thrusting his reptilian tongue at her; as if to say, she was its next victim. She ran toward the mast Crispin was hiding behind, unaware of the tentacle swinging to snatch her.

She's not going to make it!

Before he even realized what he was doing, Crispin ran to meet Rahab. He shoved her out of the tentacle's path, but in doing so, was swept overboard and into the raging sea.

Kubantu's tentacle had a tight grip around Crispin's legs, so he withdrew to the depths of the Obsidian Sea, wounded, but not empty-handed. Crispin felt himself sinking deeper into the dark waters. He opened his eyes and reached for his sword. With all his might, he sliced through the monster's tentacle. Blood encircled him, but Kubantu either tired of the hunt, or in severe pain, didn't go after him.

The prince spun around trying to figure out which direction was up. He was running out of breath. His lungs tightened. He felt himself slowly losing consciousness – the water was claiming him. His eyes closed and his mouth opened releasing a stream of bubbles. Crispin felt ice cold water fill his lungs as he sank deeper into the sea.

A hand suddenly grabbed his and dragged him back to the surface. Hoisted aboard the *Shadow of Death*, his body slammed onto the deck. He heard voices, but it sounded like they were miles away. Lips pressed against his and air filled his lungs. His eyes shot open, and he turned violently to his side to cough up water.

Once he finally caught his breath and wiped the film from his eyes, he saw Rahab lying next to him, her head tilted toward him. Her chest rising and falling quickly. She wiped the strands of wet hair that stuck to the side of her face behind her.

"You?" Crispin gasped when he realized she was the one who had saved him. "Why?"

"How else are we going to get paid if you're dead?" She stood up to hobble to her quarters.

"The *real* reason," he turned onto his elbow.

Rahab didn't bother to turn around. "A life for a life. We're even." She squished her way to her quarters, leaving Crispin with the rest of the tired and wounded crew.

Haldane patted his face dry with a rag as he squatted in front of the prince.

"She saved me." Crispin watched her disappear up the stairs.

"Aye," Haldane nodded, offering his hand to help Crispin stand. "I suppose that means she likes you."

"Or my bounty," Crispin pointed out.

"I don't care how much someone loves money; they would never jump in after a sea monster, no matter how grand the pay day."

Crispin slipped his shirt off and wrung it out. That blackhearted woman had saved him. He never expected a pirate to rescue him once he'd gone overboard, but to have Rahab save him was humbling.

"Should I go thank her?"

"Manners are wasted on pirates, lad." Haldane patted him on the back. "But if it'll make you feel like you did your mother proud by being respectable, then go ahead."

Crispin put his shirt back on and headed up the stairs to Rahab's room. As soon as he rapped on her door, he regretted it, and turned to retreat when the door opened.

"What do you want, Mainlander?" Rahab stood behind the half open door.

"I...I wanted to uh, thank you, for..." Crispin shoved his hands into his pockets, "for saving my life."

"Wow."

"What?"

"Did that feel as painful as it looked?" Rahab cocked her head to the side. Droplets of water splattered on the wooden floor from her wet hair.

"Can you just say, 'you're welcome', so we can move on?" Crispin rolled his eyes.

Rahab leaned lazily against the doorframe wearing just a bralette and pants, scrunching her hair dry with a towel. "I think it's more fun watching you squirm."

"Look," he tilted his head back in exasperation, "it's been a long day. I said what I came to say, now I'm going to lay down."

"You're welcome, Mainlander."

"You know I have a name."

"Your point being?"

Crispin shook his head and shrugged. "No point. Sleep well, Rahab." He could feel her watching him as he walked a few doors down the hall to the quarters Haldane had assigned to him in Pulau.

"That's Leeondris' room." Her voice was soft in tone but bitter in delivery.

Crispin glanced over his shoulder at her, "What is he to you?"

She frowned, "None of your business."

He nodded and lifted his arms in surrender. "Is there another room you'd rather me stay in during my time here?"

She straightened up and shook her head with a scowl. "No."

Crispin turned the knob and entered before she could say anything else, entirely too tired to play her games. She exhausted him more than fighting off that sea monster. He closed the door, leaning his back against it, and exhaled a long, weary breath. He spied the sparsely furnished quarters with gratitude. A bed and wash basin – it was all he needed. He peeled his shoes and wet shirt off before he heard a soft knock.

Crispin debated whether he should open the door or not, but he trudged over and cracked it open. *Of course*. Rahab was standing there looking like she had something else to say.

"What is it now?" He propped open the door and stood in the narrow threshold.

Rahab's brows arched and her eyes narrowed, "What?"

"Did you think of something else you wanted to say that couldn't wait until morning? How much you hate Mainlanders? How you desperately oppose me being here? How you should turn me in to the Shadows and collect my bounty? How -"

"Thank you," she interrupted him. "I came to thank you... for what you did out there."

"Like you said before," his gaze fell to the floor, "we're even."

She slammed her hand against the door keeping him from closing it. "I distrust Mainlanders because they banded together and shipped those they deemed *misfits* and *undesirables* to Pulau to die. But our people did what the Mainlanders did not expect – we not only survived banishment to islands made of solid rock with no greenery or chance to cultivate vegetation, but we thrived. We were given a death sentence years ago, but now, Mainlanders fear seeing our sails approach their shores."

"I'm sorry that was the origin of your people," Crispin's eyes rose to meet hers. "And I'm sorry for calling Pulau, *Misfit Island,* but you have to believe me when I say, I'm not like those who came before me. What they did was wrong. I hope I can help you see I truly don't wish to be your enemy."

"You saved my life, the one thing I never expected from a Mainlander," she said in hushed tones and tugged at her earlobe. "Leeondris is like a brother to me. The only Mainlander to earn our trust."

His heart raced at her revelation, but his face remained stoic. "Why are you telling me this?"

"Because I know you want to know if you're rescuing my lover. You're not."

"I don't care."

"You tilt your head slightly to the left every time you're uncomfortable," she pointed out.

Crispin straightened his head. "And you tug your ear the moment *you're* uncomfortable." He rubbed his eyes and sighed. "Whatever this Leeondris is to you doesn't matter. Once I help you and your crew track him down, I'm gone."

Rahab's lips tightened; her smile faded. "Right. Enjoy resting while you can. We should arrive to The Sisters tomorrow." She marched off; her fists closed tightly.

"Rahab," he called after her.

She whipped around, "What is it, Crispin?"

He was taken aback. "You called me Crispin."

She placed her hands on her hips and crinkled her nose. "Aye. What of it?"

A smile snaked across his face. "I told you I'd grow on you."

Rahab rolled her hazel eyes and headed back to her room, "Good night, Your Highness."

"That's worse than Mainlander."

Rahab turned around and bowed, sweeping her hand from her side down to the floor, her head nearly touching the wooden planks. "Apologies, Your Mightiness."

He muttered and rubbed his temples, "And now the bowing. Please stop."

She popped up and curtsied, "Whatever will please His Lordship."

Crispin pursed his lips and ran his fingers through his wet hair, "So is this what we're doing now?"

"Whatever do you mean, Majesty?" Rahab spread her fingers and fanned her face like one of the ladies of court.

"Look at me," Crispin closed one eye, gritted his teeth, and thrusted an imaginary sword around the narrow hallway. "I'm a scary pirate here to plunder your fields, drink your ale, and bed ugly women just because I can."

Rahab stared at him. He couldn't get a read on her. Was she amused? Offended? Angry? He holstered the invisible weapon and tilted his head slightly to the left.

"Too far?" he asked.

Rahab snickered. "Who were you impersonating? I'd like to meet that pirate."

"It's how we as children imagined," he cleared his throat, "how we imagined pirates talked," his voice trailed off.

Rahab laughed. It was a glorious laugh that made his heart soar. "You want to see our impersonation of you Mainlanders?"

"Absolutely."

She threw her hands in the air, shuddered in fear, and wailed in a high-pitched voice, "Oh no! What are we to do? The fearsome pirates of Pulau are here. We should just roll over like dogs. Maybe, if we're good, they won't spank us."

"Spank us?" Crispin roared; his deep laugh echoed through the passageway. "That's ridiculous."

"What?" she shrugged. "You've never been spanked by a pirate?"

He furrowed his brow, "You spank people you rob?"

"Nooooo," she slowly shook her head. "We would never."

After an intense stare off, they both broke out into laughter.

"You're funny," she said.

"You've got a great laugh," Crispin said without thinking. He rubbed the nape of his neck. *Was she blushing?*

Rahab sobered up at the compliment, her fingers scratching her earlobe. "Well, I suppose we should get some rest. Big day tomorrow."

"Right." Crispin nodded, realizing he'd been standing in the hall shirtless and barefoot. "Sleep well." He retreated into his room and sat on the cot. A smile inched across his face. He couldn't wait to tell Salome he battled a sea monster. She'd be so jealous.

CHAPTER TEN

RANALDA

Thanos had been arrested and taken to the dungeon located underneath the Black Tower. Ranalda had never been this far underground before and had no intention of returning. Her hood draped over her blonde hair. Her black cloak dragged behind her, collecting bits of dirt, water, and sewage. Ranalda's pale hand shot up to cover her nose – the stench was unbearable. Blood, bile, waste, and rat droppings permeated the torch lit hallways. She passed cell after cell until she reached the end of the corridor. Two Thrak sat on either side of the iron door.

When they saw her approaching, one growled, "Who goes there?"

Ranalda quickened her pace without identifying herself.

The guards grabbed their weapons; one had a longsword, the other a mace.

"This hall is off limits!" The second Thrak screeched.

Within a few feet of them, she withdrew her hand from her cloak pocket and blew a white powder in their faces. In seconds, they both slumped to the ground, asleep. She scooped the key hanging from Thrak 87624's neck and unlocked the door to Thanos' cell.

The prince sat on the slab of rock meant to be a bed with his head buried in his hands. When he looked up, his blond tresses that had fallen forward swung back to cover the shaven parts of his head.

By the look in his weary eyes, Ranalda knew he didn't expect to see her.

"Ranalda?" He straightened up and fingered his hair back, though without the proper products, it wouldn't hold the structure he was so fond of. "What are you doing here?"

"Mother plans to have you executed in the morning for murdering Father." She leaned against the doorframe, flipping the key around in her fingers.

"I didn't kill the old man."

"I know."

"You...you believe me?" He sounded relieved.

"Isn't it obvious? Mother killed father and will not allow you to stand trial for Gomorrians to find you guilty or not. She is preparing the gallows for you as we speak."

Thanos stood up and started pacing the tiny cell. If he wanted to, he could stand in the middle of the room, stretch his arms and his fingertips would touch either side of the walls. "I don't want to die, Ranalda." He stepped toward her, taking her hands in his and lifted them to his lips. "You have to help me."

"I intend to, Thanos." She gently retrieved her hands and motioned him to follow her.

As he stepped out, he noticed the guards hunched over. "Did you...?"

"Kill them?" She shook her head. "No. That's when people start asking questions." She patted her cloak, "Sleeping powder. It will look like you escaped while they slept."

His expression hardened. "Where did you get the sleeping powder?"

"Don't ask questions." Ranalda frowned. "Follow me."

The twins scurried through the prison halls, avoiding the patrolling Thrak because they were both unarmed.

"We should have taken the Thrak's weapons," Thanos whispered angrily.

"It has to look like they fell asleep while guarding you. If we took their weapons, it would look suspicious. Now hush."

They climbed up the black stone steps that led them to the street level. Slipping past more Thrak, they slithered through the sleeping city to the northern gates where a saddled horse was waiting for him.

"This is where I leave you." She untied the horse from its tether and handed her brother the reigns. "Get as far away from here as you can. Go where mother cannot find you."

"No guards?" Thanos glanced over at the oddly unguarded gate.

"I have taken care of them. But they will not abandon their posts for long. You must hurry."

Thanos embraced his sister and kissed her forehead. "I owe you my life, Ranalda." He mounted the horse. "I will return when I know I can defeat her. We will be together again. I promise."

"Then I will await your return." She wrapped her arms around herself and watched as he swiftly rode into the night.

Maltidys stepped out of the darkness and approached her daughter from behind. "You did well, Ranalda." Maltidys stood next to her and watched as her son disappeared.

"Thank you, Mother." Ranalda bowed her head. "What happens now?"

"When the Gomorrians learn the accused prince killed the two Thrak guarding his cell and that he escaped the city in the dead of night, they will know without a doubt, that he is guilty." She smirked, "No trial necessary."

"We are free," Ranalda whispered, a tear running down the side of her cheek.

Maltidys rested a hand on her daughter's shoulder. "Yes, Ranalda, we are free."

Chapter Eleven

Adonijah

Adonijah was fond of women and women were fond of him. It was a blessing, or curse, depending on how he felt that day. Visiting islands inhabited by mostly women, was nothing short of a dream come true – so, why could he only think about *her*? Salome consumed his thoughts; something he was unaccustomed to, but not upset by. She was different from other women he had met before. And his feelings for her were different.

Since leaving the Mainland, they seemed to have developed a... spark? Was that even the right word to describe what was happening between them? Was there *anything* happening between them? He wasn't sure, but the one thing he *was* certain of was his attraction to her was reciprocated. As much of a hard time as she gave him, as much as her tongue lashed out at him, her eyes betrayed her every time.

Her eyes.

Her eye.

Her marked eye.

The first day they squared off in The Hollow, he noticed something unusual about her eyes. They were different colors. It was strange, haunting even. From that moment on, he hadn't been able to stop picturing her eyes every time he closed his. He saw the crinkles along the sides of Salome's eyes when she smiled and how she scrunched her nose when she was deep in thought.

Her scars.

She had so many scars.

Even he had left his mark on her in The Hollow – and she had left her mark on him, in more ways than one.

If she only knew the power she had over him.

Adonijah shook his head as the bell tolled on Antrope, fondly known as Arena Island, and dragged him back to reality. Men weren't allowed on the training grounds, but because Salome pulled some strings with the Myridians, he and Cato were permitted to escort Salome as her protection detail.

Adonijah's gaze drifted to where Salome sat on the ground tying the leather sandals she had been given to train in. Her long, tan legs glistened as the sun kissed them. His eyes slowly travelled up her legs, up her body, to her face, to her lips... His chest burned when he realized she was watching him too.

There was that warm smile he had grown so fond of.

"How long have you known her?" Cato's voice interrupted his thoughts.

It was no secret Adonijah didn't like Cato, but Harbona insisted they spend more time together so they could get to know one another. He knew what Harbona was doing. Harbona wanted him to change his mind, to change his opinion about Cato and the Mountain Men. But that wasn't going to happen.

Adonijah knew Cato was a Stormcrag, therefore he couldn't be trusted.

What else did he need to know?

Adonijah realized he had been silently staring at the Stormcrag after he asked his question. Adonijah softened his brow.

"What was your question?"

"I asked how long have you two known each other?" Cato repeated his seemingly innocent question.

"Long enough," Adonijah snarled.

"Are you two...?" Cato motioned with his hands, touching both his index fingers together.

"Why do you want to know?" Adonijah's shoulders tensed.

"I'm not the only one who is curious."

"Well, it is no one's business." Adonijah tilted his neck to the side and cracked it. He knew it was probably Diron, Captain of *The Golden Rose*, who was the other interested party in the status of his and Salome's relationship. Another man he wasn't sure he trusted, even if Harbona did.

"So, that's a no." Cato stretched his arms above his head with a yawn. "Why do they have to train this early?"

"Hold on," Adonijah squared his chest to Cato. "What do you mean, 'that's a no'?"

"Simple really." Cato absent mindedly cracked his knuckles. "If you two were a couple, you would have just said so. Instead, you huffed your way through the question. I might not come from one of the more sophisticated kingdoms, but I'm far from stupid."

Adonijah knew arguing would be pointless. He hadn't known Salome long, but it seemed like they were meant to find one another. Or had known one another in another life? Cato didn't need to know all of that. He didn't deserve to know all of that.

Adonijah tried to push their first night in Myr to the back of his mind, but their "almost kiss" kept finding a way back into his thoughts – his desires. Maybe they could be more than what they were which was... friends? *Were they friends?* Or were they simply fellow soldiers? No. He swatted that idea down immediately. He wouldn't have this unquestionable yearning to kiss his fellow soldier. Unless that soldier was Salome.

What was she doing to him? Even his thoughts were nonsense. All he knew was he wanted to protect her.

Adonijah became very aware Cato was still watching him and he cleared his throat. "Why did you come with us?"

Cato reclined against the grassy hillside, resting his arms over his eyes to block the rising sun's rays. "I already told you. I owed Salome a life debt."

Adonijah lit his pipe and exhaled with a disgruntled huff, "As far as I'm concerned, you two are even."

Cato peeked one brown eye through his arms. "How do you figure?"

"She saved you from being held captive by the Thrak. You saved her from dying by the Thrak's blade." Adonijah shot Cato a vicious yet satisfied glance. "Even." Cato chuckled which irritated Adonijah. "What's so funny, Stormcrag?"

"Harbona told me I should ask you to train me how to fight. That you would be a good teacher. But now, I can see how ridiculous that was."

Adonijah held the tip of his pipe between his teeth. "I would make an excellent teacher if -"

"Then you *will* train me?" Cato interrupted, sitting up straight.

"If," Adonijah continued, side eyeing him, "I cared enough to teach you."

Cato released a defeated sigh. "How long are we going to be sitting out here?"

"Until she's finished."

They sat silence. Adonijah glanced at Cato, who seemed deep in thought, and remembered Salome's words. "*Should he be judged for the sins of his ancestors?*"

"Why do you want to learn how to fight?" Adonijah broke the stillness between them and immediately regretted reaching out.

Cato didn't look up from his twiddling fingers. "Had I known how to fight, the Thrak wouldn't have taken me prisoner."

"Did your Stormcrags not teach you anything?" Adonijah stretched his legs out and exhaled another puff of smoke, watching it float away. "I thought your people knew how to handle weapons."

"I'm too scrawny to be considered a worthy warrior."

Adonijah hated he detected genuine sadness in Cato's voice. It was true Cato was extremely thin; his ribs were nearly visible through his clothes. He was also clean-shaven when the Stormcrags proudly grew their beards in two sectioned pieces boasting of their victories in battle.

"My parents were taken by the Gomorrians when I was young," Cato said, "and my sister was captured by the Krazaks shortly afterwards." He hesitated. He seemed to be struggling with the memories deep within the abyss of his haunted mind. "If I had known how to wield a sword..."

"You blame yourself?" Adonijah rested his elbows on his knees. Cato remained quiet. "I lost my mother," Adonijah offered. "I was young and thought if I knew how to fight, I could have saved her."

"But?"

"But I did know how to fight, and she still died." Adonijah's misty eyes met Cato's. "You can spend the rest of your life blaming yourself, or you can get even."

"Have you gotten even?"

"Soon."

The Stormcrag nodded, shoulders hunched, defeat in his eyes.

Adonijah grumbled to himself, unsure if he was more irritated that they had more in common than he would have liked to admit, or that Harbona probably already knew that.

"Stand up."

Cato's light brown eyes flashed. "Are you going to fight me or train me?"

"Don't make me regret this," Adonijah rolled his head in a circular motion. Extending a hand to help Cato up, the Stormcrag took it and smiled as he jumped to his feet. "This doesn't mean I like you." Adonijah maintained eye contact as he stashed his pipe in his pocket.

"Of course not," Cato replied, rubbing his hands together in anticipation.

"And before I show you anything -"

"If I even think about betraying you or Salome, you'll kill me," Cato interjected and rolled his eyes.

Adonijah frowned and folded his arms across his chest. "Why would you assume that's what I was going to say?"

Cato took a step back. "Is that not what you were about to say?"

"No."

"Oh." Cato gritted his teeth. "What were you going to say?"

"I want you to answer my question from before." Adonijah stared down his nose at him. "Why did you come with us?" Before Cato could utter a word, Adonijah lifted his hand and said, "And I want the truth."

Cato stroked a hand over his short-cropped white hair, a scar zig-zagged along the side of his head. "The truth is," he clicked his teeth, "there are two reasons I joined your company."

"The first being?" Adonijah prodded.

"I have spent my entire life in the Bone Mountains fearing other Mainlanders. But then you rescued us from the Thrak, from certain death, and I had to know why."

"Salome saved you." Adonijah corrected. "I didn't want to." Cato swayed side-to-side, an immediate tell in Adonijah's mind of his nerves and discomfort. "And the second reason?"

"I noticed Salome's eyes."

Adonijah suppressed the panic rising within his chest; his fingers brushing the handle of his blade. He swore an oath to protect her. An oath he was intent on keeping. "What about her eyes?"

"Stormcrags believe in a prophecy that a woman with two colored eyes would one day bring peace to the Bone Mountains. She would be the only one to finally reunite the Stormcrags and the Krazaks," Cato explained. "So, when I saw her eyes, I knew she was the one. I had to follow her. Serve her in her quest and maybe when the time was right..." His gaze dropped to his feet.

"...she would save your people." Adonijah finished Cato's thought.

"I know you don't believe me -"

"I believe you."

"You do?" Cato whispered sheepishly.

"Aye." Adonijah nodded, unsheathing his long sword. Cato instinctively took a step back. "Here." Adonijah turned the blade so Cato could grab the handle. "Show me what you know, and I will teach you what you don't."

Cato stretched out his hand to take the weapon. His long, bony fingers wrapped around the hilt, and he raised it in front of him. He spied his reflection in the clean blade and saw a soldier. Sort of. Not really. But with Adonijah's help, he could be.

Cato smiled, "Does this mean we're friends now?"

"Don't press your luck, Stormcrag."

"What should I call you?"

"Adonijah."

"Well, that seems boring considering the fun nickname you've given me." Cato scratched his jawline. "Maybe, Northwind-er?"

"That's terrible," Adonijah deadpanned.

"Northerner?"

"Why are you doing this? Call me Adonijah."

"Will you call me Cato?"

"I prefer Stormcrag." Adonijah wasn't about to use his name. He didn't want them to be that friendly.

"Then I will call you.... Swamps." Cato flashed a gap tooth smile.

"Swamps?"

"Salome told me that's where you used to live."

Adonijah rubbed his temples, squinting his eyes. "Just... show me your fighting stance."

"As you wish, Swamps." Cato saluted before noticing Adonijah's serious expression. "Sir Swamps?"

"Your fighting stance."

Cato planted his feet wider than his shoulders and held the sword with both hands perpendicular to his thin frame.

Adonijah blinked. "What the hell is that?" He motioned his hand toward Cato's awkward posture.

"My fighting stance."

Adonijah groaned, "Almighty, what have I gotten myself into?"

"Well, that's encouraging," Cato rolled his eyes with a disgruntled huff.

Adonijah's fascination, or obsession, with weaponry began at a young age. He was from the farmlands north of Gomorrah, raised by a single mother. He hardly ever saw his father, but on the unfortunate occasion he did show up, Adonijah's mother would have him run into the fields to stay out of his father's reach.

During one of his father's unexpected visits, nine-year-old Adonijah snuck back to their two-room farmhouse, and saw his father strike his mother. The sight enraged him, and he vowed to kill his father the next time he came around.

He knew from his grandfather's drunken ramblings that his mother had been raped and he was the bastard that was the constant reminder of the attack. His mother had been seventeen when...

He didn't want to think about the cruelty his mother endured. Although his grandfather hated him, his mother loved him.

"You are my blessing," she would say as she combed her fingers through his hair while he fell asleep in their shared bed.

The next year when his father's entourage returned, his father was noticeably absent. Adonijah's mother sensed something was wrong and forced him to hide under the floorboards since he would be spotted retreating to the fields. He could still remember her golden hair in a single braid, smelling like wildflowers. Her warm brown eyes that emanated joy, and the freckles across the bridge of her nose he always wished he had.

But those memories were tainted when the disfigured Shadow – the Nameless Rider – kicked in their door and grabbed his mother by her throat, pushing his inebriated grandfather to the floor with his free hand.

"Where's the boy?" the Shadow growled.

"He's gone." His mother gasped, clawing at the soldier's tightening grip.

"Last chance, Satara. Where is he?"

"Tell him, he will never have my son."

"Have it your way." The Nameless Rider snapped her neck and dropped her lifeless body to the floor, shaking the floorboard dust and clouding his hiding spot.

His grandfather lugged himself up and threw a knife from the kitchen table at the Shadow. He caught the blade with little effort and launched it back at the old man, lodging it into his chest.

"Search the area for the boy." The Nameless Rider instructed the other two soldiers in his company. "I'll burn the house."

As flames engulfed the small farmhouse, Adonijah crawled on his belly to the edge of the house and kicked down the loose boards from under their shack and escaped.

Adonijah hid in the fields until the soldiers disappeared. With just a knife at his disposal, he wandered Adalore, doing odd jobs for a hot meal or place to rest, learning fighting techniques from strangers as he travelled. That's how he became known as the Wanderer. Now, nineteen, he had enough grief and experience to exact his final revenge. He would kill the Nameless Rider. He would kill his father. And then his mother could finally rest.

But first – he had to teach Cato.

Adonijah shook his head, rattling the sad memories from of his mind, and cleared his throat.

"Put one foot forward and one foot back. You will have better balance and a better chance to lunge at your attacker." Adonijah grabbed Cato by the shoulders and pointed to where his feet should be. The Stormcrag quietly obeyed. "Now, you look like a soldier." Adonijah nodded in approval.

"I feel... stupid."

Adonijah chuckled.

"So, you *do* know how to laugh," Cato snorted. "I was beginning to wonder."

Adonijah sighed and waved his hand forward. "Lunge."

Cato extended his front leg straight ahead and stabbed into the air with his sword. "Lesson one, complete."

"Is this a joke to you?" Adonijah crossed his arms over his chest and frowned. "Tell me now before I waste my time."

Cato sucked in a breath, "Sorry." He scratched the side of his head. "I'm nervous."

That wasn't what Adonijah had expected to hear. Mountain Men were ferocious in nature – some would say unfeeling. Cato wasn't like his kind in stature or attitude. It was almost difficult to dislike Cato. *Almost*. Adonijah had been deceived and hurt before. He wouldn't let that happen again – especially with Salome in the picture.

Adonijah wiped the nape of his neck. "Lunge." Cato once again obeyed his instructions. Adonijah nodded and clasped his arms behind his back. "Again."

He would make a soldier of him yet. And possibly a friend? Probably not.

Chapter Twelve

Salome

Salome was glad Adonijah and Cato were only forty feet away. She was nervous – but not exactly sure why. It wasn't like she really needed any training. For over a decade that was all she and her brother did. Zophar taught them all about swords, knives, archery, hand to hand combat, and even setting traps to ambush their enemies. She had put in the training, and she had the scars to prove it.

As she strapped on the leather sandals Mika had tossed her, instructing she was to wear them per Qata Vishna tradition, Adonijah's gaze had not gone unnoticed. She saw desire in his eyes, the same desire from the other night when they almost...

She cursed under her breath, inhaling a deep breath of salty sea air wafting over the cliff where the training arena had been built.

Why did she care?

Why did she want to kiss him?

She had never concerned herself with the ways of men before but now – he was taking up too much time in her thoughts. Time and thoughts she really couldn't – shouldn't – waste on him.

Her task was simple. Defeat her sister and avenge innocent blood – her family's blood. She looked at her tattoo and their faces flashed in her mind. She lost four brothers: Lykos, Mosgalath, Elias, and Jepthudar. Lykos was the responsible one. Mosgalath was the smartest. Elias was the prankster. Jepthudar was the sweet one. Although, most of her brothers teased her about her eyes, Crispin included, she missed them terribly.

She missed Crispin. She *really* missed him.

Salome fought hard not to think of him or what dangers he might be facing. But every night before she drifted off to sleep, she would recite the same prayers she had spoken for the last twelve years. She would whisper the names of her fallen family members – blessing them in the afterlife and keeping their memory alive in the present – but after they parted ways in The Hollow, she added Crispin and Zophar to her list; asking the Almighty to protect and watch over them because she no longer could. Praying she would see what remained of her family again.

Family.

Family meant everything.

Yet, family was what ripped hers apart.

Niabi had been married off to the King of Elisor, the Leader of the Andrago, before Salome had been born. The sisters had never met. At least, not formally. Salome saw her once, and it was the night Niabi attacked Northwind.

Salome remembered weaving through the chaotic city streets, sneaking past hordes of enemy soldiers undetected. Ducking into a dark alley, Zophar pushed Crispin and Salome against a white stone house and motioned for them to keep quiet.

"Wait for me here." Without another word, Zophar scurried off into the darkness.

Salome was too afraid to even breath. Neither she nor her brother knew their way around their city. In fact, they had only left the castle grounds a handful of times and hadn't bothered to observe their surroundings.

Heavy footsteps stomped on the main street. She sucked in a breath as the footsteps drew closer, hoping they wouldn't be discovered. The company of Shadows marched up the cobblestone path with the Green-Eyed-Raven leading them toward the White Keep. As they came within view, a soldier from Gershom's troop stepped forward.

"Lord Gershom has taken control of the White Keep," he reported flatly. "The city is yours."

"Not yet it isn't," the Mistress of Shadows hissed.

"The North belongs to you." The soldier narrowed his eyes and grunted, "Celebrate your victory."

Tala pointed his blood-stained sword toward the soldier, his tone too bold for his liking. "Shall I kill him, my Queen?"

"No." Niabi circled the soldier like prey. "The North still has a living king – one I must now deal with."

"He is in the throne room." The soldier's voice quivered and his breathing slowed. "They are waiting for you."

"How fitting he would be in his beloved throne room the night he dies." Even with ash and soot thick in the air and portions of the city burning, Niabi's focus on the White Keep did not waver.

"Should I show you the way?" The soldier asked, hoping to fall into her good graces for his disrespect.

"That won't be necessary." Facing him with a twinkle in her eye, Niabi stabbed him in the abdomen with one of her daggers and watched as he dropped to the ground. "I know the way." Looking over her shoulder at her Shadows, she said, "Move out."

As soon as the company was out of sight, the children sprinted down the street unsure of where they were headed. They rounded the corner and bumped into a soldier. Before they were able to scream, Zophar covered their mouths and whispered, "It's me."

"We saw her!" Crispin blurted.

"Saw who?"

Salome grabbed his hand, tears in her eyes, "She is going to kill father."

"We must get out of the city before she realizes you escaped." Zophar marched onward, dragging them forward.

"Why is she doing this?" Salome refused to take another step and ripped her hand from Zophar's grasp. "Who is she?"

"One day when we are far away from here, I will answer any question you ask of me, Princess, but today is not that day."

"But -"

"I need you to trust me." Zophar knelt before her. "If you don't, there won't be anything I can do to protect you."

Salome and Crispin followed him into a small house near the southwest side of the wall that encircled the city. Zophar closed the creaky door behind them and pushed the furniture to the sides of the room. Kicking a dusty rug up, they saw a door in the floorboards. He lifted the heavy latch and revealed a tunnel.

"Where does that go?" Crispin asked.

"Under the wall. It is the only way we can get out now."

Not needing any further explanation, Crispin descended the ladder into the tunnel. Zophar motioned for Salome to follow her brother.

"Lykos promised he would see us again." She took a step back from the hole.

"The Almighty willing, you might." Zophar once again motioned for her to follow the path.

Instead, she opened the door of the house and stared up at the White Keep in the center of the city with clenched fists. Ash rained down like snow and she no longer felt fear.

"One day when you least expect it," she hissed, "I will come for you, and I will kill you."

She was five. And she meant what she had said. One day she would kill her sister. It seemed it was now destiny for the sisters to face off. But Niabi had taken the impenetrable White City in a night. How could Salome compete with power like that?

"Salome!" Mika's voice ripped her from her thoughts. "Are you alright?"

Salome nodded, blushing, "I'm fine."

"I called out to you several times." Mika arched her brow.

Salome scratched the nape of her neck. "I guess I didn't hear you."

By the grace of the Almighty, Mika let the matter drop. "Are you ready?"

"I'm ready."

Mika led Salome to the center of the arena. The training grounds, located on Antrope, the smallest island of the Isles of Myr, was built atop of the cliff's plateau which overlooked the blue seas and the palace on the main island. Once again, Salome found herself catching her breath at the magnificent view and could feel the warm sea breeze wrap around her like a familiar and much needed hug.

Mika tossed Salome a sword with a bronze hilt. "You have skill with a blade?"

"I've been trained." Salome circled the handle around her hand.

"Trained by the Qata Vishna?"

"No, by -"

"Then you have not been trained," Mika clicked her tongue.

Salome's nostrils flared, "I was trained by Zophar of Borg, my father's Master of War."

"He might have taught you to fight," Mika conceded, "but the Qata Vishna will teach you to war." She cocked her head and flashed a confident smile.

"And there's a difference?" Salome's hand went to her hip.

"When you fight, you battle your equal. When you war, you defeat your lessers." Mika nodded her head to the weapon Salome held. "Show me what the Westerner taught you."

Salome took her stance and Mika shook her head in disapproval. "What?" Salome huffed.

"Your posture is that of a man."

Salome glanced at her footing, "It's a rooted position -"

Mika clicked her tongue again and shook her head, "You have been around men far too long, Cousin. Give me the greatest male warrior in Adalore and the least of the Qata Vishna will defeat him."

Salome straightened, "Bold talk for a people who have not seen battle in decades. "

"And why do you think that is?" Mika circled her cousin, arms securely fastened behind her back. "The Mainlanders do not pick fights with us because we are unbeaten. To war with us is a fool's endeavor."

"Unbeaten?"

"The Qata Vishna are at a level no man can touch." She stopped and stood face to face with Salome. "If you learn our ways, you will not be defeated."

"Is that how my sister defeated my father?" Salome's eyes narrowed; the words left a bitter taste in her mouth. "Her Qata Vishna training?"

Mika's expression changed, as if she was deep in thought. "Half-blood, yet she was the fiercest among us."

Salome crossed her arms over her chest, "You sound jealous."

Mika shook her head. "I would have followed her into the awaiting arms of Death..."

"But?"

"The world of men would not allow her to rise and take her rightful place at the High Table. Imagine what she could have been, had she stayed with us."

"She's a queen now -"

"Enough of your sister." Mika cut her off with what looked like sadness in her eyes. "It is not my story to share. I am here to train you. So," she pointed at the sword, "show me what you know."

Salome had so many questions she wanted Mika to answer, but the Myridian would duel her whether she was ready or not. She took her stance and Mika shook her head in dismay again. Salome grasped her sword with both hands, eyes fixed on Mika. The Red Maiden unsheathed her curved sword.

Mika reached her hand forward, fingers motioning for Salome to attack. "Begin."

Salome was used to defensive fighting, not being the aggressor. But with Mika's beckoning, she leapt forward, her sword swinging toward Mika with speed and fury.

Mika stood still and only lifted her sword to block the attack at the last possible moment. She didn't even look like she was trying.

They exchanged clashes of swords, side stepping one another. The difference between them wasn't the moves so much as the style. Salome was nowhere near as quick, seamless, and fluid as Mika was. Mika didn't appear to even be fighting – more like dancing. Her spins, twists, splits, and back bends astounded Salome. The most acrobatic move Salome had under her belt was a leg sweep and that wasn't perfect nor graceful.

Salome finally caught Mika's blade and flicked it from her hands, disarming her. Salome smirked, "It would seem Zophar taught me well."

"He taught you well." Mika leapt in the air, spun around, and kicked Salome's sword out of her hand and upon landing had unsheathed a pair of daggers that were strapped behind her back. "But he did not teach you everything."

Salome realized too late that her mouth was wide open and quickly closed it before Mika could comment. She snatched one knife strapped to the back of her pants and the wolf dagger from her thigh, flipping them around her hands.

"I'm better with my knives," Salome planted her feet and tilted her head.

"Let us hope so," Mika snorted.

Salome could feel Adonijah and Cato's eyes on her, but she refused to look their way. She didn't need to be distracted. She didn't need to lock eyes with *him*.

"You think he's impressed?" Mika asked, as if she could read her mind.

Salome attempted to keep a straight face, but the slight twitch of an eyebrow betrayed her.

Mika flashed a mischievous smile. "Let's give him something to think about later, shall we?" Mika lunged at her, blades whipping in separate directions to throw Salome off balance. Salome blocked both incoming daggers and kicked Mika away from her.

"Good," Mika cooed. "Knives are in your blood. The weapon of choice for the Qata Vishna."

Mika dodged Salome's blows, twisting side to side, flashing her back as she spun in a complete circle. Their knives sliced through the air so quickly, it didn't look like they were armed with weapons at all. Mika knocked one of Salome's knives from her hand, leaving just her wolf dagger.

Salome held the dagger tightly, the blade faced toward the ground. She hunched her body slightly, closing her chest off from attack, making herself a smaller target.

Mika flipped, kicked, swiped, and lunged to disarm Salome but she blocked the blows and held fast to her weapon.

Salome studied Mika's movements, and though they seemed chaotic and unstructured, there was a pattern. Mika lunged one of her arms forward, Salome locked her arm around Mika's, popped her elbow forcing her to drop her knife.

"Good," Mika nodded approvingly, back-to-back with Salome, arms still locked. "But I am afraid, you've lost sight of your footing."

"What?" Salome glanced down to see Mika's foot swipe Salome's leg, knocking her to the ground. Salome's dagger fell and as she reached for it, Mika's remaining knife sliced between Salome's outstretched fingers, lodging itself into the arena's grass.

Salome's eyes shot up. Mika's dagger was less than an inch from having stabbed her hand. "Did you miss?"

"Miss?" Mika planted her hands on her hips and frowned. "A Qata Vishna does not miss."

Still on her belly, Salome spat, "You could have stabbed me."

"If I meant to stab you," Mika crouched in front of her and withdrew her knife from the ground, "I would have stabbed you." She offered Salome her hand and helped her up. "Not bad for a Mainlander trained by a man from the West."

Salome retrieved her knives and holstered them. "Was my mother a Qata Vishna?"

Mika shook her head. "No. The eldest daughter is destined for the Qata Vishna. The second daughter for diplomacy. The third for the oracle."

"So, you being the oldest of your mother's daughters -"

"Qata Vishna." Mika holstered her weapons. "My sister, Marina, was meant for diplomacy. But you have seen how she treats those from the Mainland."

"I'm assuming she's not a great diplomat."

Mika laughed. "Not at all."

"Mother!" A young girl sprinted across the arena and jumped into Mika's outstretched arms.

"My little warrior! I see you outsmarted your guard detail again." Mika kissed her ten-year-old daughter on the cheek.

"It's not hard to get away from them."

"Well, I suppose that confirms what I already know."

"What's that?" Utara snickered.

Mika cupped Utara's face in her hands, "You are most definitely my daughter."

Salome was taken aback. She didn't know Mika had a daughter and she was dressed like a miniature Qata Vishna. Utara was the spitting image of her mother: long black hair, green eyes, olive skin, and a mischievous grin.

Mika stood behind her daughter, her hands resting on her shoulders and said, "Salome, this is my daughter, Utara. She has just made her tenth year and is now able to begin her training to become a Qata Vishna."

Just made her tenth year. Korah died when he turned ten. Salome had refused to think about the young boy from the Tree House Forest but seeing Utara so full of life reminded her of what sparked their journey. Korah.

"It's good to meet you, Utara." Salome managed to say with a sad smile.

"One day, when I'm older," Utara rattled off the words as fast as she could, brushing one of her feet against the back of the opposite leg, "I'm going to be the Red Maiden, just like my mother."

Mika beamed, clearly proud of the little version of herself. Salome didn't have much time with her own mother and seeing them together brewed fond memories, sad memories, too. She would give anything to have her mother back. To know if she was proud of the woman she had become.

When Salome was little, she would constantly find herself on the receiving end of a stern look and reprimand from her mother because she had been crawling through the bushes to scare the gardeners, or challenging her brothers to fight, or for ripping and setting fire to all her dresses in order to wear pants. After Bilhah fussed at her, she would flash a bright smile Salome's way letting her know how much she still loved her, though she was one of the reasons Bilhah's hair had begun turning white.

"Aren't you too old to be training to be a Qata Vishna?" Utara's question was met with an immediate frown from Mika.

"Our cousin is just the right age to become one of us, Utara."

"Sorry, Mother." Utara glanced up at her mother who was still holding her shoulders.

"We should head back to the palace." Mika wiped dirt off her daughter's face. "There is a lot to do before the festival begins tonight."

"Festival?" Salome's eyes widened. "What festival?"

"The Festival of Forbidden Fruit. Once a year, the men and women of Myr are gathered together to find a suitable mate," Mika explained as they walked toward Adonijah and Cato. "As royalty, your presence will be required, of course."

"I'm not sure I'll be any good in a festival setting," she protested.

"Don't worry," Mika tapped Salome's arm and winked. "You're not expected to find a mate tonight, unless you want to."

Salome's cheeks flushed, her eyes fluttering up to Adonijah's awaiting ones.

"We can go?" Cato stretched his arms high above his head.

"Yes," Mika affirmed. "Race you to the ship," she bumped Utara with her hip and together they took off down the hill. Cato followed them closely leaving Adonijah and Salome to make their way down to the awaiting ship.

"You held your own out there," Adonijah sparked the conversation once he knew the others wouldn't overhear them.

"I lost." Salome brushed dust from her clothes.

"Everyone loses at some point," he shrugged.

"Apparently not Qata Vishna." She didn't want to talk about the Qata Vishna anymore, so she changed the subject. "Are you going to the festival tonight?"

"Wherever you go, I go."

"It seems I have to go," she grumbled. "I'm afraid this might be the first of many royal engagements I will have to attend, if my Aunt Zara has her way."

"Ah," Adonijah clicked his tongue, "it can't be that bad."

"As long as they don't force me to wear a dress, I'll be alright."

Adonijah laughed the deepest, warmest laugh she had ever heard.

"What's so funny?" Her eyes narrowed.

"Picturing you in a dress."

She crinkled her nose, waving a hand in the air. "It isn't that funny, Adonijah."

"Someone as stab happy as you in a dress?" His eyes danced in delight. "I would break out of the deepest, darkest dungeon if it meant seeing *you* in a dress." Adonijah roared again.

"I hate you." She marched ahead of him; nose pointed upward.

"If only that were true." Adonijah took longer strides and easily caught up to her again.

"If my Aunt Zara has me parading like a peacock at this festival," she snorted, "I'll dive into the sea and pray the Almighty takes me."

Adonijah caught her arm and turned her toward him. His free hand gently stroked her jawline. "It doesn't matter what she has you wear; you will still be the most beautiful woman in the room."

Salome reached up and touched his hand, guiding it away from her face. "People might see you."

"Aye, they might."

"They might think we are..." she tilted her head side to side.

"I don't care what they think." Adonijah squeezed her hands. "I only care what you think."

Salome soaked in every bit of passion in his eyes and felt the strongest urge to kiss him. They had almost kissed the night before and she dreamt about how it would feel to have his lips pressed against hers. But before she could say anything, Cato yelled at them.

"Hurry up! We're ready to cast off."

Adonijah smiled down at her, "Come on, Princess. You have a festival to get ready for."

Chapter Thirteen

Niabi

Niabi sat at her desk in her high back chair and sliced her daily correspondence open. The light breeze blowing through her office was evidence the season was changing from summer to autumn. She preferred the warm weather over the harsh winters of the north, but Rollo loved the cold, and this was going to be the first winter without him. She reluctantly pushed him to the back of her mind. If she allowed herself to dwell on him, she would never respond to any of the letters sitting on her desk.

She skimmed through the first six letters and they were of no importance. Invitations by lords and ladies of Northwind to join them for their parties, weddings, and funerals; all of which she would decline as she always did. She had never been one for attending social events and after Rollo died, she was even more determined to be a recluse. They would not get the satisfaction of hosting their queen when she was still in such a vulnerable state.

Niabi tossed the invitations back on the black wooden desk and reached for the last folded parchment. It bore no seal and was addressed to *The Queen of Northwind.* No formality like the others. She unfolded the letter and scanned the scratchy penmanship with curious eyes.

To the Queen of Northwind.

I offer you a trade. Your sister for my kingdom.

I am staying at the White Wolf Inn.

I request an audience with you as soon as possible.

Signed,

Prince Thanos of Gomorrah, Rightful and Soon to be King.

A twisted smile tugged at her lips.

How peculiar, she thought to herself.

Word had reached the White Keep that King Cyler was dead; murdered by his own son. The son that had escaped the impenetrable Gomorrian dungeons before he could be tried and executed. The same son who now requested to speak with her, to make a trade.

Your sister for my kingdom.

Niabi had never met the prince before, but she knew he couldn't be guilty of murder. She had the displeasure of meeting Matildys years ago and had no interest of socializing with the shrew again. Niabi couldn't prove it, but she was certain the murder was Matildys' handiwork.

But did she hate Matildys enough to help her son usurp the throne? Absolutely.

Niabi quickly jotted down her response:

Prince Thanos,

I will grant you an audience.

Signed,

Queen Niabi of Northwind

Niabi folded the letter, poured a glob of hot, black wax on the seam, and sealed it with her signet ring. After passing the message to the courier outside her door, she plopped into her chair with a well-earned glass of Myridian wine. She brought the sweet-smelling liquid to her lips and enjoyed the tingle in her mouth.

A knock on her door interrupted the first bit of relaxation she had had in weeks.

"Enter." She sighed and set her glass down.

Pash opened the door and bowed, his arm crossing over his chest and touching his left shoulder. "My Queen."

She waved him inside without turning to look at him. "What news do you bring me?"

Pash shut the door and slowly walked up to her desk; his arms firmly clasped behind his back. "We might have a problem."

Niabi leaned back in her seat and motioned for him to sit. "And what problem would that be, Pash?"

He sat down on the other side of her desk, legs shoulder-width apart, bouncing his leg rhythmically. "As you suggested, I offered my services to my father."

"And?" She pressed when he paused.

"He has asked for me to silence Lord Memucan of Numbio."

"Silence as in kill him." She took another sip of wine, not surprised by Gershom's request.

"Yes."

Niabi flicked her gaze up from her glass to Pash. "Do you intend to kill him?"

"That is what my father has asked me to do."

"That is not what I asked." Niabi poured a second glass of wine and slid it toward him.

Pash gratefully grabbed the cup and swallowed nearly half its contents in one gulp. "Do you want me to kill him?"

"I want any servant of your father's dead."

"So, that's a yes?" Pash's question seemed labored. As if it hurt him to say.

"Why does he want Memucan dead?" Niabi swirled the wine in her goblet. "He's old as dirt. Death can't possibly be far from claiming the codger."

Pash ran his fingers through his hair and scratched the back of his neck. "My father didn't give a reason."

Niabi strummed her fingers on her desk, deep in thought. She played through different scenarios as to why Gershom would want Memucan dead. *What was Gershom's game?* "What exactly did Gershom order you to do?"

"He told me to bring him Memucan's head."

"Wasn't Memucan the one who informed Gershom that my brother was in Numbio?"

"Yes," Pash nodded.

Niabi kicked her legs up on her desk exposing the black leather pants that were hidden under the billowing folds of her extravagant outfit. "Perhaps Memucan knows something Gershom does not want anyone else to find out. But why silence him now?"

"He has served his purpose?" Pash shrugged and finished his glass of wine. Niabi pointed toward the decanter for him to refill it.

"Or maybe," Niabi whispered, biting her bottom lip, "he does not want Memucan dead at all."

"What?" Pash asked, cocking his head to the side.

"It's clever really." Niabi tapped her nearly empty glass against her temple, trying to make sense of the chaotic thoughts running wild in her mind. "Gershom has a strong ally in Memucan. Even I don't have servants in Numbio." She straightened up and locked eyes with Pash. "If you go down there to kill the old man, one of two things will happen. Either Memucan will be waiting for you and will have you killed on the spot," she tapped one finger and then a second one on her desk, "or you will be brought before King Osiris for attempting to assassinate his advisor. Memucan tells him that I am the one who sent you, which would be seen as a declaration of war. With the Numbio supporting Gershom's plan to usurp my throne, he could attempt to take Northwind for himself. You would be executed, and I would be left fighting two wars. One with my siblings, and one with your father."

Pash was silent for a minute, digesting everything she said, before he responded. "I suppose it's safe to assume my father doesn't trust me."

Niabi crinkled her nose, lifting her glass to her lips. "He just wants to hurt me."

Pash leaned his head back against his chair, sighing as he stared at the ceiling. "I'm afraid I'm not as useful a spy as you thought I would be."

Niabi placed her empty glass down, stood up, and glided toward him. "You have found out enough."

"You don't seem upset." Pash's brows furrowed.

Niabi sat in his lap and walked two of her fingers up his arm. "You were only meant to be the decoy. My real eyes and ears already have Gershom's trust. No need to fret, Pash. We will know more soon enough."

Pash's hand rubbed up and down her thigh. It was apparent he was trying to process the new information, but she wasn't going to volunteer more on the matter.

"I received an interesting letter today." She changed the subject when his touch became too distracting.

"From?"

"The Prince of Gomorrah," she was delighted when his eyes widened.

"What does he want?" He crinkled his nose. Pash had never liked the Gomorrians and Niabi couldn't blame him. The Gomorrians were a cruel and vile people. Even she didn't want her mind to dwell too long on the abomination of the Thrak. She shuddered.

"Thanos has requested a meeting with me." Niabi pressed on. "And I want you to be there."

His hands tightened around her hips. "What could he possibly want with you? Surely he wouldn't be stupid enough to attempt to kill you like he killed his own father."

"Hardly," she scoffed. "He wants to make a trade. My sister for his kingdom."

"You would support a murderer?"

Niabi narrowed her eyes and pushed herself off him. "I murdered for the crown. Sometimes one must bloody their hands to get what they want."

Pash sat quietly as she walked to the other side of the room. He rose to his feet and saluted. "Forgive me, my Queen. I meant no offense. I will support whatever decision you make."

Niabi whipped around when his hand reached for the door. "Pash, don't go."

"Is there something else, my Queen?"

She stepped up to him, cupping his face in her hands. "Stay with me. I don't want to be alone tonight."

"Is that a command from my queen?" he asked, resting his fingertips on her waist.

"It is a request from the woman who loves you."

Pash tilted his head to the side, eyes soft, "You have never said that to me before."

Niabi kissed his lips, "Stay."

Pash kissed her and swept her up in his arms, her legs wrapping around his waist, and carried her to her bedroom in the adjoining room.

The next morning, Niabi rolled over on her side and opened her eyes. Pash was still lying in her bed. He looked peaceful. He looked happy. She cuddled up against him, resting her hand on his bare chest. He smiled as soon as he felt her touch.

"Good morning," he kissed her forehead, wrapping his arms around her.

"You fell asleep here."

Pash was never supposed to stay the entire night. She had made that clear from the beginning of their relationship. No one was to know about them, not because she wasn't happy being with him, but because he could be seen as a weakness in her. And if there was anything she worked hard at, it was to make sure her enemies did not see a weakness they could exploit.

Pash pulled away from her and looked into her awaiting eyes. "I can go. It's still early. No one of importance should be awake to notice me."

Niabi knew she should tell him to leave. But she hadn't woken up with someone by her side in years and she didn't realize how much she missed it until this very moment. Niabi kissed his cheek. "Stay."

His eyebrows shot up. "You want me to stay?"

"Don't make me change my mind, Pash." Niabi tucked her head so he couldn't see her smile. "I wish we could stay like this all day."

"We can." Pash chuckled. "You are the queen, you know."

"Being the queen doesn't mean I'm free."

The commander caressed her arm. "Would you leave the city and never look back, if you had the chance?"

"What?" She propped herself up on her left elbow to get a better look at him.

"We could go wherever you want." Pash twirled a strand of her black hair between his fingers. "We could disappear. Change our names. Start over."

"You make it sound so easy," she whispered.

"But?"

Niabi stroked his cheek. "I can change my name, leave this world behind me, but I will always be the Green-Eyed Raven. My sins will one day find me."

Pash sat up, covers dropping to his waist. "Niabi, we could do this. We could start over and have a life together. You said it yourself. Being the queen doesn't mean you're free."

"It's a dream, Pash. A sweet, wonderful dream that I was not meant to have." She slipped out of bed and tied a silk robe around herself. She walked over to her balcony and breathed in the sunrise.

Pash cleared his throat, still sitting in her bed. "Do you still think about him?"

Niabi glanced over her shoulder to look at him. "Who?"

"Dichali."

Pash saying her dead husband's name made her feel nauseous for some reason. Though Dichali had been gone for years, she still felt she had to be a dutiful and faithful wife. That was the main reason she never allowed her relationship with Pash to be more than what it was.

"If you are asking if I still love Dichali, yes." She nodded and returned her gaze to the sun rising over the Ignacia Sea. "I will always love him."

Pash fastened his pants and took a step toward her. "Could you ever love me as much as you loved him?"

Niabi slowly turned and rested both of her hands on his bare chest. "Pash -"

He placed his hands over hers and leaned in closer. "I love you, Niabi, but it is impossible to live in his shadow."

"I never asked you to be Dichali."

"No," he shook his head. "But when you think about the man you love, he will always be your first thought."

Niabi's throat stung, her eyes burned. "I cannot forget him."

"I am not asking you to forget him. I am asking you to make room for me." Pash took a breath. "Dichali is gone, Niabi. I am here with you now. All I want is for you to be honest with me. Will I ever be enough?"

Niabi yanked her hands from his and brushed past him, beelining for the wine decanter. "You are intimidated by a dead man." The words pierced her heart.

"I am intimidated by a dead man who is very much alive in your heart." Pash leaned against the balcony doorway. "I could never replace Dichali, but am I not also worthy of your love?"

Niabi stopped pouring her drink and swung around, locking eyes with him. "I do love you, Pash."

"But not the same."

"What would you want me to do or say to make you see that I love you?" Niabi rushed toward him, her robe wafting behind her, exposing her lean legs.

"Marry me."

She stopped. "What did you just say?" she whispered; not sure she had heard him correctly.

"I said, marry me, Niabi." Pash closed the gap between them and cupped her cheeks, "Marry me."

"I told you before, I'll never get married again."

"Then come away with me." He thumbed her jawline. "Leave all this behind."

Niabi so desperately wanted to say *yes*. But she couldn't. "I can't." Her eyes watered a second before fire took its place. "Not yet."

Pash's arms fell to his sides, and he took a step back. "Why not?"

"I have unfinished business."

"You mean to say, you have unsettled revenge."

"If that is how you would like to phrase it." She crossed her arms over her chest. "Yes, I have unsettled revenge."

"When will it be enough?" Pash rubbed the back of his neck and groaned in frustration. "When your siblings are dead? Or when my father is dead? Or how about when I'm dead?"

"Pash -"

"Revenge can consume you until your dying breath and for what?" he interrupted, a ferocity in his voice she hadn't heard before. "For your dead to be avenged? What about those who are alive who love you? Why do the dead seem to always outweigh the living?"

Niabi took a deep breath, unwilling to let one tear slip down her face. "The dead cannot fight for themselves."

"Would they even want you to fight for them?"

She circled away from him, angrily braiding her hair to keep her from snapping at him. "If Issachar had just left me alone..." she mumbled.

"You would still be married to Dichali with Rollo by your side." Even without looking at him, she knew he was wounded. She could hear it in his voice.

"Yes," she nodded.

Pash sucked in a breath. "Leaving me, where?"

Niabi finished her braid. She wasn't sure how to respond. She wanted to scream how much he meant to her. How it wasn't her fault she had all these conflicting feelings. But instead, she said nothing. And that was worse.

"Niabi," he walked up behind her and reached for her hand. "I fell in love with you the moment you walked into my father's camp in the Black Forest. And I will love you until the day I draw my last breath. I just hope you don't realize too late how much you sacrificed to still be unhappy." Pash squeezed her hand and slipped on his shirt and boots to leave.

Niabi caught his arm as he past her. "Don't go."

"It's probably best if I do." He didn't look at her.

"Pash..."

Pash grabbed the back of her head and pressed his lips to her forehead. She felt the tears coming. "These moments I have alone with you are honest reminders of the ghost you aren't ready to say goodbye to." He released her and walked out the door.

A single tear escaped her eye and then there was no stopping them.

Chapter Fourteen

Salome

Just as Salome suspected, Zara had a traditional Myridian gown delivered to her room minutes after she returned from training with Mika. Her two ladies in waiting burst through the door, dress in tow, to prepare her for the Festival of the Forbidden Fruit.

Seraphina and Rosalina, identical twins not much older than Salome, began listing everything they were sent to help her with right after introductions.

"We're here to do your hair."

"Make up."

"Lotions."

"Perfumes."

"Dressing."

"But first..."

"Your bath," they said in unison.

Salome put her foot down, both literally and figuratively, when they said they were there to bathe her. "I can bathe myself."

The sisters exchanged a sharp, disapproving glance at one another.

"I'll let you do everything you were sent here to do, without a fight," Salome bargained, "as long as you let me bathe myself. Let me have a shred of privacy."

"Fine," Rosalina was the first to agree, scratching the mole by her left eye. It was the only mark that differentiated the twin sisters.

"Alright." Seraphina raised an eyebrow, her hazel eyes bouncing from Salome's face to her dirty hands. She was clearly the harder twin to please. "But if you have one speck of dirt left on you, I will personally bathe you myself. You won't have us looking incompetent to Princess Zara."

"Deal." Salome stuck out her hand for a shake, but they groaned. "What?"

"Such a Mainlander." Seraphina crossed her arms over her chest.

"More like a man, if you ask me," Rosalina whispered to Seraphina loud enough for Salome to hear.

Salome retracted her hand, rolled her eyes, and marched into the bathing room where a large bronze inground tub awaited her with warm water. Adonijah thought *she* was stubborn. She almost couldn't wait for him to meet the twins. In fact, she relished the thought of them cornering him to spray perfume on him. She laughed.

"It doesn't sound like bathing."

Salome knew by the judgmental tone it was Seraphina. "I'm working on it."

She stripped quickly, throwing her clothes in a pile, and sank into the muscle relaxing water. She closed her eyes and leaned her head back. She had not been submerged in a tub since her days in Northwind. If she wanted to bathe in the Tree House Forest, she would use the wash basin in her room and a towel. Some days, she would get up early and bathe in the lake near their treehouse, but she stopped doing that when she noticed Jacobi would creep in the trees for a peek. The thought sent shivers up her spine, and she frowned.

Salome hadn't thought of Jacobi since she left. She wondered if the Shadows had returned. And if they had, if any of the villagers had survived. If Jacobi survived. Her nostrils flared at the thought. She didn't want to think of them anymore – think of Jacobi anymore – it was ruining her relaxing bath.

A sharp knock on the door made her jump. "Do you need help?"

Rosalina by the caring tone. Salome counted, *three, two, one*, and pointed toward the door.

"If you aren't out here in five minutes, I'm coming in."

Right on cue, Seraphina. Salome shook her head and quickly washed up, knowing Seraphina was counting down the seconds until she could break down the door separating them.

Salome wrapped the silk robe that was hanging from a hook on the wall around herself and tied it tightly at the waist. She flung open the door to the awaiting twins. Rosalina greeted her with a smile while Seraphina's eyes burned a hole into her soul.

"What next?" Salome motioned to Seraphina to take control.

Rosalina and Seraphina brushed and fashioned her wild curls with pearls to look more like Myridian royalty than a 'stab happy Mainlander'. They rubbed lotions and perfumes on her neck, arms, legs, and feet, which she had to admit felt amazing. The twins either didn't notice her scars or they didn't care because there was no mention of her body riddled with them. She was grateful they kept their mouths and opinions to themselves on that matter. Although, they were extremely talkative on all other subjects.

After Rosalina darkened her eyes with kohl and reddened her lips, Seraphina helped her slip into a flowy silk gown. It hugged her curves in all the right places and when she looked at herself in the full-length mirror propped against the wall, she froze, eyes wide.

"She's taken by her own beauty," Rosalina beamed, proud of their creation.

"She does seem speechless." Seraphina, too, appeared to soften with pride.

"I look..." Salome turned; her eyes popped when she saw her exposed back.

"Beautiful?" Rosalina filled in.

"Clean?" Seraphina shrugged her shoulders.

"Tempting?" Rosalina tried once more.

"Ridiculous." Salome finished with a snort. "I mean, look at me. I don't look like myself."

The Myridians folded their arms over their chests at the same time. Clearly, she had offended them.

"Perhaps, it is good you don't look like yourself." Seraphina's eyes narrowed. "Now you can see your potential, if you tried."

"No one is going to recognize me." Salome felt her appearance was the only thing she had any true control over, and that had been stripped from her too.

"That is the point of the Festival of Forbidden Fruit." Rosalina softened when she saw the sadness in Salome's eyes. "No one is what they seem." She walked over to Salome and grabbed her gently by her shoulders and turned her back to the mirror. "Everyone will be looking and feeling their best tonight. How else would we find suitable mates?"

Salome crinkled her nose. "I'm not looking for a mate."

"Well, not with that attitude," Seraphina snorted.

A knock echoed through the room and Rosalina scurried to answer it. Salome caught Cato's reflection in the mirror. His eyes shot to her and was taken aback at the sight of a dolled-up Salome.

"What business, Mainlander?" Seraphina snapped when he stared at Salome a bit too long for her liking.

"Harbona sent me to tell Salome it was time to go to the Grand Hall for the festival." Cato fought a smirk as he tugged at his festive robes, "Have you seen her?"

Salome rolled her eyes as Cato snickered.

"Her Royal Highness, Princess Salome of Northwind," Seraphina corrected him immediately, her nostrils flared in righteous indignation. "I suggest you address her properly or not at all."

Salome attempted to protest but Seraphina marched to the door and said, "We will bring Her Highness when she is ready, not a moment sooner." She slammed the door in Cato's face, ignoring his protests.

"Men." Rosalina huffed, shaking her head. "How do you even stand being around them?"

Salome was lost in thought and didn't hear her question. *Why didn't Harbona send Adonijah to check on her?* Maybe it was better he didn't see her in this ridiculous gown. He would probably laugh at her and hold it over her for the rest of their lives.

The rest of their lives? Where did that thought come from? Would he even stay with her after everything was said and done? Would they even be alive after facing her sister for the White Throne? She shook her head, bringing her back to Rosalina and Seraphina's awaiting faces.

"What?" Salome asked, sure she must have missed them saying something.

"Are you ready, Princess?" Rosalina smiled.

Salome swallowed and took a deep breath. "I'm ready." But she wasn't ready. She didn't know what she was walking into and for the first time in a long time, she truly felt alone.

The Festival of Forbidden Fruit was more opulent than any event Salome had ever attended. The Grand Hall was exactly as it sounded. The room was three stories high with balconies overlooking the dance floor as well as the gardens. Candles filled the room and appeared like they were floating throughout the three levels where guests, men and women alike, were mingling, dancing, flirting, and coupling off, escaping to the empty rooms and romantic gardens.

Salome climbed up the stairs, more focused on not tripping over her long, silk dress than observing the male guests staring at her as if she were the prized cow at the fair. Once she reached the top level, she soaked in the entire room and gasped. The ceiling was elaborately carved into an arch with a perfect circle opening at the top to let the moonlight pour in.

As music played, she leaned over the thick stone railing and gawked as thousands of Myridians filled the floor. The light warm breeze wafted through the space and Salome was amazed it didn't blow out the floating candles.

She scanned the faces, searching for Harbona, Adonijah, or Cato. Rosalina and Seraphina had escorted her to the main doors of the Grand Hall and then disappeared, probably to ready themselves to enjoy the festivities. She found it difficult to picture Seraphina finding any male suitable enough for her liking.

"You look Myridian, but you're not from here."

Salome turned to her left as a strange man dressed in black leaned against the railing, two drinks in his hands. She could tell he was from the Eastern Lands. By the looks of his expensive clothes, he was either royalty or an ambassador. Once she accepted the drink he offered her, he raked his fingers through his short, satiny, jet-black hair. His well-groomed appearance, his almond eyes, and his alabaster skin were captivating, and she hated to admit she found him unquestionably attractive.

"You're not from here either...?

He tilted his head forward to show respect. "I am Jinn. Prince of Sakurai."

Salome reciprocated his bow, "It is an honor to meet you, Your Majesty -"

"There is no need for formality," Jinn interrupted. "Please, call me Jinn."

His smile nearly melted her. It was perfect. He looked absolutely... perfect. She couldn't even think of a different word to describe him.

"You must know who I am then," she caught herself staring and forced herself to take a sip of the fruity drink he had brought her, "if lack of formality suits you."

Jinn smiled again, "I admit, I was extremely curious to meet the surviving Princess of Northwind. But I was expecting to see someone more..."

"Regal looking?" She glanced at him.

"Pale," he chuckled. "But it seems you favor your southern kin."

Salome shifted her weight. His undivided attention made her uncomfortable. He wasn't doing anything wrong. He was just such an attractive man she found it difficult to maintain eye contact.

Pull yourself together! she internally screamed at herself before she managed to ask, "Are you here for the Festival of Forbidden Fruit?"

"I have been here for a few days on official business but didn't want to return home without attending this festival. It only happens once a year and normally Mainlanders are not allowed to participate. We Easterners call it 'The Great Fornication'."

Salome set her drink down on the railing. "I imagine in your city you don't host such festivals."

"Hardly." Jinn laughed, sipping his drink, a sparkle in his golden-brown eyes. "We are far more traditional. One's parents arrange a suitable match and that is the end of it."

"And you? Are you spoken for?" Salome spat out the question before she had a chance to think it through and immediately turned red. Had the twins not made up her face, he would have noticed her embarrassment.

"Not yet," he seemed amused by the question. "I suppose my father has not found a suitable wife of noble birth."

A woman several inches shorter than Salome with Jinn's same features emerged from the sea of faces. Her walk was slow yet purposeful and she headed straight for them.

"Princess Salome, this is Kai, my protection." Jinn motioned his hand to the petite warrior with black liner highlighting the shape of her almond eyes.

"Princess." Kai bowed, but her serious expression didn't waver. "My Prince." She bowed again, directly toward him.

"What is it, Kai?" He relaxed his back against the railing, downing the last bit of his drink.

"Your audience with Queen Nym is set for tomorrow."

Salome's eyes shifted from Kai to the prince. *How did he manage to get an audience with her grandmother, but she hadn't?*

"Anything else?"

Kai shook her head and he waved her off. Salome's eyes were glued to Kai's back when she turned to walk away. Her open back gown showcased her enormous dragon tattoo. It made Salome extremely conscious that her back was also exposed but knew it wouldn't garner the same attention. Feeling she was being watched, she turned her gaze back to the prince and found him smiling.

"Kai is known as Ryoko Naga to my people. She was one of the orphans that won the Dragon Tournament."

"Dragon Tournament?"

"Every royal is assigned an assassin to protect them. So, when a guardian is needed, we have orphans trained as assassins to compete in a tournament. Whoever is left standing at the end, is assigned to the royal. Kai is mine."

Salome crinkled her nose. "Forgive me, but that sounds rather cruel."

"What else are we supposed to do with the orphans?"

Somehow, he didn't seem as attractive to her anymore. Had they been in the forests, she would have punched him.

"Why the tattoo?" she asked politely, not wanting to cause a scene and risk Zara's wrath.

"Every winner of the Dragon Tournament has one."

"And her name, Ryoko Naga, what does it mean?"

"It means Dragon Queen." Jinn cleared his throat and stepped closer to Salome, their bodies now touching. "She is the only female ever recorded to win the tournament."

Salome caught sight of the girl as she slithered through the horde of guests. Although she felt compassion for Kai, she knew she had to be leery of her as well.

"And your tattoo?" Jinn lifted her arm, cradling her left hand in his.

"One line for each member of my family that... died."

"A tragedy." They looked at one another and Jinn stared at her left eye. "Might I be bold and ask about your eye?" He still held her hand in his.

Salome became indignant but couldn't hide the flush to her cheeks. "It's a birthmark.

"A curious birthmark." He kept his eyes locked on hers. "You are lucky Myridians are not superstitious like the Mountain Men or even the elderly in my city. They would think you were a witch."

The way he kept staring made her uncomfortable. Her shoulders tensed. Even though Rosalina and Seraphina insisted she not carry any weapons on her, she secretly strapped her wolf dagger to her upper thigh when they weren't watching her. If she needed to defend herself, she would be able to.

"Then perhaps, I will refrain from visiting either kingdom." Salome retrieved her hand from his grasp.

"You mustn't let a few batty old people keep you from visiting my homeland." Jinn rested his hand on her lower back and whispered in her ear, "I would be honored if you would accompany me to Sakurai as my guest."

"You flatter me, Prince Jinn." She stepped to the side, hoping he would withdraw his hand from her person, but he stepped with her, his face still unnecessarily close to hers.

"Dance with me," he glided his hand from her lower back and took her hand.

"Excuse me, Princess." Salome whipped around, her heart skipping a beat when she recognized Adonijah's voice. "Harbona sent me to escort you to meet with him on an urgent matter."

Salome pulled away from Jinn's grip. "You will have to excuse me, Prince Jinn."

"Of course," Prince Jinn smiled and brushed a loose strand of her hair behind her ear. "Another time."

Salome noticed Adonijah and Jinn exchange a look before Adonijah escorted her down two flights of stairs and through one of the side doors into the gardens. She looked around the garden lit by lanterns but didn't see Harbona anywhere. She turned around and saw Adonijah leaning against the doorway, arms folded over his chest. "Where's Harbona?"

Chapter Fifteen

Adonijah

"Harbona didn't ask to see me, did he?" Realization sparked in Salome's eyes.

"No," Adonijah flashed a mischievous smile. "I saw how you were acting with the Easterner and thought you needed an excuse to escape him."

"How was I acting?" She squared her body to his, arms folded over her chest.

"I've not known you long, but I've known you long enough to recognize the look in your eyes when you're looking for a reason not to stab a man."

Salome paused before responding, a coy smile spreading across her face. "If you wanted to be alone with me, that's all you needed to say." She laughed.

Oh, how he adored her warm, silky laugh.

Adonijah curled up from the archway and stood in front of her. His eyes rested on hers – she looked different. When he spotted her in the Grand Hall, he couldn't believe his eyes. She was a vision, but he could sense how uncomfortable she was. If only she saw herself through his eyes. If she knew he was at her mercy. She looked like a true royal and it reminded him of the vast differences between them.

Salome's eyebrow arched playfully. "Don't tell me you were jealous."

"Of *him*?" Adonijah snorted. "Don't be ridiculous."

"Then why tell me Harbona wanted to see me when he clearly didn't summon me?" She popped a hip. Her white dress wafted in the light breeze exposing the slit up her leg to her thigh. He could have sworn he saw the tip of one of her daggers but dismissed it.

"Adonijah?"

He'd been staring. He blinked, returning to himself. "Like I said, you looked like you needed a break from him."

Adonijah knew Salome was perfectly capable of protecting herself, but he still felt responsible for her. And maybe, if he were honest with himself, he was a little jealous.

Which was unfamiliar territory. Adonijah was not the jealous type – or at least, he wasn't before. It irritated him to have those feelings. But he saw how Jinn looked at her, how he touched her. Saw how all the men in the room watched her the moment she walked in.

"Admit it." Salome sliced through his thoughts.

"Admit what?"

"Either you wanted to be alone with me or you were jealous." Her smile was gone, the intensity of her eyes drew him in.

"Both," he whispered.

"What?" She seemed surprised by his admission. He was too.

Adonijah stepped to her, placing one hand on her hip and the other against her face, gently running his thumb across the curvature of her jawline.

"I know you didn't want to wear that dress -"

Salome's eyes dropped to the pavers, "You think I look better this way."

Adonijah lifted her chin, their lips so close they could feel the tension, the electricity, between them. "I know you didn't want to wear that dress because you were afraid no one would be able to see you anymore. But *I* see you. And even though you are a pain in my ass, I can't help wanting to be alone with you. Wanting to hold you. Wanting to kiss you. But seeing you with him... I'm not a jealous man, Salome..."

She rested her hands on his chest when he trailed off, staring up into his eyes, her sight drifted down to his lips.

Adonijah wanted to kiss her – to feel her lips on his, to run his fingers through her hair. And by the lack of space between them, he knew she wanted him, too. He moved his face to hers, his heart racing.

"Adonijah," she whispered.

He opened his eyes and felt her gently push him back. "What's wrong?" he asked, caressing her cheek.

Salome placed her hand on top of his. "I can't..."

Adonijah's arms fell to his sides, and he took a step back from her. "It's alright."

"It's not you," she reached for him but stopped short.

"You don't have to explain anything to me," he cleared his throat. He wasn't sure what happened, but he wasn't going to pressure her for answers.

They silently stared at one another; tears welled in her eyes – but why?

"Are you alright?" Adonijah asked.

Salome let out a half laugh, half groan. "I push you away and you're more interested to see if I'm alright?"

"Of course, Princess -"

"Don't call me that," she snapped.

"Alright." He rubbed the back of his neck. He'd called her that before, but it never drew that vicious of a response. "You realize that's your title."

"I am Salome. Just Salome." Her nostrils flared; she wiped her eyes. "Overnight, I became princess – her majesty – Hunter – chosen one. It's all too much." She turned her back to him and wrapped her arms around herself. "And now this," she flicked her dress and spied her reflection in the still waters of the pool in the garden. "I don't even look like myself anymore."

Adonijah braved being on the receiving end of another tongue lashing or worse, a physical altercation, to come up behind her and wrap his arms around her. Holding her, his face next to hers, he felt her exhale a deep breath and heard a muffled sob.

"Do you remember what I said to you in Valley Pass?" Adonijah asked in a raspy whisper.

"I have a lot of scars."

"Aye," he nodded, "but I also said that to me you were the same Salome. It doesn't matter if you wear dresses and crowns or if you run wild hunting in pants armed to your teeth in weapons." He kissed her temple, "You are always you." Salome released the tension in her body and relaxed into his embrace.

Holding her told him everything he needed to know. She was willing to let him comfort her, and she trusted him. It felt good to hold her, to feel her body wrapped in his. He could spend all night embracing her, but he released her instead.

Salome faced him, and grabbed his hand4. Adonijah wiped a stray tear that slipped down her cheek.

"I should go," he said.

Her eyes. Filled with such sadness.

She nodded and he walked back inside, letting her have time to herself, knowing it was important to her. But he didn't dare leave her unprotected. He sat on a bench on the opposite side of the wall and leaned his head back, gearing up for a long night.

Chapter Sixteen

Zophar

Three days.

It took the beaten down and weary warriors three days to find another way out of the Cavern of the Undead. With their resources depleted, half of their horses dead, and exhaustion setting in, the Numbio crawled into the moonlit sands of Dead Man's Lands with subdued happiness.

Relief washed over Zophar as he inhaled the deepest breath of fresh air his lungs could hold. He had never been so happy to see the Sand Lands in his entire life and that not only his horse, Midnight, had survived the Caverns of the Undead, but Crispin's horse, Freya, also made it out alive. Collapsing to the ground, he didn't care that sand seeped into every orifice of his body. He was just elated it wasn't the musty, damp rock of the caverns touching his skin.

Not knowing where exactly they were, Zophar could only hope and pray a rare passing caravan would catch sight of them and help them. If they were within walking distance of Jannat Sin, Ibrahim and his people would gladly welcome them to rest and regain their strength.

Zophar spied Heru sprawled in the sand and if he didn't know any better, he would have sworn the prince was kissing the sand.

"If we can make it to Jannat Sin," Zophar forced himself to stumble toward Heru, "we will receive aid. I know Sheik Ibrahim. He's a good man."

Heru's tired eyes found their way to meet Zophar's equally exhausted gaze. He nodded, his lips were so chapped Zophar could see dried blood around his mouth. "Then let's hope we can make it there tonight. I fear we won't last a day in the unforgiving desert sun without food, water, or shelter."

Agreed, they mobilized the Numbio to their aching feet and encouraged them onward. Zophar whispered prayers to the Almighty, asking for a miracle. It was all they could hope for at this point.

Walking slowly but steadily, the company trudged their way through the moonlit desert for hours until the dawn threatened to end their quest for the oasis village. One by one, Numbio began to fall to their knees until Zophar, too, couldn't take one more step. With the scorching sun rising, Zophar laid on his back, accepting that Death would be coming for them all before noon.

Extremely dehydrated, he closed his eyes, accepting the sun's burn upon his pale skin. He was wishing for a drop of water to quench his thirst when a splash hit his face. He squinted and saw a camel hovering over him.

A camel?

Zophar groaned as he propped himself up on his elbows, gazing up at the rider wrapped in black robes. "Please," Zophar's voice came out raspy and strained, "help us."

Sounds of laughter, running water, and the smell of freshly roasted lamb filled Zophar's ears and nose. As his eyes fluttered open, he saw a familiar sight. It was the luxurious tent he and Crispin had shared in Jannat Sin.

They had made it. But how?

Zophar's mind flashed back to the camel that had slopped a watery kiss on his nose and its rider who had looked down at him with pity. Reluctantly pushing himself up from the soft and warm bed, Zophar rinsed his hands and face in the water basin and cherished the cool liquid sloshing through his hands.

Dressed in the clean clothes that had been left on a chair in the corner of his tent, Zophar ducked out of his quarters and made his way toward Ibrahim's dwelling in the middle of the village. As he passed other tents, he saw the Numbio eating their fill, drinking as much water as they could, and laughing. They were smiling for the first time in weeks.

Zophar caught sight of Midnight and Freya with the other horses in the fenced stables being tended to, looking healthy and strong. He whispered a prayer as he glided past, thanking the Almighty that both horses survived. Thankful that his last piece of Crispin was still living and keeping his memory alive.

"My friend!" Ibrahim's voice sang out to him as he approached the largest tent. His arms were stretched wide, and a friendly smile spread across his brown face. "It is good to see you."

Zophar embraced the Sheik and flashed a smile of his own in return. "I don't know how we got here but thank you."

"Some of my riders were on their way back from Numbio, having done some trading in the city, and happened upon you and your friends." Ibrahim ushered Zophar into the tent where a gluttonous feast was already out on display. Heru and Rayma were inside looking refreshed from a good night's sleep. "We are just glad we found you in time."

"How can we ever repay you for your generosity?" Zophar plopped down on the pillow Ibrahim motioned him toward.

"How could we let the desert claim you when we have the resources and good will to help?" Ibrahim shook his head and served himself a plate. "As long as my people can offer aid to those who are in need, we will continue to prosper. The Almighty blesses those who give."

"Thank you, Sheik Ibrahim," Heru chimed in, a hand over his heart. "The Numbio owe you a debt."

Ibrahim mirrored the prince's hand to heart motion but again declined payment or offer of any kind. "I just thank the Almighty you are alright." He dared a glance at Rayma. "Our healer said he wasn't needed. Despite the dire state we found you in, your men's injuries have been cared for."

Rayma nodded her head in gratitude for the compliment but something about her seemed haunted. Zophar had noticed Bantu creep toward her to assault her. He wanted to rip the man limb from limb but by the time he reached her, she had stabbed and killed Bantu. They hadn't spoken about it since. They hadn't spoken at all since the incident.

"Where is Prince Crispin?" Ibrahim asked between bites of mutton. "I am eager to see him again." His eyebrows bounced, "And I am positive he will enjoy tonight's entertainment."

The room fell silent, and Zophar met the Sheik's gaze. Tears pricked at the Westerner's blue eyes. That was all it took to convey the message.

"I am sorry," Ibrahim was somber as he trailed a finger from the top of his head down to his heart. "How did it happen?"

"He..." Crispin being swept down the River of Lost Souls flashed in Zophar's mind, and he couldn't utter another word.

"The River of Lost Souls claimed him," Heru said with great difficulty. "We don't know if he made it out alive or not."

"You were in the Caverns of the Undead?" Ibrahim's mannerisms were calm and graceful, but his eyes were filled with terror.

"When your people found us in the desert, we had just escaped." Zophar explained, his appetite now gone.

Ibrahim set his plate down, as if he also was no longer in the mood for food. "We shall keep our eyes open just in case the prince reappears. But as always, you are welcome here amongst our people. Rest, restock for your journey. I have a feeling you are not returning to Numbio yet."

Zophar and Heru exchanged a quick glance before the prince said, "We are headed north to Oakenshire. We are to meet Crispin's sister there."

Ibrahim nodded. "If I could offer you a word of caution..."

"Of course," Zophar motioned for the Sheik to continue.

"My scouts have reported quite a bit of movement from the Thrak of Gomorrah." Ibrahim's nose crinkled in disgust when speaking of the cannibalistic warriors. "They are looking for someone. From what we have gathered, they are searching for a woman."

"Their search stretches this far south?" Heru was dumbfounded.

"Where the Sand Lands and The Hollow meet and as far west as Port Daelon." Ibrahim crisscrossed his legs. "If you intend to continue your journey north, I would avoid the main roads and travel through the Bone Mountains."

"But aren't the Mountain Men just as cruel?" Rayma spoke for the first time in days.

"The Krazaks are," Ibrahim bobbed his head, "but the Stormcrags would help you if you asked. Their quarrel is only with the Krazaks and the Thrak."

"Thank you," Zophar put a hand to his chest, showing his respect and gratitude. "We appreciate the warning."

Ibrahim smiled at Zophar before turning his gaze to the prince. "Whatever you need, let me know and we will provide. I have a feeling the journey ahead will be a difficult one."

Chapter Seventeen

Odelia

Odelia's eyes shot open when she heard what sounded like footsteps outside her bungalow. It was dark, the middle of the night. She sat up from her bed and softly planted her feet on the creaky wooden floors. Having lived in that house for decades, she knew where she could step and not make a sound. As quickly as she dared, she hopped spot to spot until she reached her modest kitchen and grabbed the biggest knife she owned.

Reaper's growl rumbled low, but Odelia held her index finger to her lips to silence him. He stood alert; his nose pointed toward the front door.

Odelia's back was pressed tight against the wall with the door next to her. She inhaled and exhaled rhythmically to keep herself calm. If someone had come to kill the Enchantress, they would not leave the swamp alive. It was not the first assassination attempt, and it would not be the last. At least Reaper could claim another soul or two, adding to his own lifespan.

The intruder's feet stepped onto the front porch. Odelia clutched the hilt of the knife tighter and watched as the handle of the door turned. Going on the offensive, she sliced her weapon down to stab whoever was on the other side of the door: a Shadow, one of those grotesque Thrak, a mercenary for hire. But she stopped short of piercing *her*.

"Makeda?" Odelia stepped back, her mouth agape.

"Mother!" Makeda wrapped her arms around Odelia's neck. "Thank the Almighty I got here in time."

The Enchantress dropped the knife on the kitchen table directly behind her and returned her daughter's embrace. She pulled away to close the door and lit lanterns to get a better look at Makeda.

Odelia hadn't seen her in years, since she left the swamp for a life in Northwind. Makeda had wanted to join the rebellion in Northwind, to make a difference in the lives of the oppressed. A decision that left a sour taste in Odelia's mouth. The Northerners were not their people, therefore, they were not their problem, yet, Makeda abandoned the swamp, abandoned her mother, abandoned her future, to pursue a life underground.

"What are you doing here, child?"

"Niabi dispatched Shadows to find you," Makeda accepted the seat Odelia motioned her to take. "She has instructed them to bring you to Northwind."

Odelia put a kettle of water to boil. "And why should she want me?"

"We think she wants to harvest your magic." Odelia furrowed her brow when Makeda said, "*we*". "There is no time for tea, Mother. I need to get you out of here before they find you."

"*If* they find me." Odelia smirked.

"They will find you."

"How can you be so sure?"

"It wasn't Niabi's idea to send them. She didn't know you existed until that witch told her."

Odelia's eyes widened, although she kept her back to her daughter as she fiddled with the tea bags. "What witch?" she asked calmly.

"The Old Witch of Endor. Apparently, she is Niabi's -"

"Aunt." Odelia finished the statement.

"You know of her?"

"I met Vilora a very long time ago." Odelia could see a young version of the witch flash in her mind. "It would seem she has never forgotten me."

Makeda slammed her palms on the table. "We need to go. Now."

"And where would we go? To your *friends* in Northwind where they can keep me underground? No, no. I am the Enchantress of the Swamp. No one invades my home and lives to tell the tale."

"Mother, please don't be stubborn." Makeda pleaded. "I am here to rescue you."

Odelia chuckled, patting Reaper on his square head. "It is not I who is in need of rescuing."

"Is this about me not staying?" Makeda hunched over Odelia. "Because I didn't want this," she motioned around the room.

Odelia knew she didn't mean the bungalow, but the swamp itself. "I should have known the swamp would never truly have your heart. After all, you are not fully mine."

"You still won't tell me where to find my father?"

"As I have told you before, Makeda, your path and his are destined to cross." The kettle sang, releasing its steam. Odelia snatched it from the heat and placed it on the counter. "Why spend time aimlessly searching when you were fated to meet?"

"Riddles. So many riddles." Makeda paced the small house, rubbing her forehead.

"I appreciate you warning me of the Shadows, dear." Odelia poured the boiling water in a cup but paused over the second mug. "Tea?"

"No!" Makeda lurched forward, pointing at the door. "Those Shadows can't possibly be far. They had a head start on me. Fortunately, I know my way around the swamp. Let me help you."

"I don't need your help, Makeda. You might have rejected the swamp, but I did not. The swamp fuels me, sustains me. I am strongest here. I am safest here."

"Have you used your magic recently?" Makeda popped her hip to the side, narrowing her eyes.

"Watch your tone, Makeda." Odelia blew the steam from her tea. "I am still your mother and won't hesitate to put you in your place."

"Is your boat still in working condition?" Makeda peeked through the drawn curtains toward the dock. "I released my horse before I arrived in the swamp so no one could follow my tracks."

"If you need it, take it."

Makeda squinted.

"What is it?" Odelia asked as soon as she noticed her daughter's sudden shift.

"I thought I saw something." She gasped and slid to the floor. "They're here."

"You saw them?" Odelia didn't bother to get down on the floor, instead remaining in her seat to enjoy her cup of tea. "How many are there?"

"Get down here!" Makeda whispered as she crawled over to the lanterns, blowing them out one by one.

Odelia sipped her drink. "I asked, how many are there?"

"I don't know," Makeda spat. "Could be one, could be a hundred. What difference does it make?"

"No difference."

"Then why ask?" Makeda rolled her eyes. "We can still get out of here." She felt around the wooden floorboards until she found the brass handle to a secret exit. "Come on."

"Go ahead, dear. I'll make sure they don't see you."

"Mother, please!"

Odelia was caught off guard by Makeda's unusual tone. She softened her gaze. "Take Reaper to the boat. I'll be right behind you.""Mother -"

"Trust me."

Makeda reluctantly nodded and patted her thigh for Reaper to follow. Reaper sat loyally by Odelia's side until she shifted her eyes ordering him to go with Makeda. Once the hatch closed, Odelia set her cup down. She cracked her knuckles then her neck.

"Let's have a little fun."

Odelia opened the front door and stepped out onto the porch. The moon lit the swamp enough for her to see the dark figures approaching. There were at least twenty of them.

"Consider this your only warning to leave my swamp." Odelia trotted down the steps and stood on the wet ground barefoot.

"We don't take orders from you," a voice hissed in the darkness.

"Then," she shrugged with a grin, "you will all die."

Odelia slammed her palms to the earth and a low rumble followed. She willed the ground to shake and heard the Shadows shouting orders at one another. She couldn't make out their words but knew she wouldn't have much time before the assassins reached her.

She dug her fingernails into the soft ground and yanked dirt up. Holes large enough to swallow some of the Shadows opened and claimed the soldiers. She slowly stood, lifting her arms with great resistance. As her arms rose, so did the roots she was controlling. They grew around the Shadows that remained. Odelia started closing her arms and the roots closed in on the men and entrapped them.

Odelia suddenly felt a piece of metal slice into her left shoulder and it relaxed her arms slightly. One of the Shadows had launched an arrow at her before the roots swallowed him. She heard Makeda shout from a distance. Pain or not, she had to finish this.

The Enchantress let out an unearthly scream and forced her arms to close, her palms meeting in front of her. The Shadows screeched in pain as the roots squeezed the life out of them. Odelia slammed her fists down to the ground and the roots pulled the Shadows into the earth.

Although it appeared she had killed all the intruders, she sensed one had survived. Her vision was blurry. The pain in her arm was slowly taking over all her other senses. In the moonlight, she caught the glint of the Shadow's sword as he slid down from his hiding spot in one of the trees. Blood oozed down her arm, and she was unable to stand up.

The Shadow in the distance lit his torch and dropped it on the ground, disappearing into the darkness, no doubt to inform his queen of what happened. The Swamp was thrown into chaos as the fire spread.

Her swamp. Her home. It was all burning around her and there was nothing she could do to save it. She didn't possess the power of water – just earth.

Odelia's eyes blurred to the point she couldn't see anymore, so she closed them. She felt the heat and smelled the trees burning. But she swore she heard the sound of rushing water spraying across the earth. She felt its coolness on her skin. She forced her eyes to open and used every bit of strength she had left to focus on what she could see. The fire had been extinguished. Billows of smoke stretched to the heavens, but there were no flames.

How was that possible?

"Mother," Makeda knelt in front of her and focused her attention on the arrow sticking out of her shoulder.

"Makeda." Odelia embraced her dripping wet daughter. "The swamp, it was on fire. What happened?"

"I put it out." Makeda wrapped her fingers around the arrow. "This is going to hurt."

"What?" Odelia screeched in pain as Makeda snapped the arrow shaft in half.

"We need to get you to a healer."

"Makeda, do you have magic?" Odelia grabbed her daughter's shoulders.

"Water." Makeda admitted.

"Why didn't you tell me?" Odelia felt herself fading. She grabbed Makeda's hand for balance.

"I've got you." Makeda's voice sounded as Odelia's consciousness faded to black. "I've got you, Mother."

—•—

Chapter Eighteen

Salome

If Salome hadn't attended the Festival of Forbidden Fruit, she wouldn't have believed it even happened. As she strolled through the Scarlet Citadel, after another grueling morning training session with Mika, there wasn't a trace of a party. It was still mid-morning when she returned from Antrope, and she managed to sneak out of her chambers before the twins arrived to dictate her schedule or Almighty forbid, try to make her up again.

Since arriving in Myr, she hadn't had the opportunity to go for her morning walks and was fully aware of how important they were to her. How necessary they were. Stretching her arms around her torso, she inhaled the sea breeze as the sun's rays lit up the castle. She wished for a split second that she could stay in Myr, but that wasn't her path.

"It's a beautiful view."

Salome jerked back from the banister overlooking one of the gardens. She never heard Jinn approach her and that was unsettling. What if he had meant to harm her?

"I apologize for startling you." Jinn said warmly. "I thought I was the only one walking in the gardens."

"It would appear we agree on something, Prince Jinn." She steadied herself, unsure of his intentions as he approached her.

Jinn gave her a look over and flashed a perfect smile. "So, this is what you really look like."

She glanced down at her loose-fitting green shirt, dark pants, and boots. Her hair was down and curly and whatever make up she had on her face was whatever she didn't wash off before tumbling into bed the night before.

"Surprised?" she asked, one eyebrow arched.

"Intrigued." Jinn leaned his elbows against the railing next to her. His fingers intertwined, the sun hitting him just right to make him look undeniably enticing.

Salome hated that she was attracted to him, especially since she found his personality grating. She found him arrogant, unfeeling, and invasive.

"You don't like me, do you?" Jinn asked, eyes fixed on the sea.

Was he a mind reader? How did he know what she was thinking?

"I didn't say that."

"But your eyes did." Jinn met her gaze. "It's alright. You're not the first woman to look at me that way. Despite my best efforts, I'm afraid I'm not good at first impressions." He shrugged. "Kai tells me I try too hard."

Salome flushed, heat rising through her body. She broke eye contact with him. "Prince Jinn -"

"Jinn," he softly interrupted. "Please, call me Jinn."

"Jinn," she complied. "Perhaps, I've rushed to judge you."

"It's because of Kai, isn't it?"

"What do you mean?"

"How Kai came to be in my service," he explained. "How my people treat our orphans."

Salome tried to hide her disgust thinking about children being trained to kill but it was impossible. He nodded, as if to say he understood her reaction.

"I don't like it either." Jinn rubbed his thigh. An obvious nervous twitch. "But it's tradition."

"Some traditions should be changed."

"Maybe," he nodded, gracious in his responses, just like a nobleman. "Might I ask you a question?"

Salome shifted her weight, leaning against the railing next to him, their elbows inches apart. "Sure."

"How old are Northern boys when they begin their military training?"

Salome felt her throat dry as soon as he asked his question. "All firstborn males begin training at ten."

"And how old were you when you started?"

"Girls aren't allowed -"

"Please, Salome," he shook his head with a chuckle. "I might not look like much of a soldier, but I can certainly identify one. And you carry yourself like a soldier." His eyes scanned her up and down. "You have at least four knives on you as we speak."

"Three actually," she admitted. The wolf dagger against her thigh, one sheathed to her lower back, and a small one in her right boot.

"So, when did you start your training?" Jinn asked again.

"I was five."

"And Myridians. How old are they when they begin training as a Qata Vishna?"

"Ten."

Jinn ran his fingers through his hair, slicking it back from his face. Such a beautiful, symmetrical face. "In Gomorrah, the firstborn son is dedicated at birth to become a Thrak. The Andrago teach their sons the way of the sword as soon as they take their first step. And I'm pretty sure the boys and girls of Borg are birthed clutching a weapon."

Salome smirked at the last one, thinking of Zophar as a baby armed with his battle axe.

"Families willingly offer their sons and daughters to honor their kingdoms and it is applauded. But children without a family: no one to feed them, shelter them, clothe them, protect them – it is wrong to have them trained in sword play? Housed in youngling barracks and given a purpose? What is so different about our peoples' traditions? You draw the line of training children to kill if they have parents?"

Salome dropped her eyes to her twiddling fingers. She didn't know what to say. He was right. What she scoffed at last night, she and her people were guilty of too.

Jinn placed his hand gently on top of hers. Their eyes met. His golden eyes were so warm, so inviting. It was as if she was melting into him, being drawn in by his spell.

"In Sakurai, to be a Ryoko Naga is the highest honor. To serve our kingdom, honor our people, and uphold our traditions. Without our ways, we would be lost. If you ever graced my kingdom with a visit, I would show you. You might actually like it there."

Jinn swept her hand into his. His fingers were calloused, a sign he might know how to wield a weapon. Based on appearance alone, she wouldn't have pegged him for a warrior. A politician, yes. A soldier, no.

Adonijah, although caring, had hands that matched his rugged appearance. When Adonijah touched her, she felt something surge through her entire body. A feeling that paled in comparison to how it felt when Jinn held her hand.

Why was she even comparing them?

Salome shook her head, retracting her hand. "I have to thank you, Jinn. You've opened my eyes to my own shortcomings and hypocrisy. I judged you and I judged your people when my people are not much different. Please accept my apology."

"There is nothing to forgive." He touched his fingertips to his chest, bowing his head. "Until our paths cross again."

"Are you leaving the Isles of Myr?" She hated that she cared.

"We sail to Sakurai tomorrow." His eyes were filled with expectation. "You are always welcome to join me."

Salome hesitated. An opportunity to see the first kingdom Malachi the First helped establish. A kingdom that still celebrated and upheld the traditions they were founded on a thousand years ago, whether she agreed with them or not. What a tremendous honor. What an incredible opportunity. A dream of seeing Adalore within her reach.

"Thank you," she whispered, "but I can't."

Jinn smiled. "It's because of your bodyguard, isn't it?"

"There are many reasons why I can't go with you." Salome kept a straight face, even though her mind was screaming at how it felt like he could see right through her.

"Him being one of them?"

"Have a safe journey home, Jinn." She wasn't sure what was going on between her and Adonijah, but it was not a topic she was willing to speak openly about, especially with Jinn.

Jinn nodded, folding his arms behind his back, and left.

"It would not be the worst match." Harbona walked up the garden steps to her right.

"How long have you been there?" Salome pushed away from the railing and squared her shoulders to his.

"Long enough to gather he is quite taken with you." Harbona's smile was meant to reassure her, but it made her feel guilty because Adonijah popped into her mind. "Come with me."

As he passed her, she asked. "Where?"

He flashed a toothy grin. "She is waiting for us."

"Who?"

But Harbona didn't answer. He pressed onward, weaving through the castle halls. Salome's curiosity got the better of her and she quietly followed him until they reached an enormous set of arched doors.

"We are here." Harbona reached for the handle.

"Wait." Salome touched his hand and was suddenly flooded with visions of what seemed like a hundred lifetimes. Faces, battles, places, all images she had never seen before. It happened so fast, within a split second, but she couldn't release her hold on him. She snapped out of her visions once they released her. She fell to the floor. Beads of sweat bubbled across her forehead.

How was that even possible?

Harbona stared at her wide-eyed, half curious, half pleased.

"What just happened?" Salome huffed, breathing rapidly.

"Remarkable." Harbona whispered, more to himself than her.

"What's going on?" She tried to stand up, but her legs wobbled as if she'd run ten miles. "What is happening to me, Harbona?"

"That has only happened to one other person who has touched me."

"Harbona!" Salome's fear consumed her. "What's going on?"

"What did you see?" Harbona reached to grab her hand, but she pulled away, keeping a few feet between them.

"Don't touch me," she hissed.

"What did you see?" he pressed, ignoring the panic in her eyes.

"Nothing," she whispered. "Everything. So many faces I've never seen before." She rubbed her eyes as if scrubbing them hard enough would erase what she saw. "Please, tell me what's happening."

"You saw the past," he said, simplicity in his tone. Like she should have known that. "You saw *my* past."

"How is that possible? I didn't see you in any of the flashes."

"Why would you?" Harbona smiled and took a step toward her. "You saw it through my eyes."

"Am I... am I going crazy?" she whispered after looking up and down the hall.

Harbona leaned forward and said, "Not yet, Princess." He turned on his heel and returned to the doors. "Come. She can tell us what we need to know."

Salome followed Harbona inside and saw an enormous circular table in the middle of a ceiling free room. Already seated were Adonijah, Cato, and Damaris.

"What is this?" Salome asked, still glancing around the atrium.

"Come, sit, Cousin," Damaris instructed and motioned to the seat beside her.

Salome was reluctant but was too exhausted to argue. She plopped down in the chair to Damaris's right and Harbona sat on Damaris's left. Salome could feel Adonijah's gaze on her from across the table and Cato's bouncing knee to her right frayed her nerves. She wanted to grab his thigh and force him to stop but she kept her hands to herself.

"Harbona asked me to meet with you," Damaris began.

Salome's eyes flashed in her direction. "About what?"

"What do you know of the Hunters?"

"Harbona already explained to me about Malachi the First." Salome shot her question down.

Damaris leaned closer to her, "Salome, what is a Hunter?"

Salome rubbed her eyes and groaned, "A Hunter is chosen by the Almighty, marked, and tasked to avenge the blood of the innocent." Damaris did not seem impressed. "What?" Salome shrugged, eyeing Harbona.

"Hunters are so much more than just one charged to avenge innocent blood." Damaris kept a fixed gaze on Salome, but her question was directed to Harbona. "You haven't told her everything, have you?"

Harbona shifted in his seat, "It is beyond my expertise, beyond my understanding."

Salome's nostrils flared, "More secrets, Harbona?"

"It is wise not to speak on matters one knows nothing about," Damaris came to Harbona's defense. "It is my destiny and my duty to help you understand your magic."

Adonijah and Cato's mouths dropped simultaneously when the word magic was casually thrown into the conversation.

"Magic?" Salome crinkled her nose. "I don't have magic."

Harbona cleared his throat, grabbing her attention. He nodded his head toward Damaris, as if suggesting she tell the oracle what happened just before this gathering.

"I *don't* have magic," Salome insisted, crossing her arms over her chest. "If I did, don't you think I'd know about it?"

"None of the Hunters knew they had magical abilities until they were called into the Almighty's service, Salome," Damaris said.

"You're telling me every Hunter before me had some kind of powers?" Salome was skeptical.

"Malachi the First was a creature summoner. Tolemy the Red could breathe underwater." Damaris seemed impassioned by remembering the old world and their Hunters. "Raego the Mighty could manipulate metal. Lor the Meek could read human aura, see people's emotions as colors around their bodies. And Polantis the Peacemaker controlled the weather." Damaris focused on Salome. "So, tell me, Cousin, what is your power?"

Harbona cleared his throat, louder this time, drawing everyone's attention. Salome's nostrils flared, irritated at the eyes that now drifted back her way. An explanation. That is what their faces demanded.

Salome grunted, "Sometimes, I hear..." she turned her head to the side and grimaced, "trees."

"You hear trees?" Cato tried to steady his voice, but Salome picked up traces of panicked laughter. "You can hear trees talking to you?"

"I... uh... Yes. No." She scraped her fingers down her face. "I don't know. But what I do know is it's not magic."

"A rare gift, indeed," Damaris mumbled, running her thumb across her fingertips.

"What do they say?" Cato leaned forward, resting his elbows on the table, cupping his jaw in his hands.

"My name."

"Your name?" Cato asked, disappointed. "That's it?"

"That's it."

Damaris turned her face toward her and smiled. "Salome, the trees themselves are not speaking to you, they are merely the vessel our departed use to communicate."

"The departed?" Salome blinked. "You're saying dead people are trying to talk to me?"

"The spirits of our ancestors, of our loved ones," Damaris watched Salome closely. "They are reaching out. But that is not all you have experienced lately."

Salome squirmed in her seat, feeling sweat dripping down the middle of her back. "I see things."

"What things?" Cato's eyes widened.

"You mean visions." Damaris clarified.

"Of the past." Salome nodded.

"How long has this been happening to you?" Damaris asked.

"A few months. At first it was just when I was asleep, but now," Salome leaned back in her seat, and puffed, "I see them even when I'm awake. When I travel, when I eat, when I hunt." Her voice trailed off, "They look so real."

Damaris reached her hand forward and gently rested her fingers on the six lines tattooed on Salome's arm. "Someone is trying to reach you. Have you asked what they want?"

"No," Salome furrowed her brows. "Why would I ask the trees or spirits or the dead what they want?"

"Next time you hear them call you, answer." She patted her arm and retracted her reach. "There is something they need to say."

Salome nodded, unsure if she really believed it was a departed spirit sparking a conversation, but she was willing to at least take Damaris's advice. What was the harm in responding to trees that whispered her name? *What an insane question to ask herself*, she shook her head. She remembered how Crispin looked at her when she told him the trees in The Hollow were speaking to her. As if she was diseased or had descended into insanity. She refused to meet Adonijah's gaze, she didn't want to know what he was thinking of her now.

"That's not magic," Salome said, bringing every eye in the room back to her.

"What do you mean?" Harbona spoke for the first time in several minutes.

Salome looked at him. "She said that Hunters have magic. Talking to trees or spirits can't possibly be all I can do." She bounced her gaze back to Damaris. "Can it?"

"Do you have other abilities you care to mention?" Damaris asked.

Salome wanted to ask Damaris about how they had spoken to one another with just their thoughts but clammed up at the thought of what the others would think. She shook her head. "No. But shouldn't I be able to, I don't know, be able to breathe underwater like Tolemy the Red or manipulate metal like Raego the Mighty? Something more powerful?"

"The Almighty gives the Hunters the abilities they will need to succeed. Perhaps, your strength will come from those who have already crossed into the afterlife." Damaris rose from her seat, signifying the end of their meeting. "Do not compare yourself to others. Peace and strength do not dwell there."

Chapter Nineteen

Crispin

After fighting alongside the pirates and saving Rahab from being swept into the Obsidian Sea by Kubantu's tentacles, Crispin had earned some favor and respect from the crew of the *Shadow of Death*.

Rafi no longer shot Crispin dirty looks whenever he walked around a corner.

Ondrej was more than willing to show him every nook and cranny of the vessel with pride since he had reconstructed most of it over the years.

Phex eagerly showed him the secret, but terrifying, projects he was working on. At some point, all of them would go, "Boom!" the madman explained.

Corwin gave him one of his prized knives. Apparently having just a longsword wasn't good enough to be a member of the crew. The dagger looked like it was of Borgian design; a weapon Zophar would be jealous of.

Haldane was eager to share stories of their exploits and adventures. And Crispin wished for a fleeting moment to be able to have a life on the seas and enjoy the freedom and excitement that came with it. The captain even allowed him to take the helm for a couple of hours, igniting a passion in him for the sea.

But since their run-in with Kubantu, Rahab kept her distance from Crispin, and it had not gone unnoticed. He knew she was watching him. He could sense her eyes on him as he learned the rigging system from Rafi and Ondrej, even though he was supposed to be learning that from her, the First Mate.

Rahab stood on the quarterdeck next to Corwin as he steered them toward the cove where The Sisters was. Her hazel eyes homed in on him and he didn't back down from their stare off.

"She's pretty," Ondrej cut through Crispin's thoughts, causing him to lose the unspoken competition between him and Rahab, "dangerous. She's pretty dangerous."

"I've heard." Crispin sat against the mast and chewed a hunk of bread he'd snatched from the galley. "What is she to Leeondris?"

Rafi plopped down next to Crispin, resting his elbows on his knees. "You want to know if they are lovers?"

Crispin tried to hide his embarrassment by sinking his teeth into another piece of bread. "Are they lovers?"

Rafi furrowed his brow into a furry, white unibrow. "No."

Crispin nodded and accepted the one-word answer. He wasn't much closer to learning the extent of Rahab and Leeondris' relationship, though he wished he didn't care. At least someone other than Rahab confirmed they were not romantically involved.

Boots thudded toward the trio. Crispin looked up, holding a hand above his eyes to block out the sunlight beaming down on him. A dark silhouette stood in front of him.

"Captain wants to see you in his cabin, Mainlander." Rahab turned on her heel, expecting him to follow her without explanation.

Crispin hopped up and jogged to catch up with her. "You've been avoiding me."

"Hardly."

"Which begs the question," he ignored her feeble attempts at denial, "*why* have you been avoiding me?"

"I am the First Mate of the *Shadow of Death*. The fastest and most dangerous ship in the Obsidian Sea. I have more important matters to tend to than to worry about your whereabouts." Rahab didn't break stride as she hissed each word, refusing to look in his direction.

"Yet I've caught you staring at me several times."

Rahab didn't take the bait as she bounded up the steps that led to the hallway that housed their sleeping quarters. "Keeping a watchful eye on you is far from staring."

Once inside the narrow hall, Crispin slammed his hand against the paneled wall, not allowing her to pass. "So, you admit you can't keep your eyes off me."

"Move," she demanded hoarsely.

"Make me."

Rahab moved so quickly he had no idea what happened until it was too late. She grabbed his arm, whipped him around, and slammed his back against the wall.

"Are you always this stubborn?" Rahab hissed, holding her ruby hilted dagger against his throat.

"Are you always this aggressive?" Crispin fired back.

"I would have died a long time ago if I wasn't."

Crispin suspected she could feel his heart beating rapidly against the forearm she pressed to his chest. She had him pinned and therefore, had the upper hand.

"We don't have to be enemies." He rested his head against the wall, eyes still glued to hers.

"Who said we were enemies?"

"Don't tell me this is how you treat your friends," his eyes widened. "Your contempt for me couldn't be more obvious."

"What tipped you off?" Rahab relaxed her arm and tilted her head to the side. "When I told you, I'd slit your throat if you touched me again or that we should have turned you over to the Shadows the moment we had the chance?"

He smirked, mischief in his eyes, "The slitting my throat bit. So, either do it, or let me go."

Rahab's body tensed. Her lips curled, her eyes wild and vicious. What he would give to know what she was thinking that very second. Her gaze softened and she lowered her knife slowly.

"Letting me go," he was both relieved and surprised.

"With you dead," she holstered her weapon, "we don't get paid. And if there's one thing I value more than human life, it's money."

Crispin brushed the imaginary dust from his shirt with a smile creeping across his face. "See, I'm growing on you. I told you I would."

"What's to say, I don't kill you once you pay us? Or hand you over to the Shadows and collect on your bounty?" Rahab flashed a mischievous smile of her own – yet hers looked more menacing than playful.

"By the time money exchanges hands, you'll be in love with me." Crispin followed her as she turned on her heel to walk down the hall.

"Oh really?" she snorted. "Very cocky of you, Your Majesty."

"No," he shook his head, "just confident."

"Next thing you'll tell me is you've never met a woman who hasn't fallen for your charm."

"You think I'm charming?" He stepped in front of her, stopping her dead in her tracks.

"No, I find you annoying."

"If I'm being honest, I don't have very much experience with women. At least, not pretty women my own age. More like the wrinkled, old ladies who need help with odd jobs and ogle my body." Crispin rubbed his hands up and down his chest with a wink.

Rahab popped her round hip to the side, crossing her arms over her chest, and chuckled. "Funny."

Crispin ticked his fingers, "So, you think I'm charming -"

"Annoying."

"And funny."

"When I look at you, all I think is how -"

"Impossibly handsome I am?" He flipped hair from his eyes.

"How out of your element you are," she corrected.

"So," he lowered a finger, leaving two up, "not impossibly handsome?"

"You aren't..." she cocked her head to the side, examining his face, "...ugly."

Crispin slapped a hand to his knee and pointed his finger in her direction. "I'll take it. One step closer to you falling madly in love with me."

"For all your cockiness -"

"Confidence," he interrupted.

"Cockiness," Rahab held steady, her brow arched. "There is one thing you haven't taken into consideration about this whole 'me falling in love with you' ploy."

"Which is?" Crispin leaned his shoulder against the wall.

"You aren't my type."

"You mean, because I'm a Mainlander."

Rahab's eyes narrowed, "Unlike *your* people," she rested her hands on her hips, "skin color has nothing to do with who I love."

"My mother was from the Isles of Myr and married my father who was the King of Northwind. Skin color has nothing to do with -"

"You're a prince," she blurted. "And I'm a pirate. Our kind don't settle down to raise a family together."

"You think I'd be shallow enough..."

"Not to commit to someone like me?" she motioned up and down her body. "Absolutely. What do I offer? Nothing a princess or lady or ambassador with royal blood could."

"Rahab -"

She shot a hand up to silence him. "It's alright, Mainlander. I'm not offended, just realistic." She stepped up to him and whispered, "So, before you go through the effort of winning my affection, ask yourself if this is really what you want or if it's just a game."

Crispin grasped her hand as she tried to pass him and pulled her back to face him. "It is my choice who I love – and if that is you, then nothing and no one can change my mind."

Rahab's gaze bounced back and forth from his lips to his eyes.

"Tell me I really don't stand a chance of you loving me and I won't mention it again." Crispin dragged his thumb along her jawline, brushing over her mouth.

Rahab leaned in and closed her eyes. He lowered his head, ready to feel the touch of her soft lips against his, when he heard her laugh.

"What?" he whispered.

Rahab patted his cheek, "You really are good. You almost had me."

"What are you talking about?"

She smiled, inches from his face, "A lesser woman would already be in your bed. Thank the stars I am not a Mainlander wench."

This time, he didn't attempt to stop her from leaving. He smirked and ran fingers through his wavy hair as her hips swayed side to side. He didn't know why it mattered to him, but he was determined to change her opinion of him.

As Rahab lifted her fist to knock on Haldane's door, it swung open, and the captain filled the threshold. He smooshed his hat atop his head and Rahab stepped back, allowing him access into the hallway.

"What took you two so long?" Haldane's eyes bounced from Rahab to Crispin.

"I'm a slow walker." Crispin shrugged his shoulders. Rahab seemed to stifle a giggle. Maybe she did have a sense of humor after all.

"Well, no time for chit chat." Haldane marched to the end of the hall with the two of them fast on his heels. "We're here." He climbed the steps to the quarterdeck and motioned toward The Sisters.

Crispin turned toward the bow of the boat and sucked in a quick breath. The Sisters was breathtaking. He had never seen towers built so high before, and there were two of them inhabiting a small island with the pine trees of the Western Lands directly behind them on the Mainland.

Rahab pointed, "The left tower belongs to the Witnesses. The right tower belongs to the Keepers."

"And the bridge connecting them?" Crispin asked, pointing at the two-story connection at the top of the towers.

"That is where the Sovereign stays." Rahab inched closer. "He connects both sects, ruling them in harmony, keeping them balanced."

"He can tell us where to find your friend?" Crispin's eyes trailed down to hers.

"Aye." She met his gaze. "If he is feeling generous."

"And if he isn't feeling generous?"

"Let's hope that's not the case." Rahab stepped up to take her place on Haldane's right as they approached the harbor.

Once they docked, two Keepers approached their ship, spears pounding against the stone pavers with each step they took.

"State your business," one of the Keepers barked.

"We're here to meet with his Holiness, the Sovereign," Haldane's boots thudded down the wooden ramp toward the warriors.

The shorter Keeper crinkled his nose, "Pirates."

"You are ordered to leave our city immediately," the Keeper closest to the ramp commanded.

"You don't understand," Haldane protested, "we mean you no harm, oh mighty blind ones. Prince Crispin of Northwind is with us. See!" Haldane motioned with an exaggerated swipe behind him to Crispin but then smacked his palm against forehead. "I don't mean see as in actually... I mean see as in – uh." He exhaled in defeat, so Crispin jumped in..

"I am Crispin, son of Issachar of Northwind. I humbly request an audience with the Sovereign."

"And why would a *prince* keep the company of Pulauan pirates?" The Keeper folded his arms across his broad chest, his spear hugged against his body.

Haldane stuttered, clearly insulted, "L-L-Look here, we are -"

Crispin gripped Haldane's forearm. "These pirates rescued me when I was separated from my company. Please, allow me five minutes with the Sovereign and I swear we will be on our way."

The dark skinned Keeper sniffed the air loudly. "Smells like filthy pirate tricks to me."

"Be on your way!" The first Keeper demanded. "Or we will sink your ship and throw you in the dungeons."

Haldane growled, "Do you know who we are?"

"Does it matter?" The second Keeper scoffed.

"Now, listen here -"

"We're leaving." Crispin interrupted Haldane, silencing the captain.

Haldane's nostrils flared, ready for a good, old-fashioned fist fight, but he turned and marched back up the ramp. "Looks like we be leaving, lads!"

Rahab also fought spouting off and followed Haldane and Crispin up the steps to the quarterdeck. She took ahold of the helm, guiding their ship from the docks.

Haldane whipped around and pointed a finger in Crispin's chest. "You better have a damn good reason for overstepping your command and having us run like whipped dogs with our tails between our legs."

Crispin rubbed his chin, eyes still fixed on the towers as they sailed out of the cove and around the cliffs that bordered the Western Lands. "How hard would it be to break into The Sisters?"

Haldane's eyes nearly popped out of his head. "How hard? How har-" He slapped his tricorn hat against his leg. "I'd say it's impossible. Has the heat finally warped that brain of yours, lad?"

"Can you scale a wall?" Rahab asked.

"I don't know about walls," Crispin scratched the stubble along his jawline, "but I can climb trees faster than a monkey."

"You can't be serious," Haldane quipped.

"I'll race a monkey right now -"

"No, you twit!" Haldane waved his arms in the air. "No one cares about you racing monkeys. Are you two seriously considering breaking into one of the most secure cities in Adalore?"

"I made a deal to help you find your friend," Crispin leaned against the railing. "I will do what needs to be done to get back to my companions."

"Then I'm going with you," Rahab stepped forward, volunteering for the stealth mission.

Haldane took over steering when Rahab released the helm. "I don't like this. We're pirates, not thieves."

Crispin turned around to look at Haldane, "Do you even hear yourself? What exactly do you think a pirate is?"

"You know what I mean," Haldane snorted. "We belong on the seas, not breaking into fortified cities."

"How else do you expect us to get the information we need to find Leeondris?" Rahab asked. She grabbed Haldane's arm, drawing his gaze. "We can do this."

Haldane chewed on the inside of his lip. "Take Phex with you, just in case."

"Hell, Captain, we might as well just bang on the front door." Rahab shook her head.

Phex ascended the steps with a menacing smile that made Crispin shudder. He reminded Crispin of a sleepy fox, but a dangerous one that liked to blow things up. "I'll take that as a compliment."

"Take it however it suits you, Phex." Rahab watched as Corwin, Rafi, and Ondrej followed Phex up the steps to join them. "This is a stealth mission. Give me Corwin."

Haldane looked over at the crew and reluctantly nodded. "Fine. But any sign of trouble breaking in, you bail. Understood?"

"Aye, Captain." Rahab nodded in agreement.

Corwin flipped his knives around his hands. "Let's go rob the blind."

Chapter Twenty

Ziggy

Ziggy laid in Gershom's bed, hating herself more than the last time they were together. Each time they rendezvoused, she felt cheap, dirty, and used. But no one else in the Order had gotten this close to Gershom or Niabi. They kept a close-knit circle and outsiders were rarely welcomed into the fold. Neither the queen nor her second in command trusted easily, so the fact she had been chosen, hand-selected by Gershom himself to be his female companion, was a reason to rejoice.

Oden had grinned ear to ear when she told him and the Order of her first encounter with the Bear. She had hoped Oden would tell her it was too risky being that close and in that vulnerable of a position, but he didn't. He just clapped his hands together, whispered a breath of thanks to no one in particular, and instructed her to see Gershom in whatever fashion he deemed worthy. Ziggy was to get close to Gershom, to learn everything she could, and report her findings.

"It is your duty," Oden had said, hands gripping her shoulders. *"You must do everything you can to please him so we might know his weaknesses."*

That had been nine months ago to the day, and she hadn't gotten much useful information. Instead, it had put her in the queen's sights and now service. Not only was Oden pressuring her to bring him intelligence worth his time, but the queen was too. And one would think Niabi would be far more frightening, but it was Oden's face that stopped her heart.

Gershom sat up in his enormous bed covered in furs, interrupting her thoughts. He planted his feet on the ground and turned his back to her. If she was determined and quick enough, she could snatch one of the swords he kept mounted above his headboard and strike him down. She could escape his calloused fingers roaming across her smooth, pale skin. She could tell Oden she eliminated one of their enemies and be reassigned to something less humiliating.

But as she tore her eyes from the three swords above her, her gaze rested on Gershom's battered back. For the first few months, he refused to let her stay the night, and warned her never to ask him personal questions. She learned to avert her eyes most of the time they were together. But tonight, she let her focus remain on his scarred body. Whip lashes by the look of them. There were so many. They were deep, too. She almost felt sympathy for him.

"Does my appearance frighten you?" Gershom's voice caused her to avert her gaze. He must have sensed her staring.

"No, my lord," she managed to spit out.

"You do not need to fear me," he twisted his torso so he could look at her. She sat up and leaned against the wooden headboard, pulling the furs up to cover her body. "I know of my scars."

"All great warriors have scars."

"Yes," Gershom nodded, "but most of my markings did not come from battle."

Ziggy opened her mouth but hesitated and snapped her lips shut. She knew she needed to ask him deeper, more intimate questions, if she was going to learn anything she could deliver to the Order, but she wasn't sure if Gershom would answer or smack her like past clients had.

"Go ahead." Gershom walked to a small table against the wall and poured two glasses of wine.

"My lord?"

"I can see it written all over your pretty face." He climbed back into bed, handing her one of the glasses. "You have questions. Go ahead and ask."

Ziggy couldn't mask her surprise. She had earned his trust. The poor fool. "If I may be so bold, my lord, where did you get those scars?"

Gershom gulped half of his wine down in one sip and cleared his throat. "Before serving the queen, I served her father. I was his commander, his friend. But something changed him."

"What changed him?" She sipped her drink, leaving a red lipstick stain on the rim of her glass.

"Her." Gershom polished off what remained in his glass and set it down. "Issachar did everything in his power to rid himself of a firstborn daughter. With plans to marry her off to the heir of Borg, he hoped he would never have to deal with or see her again. But King Benaiah wasn't interested in peace as much as he was in power. Knowing Northern laws, he understood Niabi's rightful claim to the White Throne and insisted his second born son, Antilles, marry her instead. Issachar was enraged by this proposal. When he learned Niabi and Antilles had grown quite fond of one another during one of the Westerners' visits, he ordered me to kill the young prince and make it look as if the Andrago had ambushed them during one of their northern hunting excursions. When I refused, Issachar had me arrested for treason and thrown into the dungeons." He cleared his throat and pressed on, as if he needed to tell someone or he would burst. "I was tortured for weeks until my brother, Ophir, rescued me."

Ziggy couldn't hide the horror in her eyes. Gershom had been mutilated for doing what she thought the Bear incapable of doing: the honorable thing; the right thing.

"But..." she scooted closer to him. "But you were his friend. How could he do that to you?"

Gershom rested his hand on her thigh and sighed. "Kings tend to forget their friends when it suits their agenda. Issachar was not interested in truth or honor – only power and blind obedience."

"Is she like him?"

Gershom's eyes shot up to meet hers. "The queen? She is far worse."

Ziggy shuddered, "She frightens me." A truth she would willingly admit to anyone.

"You would be a fool not to fear her." He mumbled to himself, "She will be my undoing when the endless night comes for me."

Without thinking Ziggy grasped his hand in hers and said, "I'm sorry that happened to you. I think you would make a great king."

Gershom glanced down at their hands clasped together and she instantly paled. She stammered an apology as she snatched her hand back.

"A man should never drink around a beautiful woman." He smiled. "He says more than he ought."

"My lord," her lips quivered. "Forgive me."

Gershom kissed her forehead, "You would make a lovely queen, Ziggy."

Her heart skipped a beat. "Such kind words -"

"Not just words," he grasped her petite hand. "If I bore the crown and sat on the White Throne, would you want to be my queen? To bear me sons? To be by my side?"

Ziggy's mouth opened but she didn't know what to say. She had to tread carefully because she was now wading in treasonous waters.

"I see you are speechless," he grinned.

"Of course, I am, my lord." Ziggy brushed rebellious red curls out of her face. "It is an honor to be by your side in any capacity."

"So, you would be my queen?" Gershom's eyes were filled with expectation, hope, if she dared to read into the emotion he had written across his scarred face.

She had a role to play. The Ziggy who Gershom knew wouldn't hesitate to accept this treacherous proposal. Ziggy mustered a bright smile and nodded her head.

"My lord," she whispered, "I would be your queen and I would bear you as many sons as I could give if you were King of Northwind."

Gershom squeezed her hand. "Soon, my dear, you will be dripping in gold and jewels." He brought her hand up to his lips where he planted a kiss. "When the time comes for me to bear the crown, I will send my men to ensure your safety."

"What of the queen?"

Gershom frowned at the mention of Niabi, "She will be forgotten. I just need more time."

Ziggy lifted a hand to his chin and gently forced him to look at her. "I will be here for you in whatever way you need me to be."

Gershom smiled and kissed her forehead, lingering a bit longer than normal. "That will be all tonight, Ziggy." He draped a fur over his shoulders, and left the room, allowing her to finish dressing in private.

For the first time in nine months, she finally learned of a potential plot to usurp the queen. She should have been excited to give Oden something to chew on, but she felt something for Gershom she never thought possible. She felt sorry for him. For a split second, she believed in his cause and pictured herself as his queen. Dressed in the finest clothes money could buy and dripping in beautiful gems.

Her thoughts were ripped from her mind when she heard Gershom and another man in the adjoining room in a heated discussion. She threw on her dress and as quietly as possible, tip-toed to the door, and dropped to her knees to listen through the keyhole.

Gershom sounded angry and was caught off guard by the unexpected visitor. She strained to hear what they were saying, so, Ziggy peeked through the keyhole to see if she could get a good look at whoever Gershom was talking to and was surprised to see a man from Numbio. Ziggy watched as Gershom pinched the bridge of his nose and snarled at his company. He pointed a massive finger at the bald, old man.

"You are a fool for coming here, Memucan," Gershom hissed.

"And what did you expect me to do?" Memucan asked angrily. "Stay in Numbio and have the king execute me for treason? Have him discover our plot to usurp him and Niabi?"

"Hush!" Gershom growled. "The walls have ears. Why do you think we have never met here before?"

"My life was in danger. The king and his priestess were putting the pieces together faster than I anticipated. I had no choice."

"And what do you think I will be able to do for you here?" Gershom shrugged his fur from his shoulders and made his way to the decanter of Myridian wine he loved so much. He shakily poured himself a glass but didn't offer one to Memucan. "If the queen doesn't already know of your arrival, she will soon enough. I cannot risk her wrath again. Not when we are getting closer to achieving our goal."

"I didn't sail here on a Numbio ship." Memucan sank into one of Gershom's leather chairs. "I came by way of Port Daelon. There is no way your queen would know of my presence. If anyone asks," the old man twisted his fingers to crack them one by one, "I am one of your servants."

"No." Gershom shook his head. "We need to find somewhere for you to hide. Maybe at one of the inns by the harbor."

"You want me to hide in this filthy city?" Memucan scrunched his nose in disgust.

Gershom squared his shoulders to face the door Ziggy was spying from. He tilted his head to the side and marched for her hiding spot. She scurried to the bed and started throwing more of her clothes on. When he burst through the doors, she was sitting on the bed tying her boots.

"My lord?" Ziggy feigned confusion. "Is everything alright?" Gershom stared so deeply into her eyes it made her skin crawl. "My lord?" she asked again, sure she had been made.

"Can I trust you, Ziggy?" he asked the question as if she were one of his soldiers.

Ziggy bobbed her head and flashed a nervous smile, "Of course."

Her answer seemed to satisfy him. "Do you know of an inn near the harbor that Her Majesty's soldiers don't patrol?"

She knew of several but the one she would recommend was a block away from *The Whispering Fox*. Whoever this Memucan was, the Order would want to keep an eye on him, and the proximity would make that easier.

"I could make arrangements at *The Black Lotus* if that pleases you." She finished tying her laces and stood up, his eyes roaming freely over her clothed body.

Gershom nodded. "See to it then. Send word when you have acquired a room."

With a quick bow, Ziggy slipped out of Gershom's chambers and made her way down the secret corridors to return to her small apartment in Northwind. She didn't know when Gershom would stage his coup, or who exactly Memucan was, but what she did know was she was now in dangerous territory. Up until this point, it was all hypothetical. Now, the game had truly begun, and she would have to be careful to remain on the victor's side, lest she die a victim's death.

Chapter Twenty-One

Crispin

Well after darkness had shrouded the cove, Crispin, Rahab, and Corwin disembarked the *Shadow of Death* anchored beyond the cliffs and swam back to The Sisters. They crouched behind a cluster of boulders near the harbor shores and scoped out the movement of the Keepers patrolling the perimeter of the Witness Tower. Being blind didn't hinder them. If anything, Crispin knew their hearing would be heightened. And if Corwin got too close, they'd be able to smell the mix of musk and tobacco easily.

"They have eight patrols, two Keepers in each." Rahab whispered near Crispin's ear, wringing her shirt. "There are seconds in between their paths crossing as they circle the Witness Tower."

"So, that's our way in." Crispin rubbed at the stubble growing on his face. He had made a point to keep his face clean shaven like Northern royalty, but he was liking the facial hair. Zophar would be pleased he looked more rugged.

Corwin scraped dirt from underneath his fingernails with one of his knives, his back rested against the boulders facing away from the Keepers. "I didn't spy any doors other than the main ones. How do you suggest we get in if we sneak by the patrols?"

Rahab turned from Corwin on her right to Crispin on her left. "Remember when I asked how good you were at scaling walls?" She smirked and nodded her head up the side of the tower.

Crispin's eyes followed hers and rested on the first of seven wraparound balconies. The lowest balcony was a good distance above the ground.

"How high do you suspect that landing is?" Crispin asked.

Rahab pursed her lips and scratched the side of her head. "If I was the guessing sort, I'd say fifty feet at least."

Crispin nodded, "I would have said the same."

"Well, good luck with that." Corwin huffed, folding his enormous, tattooed arms over his chest. "I'll let the captain know when you die."

"That's the spirit." Crispin forced a smile.

Rahab smacked the back of her hand against Corwin's bicep, clicking her tongue. "We all go."

"Oh, hell no!" Corwin shook his head.

"Corwin!"

"You said we were going to break in. No one said anything about scaling up the tower in the dark," Corwin snorted.

"Don't tell me you're afraid of heights." Rahab rolled her eyes.

"Not afraid." Corwin cracked his neck. "Just prefer to keep my boots on the deck of a ship."

"Look at it this way," Crispin offered, leaning closer to the pirates. "You won't be nearly as high scaling to that landing as you are on the deck of the *Shadow of Death*."

Corwin's brows formed a unibrow as he frowned at Crispin. "How do you figure?"

"Do you know how deep the Obsidian Sea is? More than fifty feet, that's for sure." Crispin squatted next to Corwin. "What happens if you fall into the sea? You sink and it's a long way down."

Corwin grimaced and Rahab rubbed her eyes with a sigh.

"I..." Corwin wheezed, wiping his sweaty hands down his pants. "I never thought about it that way. More than fifty feet, huh?"

"Great. Now you've done it." Rahab fussed at Crispin. "He won't be able to scale that wall or sail the Obsidian Sea now."

Crispin patted her hand which she ripped away. "Give him a minute. He might surprise you." He pointed with his mouth back to the pensive pirate.

"I," Corwin relaxed his face. "I suppose it isn't much different, distance wise.

Crispin nodded his approval. "See?" he whispered to Rahab with a smug smile tugging at his lips. "Just needed to give him a minute to put it together."

"You got lucky."

"Was it luck or was it my charm?"

Rahab thrust the rope they had brought with them into his chest. "Luck."

Crispin heaved the rope over his shoulder and followed Rahab toward the tower. Two patrols were crossing paths; his short window was about to open.

"Don't fall," Rahab side-eyed him.

"And hope *you* catch me?" Crispin chuckled. "I'm not that lucky."

She rolled her eyes and tugged at her left ear. "I'll be right behind you as soon as you lower the rope.

"Can't get enough of me." He noticed her nervous tell and tried to lighten the mood.

"You can't help yourself, can you?" she laughed softly.

"Where's the fun in that?"

"It's now or never," Corwin interrupted.

Crispin nodded and locked eyes with Rahab once more. Her lips parted as if she wanted to say something, but he took off before she had the chance. He hoisted himself up onto the stone landing and slipped behind the four Keepers walking in opposite patrol directions. He made it to the tower and exhaled a low breath, having held it since he left his companions. Crispin double checked to ensure the rope was still secure over his shoulder and across his chest before finding grooves to put his fingers to climb up the side to the balcony above.

Crispin kept a steady pace as he climbed up the side of the Witness Tower. He was about half-way when his fingers slipped, and he clung to the stones with his right hand. Fragments of stones fell and bounced off the pavers below. What would have gone unnoticed to Crispin's ears was magnified to the four passing Keepers who halted their patrol and turned around to investigate.

Grasping the building, Crispin picked up the pace. The last thing he needed was to draw their attention, hindering Rahab and Corwin from following him. He risked a glance downward just in time to see the Keepers resume their rounds. He exhaled a huge sigh of relief and focused on finishing the last ten feet to the landing.

The last few feet nearly took his breath away. That was the hardest and highest climb of Crispin's entire life. His forearms, biceps, and shoulders were on fire. His arms began to shake as he suspended himself just below the balcony to check for Keepers. Seeing it was clear, he hopped over the railing and ripped the rope from his chest, tying it around one of the columns that stood on the side of the open doorway into the tower.

Quickly and quietly, he lowered the rope for Rahab and Corwin to climb. Once Rahab sneaked past the Keepers and started her ascent, Crispin poked his head around the entryway and was relieved and surprised no Keepers were patrolling. He stared up to the top of the tower and was awed by the stained-glass ceiling that whisked moonlight inside.

His concentration shot back to Rahab as he heard her grunting near the top of the railing. She had scaled the wall faster than he thought she could and was impressed. He extended his hand to help her over, but she slapped his hand away and whipped her legs over onto the balcony.

"What?" Rahab huffed when she noticed Crispin's odd grin. "What is that smirk for?"

"You are an impressive climber."

"When you spend most of your time on a ship, you get really good at climbing up ropes." She turned her attention to the ground where Corwin had yet to appear. "Blast!" she whispered, a tinge of anger in her tone.

Crispin leaned closer to her, their arms touching. "What is it? Did the Keepers -?"

"No," she shook her head. "If that brute of a sailor chickens out..."

"You'll make him walk the plank?" Crispin flashed a smile, elbowing her arm.

She flitted her eyes at him. "Is that what you Mainlanders think we do to cowards?"

"Ye-es."

Rahab rolled her eyes.

"So, that's *not* what you do?"

"No, we give them a big hug and hand them a pint." Before he could say anything, she smacked his arm and clicked her tongue. "Of course, they walk the plank! We haven't the time or space for cowards."

"Wait. But you just said -"

"I asked if that's what you Mainlanders believed. I never said you were wrong."

Crispin rubbed his eyes with a groan. "You are honestly the most frustrating woman I have ever met. Truly. You should be proud of your accomplishment."

Rahab saluted him. "An honor I shall cherish always, Your Mightiness."

"Again, with the titles." He squinted his eyes to see if he could spot Corwin. "How long should we wait -"

"Would one of you two jabbering fools help me up before I fall?" Corwin startled them as he heaved his arms over the railing. Their attention had been on each other, so they hadn't noticed Corwin scrambling up the rope with great difficulty.

Crispin grabbed ahold of Corwin's arms and dragged his heavy body onto the balcony, both falling to the tiled floor.

"Seven hells, Corwin!" Rahab wheezed as loud as she dared, a hand pressed against her heart. "You nearly caught a fist to your face."

"Thank the Seas, for once you kept those fists of yours to yourself." Corwin huffed, slowly standing to his feet. "Tell me we have another way out of here."

"Or what?" Rahab popped her hip and cocked her head to the side. "You going to stay here with the blind?"

Corwin turned to Crispin, a glimmer of hope and pleading in his brown eyes. "Tell me you have another way out of here."

"We have another way out." Crispin patted Corwin on the back. He could feel the trembling in Corwin's body. Heights was not Corwin's friend. Corwin inched his way toward the entryway, not daring a glance down to the pavers below.

"You lied." Rahab grasped Crispin's arm before he could follow Corwin inside. "We don't have another way out."

"I think you should say that a little bit louder, Rahab. I don't think the second tower heard you."

"What do you intend to do if Corwin refuses to repel from the tower?" She blocked his pathway, ignoring his snarky remark.

"We need him focused on our mission. There is no need for him to worry the entire time we're here. We need Corwin at his best and most focused." Crispin nodded back to the rope still tied for their return. "We will cross that bridge when we get to it."

The three intruders walked around the circular hall, open to the center of the tower, until they reached a set of spiral stairs. The staircase led them into the most impressive library Crispin had ever laid eyes on. Shelves that extended up the walls all the way to the ceiling at least a hundred feet above them. Crispin was taken aback at the grand space; it was hard to believe it even existed inside the tower. No matter which direction he turned, the rows of books, scrolls, and loose parchments seemed endless.

In Northwind, Crispin's mother had taken a special interest in the library. He spent many punishments helping her sort and restore book after book. What Bilhah never knew, or at least he assumed she never knew, was how he would purposely get into trouble so he could spend time with her. Books were their special thing. It's how he learned about the different Kingdoms of Adalore: their customs, their traditions, their laws. He never expected that knowledge to come in handy, but now standing in the middle of the Witness Tower, the ultimate library that housed the Hall of Records, he was awed by how much he still had to learn.

Rahab whistled a low drawn-out sound, pulling him from the memories of his mother. "This is going to be harder than I thought."

She was right. They had broken into the tower to find where Leeondris' was being held captive. Without a general idea of where they should look, there would be no way they'd find what they were looking for.

"Well, I guess we start here and work our way around?" Corwin scratched the tattoos on his cheeks so hard, Crispin was positive they'd peel right off.

"This is impossible." Rahab clasped her hands behind her neck, exhaling a sigh. "Maybe we should snatch a couple of the Witnesses from their beds and force them to find it for us."

"So now we're kidnapping people?" Crispin tsked. "Let's not disturb the hornet's nest, shall we?"

"Fine. No kidnapping." Rahab dragged her fingernails down her face. "But without some idea on how to look up information, we could be down here for years, and we obviously don't have that kind of time."

"It's your call," Crispin turned to her. "We either try to find what we came here for, or we leave and try to find him some other way."

"You'd do that?" She was surprised.

"My word is my word." Crispin nodded. "So, what's it going to be?"

Rahab didn't hesitate. "We find what we came here for."

"And what is that exactly?"

The trio hadn't heard the Keepers surround them in the library. The soldiers were hidden in so many places and because Crispin was distracted, he didn't check the room for Keepers.

"And what is that exactly?" The Keeper who appeared to be in charge stepped forward, asking the same question again. "You didn't think you would actually rob us, did you?"

Crispin stepped between her and his companions. "We were looking for information, Master...?"

She smiled, stretching the black wrap around her eyes. "Master Penn."

"From your wrap, you must be in charge of these Keepers."

"You are a well-informed thief." Penn nodded. "But that won't help you here. Without the help of a Witness, you would spend a hundred years in here and never find what you are looking for."

"Perhaps, you'd be willing to fetch one of them for us?" Crispin's snarky remarks didn't work on Penn.

"We are going to take a little walk." She snapped her fingers and twelve spears pointed toward them. "You are charged with trespassing and attempted robbery. The Sovereign will determine your fate."

An old man hobbled toward them; his cane echoed with each step he took. "It seems you have apprehended the intruders with little trouble, Master Penn."

"As I have told you before, Master Balor," Penn said, "we Keepers were bred for this."

"You are taking them to the Sovereign?"

"I am."

"I shall accompany you."

"If you like." Penn snapped her fingers again and six Keepers grabbed either arm of the three intruders. "But do try to keep up."

—•—

Chapter Twenty-Two

Adonijah

Adonijah hungrily forked at the pork on his plate, shoveling bite after glorious bite into his mouth, as if he hadn't eaten in days. He had never eaten better than during his time in the Isles of Myr. He was going to miss the endless options paraded into his suite every day, but he was ready to return to the Mainland. He was growing tired of all the judgmental stares he received from the Myridian women, especially Seraphina, the mean twin. Although it was clear she despised every man that crossed her path, she seemed to have it out for him in particular.

He leaned back in his chair once his plate was cleared and lit his pipe. With a leg resting on his lap, he exhaled a puff of smoke across the table where Cato was scarfing down his second helping of roasted potatoes. Salome was pushing her fish aimlessly around her full plate, not having eaten one single bite since they sat down.

She hadn't said much since Damaris and Harbona told her about her magical abilities – or lack thereof. And for her not to devour her food like she normally did, signaled she was deep in thought, stewing in disappointment. Or anger. He wasn't quite sure.

Cato finished his dinner with a gratifying burp and sighed as he patted the small belly protruding from his skinny frame.

As much as Adonijah hated to admit it, and would never tell Cato because he didn't want him to get a big head, he had come to like the Stormcrag. Cato was entertaining and, on an island filled with man-hating-women, having him for a companion was oddly comforting.

Cato picked at his teeth with his golden fork. "What do you think your Hunter name will be?"

Salome only realized Cato was talking to her once Adonijah cleared his throat. "What?"

"Your Hunter name," Cato smiled with excitement. "Like Malachi the First or Raego the Mighty. What do you think yours will be?"

Salome tossed her utensil on her plate and shrugged. "I don't know, Cato."

Cato hummed. "Hmmm... Salome the..."

"Stubborn," Adonijah filled in the blank.

"Stubborn! Stubborn?" Cato gulped audibly, he glanced at Salome seated next to him. "Has a nice ring to it?"

Salome snapped out of her silence and glared at Adonijah across the table. "And you would be Adonijah the Ass," she snorted.

"Also has a nice ring to it," Cato chuckled, patting his mouth clean with his linen napkin.

"Aye." Adonijah kicked his boots up on the table and exhaled another ring of smoke above his head. "Salome the Stubborn it is. I'll spread the word."

She folded her arms over her chest, "You'll pay for that later."

"Oh, I'm counting on it, Princess." He flashed a mischievous smile, tucking a hand behind his head.

Cato's eyes bounced back and forth between Salome and Adonijah. "Should I give you two some privacy?"

Simultaneously, they said:

"No."

"Aye."

Cato leaned in closer to the table until his chest touched the edge. "What should I do in this situation?" he whispered. He turned to Salome, "Do what you say?" He turned to Adonijah, "Or do what you say?"

Adonijah's eyes were locked on Salome. "Always do what *she* says."

"So, I should stay." Cato reached for the bowl of green olives in the center of the table and popped one in his mouth.

Salome kept her gaze on Adonijah, as if she would lose some contest if she broke eye contact first. "Give us a minute alone, Cato."

"Right." Cato huffed and grabbed the entire bowl of olives. "Don't kill each other."

Once Cato disappeared around the corner of the suite's dining room, Salome stood up and slapped his boots off the table.

"Stubborn? Really?"

"Am I wrong?" Adonijah planted his feet on the tiled floor, his legs the same distance apart as his shoulders.

Salome slithered around the circular, wooden table and stood in front of him. Her thighs pressed up against his knees. "That's the best attribute that comes to mind when you think of me?" Her hip popped to one side and she rested her hand on it.

His sight floated from her hips up to her narrowed eyes. "Not the best," he rose from his seat and looked down at her, "just the first."

"So," she smiled, "you admit you think about me." She chuckled at her own cheekiness, and it warmed his face.

"Aye." Adonijah stroked her chin with his thumb. "I think about you."

Her voice softened, as if under his spell. "Do you think about our first night in Myr? When we almost...?"

"Kissed," he whispered and nodded. "Aye."

Salome slowly wrapped her arms around his neck. He rested his hands on her hips and leaned in to kiss her, but just before their lips touched, someone by the doorway cleared their throat announcing their presence.

Salome and Adonijah's heads whipped toward the arched threshold and spotted the twins, Rosalina and Seraphina, standing shoulder to shoulder. Rosalina blushed, looking uncomfortable with seeing them locked in such an intimate embrace. Seraphina, on the other hand, had her arms crossed over her chest and shook her head in palpable disgust.

How he had grown to loathe those meddlesome twins. Always appearing at the most inconvenient moments.

"Your Highness," Rosalina curtsied.

"Your Highness," Seraphina followed suit.

Salome released Adonijah and faced her ladies in waiting. "What is it?"

"Your grandmother, the queen," Rosalina started.

"Has requested you join her for an audience," Seraphina finished.

"When?" Salome tried to mask her irritation, but Adonijah knew her better than the twins, and by the tone in her voice, she was seething.

Please say tomorrow, Adonijah wished.

"Now," Seraphina flashed a satisfied grin.

"Now?" Salome scratched the side of her face, her eyes met Adonijah's.

"Yes, Your Highness." Rosalina nodded. "We are here to escort you."

"I'm sorry," Salome whispered up to Adonijah.

Not as sorry as he was. He kissed her forehead, drawing a grunt from Seraphina. Without looking at her, he knew the twin's eyes were rolling back in her head. "Go," he said softly.

All Adonijah could do was watch as Salome disappeared with the twins. He rubbed the nape of his neck with a heavy sigh. It seemed like the Isles of Myr didn't want to see them together. All the more reason to return to the Mainland. He would miss the food. He would miss the sea views. But he would *never* miss those damn twins.

Chapter Twenty-Three

Crispin

Master Penn and her Keepers escorted Crispin, Rahab, and Corwin up what seemed like a never-ending staircase to the two-story bridge where Neempo, the Sovereign, dwelled. Once they reached the top of the enclosed bridge, they were able to see the Obsidian Sea on their right and to their left was the Mainland. The *Shadow of Death* wasn't docked in the cove, so it was safe to assume the Keepers hadn't tracked them down and brought them in for punishment.

The windows of the hallway ended on the right, and they marched another twenty feet before they were pushed up to a set of arched double doors. Two Keepers guarding the entrance slammed the butt end of their spears onto the wooden floors and the Keepers escorting the intruders echoed the movement. The doors swung open. Penn entered and Crispin, Rahab, and Corwin were shoved inside after her.

Neempo, dressed in his sleeping robes, sat stoically in his office, sipping a cup of late-night tea. It appeared he rolled out of bed for the sole purpose to sentence them, so the Keepers could execute judgment.

"The intruders, Sovereign." Master Penn announced, her hand resting on the sword that hung by her hip.

"Very efficient of you, Master Penn." Neempo blew the rising steam from his mug. "Master Balor, good of you to join us this very late evening. Or should I say, very early morning?"

Master Balor hobbled up and set his cane in front of him, setting both his hands on top to keep him steady. "Sovereign."

Neempo motioned toward the bonds around the prisoners' wrists. "Those bonds won't be necessary."

Penn tilted her head. "Sovereign, they could be dangerous."

"Cut their bonds." Neempo instructed. "Bonds are not necessary. None of them are foolish enough to attempt an assassination with both my Master of Keepers and Master of Witnesses with me. No. We are simply going to have a nice chat."

Penn obeyed and cut their bonds. Rahab rubbed her wrists, her nostrils flaring.

"Please," Neempo motioned for them to take seats around the study. "Have a seat. There is much we need to discuss."

Penn and Balor sat on either side of Neempo, ensuring an attack would not be so easily accomplished. The Keepers backed away to the doorway.

"This will be a private conversation. Your services are not needed." Neempo dismissed the Keepers. Once the doors closed, Neempo flashed a friendly grin in the pirates' direction. "So, you were found trespassing in the Hall of Records. How very naughty of yo u."

"We beg pardon, Sovereign," Crispin leaned forward. "We are not here to harm you or your people. And we were not here to rob you."

"Then tell me, why would you risk scaling the Tower of Witnesses if not to harm or rob us?" Neempo didn't seem angry; he was amused more than anything.

"We were looking for a missing companion of ours. We figured..."

"You thought our Hall of Records could enlighten you." Neempo smiled, filling in the rest of what Crispin was trying to say.

"Yes."

"Surely you must know the penalty for trespassing."

Crispin shrugged. "Death, I'm assuming."

Neempo slapped a hand against his thigh and chuckled. "You speak without a trace of fear. And you don't sound like a pirate. Who are you?"

"I'm just a man looking for my companions." Not a lie, but definitely not the whole truth.

Neempo set his teacup and saucer down on the small table in front of him. "You are far too humble, Crispin, son of Issachar. Secrets do not exist here."

Rahab shot Crispin a look of panic. Crispin, too, was taken aback by how the Sovereign knew who he was.

"Do not look so surprised, Your Highness." Neempo continued, as if he could read his thoughts. "Perhaps, I can be of service."

"You..." Crispin scratched the back of his neck. "You want to help me?"

"Your visit has been foreseen. I have taken the liberty of having the information you need pulled from our Hall of Records. Master Balor."

Balor pulled a scrolled-up parchment from underneath one of his long sleeves and placed it on the table.

Crispin and Rahab eyed one another suspiciously. It couldn't possibly be that easy.

"What is it that you want in return?" Crispin asked, one eyebrow arched.

"I ask that you save my life."

Crispin saw both Penn and Balor tense up after Neempo's request. It seemed like they didn't expect that response either. "What do you mean save your life? What can I do for you that your own cannot?"

"They are coming for me." Neempo was calm. He kicked one leg up and crossed it over the other. "She has sent them, but she cannot succeed. I need to know that if protecting me fails, and if rescuing me fails, that you will be strong enough to do what needs to be done."

"Who is coming for you?" Crispin asked. "Who is *she*?"

"I think you know exactly who *she* is," Neempo said. "Do I have your word?"

Crispin risked a glance at Rahab. Her eyes were glued to the scroll sitting unopened before them. She made her decision. Anything for that information.

"Alright." Crispin nodded. "It's a deal."

"Good," Neempo stood with his back to the windows that faced the harbor and the Obsidian Sea. "Keep that scroll close. You haven't time to read it now."

"What do you mean?" Rahab spoke for the first time, growling each word.

"You have more important things to do."

"Like what?" She shot back.

"Fulfilling your promise to me." Neempo moved his head to face Crispin. "They're here."

The night sky erupted in explosions and the alarm bells rang. Crispin looked past Neempo and saw the harbor, which had been empty minutes ago, was now filled with pirate ships.

The Sisters was under attack.

Crispin walked up to the window and placed a hand against the cool glass. It rattled underneath his fingers as another explosion sounded. He felt Rahab join him.

"Did you know?" Crispin asked her, brows furrowed.

Rahab didn't look at him. Her eyes were wide, glued to the largest ship in the harbor. Crispin realized she was not only surprised by the attack, but she was afraid.

"Whose ship is that?" Crispin stared at the enormous pirate ship where the explosions originated from.

"That is *The Leviathan.*" Rahab's fear-stricken eyes met his. "That is the Pirate King Uri's ship."

The Leviathan was three times bigger than the Shadow of Death and would easily require three to four hundred crew members. And if that wasn't enough muscle, the Pirate King brought seven more ships with anywhere between fifty to one hundred sailors aboard each vessel.

Crispin turned around. Master Penn was instructing some Keepers to guard this level from intruders. The remaining Keepers were sent to the other two towers to deliver her orders until she could join them.

"Is there a way to get you out of here unseen?" Crispin asked the Sovereign.

"There will be no need for sneaking." Master Penn shook her head and rejoined their group. "Our towers have never been breached. And they would be fools to attack us on level ground."

"And if they scale the walls like we did?" Corwin spoke for the first time in almost an hour.

"We allowed you to get inside our walls." Penn snipped, a snarl flashing from underneath her black wrap. "You really think you can outwit the blind?"

Corwin pointed a large, shaky finger toward the pirate ships in the harbor. "They won't stop at scaling walls. They will destroy these towers, stone by stone, until there is nothing left. Those are men you should be afraid of."

"I'll leave the cowering to you," Penn rolled her shoulders back and held her head high. She gripped the handle of her sword tighter and brought the blade up to tap her forehead. "Sovereign."

Neempo bowed his head, a silent thank you and good fortune. "Master Penn."

Penn stomped toward the doors to leave when an explosion shattered the wooden entrance and sent her flying.

Crispin had instinctually wrapped his arms around Rahab, shielding her from the shards of glass and wood that flew through the room. He looked around the Sovereign's chambers and saw everyone lying on the floor. The lights had been snuffed out, but

Crispin was able to make out two dead Keepers sprawled over the threshold, blood pooled around their lifeless bodies.

Penn reached for her side. A piece of wood had sailed through the air and stabbed her. She grimaced but grabbed ahold of the spike and pulled it out with nothing more than a small groan.

Crispin ripped a piece of the curtain hanging behind him and slid over to her. "Let me wrap your waist to stop the bleeding."

Penn nodded, allowing him to help her. As he did, she whispered, "There is no way to slip past my Keepers. We have ancient magic shielding the Sovereign's chambers from invaders."

Crispin finished bandaging her wound and peered around the room. Master Balor was struggling to his feet. Neempo had found his seat and plopped down, blood trickling down his forehead from the impact. Rahab and Corwin had drawn their weapons, and had their eyes fastened to the smoke billowing in from the hall. Someone was coming. The pirates knew it. And they were afraid of who was coming. His eyes darted to the entrance as he heard boots stomping inside.

"Well, well, well," a deep, booming voice echoed through the decimated chamber. "It seems we have traitors in our midst."

Crispin saw the giant of a man staring directly behind him at Rahab and Corwin. Whatever fear had been in their eyes before was gone, replaced with anger and hatred. They had the appearance of cornered animals and were ready to launch an assault, if necessary.

Rahab's shoulders were rounded, her hand tightened around her dagger. She spat at the man, now surrounded by ten other pirates filing inside the room. "May your name be forgotten when your bones turn to dust."

The man stepped forward, a cruel smile stretching across his face. Now out from the haze, Crispin could see him fully. His dark skin was peppered with identical notched markings all over his body. He was bald except for three braids that reached down to his mid-back. By his commanding presence, and the terror on his companions' faces when they saw *The Leviathan* in the harbor, Crispin assumed he was the Pirate King.

Crispin stood up, helping Penn to her feet. "You must be Uri."

The Pirate King's blazing glare shot to him. He gave him a quick once over and if he recognized him from the wanted posters, he did not indicate it. "You seem to have the honor of knowing who I am. But who the hell are you?"

Penn reached for Crispin's forearm and squeezed it, warning him to keep his identity a secret. For once, Crispin heeded the warning.

"Take your thugs and get out," Crispin growled. "The Sisters is neutral territory."

"Not anymore." Uri rumbled a wicked laugh. "Don't worry, Masters." He mocked a bow. "We will leave your pathetic city intact. We only came for him." He pointed at the Sovereign, calmly sitting in his armchair.

Penn lifted her sword. "You will not touch him."

Uri sniffed the air and grinned. "Ahh, a challenge. I was hoping to bloody my swords tonight." He pulled two identical blades from their sheathes on his hips.

Penn dug her heels into the floor, ready to fight to her death, if need be, to protect her Sovereign.

"How did you get past our wards?" Neempo asked, no trace of fear or animosity in his voice.

"Hello, Neempo." A silvery voice sliced through the room. The woman dressed in a black, skin-tight robe floated to Uri's side. She had a thick strip of black paint across her eyes and gold liquid streaks from her forehead to her chin. "Miss me?"

"Nezreen." Neempo nodded. "I heard you died."

"A vicious rumor."

Crispin saw her eyes had a milky white film. She was blind.

"When you banished me," Nezreen wrapped her hand around Uri's outstretched arm. "My king found me and gave me shelter. Where you saw weakness in my gifts, he saw strength."

"All of this," Balor motioned around the destruction, "because you were not chosen to be Sovereign?" He rested a hand against his heart. "Nezreen, child -"

"I am no longer one of your Witnesses, Balor," she spat like a venomous serpent. "You are no longer my master."

King Uri smirked. His enormous, scarred hand stroked her petite, pale one. "Come with us, Neempo, and we will spare the rest of your order. Resist, and I will take delight in slaughtering all of your citizens one by one."

Neempo stood up slowly. "I will go with you."

Master Penn moved to protest but stopped. Her Sovereign had spoken.

As Neempo neared Crispin, he whispered, "You know where they will take me. If a rescue fails, you must do what needs to be done."

Crispin didn't dare a glance at Neempo. He didn't want Uri or that witch of his to ask what the Sovereign had said. Although, it was still as much a riddle to him as it would be to them.

Neempo stood in front of Nezreen and that's when Crispin's breath hitched. Something about them standing together sent an unwelcome shiver up his spine. Crispin felt eyes on him. The Pirate King was watching him closely. Realization hit Uri and a malicious chuckle erupted from him.

"Now I know who you are," Uri cooed, "Crispin, son of Issachar. Your sister might even reward me with a night in her bed for delivering you to her."

Crispin unsheathed his sword, taking a fighter's stance. "You'll have to fight me first."

Uri roared in wicked delight. He licked his chapped lips and took a monstrous step toward the prince. But he was stopped by Nezreen's voice.

"This is not your fight, my King." Nezreen's solid white eyes met Crispin's. "Not yet," she smiled.

Uri sheathed his swords without batting an eye. "Until we meet again, Prince." He cocked his head to the side. "I will take great delight in killing you when the time is right."

Crispin pointed the tip of his blade at the pirate. "I'll make sure to mount your head from the tallest tower in Northwind."

Neempo was shackled and dragged from the room. Nezreen followed the soldiers out but paused, waiting for Uri to fall in line.

Uri smirked at Rahab and sniffed the air. "Tell Haldane, Palma lasted longer than I expected her to." Rahab flinched; tears welled in her eyes. "Do you want to know what her last words were?"

Crispin stepped in between Uri and Rahab, halting his approach. His stomach was churning, picturing the kind woman who had saved him being tortured at the hands of this monster.

Uri snickered, "Her last word was *Haldane.* She repeated it over and over again, hoping he would save her from me."

"I'll kill you," Rahab rasped through tears. Corwin grabbed her arm, keeping her from attacking the Pirate King.

"Get in line." Uri pointed at Crispin. "I'll be seeing you again." He turned on his heel, joined Nezreen, and they vanished over the other side of the bridge.

Chapter Twenty-four

Niabi

The Royal Healer was instructed to tell the members of Niabi's small council that she was fighting off a cold and was instructed to rest, but that wasn't the truth. The truth was she was pregnant and only she and the healer knew. And that was exactly how Niabi wanted it. The Royal Healer obliged, being more afraid of suffering the queen's wrath than spilling the juicy gossip to her companions. She did as she was told and left the queen to rest, to process her thoughts.

That was three days ago and Niabi had refused visitations from everyone, including Pash.

How could this have happened?

What would she tell Pash?

Should she tell Pash?

She was still mourning Rollo – was it appropriate to be happy to welcome a new life?

Rollo would have been the first person she would have told. And he would have been overjoyed to finally become a big brother. He had begged her, year after year, to give him a brother or sister, but Niabi would kiss his face and tell him, *"Why should I have another child when the Almighty already gave me a perfect one?"*

She smiled fondly at the memory before softly sobbing and rubbing her swollen belly.

"Ivaylo if it's a boy and Suni if it's a girl," Rollo would say.

Niabi's pregnancy with Rollo was euphoric. She radiated joy and her vindictive and vengeful nature seemed to dissipate with every passing month. She never even suffered morning sickness; no pain plagued her. It was the perfect pregnancy with the perfect child. This second pregnancy, although still within the early stages, already had her suffering with nausea and lack of appetite.

But Rollo would be so happy.

Pash would be over the moon. All he wanted was for them to be together – to have a life away from all of this.

But who was she without her kingdom, her crown, her throne? It had been a long time since she was no one of importance.

Where would they be able to go and live in peace, unafraid of their enemies finding them?

If she asked Tala to take her to Elisor, he would. If she asked Tala to accept Pash into the fold, he would not.

But above all else, Niabi could never leave Rollo. She could never abandon her son, even in death.

After all, it was her fault Rollo was dead. She lowered her guard and gave her father an opportunity – a moment of weakness to destroy her; to take the man she loved. She believed in Vilora's prophecy. She trusted in Gershom. All of them were mistakes. Had she been vigilant when Dichali was alive, Issachar's assassins would never have gotten past her to kill him. Had she not listened to the witch, she never would have aligned herself with Gershom. Had she not sought out the Bear to help her get revenge, he would not have failed to execute Crispin and Salome, and Rollo would still be alive.

She jumped up from her chair overlooking her kingdom and snatched every glass cup and shattered them against the floor and the walls, one by one. She screamed. She wept. She allowed herself to wallow in misery, even though she hated herself for it.

Sinking to the white marble floor, in the midst of thousands of pieces of glass, Niabi swore no harm would come to her second born.

She would trust no one.

She would make deals with no one.

She would listen to no one.

Niabi would not make the same mistakes. She would not risk this child like she unknowingly did Rollo. She would not lose another baby. She would not fail again as a mother.

A knock echoed through her chambers. The sun had set and without any lights lit, the room was pitch black. She opened her left palm and let a flame flicker until she sent the fireball toward the fireplace, lighting it.

"Go away," she hissed feebly.

But the door opened anyway.

Niabi didn't have the strength nor desire to bark out more commands. She didn't bother to look over at the visitor who quietly shut the door and glided toward her. As always, she was armed with daggers underneath her sleeves; fearing assassins wasn't something she wasted her energy on. But she already knew who was approaching just by his footsteps.

Tala used his foot to push pieces of glass away from her and sat down beside her. He stretched his long legs in front of him and said nothing. Tala was a good friend, knowing when to speak and when to just be present. She placed her open hand down in between them and he grasped it. Neither of them spoke. His warm hand tightened around hers and she felt at ease.

Niabi lowered her head and rested on his shoulder, allowing tears to run down her cheeks. "I miss him," she whispered.

Tala kissed the top of her head and squeezed her cold right hand. "We will see them again."

Niabi knew when he referred to *them,* he wasn't just thinking of Rollo, but of Dichali and Tallulah, as well. Riding their horses through the endless fields and valleys of the Great Beyond.

"There is something I have to tell you." Niabi wiped the snot from her nose with her sleeve.

Tala reached into his breast pocket, pulled out a handkerchief and handed it to her. "Rollo would have been the first to congratulate you, so allow me to be the second."

Niabi's eyes flicked up at him. Of course, Tala already knew she was pregnant. He wouldn't risk her wrath without reason.

"I will have that loose-lipped healer flogged."

Tala chuckled and patted her arm. "Spare your punishments, woman. I know you well enough to know you wouldn't allow something as simple as a cold prevent you from stomping through these halls."

"Then how did you know?"

"I could tell as soon as I opened the door and saw you."

She shot him a look; her lips pursed. "Are you insinuating your queen already looks to be with child?"

"You had the same fearful look on your face when you found out you were expecting Rollo."

Niabi inhaled a deep breath, commanding the tears welling in her eyes to stay put. "How can I be happy?"

"Because Rollo would be happy." Tala leaned his head back against the wall. "A new life is a blessing, Niabi. Consider this child Rollo's gift to help you heal." He squeezed her hand. "He is watching over you. So don't wither away in this room. Be the queen he always knew you to be. Make him proud and thank him for his gift."

"I won't make the same mistakes." Niabi vowed.

"If I might be bold enough to risk your wrath," Tala's eyes met hers. "Does the commander know, yet?"

Niabi shook her head. "And I'm not sure if I should tell him."

"Are you involved with someone other than the commander?" Tala asked, though he already knew the answer.

"You mean to say, whether I tell him or not, he will find out I carry his child." Niabi narrowed her eyes, drawing a chuckle from Tala.

"Of all the men in Adalore..."

Niabi laughed. "I chose your favorite."

Tala crinkled his nose in disgust. "What a disappointing statement. So, you'll tell him?"

"I'll tell him when the time is right." Niabi promised, although she wasn't sure when that would be. "Will you take me to see him?"

Tala escorted Niabi to Rollo's crypt but stayed outside so she could have a moment with her son. She slowly closed in on the white stone statue of her son guarding his final resting place. She ran her fingers over its face – such an incredibly accurate likeness.

"You always did look out for me, even before you could walk." Niabi's lip quivered. She cleared her throat. "No one could ever replace you, Rollo, my love. My sweet boy. But I thank you for your gift. I thank you for your continued love from the Great Beyond. I will make sure this little one knows all about you and never forgets you." She rested her forehead against the statue's and closed her eyes. "Tell your father, I miss him. And we will all be together again soon."

Niabi rested her hand on her belly and inhaled deeply. “Ivaylo if it’s a boy and Suni if it’s a girl.”

Chapter Twenty-Five

Crispin

As the sun rose, the harbor was once again empty and calm. If Crispin hadn't seen the forces of the Pirate King with his own eyes, he never would have believed The Sisters had been attacked.

Crispin nursed a cup of tea as he stared out the blasted windows at the docked *Shadow of Death*. "Who is she?" Crispin asked. "The witch?"

"Nezreen is Neempo's twin," Balor grasped his cane tightly. "They were brought to The Sisters as infants.""Both of them were born blind?" Crispin picked up an overturned chair and plopped down across from Master Balor and Master Penn.

Balor nodded his head. "I could sense great power in them the moment they arrived. When our last Sovereign died, his spirit had to choose who would replace him. Nezreen and Neempo were two of five potential candidates for Sovereign. I thought Nezreen would be chosen. She was more powerful than Neempo. But he was selected because of his kind heart. Nezreen was angry and for years she refused to speak with her brother. She poured all her time and energy into her duties as a Witness. But instead of accepting the visions as they were given, she tried to look into the future and that's when darkness grew in her."

"She tried to kill Neempo." Penn cut in. She reclined in her seat, massaging the freshly stitched wound on her side. "She tried to become Sovereign by force, believing her destiny had been stolen."

"Did you always hate her?" Crispin cocked his head to the side and flinched when Penn flashed him a menacing look.

"Hate is not a strong enough word to express how I feel about the witch." Penn cracked her knuckles before continuing, "Weeks before her attack, Neempo had been blessed with a vision into the future by the Almighty. A warning of her betrayal."

"Neempo did not wish to see his twin sister executed." Balor set his teacup down on the splintered table and brushed his fingers against his brow. "So, he banished her instead."

Crispin rested his elbows on his knees and leaned forward. "The Sovereign said he heard Nezreen had died. Couldn't he have checked by using his sight?""Witnesses are not Seers." Balor shook his head. "We see what we are meant to see for record keeping purposes. Seers can look into many possible futures, but even with their sight, nothing is certain."

"So, is Nezreen a Seer?" Crispin asked.

"She has limited sight as a Witness," Balor explained, "but whatever she does not see, her shadows whisper to her, warning and advising her along the way."

"Her shadows?" Crispin rubbed his hands over his face. Exhaustion was starting to take ahold him. "I thought that was smoke from the explosion."

Penn shook her head, "From what we know, the shadows are her closest companions. Wherever she goes, they go."

"It's rumored," Rahab marched into the room, drawing Crispin's undivided attention, "while wandering the shores of the Mainland, Nezreen made a deal with the Grim." Rahab sat in the chair next to Crispin when he kicked up to a standing position. "She sold her soul to him. She swore she would serve him for eternity in exchange for power to destroy her enemies."

Crispin strummed his fingers against the armrests of his wooden chair, deep in thought. "So..." he cleared his throat, "these shadows are the source of her power. How do we get rid of them?"

"One would assume by killing the vessel, the shadows would disintegrate." Balor scratched his beard. "But there is nothing to suggest that it would work."

"But in order to kill her," Crispin slid lower into his seat, tapping his foot against the dusty floor, "we would have to hide our plan of attack from her shadows. And from what you're saying, it's damn near impossible."

"Perhaps, if we found someone with cloaking magic, we could have the element of surprise." Rahab suggested, crossing one leg over the other.

Crispin looked at her. "Do you know someone with this ability?"

"The cloaker I knew is dead." She twiddled her fingers, eyes glued to the floor. Before Crispin could ask about the cloaker, she changed the subject. "The Pirate King said he had a dream of a powerful witch who would help him establish his kingdom. When Nezreen arrived on our shores, he welcomed her with open arms and a lustful smile. That was almost nine years ago."

"Are they a couple?" Crispin turned to her, kicking a lazy leg over the armrest of his chair.

Rahab grimaced and wiped her dirt-stained face. "Uri will never take a wife. His bed is open to anyone, willing or unwilling."

There was something about the way she said, "unwilling" that sent an unwelcome shiver down Crispin's spine. Had she been one of the unwilling ones in Uri's bed?

"Rahab?" Crispin whispered, but she waved her hand in the air, brushing him off.

"Do you have a plan?" she asked, not daring to meet his gaze.

"Not exactly," Crispin's gulp was audible to everyone in the room.

"The Sovereign said you would know where they are taking him." Rahab tilted her head, clearly looking for answers.

Crispin bobbed his head, meeting her calculating gaze. "Northwind."

"Why?" Rahab rubbed the back of her neck, looking defeated. She knew as well as Crispin did, that once Neempo was in Northwind, it would be a monumental task to rescue him.

"We have received report of a witch joining your sister's small council," Penn stated.

Instinctively, Crispin wanted to bark out that Niabi wasn't his sister, but he swallowed the argument. "Why bring Neempo to Northwind? Does he possess powers that Niabi would want to exploit?"

Master Penn and Master Balor tensed up at the same time. They knew something and seemed unwilling to speak on it.

"What is it?" Crispin pressed. "If I am expected to break him out of the White Keep's dungeons, I deserve to know everything."

"One of the reasons a Sovereign is chosen is because of their heart," Balor answered Crispin's question. "We call it the Heart of the Righteous."

"From what we understand," Penn added reluctantly, "your sister intends to use our Sovereign's heart to raise her son from the dead."

Crispin's eyes widened. He never thought resurrecting someone was even possible. "Sh- she can do that?"

"It's a difficult spell to perform." Penn stood and paced around the room with arms clasped behind her back. "But it worked once, a long time ago. With enough magic and the Sovereign's heart, it is possible."

Rahab exhaled as Balor continued. "For the resurrection spell to work, the heart must still be beating."

"You mean," Rahab brought a hand to her breast, "they are going to carve his heart out of his chest while he is still alive?"

Balor nodded in confirmation. "It is the only way."

An eerie silence engulfed the room. No one moved, no one uttered a sound. Crispin glanced at Rahab who went from looking ill to indignant. She angrily stood up, her chair falling behind her.

"Then we rescue the Sovereign," she said, "and kill Uri while we're at it."

"We'll need a ship," Crispin looked out the shattered window at the harbor.

"Then it's a good thing we have the fastest ship in Adalore." Rahab nodded with a cocky smile.

Penn planted her feet shoulder-width apart as she stood, and said, "I will bring twelve of our fiercest Keepers to rescue our Sovereign. We leave the Pirate King and his demon to you."

"Twelve Keepers?" Crispin was shocked at how few soldiers Master Penn was planning to bring to Northwind.

Penn tapped her fingers to her chin before bobbing her head slightly. "You may be right." Crispin breathed a short-lived sigh of relief. "Twelve Keepers seems excessive. I will bring our best six."

Crispin nearly choked, "What? No, I meant, shouldn't you bring as many Keepers as you can?"

Penn threw her head back and laughed heartily. "I haven't laughed so hard in ages." She collected herself before saying, "Six will be more than adequate, Prince Crispin. I will ready my Keepers and meet you aboard your ship." Penn squared her shoulders to Master Balor who slowly rose to his shaky feet. "Master Balor."

"Master Penn."

The Masters walked to the opening where a door once stood and went their separate ways to their respective towers.

Crispin walked up behind Rahab who stood by the windows overlooking the *Shadow of Death* docked in the harbor. "How is he?"

Rahab knew he was asking about Haldane. Her gaze didn't waver from the black ship whose deck was being scrubbed by the youngest crew members. "Shattered." Her lip quivered and she cleared her throat. "As shattered as a human can possibly be."

"I'm sorry about Palma." Just speaking her name made his heart ache.

Rahab turned around to face him, but he refused to meet her gaze. "Her death wasn't your fault." Her voice was soft and compassionate, but it did nothing to ease Crispin's guilt. Rahab's fingers grazed his and he finally looked at her. "Whether you had crossed paths with Palma or not, Death had called for her."

"She took me in, healed me, aided me," Crispin shook his head and withdrew his hand from her warm touch. "How am I not to blame for her death?"

"Uri and that witch weren't here for you," Rahab pointed out with a frown. She grabbed his chin, pulling his face toward hers. "Palma kept her knowledge of you hidden from Nezreen's sight. They were here for the Sovereign. This is not your fault."

"Then why go after her in the first place?" Crispin's nostrils flared. "Why kill her?"

Rahab tentatively stroked her thumb up and down Crispin's stubbled jawline. "When Nezreen came to Pulau, she convinced Uri that all diviners, fortune tellers, cloakers, and oracles on the islands were a threat to his power and should be eliminated. Hundreds of men, women, and even some younglings were slaughtered over the years. There were some of them, cloakers mostly, who hid, but eventually her shadows found them."

"Your friend?"

"His name was Desi." She rested her hand on Crispin's chest. His heart thundered underneath her palm. "He was fifteen."

"I'm sorry."

"Haldane blames himself for him and Palma separating. But the truth is, Palma distanced herself from all of us." Rahab's eyes were glossy as she remembered her friend. "She tried to shield us from any danger because of her gifts. Last I heard, she stopped using her power so her magic wouldn't leave a trail for Nezreen's shadows to pick up."

"She gave all of you up..."

"To save us." Rahab bobbed her head, a tear slipping down her cheek, which she quickly flicked away.

"But," Crispin cleared his throat, "Palma told me she saw me in a vision."

Rahab knew where he was going. "A vision she could have ignored but didn't. She believed in saving you more than she feared Nezreen."

Crispin thought back on his short time with Palma. It now made sense why her hovel didn't have any windows, why she didn't go into *The Dancing Lady*, why she refused to set foot on the *Shadow of Death*. And then realization sliced through him like a hot blade cutting through butter. Palma asked for her and her parents to be allowed to live in Northwind once he became king. But she knew Nezreen's shadows would more than likely track her down before he even left Pulau.

Crispin's heart raced. He thought he was going to throw up.

"Your word is all I need." Palma's sounded in his head.

"Are her parents still alive?" Crispin opened his eyes and scanned Rahab's face. But he knew the answer before she spoke.

"She was the last of her name."

Crispin couldn't stop the tears from streaming down his face. Rahab gently wiped them away.

"I asked what her price was for helping me off of Pulau." Crispin rasped. "All she wanted was to live in Northwind with her sick parents, so they could live peacefully."

"Would you have followed her to *The Dancing Lady* had she not struck a deal with ye?"

Crispin hesitated. "I suppose I wouldn't have."

"Palma would have known that." Rahab interlaced her fingers with Crispin's, which caused his heart to skip a beat. "She knew her fate when she saved you. Don't let her death be a waste."

Crispin's eyes dropped to their hands clasped together. "What did the scroll say?"

Rahab's eyes widened at the sudden change in subject. Her free hand dipped into her coat pocket and retrieved the unopened scroll Neempo had given her. "I forgot I had this."

Crispin looked at her in anticipation, but she didn't unravel it.

"Whenever a girl in Pulau celebrates her sixteenth Name Day, the Pirate King has her snatched from her bed in the middle of the night and brought to his fortress. He is known to be cruel in his chambers but if you don't fight back, it won't be as painful."

Crispin tilted his head, horrified by her story and where it was headed. Rahab's eyes were glued to his chest where her hand still rested, fingertips caressing his skin.

"I was taken from my home four years ago. I didn't want his calloused hands roaming my body, so I fought back." She paused, inhaling a deep breath, "And he..." Rahab lowered the waistband of her pants an inch. There was a jagged scar across her lower abdomen.

Crispin reached to touch her but stopped. She grabbed his wrist and pressed his hand against the dark scar.

"The healers say I will never be able to have a child." Rahab's voice cracked. She tapped the side of her neck. "But I left a mark on him as well."

Crispin flashed back to Uri standing before them with a malicious grin and remembered seeing a long scar from the bottom of his earlobe to the center of his thick neck.

"And the notches all over his body?"

Rahab whispered, "One notch for every woman he has bed."

Uri must have had thousands of notches on him. Crispin shook his head trying to rattle the image of the Pirate King raping all those terrified women. He glanced down at Rahab, his hand still resting on her lower belly.

"He didn't rape me," Rahab shook her head, reading the question in Crispin's eyes, "but he had me thrown into his dungeons to bleed to death after I cut him." She lifted the scroll. "You want to know who Leeondris is to me?"

"He rescued you." Crispin pieced that part of the story together.

Rahab nodded. "He had broken into Uri's prison to free Phex. Phex had been captured and tortured for refusing to construct explosives for the Pirate King. After breaking Phex out, Leeondris passed by my cell and saw what Uri had done to me. He refused to leave me there to die, so he carried me to the *Shadow of Death* and sat by my bedside every night until I was able to walk again." Her eyes glistened with tears, but she held them back. "If he hadn't saved me that night, I would have died on that cold, damp dungeon floor."

Crispin fingered through her icy blue locks, moving hair out of her face and tucking it behind her ear. "I can't believe you suffered through all of that."

"I guess I'm a lot harder to kill than most people think," she flashed a smirk his way.

"I guess so," he said softly, removing his hand from her abdomen to cup her face, "I'm glad you survived, Rahab."

Her gaze lingered on his lips. "I am, too."

"If the Pirate King knows about you and Phex, then why hasn't he tracked you down?" His hands trailed down her arms.

Rahab motioned with her hand from her head down to her feet. "You dye your hair blue, change your name, and hide in plain sight, counting down the days until you can seek revenge." She cocked her head to the side with a wicked grin, "You really think Uri loses sleep thinking about people like me? People like Phex?" She shook her head. "The Pirate King looked me in the eye and there was no recognition, no realization, that I'm the one who gave him the scar he stares at in the mirror every day."

Crispin traced a circular motion in her palm, "He'll remember you the next time we cross his path."

"We will rescue the Sovereign. We will kill the Pirate King and gut the demon witch." Rahab's eyes were filled with a fire that made his stomach do somersaults.

"And Leeondris?" Crispin tipped his head toward the scroll she gripped tightly in her left hand.

Rahab thrust the parchment back into her pocket. "What if..." She inhaled and exhaled deeply. "What if he is not in need of rescuing?"

"You don't think he abandoned the crew -"

Rahab shook her head ferociously. "Leeondris would never abandon the crew." She tilted her head upwards, keeping whatever rebellious tears that stung her eyes at bay. "What if he is dead? I'm not sure I'm ready to find out what is in this scroll."

Crispin took both of her hands in his and clutched them against his chest. "We rescue the Sovereign. We kill the Pirate King and gut the demon witch. Then we open this," he eyed her pocket where the scroll was tucked.

Rahab shook her head. "What about your men?"

"I swore an oath to help you find Leeondris," he whispered, leaning closer to her, his fingers stroking from her temple to her chin. "I swore an oath to rescue the Sovereign. If I don't honor my word as an exiled prince, no one will trust me when I am..." He trailed off, for some reason he was unable to finish with...

"King." Rahab finished it for him. "When you're king."

Crispin nodded; eyes glued to hers.

"Does that frighten you?" she asked, leaning into his touch.

"Being king?" Crispin shrugged. His grip tightened around her hand. She was so close to him; she could probably feel his heart pounding in his chest. "I suppose I never looked at it as me being king so much as me killing my sister." He had never acknowledged Niabi as his blood before and the word *sister* felt bitter on his tongue when associated with her.

"But if you defeat her, you would be crowned king?"

Crispin arched an eyebrow. "Why the sudden interest? Are you inquiring into the position of queen?" He flashed a coy smile and she reciprocated with a grin of her own.

"If I ever need a pardon in Northwind, I know who I need to speak to." She retrieved her hand from his and lowered her eyes. "Besides, a queen would need to give you heirs."

Give him heirs. That phrase struck him like a knife to the chest. All the years he spent training and brooding in the Tree House Forest, not once did he think about being a father. His thoughts were solely focused on exacting his revenge, not being king. Crispin was his father's fifth son. He was never meant to sit on the White Throne. But now...

"I should check on the captain before everyone boards." Rahab's voice sliced through his thoughts.

"Right," Crispin bobbed his head, tucking his hands in his pockets.

"I'll see you down there." Rahab walked out before he could say anything else.

Crispin stood in silence, looking around the Sovereign's office that had been blown to bits. It was a wonder more of them weren't injured or killed in the blast.

Though he tried to push her to the back of his mind, he could still feel Rahab's warm touch on his skin. His eyes skimmed to the *Shadow of Death* and the longing for adventure on the high seas rippled through him. Being aboard the ship, finally living out his childhood dream, lit a fire in his heart that had been extinguished years ago. He never expected to be king. But that was now his future.

Why did Rahab make him question everything he thought he wanted?

"She's right."

Crispin whipped around and found Master Balor standing in the threshold, propped on his cane.

"What?" Crispin asked.

"A king will need heirs."

"Forgive my bluntness, Master Balor," Crispin hissed, "but you speak too boldly on a matter that doesn't concern you."

"Perhaps," Balor hobbled closer until he was standing a few feet in front of the hot-headed prince. "But I have lived for seventy-four years and have seen far too many lineages of good princes and great kings end with wicked men and women taking their place. Though battle is important for you to reclaim your father's throne, it is not the only priority."

Balor sank into the chair he had occupied earlier and set his cane to the side. He stretched his legs out and rubbed his wrinkled hands up and down his knees. "What a tragedy it would be for you to win your crown with ash and blood, only to lose it by loving a barren woman."

"I will do as I please," Crispin spat, shoulders tense like a predator about to launch an assault on its prey. "I will love who I please. I will rule how I please and I will die how I please. You, nor anyone else, will persuade me differently."

Balor shook his head in disappointment, "You really are no different than her."

Crispin knew Balor was referring to Niabi and his nostrils flared at the disrespect, the insinuation that he and his sister had anything, other than blood, in common. "For someone with age, you lack wisdom."

Master Balor smirked, crinkling the lines of the white wrap over his eyes. "And for someone with sight, you lack vision." He snagged his cane and struggled to his feet, shakily making his way back toward the chaotic hallway. "Marry the pirate and your line will end. Put your people before your own desires, and your sons and daughters will rule for an age." Balor squared his shoulders to Crispin who hadn't moved an inch and bowed his head. "Favor and fortune on your journey, Prince Crispin." He turned the corner and disappeared.

Crispin watched as The Sisters faded from view and the open waters drew him in. In a few days, he would be home. Home for the first time in twelve years.

This was risky. Going not only into the heart of Northwind, but venturing into the belly of the beast, to rescue Neempo from Niabi's dungeons.

What if he saw her? Or came face to face with her?

He could possibly end a war before one was officially declared. He could avenge his dead and claim the crown and throne. He could finally return home for good. Crispin swore to himself right then and there, if he had the chance to kill Niabi, he would do it. He wouldn't hesitate. He would show her no mercy. He would do what needed to be done .

Crispin was going home. But a warm welcome didn't await him; vipers did.

Chapter Twenty-Six

Rayma

Dark shadows danced around Rayma, coaxing her to follow. She pushed herself up from the wet grass and found herself surrounded by lifeless trees that stretched upward farther than she could see. Grey skies and an eerie cold wind enveloped her as she let the shadows lead her through a graveyard filled with broken and crumbling headstones. She saw a crow perched on a tombstone covered in moss before a chilly voice beckoned her forward.

"So," the Grim sat on a floating throne comprised of shadows. "You're the one who stole from me."

Rayma tried but failed to tear her eyes from his skeleton face. His ruby red eyes flickered like flames and bits of flesh hung from his ivory bones.

"I..." she gulped to coat her dry throat. "I didn't steal from you."

"You killed Pyke," the Grim hissed through his lip-less mouth. "With her dead, you eliminated my Wagura. All those souls had years of servitude left to pay their debts to me."

"I had to free my friends," Rayma rasped, gripping her clothes tighter.

"Who is going to pay me now?" The Grim's bone fingers stroked the hilt of his scythe.

Rayma stifled a whimper. "Pyke said I could free her – free my friends."

"And you did." His red eyes flared beneath his black hood. "But now you must pay the price for their freedom."

Rayma clawed at Pyke's crystal dagger hanging at her hip and extended it to him. "Take it, it's yours."

The Grim lazily twirled his hand in a circle and another crystal dagger appeared. "You think that dagger is special? That it would be enough to tempt me?" He laughed, and the rattly sound sent a chill up Rayma's spine. "I care not for trinkets, jewels, or weapons. If I did, then many rich and royal humans would have escaped making deals with me." The

Grim rose from his shadow throne and crunched the grass underneath with his skeletal feet as he approached her. "I deal in souls, Rayma. What is yours worth, I wonder?"

Rayma stood still when he circled her and his decaying fingers tugged her braids. "What do you want?"

"I'll make you a deal, Healer," the Grim stopped in front of her, whether he smiled she couldn't tell, but by his tone, she detected a wicked playfulness. "When Death calls for you, you can be the new Queen of the Wagura for a hundred years, a bargain considering all the years of servitude you stole from me."

Tears stung her eyes as she whispered, "Please -"

"Or," he continued, unmoved by her pleas for mercy, "you can offer Prince Heru's soul in your place for twenty years as a Wagura. After all, it was your love for him that got you into this mess in the first place."

"Don't touch him!" Rayma hissed.

The Grim stretched his cold, boney finger and touched Rayma's cheek; the contact made her skin crawl. "I will let you have some time to think it over before you decide. I look forward to doing business with you."

"No!" Rayma reached for the Grim, but he vanished, and she felt herself falling into a pitch-black abyss. "No! No!"

Rayma swung her arms to fight off whatever creature had grabbed ahold of her but realized it was Heru. His strong arms wrapped around her, pulling her against his warm, bare chest.

"You're safe, Rayma," Heru whispered in her ear. "I'm here."

"The Grim," Rayma squirmed out of his embrace, jumped up from her bed, and distanced herself from the prince. "It's the Grim. He's ... I... I stole from him. I stole all those souls from him."

Heru stood up and crossed the tent to her, but she threw her arm out to stop him from getting too close. "Please, don't get any closer. Don't you understand what I'm saying? I'm marked."

"Rayma, what are you talking about?" His eyes were wide, and she could tell he was afraid of her.

"I stole from the Grim," she hugged herself, eyes watering, "and he wants me to pay him back."

"It was just a bad dream," he said calmly, but she knew he didn't believe that. No one had dreams of the Grim unless he wanted something. Or someone.

"A hundred years." Rayma straightened, the gravity of the Grim's words hitting her all over again. "When Death comes for me, he wants one hundred years of servitude before I can pass to the Second Death."

Heru shook his head. "We'll find a way to get you out of this. I won't let that happen to you."

"I deserve it." Rayma sank to the carpeted floor and rubbed her face. "I deserve worse than one hundred years in debt to the Grim."

The prince knelt before her, clasped her hands in his, and forced her to meet his gaze. "No one deserves such a fate. You are a good woman with an even bigger heart -"

"Stop," she begged.

"I love you, Rayma," he kissed her hands. "I won't let you suffer this fate. We will consult every wise man, seer, oracle, and record keeper, if that is what it takes to find a way to defeat the Grim."

"I'm not who you think I am."

Heru sucked in a breath as if she had struck him across the face. "What do you mean?"

"I'm not who you think I am," she repeated. "I'm not the woman you love."

Heru dropped her hands. "What are you talking about?"

Rayma wiped tears from her cheeks and pulled her legs into her chest. "I was ordered by Lord Memucan to get close to you. When it was evident you had feelings for me, Memucan ordered me to return those affections, to earn your trust."

"No, that can't be true," Heru distanced himself and stared at her.

"Along the way I did fall in love with you, Heru. I do love you. I swear it. But..."

"But what?" Heru's voice carried a lethal tone. "What did Memucan want you to do once you earned my trust?"

Rayma didn't want to see his face when she revealed the entire truth, but she maintained their eye contact. "He wanted me to kill you. Slip something in your drink."

"You were going to kill me?" Heru rasped, but she didn't know if it was out of anger or pain.

She lowered her head, a lump rising in her throat, "If I killed you, he promised to return my brother to me. He's had him in prison for years. I didn't want my brother to suffer anymore. He's the only family I have left."

Heru paced like a caged animal, running a hand over his head, brow furrowed.

"Please say something," Rayma whispered.

"What do you want me to say?" Heru shot her a vicious look. "That it's alright you deceived me into thinking you loved me? That I forgive you for plotting my assassination? That I'm not angry you betrayed your crown prince and future king?" He sank onto her bed with his elbows resting on his knees. "What is it you want to hear, Rayma?"

Rayma's bottom lip quivered, and her voice cracked. "It might have started as a lie, but I do love you, Heru. I never intended to go through with it."

"I suppose you think that brings me some comfort?" Heru refused to look at her. After a moment of silence, the prince stood and said, "You are the only healer the Numbio has on this journey, so I won't order you to leave our company. But once this war is over, you will find a new home to return to."

"Heru -"

"It's Prince Heru." He interrupted, a brokenness in his tone. "Had you come to me with the truth about Memucan from the beginning, I would have done everything in my power to get your brother back to you." Without waiting for her to respond, he slipped out of her tent.

Chapter Twenty-Seven

Salome

Rosalina and Seraphina walked Salome down the hall that led to the throne room but instead of stopping at the double doors to enter the Inner Depths, they walked past them. Salome was going to protest but was too irritated with them interrupting her time with Adonijah, so she followed them quietly. After a few more twists and turns down the mosaic tile hallways, they arrived at an archway that emptied into a garden Salome hadn't seen before.

It was much smaller than all the other gardens and by the stone wall and sizable hedges enclosing it, it was safe to assume it was the most private as well. Salome caught whiffs of roses, poppies, and pomegranate flowers. It was floral overload and yet, not revolting. Her nose welcomed the sweet smells, reminding her of what her mother used to smell like. She closed her eyes and allowed the moonlight to envelope her, not even noticing when the twins left.

"Salome," a soft voice called out.

"Yes?" Her eyes flashed open, but when she looked around the garden, she was alone. "Is someone there?"

"Salome." The voice grew louder. "Salome."

"I know your voice," Salome followed the voice.

"Salome," the sweet, breathy voice echoed.

She drew nearer, "Who are you?"

"Salome!" The voice wrapped around her in a familiar embrace.

"Mother?"

Salome found herself standing in front of a bronze statue of Bilhah. Maybe she was losing her mind. Maybe she was desperate enough to hope Damaris and Harbona were right about her ability to commune with the departed. Tentatively, Salome reached out and touched the statue's hand.

Salome blinked and was no longer in the Myridian garden, but in the White Keep. She was in her mother's chambers. A fire was roaring in the hearth, snow cascading like droplets of rain outside the window. Furs and bear skin rugs were strewn throughout the room. And then she saw her.

"Mother?" Salome exhaled, eyeing the dark-haired woman sitting on a tufted bench near the fire doing needle point. Bilhah turned to her with a warm and welcoming smile. Salome instantly felt the comfort of home envelop her.

"Hello, Sweetness." It was the nickname Bilhah had given her the moment she was born. "I've missed you."

Bilhah stood with her arms outstretched. Tears flowed from Salome as she ran to her, hoping unlike the Enchanted Swamp, she would be able to feel her mother's embrace.

Bilhah wrapped her arms around her daughter and whispered in her ear, "What took you so long?"

"What do you mean?"

"We've been calling you." Bilhah pulled away from Salome, tracing a finger down her daughter's cheek. "Why have you not answered us?"

"I didn't know it was you."

Bilhah flashed a sad smile. "You've forgotten our voices."

"No!" Salome denied it, even though she knew it was true.

"It's alright." Bilhah squeezed Salome's hand reassuringly. She spied the six lines tattooed around Salome's left arm. "You might have forgotten our voices. One day you might forget what we look like, but never forget how much we love you."

Trying to hold back the tears, Salome ended up making an unflattering grimace. "I miss sitting here with you."

Bilhah tapped her finger playfully on Salome's nose. "You hated needle point."

"I did," she nodded, "but I loved you. I loved our bench and the stories you told me. I loved how excited we would get during the first snowfall of the year. I loved how when I was scared, you would sing me Myridian lullabies and let me cuddle with you in bed. I wish that life wasn't over."

"I miss all of those memories too, Sweetness." She led Salome to their bench. Bilhah strummed her fingers through Salome's curls. "Northern curls."

"I always wanted your straight hair."

"Curls suit you. They're wild and rebellious, just like you." Bilhah cleared her throat. "Do you know why I called you?"

"You want me to avenge your death." Salome said confidently.

Bilhah shook her head. "To warn you."

"To warn me?" Salome tilted her head, confusion running rampant in her mind. "Warn me about what?"

"Soon, you will find yourself very much alone -"

"I'm not alone, Mother -"

"Listen," Bilhah interrupted her with the softest voice. "When the time comes and you find yourself standing on your own, you will have a choice to make. Rise from the ashes or crumble into dust."

Salome's mind was flooded with images of Crispin, Zophar, Adonijah, Harbona, Cato, and even Mika.

Would they abandon her?

Would they die?

Why, when surrounded by so many, would she have to walk alone?

"Will I be alone for the rest of my life?" Salome dreaded asking the question but dreaded the answer even more.

Bilhah smiled, cupping her face, "No, Sweetness, you will not spend the rest of your days alone. But the choices you make during your loneliest moments will determine who you will find on the other side."

"I don't understand." Salome looked into her mother's green eyes expecting her to explain but she didn't.

"Our time together is coming to an end. It's time for you to return."

"Please don't make me leave you."

"We will be together again, Sweetness. But when you hear us call you, don't be afraid to answer." Bilhah kissed her daughter's forehead.

Instantly, Salome felt a surge shoot through her body and upon opening her tear-filled eyes, saw her mother's statue crying.

"How can that be?" Salome whispered.

"Zara told me you favored your mother."

Salome whipped around to see an old woman standing stoically behind her with a bouquet of flowers.

"I am glad to see that is true."

"Are you...?"

"I am Nym." She flashed a half-smile, accentuating the wrinkles around her fading green eyes. The top layer of her long hair was white as snow, while the bottom layer was still raven black from that of her youth. Around her aging neck was a necklace of green aventurine fashioned in the shape of octopus tentacles. Nym's eyes were like Bilhah's and oddly enough, brought Salome comfort. "Our dead never truly leave us," the olive-skinned queen pointed at the statue's tears, not at all surprised by the sight.

"You are Queen Nym?"

"And your grandmother." She gently set the floral offering before her daughter's memorial. "I should have known Bilhah would eventually bring us together. All these years, I thought all her children had been killed. But when word reached my ears that you may have survived, I was both overjoyed and saddened that I had not been able to give you a proper home."

"My mother told us stories of the Isles of Myr." Salome faced her grandmother, who was just about her height. "Being here, makes me feel close to her again."

"Of course, you can feel her," Nym glanced at the statue. "She never left."

Salome looked at her mother's bronze likeness. "I would love to erect a memorial for her in Northwind."

"Northwind?" Nym shot a disappointed glance at her granddaughter. "Do you mean to tell me you actually plan to challenge Niabi?"

Salome was confused. "Yes."

"If you are to risk your life for a throne that is not rightfully yours, should you not know the truth?"

"What truth?" Salome scrunched her nose, taking a giant step back from Nym.

"Come with me. There is something you need to see."

Nym turned on her heel and glided down a set of steps Salome hadn't noticed were there. As they weaved through the labyrinth of hedges on the lower tier of the garden, they rounded a corner, and found a rectangular, inground pool.

"What is that?" Salome stared at the glowing waters.

"The Pool of Enlightenment." Nym ushered her toward the mystic pool. "If you wish to know the truth of what happened all those years ago, submerge yourself."

"I know the truth. I was there that night."

"You know what you witnessed but you know nothing of the truth."

Salome's eyes darted around the pool, looking for signs of a trap. She patted the dagger attached to her thigh, glad it was there. She would be lying if she said she wasn't curious about this so-called Pool of Enlightenment, but she was wary of the woman she just met.

"Well?" Nym ripped her from her thoughts, hand still motioning her toward the pool.

Salome slowly stepped forward and sat on the edge of the mosaic tiles that bordered the basin. Her grandmother hadn't moved, her eyes fixed on Salome. She slid her legs into the warm water and peered back at Nym. With a final nod from the old queen, Salome inhaled deeply and submerged into the water.

When she opened her eyes, she saw she was no longer in the Myridian pool, but in the White Keep years before her own birth. She sucked in a breath; she knew these halls. She reached out and ran the tips of her fingers over the white walls; a tear ran down her cheek when she felt the coolness against her skin.

The halls were bustling as the workers were talking about the birth of a royal baby. She followed one of her old nursemaids, Bertie, who looked so much younger than she remembered. She was carrying armfuls of blankets down the hall. Salome stopped dead in her tracks when she happened upon another familiar face. A decades younger Issachar paced outside her mother's quarters. Anxiety smeared across his unblemished face; the dark-haired king appeared frightened; a look she had never seen from him before.

"Father?" she called out, her voice cracking.

"He cannot hear you, Cousin."

Salome looked to her left and saw Damaris in white linen standing next to her. "What are you doing here?"

"You submerged yourself in the Pool of Enlightenment. There are truths I must show you."

Salome's gaze focused once more upon Issachar. "He looks frightened."

"He is," Damaris said. "That is what a man looks like when he is about to become a father for the first time."

"You mean..."

"Watch," she hushed her.

"Your Majesty," an elderly midwife bowed before the king. "The queen is ready to see you now."

Issachar barreled past her into the room and as he rounded the corner he stopped as he saw Bilhah holding the smallest baby he had ever laid eyes on.

"She looks so happy." Salome couldn't peel her eyes off her mother's joyful face.

"Bilhah always wanted to be a mother." Damaris' eyes were fastened on Salome. "It was her dream."

"Come closer, my love," Bilhah extended her hand to Issachar. He slowly approached his newly born heir with a proud smile. "The Almighty One has blessed us with a daughter."

"A daughter?" Issachar frowned.

"Is it not wonderful?" Bilhah was so happy she nearly sang. "The heir to the White Throne – the first Queen of the North."

"Queen?" He fumed. "Queen of the North? She will be no such thing!"

"What do you mean?"

"If you believe that girl will one day, be the ruler of Northwind then you are gravely mistaken."

"But Northern law states that any firstborn child can be heir to the throne," she protested.

"You were to bear me sons and you give me," he motioned with a snort toward Niabi, "this!"

"Issachar, please, just hold her -"

"I will do no such thing," he growled. "Until you bear me a son, you will no longer be in my good graces." Tears streamed down Bilhah's cheeks as she watched her husband disappear from her quarters, slamming the door behind him.

"He..." Salome was left speechless by what she saw. "He just..."

"He wronged Niabi from the beginning." Damaris stood beside her, knowing there was far more for her to see.

"All because she was a girl?"

"Never before had a daughter been born first in the North. Issachar had made a hefty wager with the King of Borg, that he too, would continue the tradition and have a son. He lost."

"Must I continue to watch my mother cry, Damaris?"

"Listen."

"Forgive your father," Bilhah whispered to her newborn. "He does not understand the power a woman possesses."

The bubbly midwife returned with fresh linens. "Have you thought of a name, my Queen?"

After a slight pause, Bilhah smiled. "Niabi. Her name is Niabi."

"A lovely name for a princess."

"Yes," Bilhah caressed her small, sleepy face, "and one day she will be queen."

In the blink of an eye, a year passed, and Salome found herself watching her father cuddling a newborn as he walked to the royal balcony that overlooked the White City. Two guards opened the double doors and Issachar proudly announced the birth of his son and heir, Prince Lykos, to the cheering citizens of Northwind.

"Your mother gave him his son," Damaris broke the silence.

"What of my sister?"

"See for yourself." The Oracle had her turn around to see her mother holding a one-year-old Niabi. "He never once held her."

"Even after Lykos was born?"

Six-year-old Niabi ran past them with a five-year-old Lykos nipping at her heels. Laughter filled the hall as they played together until their father turned the corner.

"Father, play with us!" Niabi attempted to hug him only to be pushed away.

"Go to your mother!" he barked.

"But father -"

"I said go!" Downtrodden, the children turned to leave. "Not you, my son. Come with me. I have much to teach you." Taking the young boy by the hand, he ushered him away with a smile.

Salome wasn't sure if she was more angry or heartbroken, but she wished she could wipe her sister's tears from her face. "Father never treated me like that."

"You were not his firstborn." Damaris grabbed Salome's hand and led her down a different corridor and as they turned the corner, she found herself walking the training grounds in Myr. "When your sister made ten, your mother sent her to Myr to be trained in our ways. She was a quick study and within a few years, earned the title of Red Maiden."

Salome suddenly remembered what Harbona told her when they first arrived in the Isles of Myr, that there was a living Red Maiden that did not don the red armor. Now, she knew it was Niabi.

A proud Nym stood off to the side as she silently watched her granddaughter spar with Zara and beat her in a duel. The Myridian female warriors cheered as the student had defeated her mentor; a rare feat to bear witness to in such a short amount of time.

"She had more Myridian blood flowing through her veins than Northern blood."

"Why didn't she stay with you?" Salome watched her grandmother bow her head to Niabi, showing her the utmost respect.

"Our queen appealed to your father, requesting he allow her to remain with the Myridians, but he refused. Issachar might not have loved Niabi, but he was not against using her." Damaris waved her hand in front of them, and they stood at the Myridian docks watching a teenage Niabi board a ship set to sail her to Northwind.

"Please," Niabi grabbed Nym's hand, "do not force me to return to Northwind. Please! He hates me. You know he does!"

Nym gently brushed her granddaughter's raven black hair behind her ear. "Never forget who you are, Niabi. You are the Red Maiden, Princess of the Isles of Myr and of the Northern Lands, heir to the White Throne of Northwind and one day, you shall be queen. Let him have this victory for it shall be short-lived." Showing an extraordinarily rare display of emotion, Nym embraced the teenager tightly. "Know that wherever you go, you are loved here in Myr."

Salome closed her eyes and the image of her sister faded. She emerged from the pool, coughing up water. Once she climbed out of the pool, she caught her grandmother's gaze and asked, "Why show me this?"

Nym knelt with a blanket and wrapped it around Salome's shoulders. "Your sister is not the villain in this story, child."

"You hated him, didn't you? My father?"

"Men of power are not to be trusted. He was one of those men."

"That is not true." Salome jumped up, hands tightening around the edges of the blanket hanging from her shoulders. "My brother is not -"

"What do you expect will happen, if by some miracle, you should defeat your sister for the White Throne?" Nym interrupted her, rising gracefully from her crouched position. "Your brother will be crowned King of the North. Do you think he will treat you as his equal? Do you think he won't turn out to be just like your father and use you as a pawn in his game? Do you think he would not marry you off to a foreign dignitary the first opportunity he sees to expand the reach of his power? Foolish, girl! You see Northwind as your home, but until now, the North has only been run by men. Do not do as my Bilhah did. You have Myridian blood coursing through your veins. Know who you are, Salome. You are meant for a far greater purpose than being in a man's shadow."

"How can you expect me not to challenge her?" Salome spat, the wetness of her hair and clothes dripping onto the stone pavers. "How can I allow her to live in spite of what she has done?"

"You believe she should die?" Nym arched her brow.

"For what she has done, she deserves to die."

"Your sister did what a true warrior would do. She rose from the flames meant to consume her and faced her enemy as a queen. For everything your father stole from her, she made him watch as she took it back." Nym straightened, her nose pointed slightly upward.

"She killed my family. She murdered your daughter! Surely you must see what she truly is!"

"I will never forgive her for what she did," Nym said sternly.

"But?"

"If you were Niabi, what would you have done?"

"I *am* Niabi." Salome fought back tears as she spoke. "What our father did to her, she has done to me. The pain, the suffering, the loss; we share the same story."

"Then do not follow in her footsteps." The queen took Salome's hands in her own. "There is an alternative to war. Stay here in Myr. Learn our ways. Take your mother's place in our high council. You belong here."

"You want me to forget about her?" Her was nothing more than a raspy whisper. "Forget about Gershom? Let them win?"

"Think, Salome, think!" Nym cupped her granddaughter's tear-stained face in her withering hands. "If you are anything like your mother, you would not want this war. So many people will die and for what? What is done is done, nothing will bring back your dead. Did you learn nothing from Niabi's past?" Nym sighed, "You can have a real life here; do not throw it away for your brother to reap the glory."

"But Niabi -"

"You speak of her as if she was some type of monster."

"Monsters come in many forms." Salome felt a lump of emotion bobbing in her throat. "Most of the time, they look like people."

Nym inhaled deeply before she spoke, her hands falling to her sides. "Consider what I have told you, and what you have seen, before making your decision."

As her grandmother began to walk away, Salome quickly extended her hand to stop her. "You are afraid."

Nym's brow furrowed, "Afraid of what?"

"When you look at me you don't see my mother, like you claim. You see my sister and that frightens you." Salome took her silence as confirmation. "Tell me I'm wrong, Grandmother. Tell me I'm wrong."

Nym sighed heavily as she sat on a padded bench overlooking the sea. "Niabi was a bright student; clever, kind, disciplined, hardworking. She deserved better than your father." She smiled slightly, "While she was here, she earned the honor and title of Red Maiden.

Salome sat next to her. Even though there was a warm breeze, she clutched the blanket tightly, still feeling the effects of the Pool of Enlightenment.

"Your sister was the deadliest warrior to walk the Isles." Nym studied her granddaughter's face. "Niabi was loved, respected, and admired. She belonged here, with us. I never should have let your father take her."

"You still care for her."

Tears welled in the matriarch's green eyes, regret deep within her soul. "If war can be avoided, and lives spared, should you not at least consider it?" Before Salome could answer, Nym stood to make her way back inside the castle. "The Isles of Myr can be your home. Consider my offer, child. Please." The queen walked away, leaving Salome to her thoughts.

Chapter Twenty-Eight

Niabi

Prince Thanos strutted to the throne with an arrogance that could be felt the moment he walked into the room. With his chin tilted upwards and his malicious, beady eyes fixed on Niabi as she lounged in her throne, the Prince of Gomorrah approached without giving Tala standing on her right, Pash positioned on her left, or Anaktu stationed at the bottom of the dais, a second glance. Niabi was thoroughly protected should the young heir mean her harm, but if he attempted to assassinate her, she would slit his throat faster than they could.

Anaktu lifted an enormous hand to halt the prince before he could ascend the steps to the throne. Thanos stopped and bowed, but his shifty eyes bounced from Niabi to her Nephilim.

"You seem frightened, Prince Thanos." Niabi purred from her white throne, a wicked grin stretching across her face. "You can't possibly be alarmed by one Nephilim, after growing up with the Thrak."

Thanos attempted to hide a gulp but failed. He reluctantly withdrew his gaze from the giant to look up at the queen. "The Thrak are flesh and blood. But that thing is -"

"He." Niabi interrupted with a hiss.

Thanos crinkled his nose but amended, "*He* is more demon than man."

Niabi shrugged lazily, bored by him. "You're right to fear him, but to be a king, you must never show it."

Thanos stiffened. "Have you considered my proposal?"

Niabi smirked, her eyes scanning him from head to toe. "I have considered it. But seeing you now makes me wonder why I should waste my time and soldiers on *you*." She threw the last word out with disdain. She was not impressed by the scrawny, haughty boy that stood before her. "Tell me, Thanos, why shouldn't I just kill you now and spare myself this aggravation?"

Thanos narrowed his eyes, "I am the Prince of Gomorrah!"

"Hair has not yet grown on your face, and you dare raise your voice to me, boy!" Niabi gripped the armrests of her throne, her eyes blazing. She leaned forward and rasped, "I wouldn't lose one night of sleep if I slit your throat."

Without realizing it, Thanos took a step back, distancing himself from both the vicious queen and her Nephilim. Thanos' voice was shaky, but his head was still held high. "If you kill me, my mother will wage war against you."

"Or would she thank me for ridding her of the one problem that stands in her way of being sole-ruler?" Niabi cocked her head to the side, the movement predatorial. "Clearly you are not her choice to rule. Your death would be the best present she could ever receive."

"You believe Maltidys needs a lesser reason to come for your neck?" Thanos spat, his fingers twitching at his side. "That woman won't stop until you are dead."

At the word *dead*, Tala and Pash drew their swords. Niabi threw an open hand in the air, halting them from approaching the hotheaded royal. She stood slowly and glided down the steps, her black train cascading behind her, and circled him like prey.

Niabi stopped behind him and whispered in his ear, "I welcome the challenge."

Thanos shivered as her breath touched his neck. "But I said I could help you."

Niabi let out a menacing laugh as she rounded in front of him, standing beside Anaktu. "If you live to be king, you will learn not to trust so easily." She stared into Thanos' eyes and said, "One battalion. I will send one battalion to claim your throne."

Thanos grinned and Niabi saw the features he had inherited from his wicked mother. "I will lead them to victory -"

"Don't be ridiculous," Niabi snorted and waved a dismissive hand. "Commander Pash will lead them." Pash stepped forward; sword now sheathed.

Thanos was nearly rendered speechless at the insult. "I should be the one to lead them if I am to be king."

"Commander Pash will lead *my* soldiers, or you can go elsewhere for aid." Niabi motioned for Thanos to come closer. "But before my men march, you must swear fealty to me."

Thanos wrinkled his nose, eyes burning as they bounced from the commander back to the queen. "I am to be King of Gomorrah. I will not bend the knee to anyone."

Niabi nodded her head in understanding, though her smile didn't falter. "You have so much to learn in the world of rulers and makers. You need me. I do not need you."

"But your sister -"

"Will be found with or without your assistance." Niabi interrupted with an iciness that sent shivers up Thanos' spine. "What will it be, *Prince*?" the word shot from her tongue like a poisoned dart. "Bend the knee to the woman who holds your future in her hands or walk away with your pride and no army to fight your battles."

Thanos gritted his teeth. "Perhaps the King of Borg -"

The queen erupted in laughter. Thanos' cheeks flushed with embarrassment. "By all means, go to all the other kingdoms for aid. Perhaps it will be a humbling experience for you." She clasped her hands in front of her and took a step toward him. "You came to me because you know I am not only your best chance at the throne, but your only chance. The West won't let you step one sooty foot before them. The Andrago," she motioned a hand to Tala, "answer to me. And quite frankly, none of the other kingdoms will care of your claim. They would delight in seeing you and that shrew you call a mother dead."

Thanos flashed her a dirty look. She had rattled him, and she enjoyed seeing the desperation in his eyes.

"Whenever you are ready to kneel..." She pointed to the floor before her.

Thanos hesitated before he slowly knelt before her, lifting his eyes to meet her awaiting gaze. "I, Thanos, Prince of Gomorrah, swear in life or death, my house shall serve yours."

Niabi clapped her hands together and grinned. "Now, was that so difficult?" She winked and Thanos flinched, as if she had slapped him. "Commander Pash, ready the battalion."

Pash crossed an arm across his chest in salute. "It will be done."

"I request to go along." Leoti's voice echoed through the throne room as she marched down the carpeted aisle.

Tala and Pash exchanged a quick glance before Niabi waved her to come closer. She was the only one in the room who didn't seem surprised by Leoti's unannounced arrival.

"And why would you like to join them?" Niabi asked.

Leoti bowed to Niabi before saying, "I have a set of skills -"

"Leoti, no," Tala whispered, panic in his eyes.

"I have a set of skills," Leoti continued, disregarding her father's warning, "that I have not used in quite some time, but I know can be an asset in this war."

"What skills could you possibly possess to help me?" Thanos refused to even look at her when he asked the question.

Leoti extended her leather-wrapped arm, and a falcon flew in the window behind the throne, perching on her outstretched limb. "This is Tiki." She handed him a treat. "Tell me what you wish to know, my Queen, and we shall tell you."

Niabi tilted her head to look at Thanos and flashed a vicious smile. "How many guards does Prince Thanos have in the courtyard?"

Leoti moved her arm and Tiki shot back out the window.

"Prince Thanos," Niabi instructed, "whisper to Commander Pash how many soldiers you have in your company."

By the look on Thanos' pale face, Niabi knew he was reluctant to admit how few men he had managed to scrounge up on his journey north, but he did as she bade him.

Leoti blinked and her brown eyes were replaced with solid white. They watched in awe as she sat completely still. At the right moment, she rose from her cross-legged position in time for Tiki to perch upon her awaiting arm.

Leoti smiled, her eyes back to their natural color. "Eight soldiers, Your Majesty."

Niabi eyed Thanos and Pash.

"Eight," Pash confirmed as Thanos nodded.

Niabi glided to Leoti, amazement and wonder in her eyes. "You are a warg."

"I am," Leoti bowed her head.

Niabi whipped her head around to look at Tala who looked ill. "Leave us," the queen commanded.

Everyone except Tala emptied the throne room. Once the doors closed behind them, Niabi's face softened, and she grabbed Tala's hand. "I didn't know."

"If word had gotten out that she had these powers..." Tala ran fingers through his hair and sighed. "I don't know who might have tried to get their hands on her for her power."

"Are you...?" Niabi whispered.

Tala shook his head. "No. Neither was her mother. There hasn't been a warg amongst our people in generations. The last one..." He forced himself to speak. "The Gomorrians kidnapped her."

"Looking for the Tears of the Gods and the City of Bones, I would imagine." Niabi pieced that bloodthirsty lot's motive together easily.

"And when she couldn't find it, they sent her back to Elisor in pieces. They kept her eyes though; a mockery and an insult of her gift."

Niabi cupped Tala's chin. "I won't send Leoti, if you do not wish it."

Tala had tears in his eyes, and it pained her to see him like this. "Thanos knows about her power now. If she doesn't go, he might try to come back for her, if he's crowned king. Not many people have magic like her anymore."

"Tala," she said gently. "There's something I need to show you." Niabi lifted her left hand and conjured a small flame to dance in her palm. Tala scooted back, eyes wide. "Vilora's magic is in my blood." Niabi shrugged with a half-smile. "I never knew."

Tala glanced to her arm, "The blackness...?"

"I didn't use my power and it began to consume me."

"You think Leoti may suffer the same fate?"

"That I cannot say," Niabi shook her head and closed her palm, extinguishing the flame. "But if she doesn't use her power, it may very well turn on her."

"I worry about her leaving my sight with this power," Tala said.

"But?"

Tala looked gutted to admit the next part but did anyway. "I am terrified of what she might do, if she stays here."

"Meaning?"

"I think..." Tala breathed in deeply. "I think she might attempt to assassinate *him*."

"I see." Niabi understood he meant Gershom. "I will have Pash watch over her. No harm will come to her."

Tala squinted and she knew exactly what he was thinking.

"I know you and he aren't on good terms, and I respect that," Niabi patted his arm. "But trust me once more, my old friend. If I tell him to protect her, he will give his life for her, if it comes down to it."

"Do you trust him?" Tala asked.

"Of course, I do," she narrowed her eyes, confused by the question.

"Then he knows of your magic? Of the baby you now carry?"

Niabi lifted her chin. If anyone other than Tala had spoken to her with that tone, she wouldn't have hesitated in claiming their tongue. She rolled her shoulders back and cracked her neck.

"He knows what I want him to know."

"Whether I like him or not," Tala rubbed the nape of his neck, "he deserves to know about his child."

"And he will know when I am ready to tell him." This was where she drew a line in the sand. The mountain she was ready to die on. She would not be pushed or pressured. Niabi felt heat in her left arm as it trailed down to her fingertips. She glanced at her balled-up fist and saw a faint orange glow.

"It seems I have upset you," Tala noticed it, too.

Niabi shook her hand to rid herself of the fire itching to erupt. "I... it's never done this before." She met his gaze and the worry in his eyes matched what she was feeling in her thrashing heart.

"For years you have stifled it," Tala tentatively reached for her left hand, "but now that it has tasted freedom, it craves more. That's the danger of magic. Once it is released, it has no intention of being caged."

"I can control it." Niabi retracted her hand before he could touch her.

"You are afraid." Tala knew her well.

"My fear will not cripple me." Niabi ascended the steps to her throne, flexing her fingers, the glow now gone. She sat, her train pooled around her leather boots and the hem of her black pants. "And Leoti? What would you have us do?"

Tala grimaced. "She goes."

Niabi nodded in agreement before calling for Leoti and Pash to come back into the throne room.

"Leoti, you will go with them." Niabi met Pash's gaze. "Consider Pash your commander and protector."

"My Queen," Leoti bowed with satisfaction.

Pash crossed his arm over his chest and the softness of his eyes nearly shattered Niabi's heart. She had to make sure her hand wasn't resting on her belly where his baby was now growing. She knew he understood she was trusting him with her daughter-in-law's life, and he wouldn't fail either of them.

Niabi turned her focus back to Leoti. "Is it just the falcon's eyes you can see through?"

Leoti smirked and looked every bit the predator as Niabi. "Any beast is prey to me."

Niabi smiled. "Good."

Chapter Twenty-Nine

Salome

Salome left a trail of water from the gardens to her chamber doors. Though she had wrung her hair and clothes by the Pool of Enlightenment, she was still wet and uncomfortable, looking more like an angry cat than Myridian royalty.

I never should have let him take her. Her grandmother's words hovered over her like a dark cloud.

She pushed the door open to find her sitting room dark, except for the moonlight that glistened off the sea and filled the space with a silver glow. The door latched and a hand from behind her clamped down over her mouth, an attempt to stifle her screams. Salome elbowed the attacker in the gut, grabbed their forearm, and flipped them onto the ground. She snatched the wolf dagger from its holster, dug a knee into the intruder's chest, and put the tip of her knife against their throat.

"Salome, it's me!" The deep male voice rang out. "It's Jinn."

Her eyes began to adjust to the darkness and she saw his Eastern features. "What are you doing here?" she growled.

"I came to warn you."

"Warn me? You attacked me!"

"I didn't attack you," he spewed. "I didn't want your scream alerting your watchdog across the hall."

Salome knew he was referring to Adonijah and fury shot through her body. She poked her knife a little closer into Jinn's neck. "He is *not* my watchdog."

"Your protector, your lover," he waved a dismissive hand in the air. "It doesn't matter to me one way or another. But you need to listen to me. We don't have much time."

"Time for what?"

"Whispers have reached my ears of an attempt on your life."

Salome narrowed her eyes and hissed, "The only intruder in my room has been you."

"I'm not here to harm you." Jinn rested the back of his head against the floor, exasperated. "Do you really think an assassin hasn't been sent for you?"

"Perhaps," she scanned the room. "Perhaps not."

"I lied to you before." His statement caught her attention. "I'm not here on business. I'm here for you."

"For me?"

"I've been sent by one of your father's allies to help you."

Salome shook her head slowly, shoving her knee deeper into his chest, feeling nothing but solid muscle and hating herself for picturing him shirtless. "I don't believe you," she spat.

"Salome, please," Jinn pleaded. "You have to believe me."

"No, I don't."

"Salome -"

Her eyes scanned the room again, sensing they weren't alone. "And *your* watchdog? Where is she?"

Kai stepped out of the shadows on the opposite side of the room, moonlight flashing across her belt filled with knives of varying sizes.

Salome smirked and tightened her grip around the hilt of her dagger. "I have a knife to your prince's throat. Do you not care, Ryoko Naga?"

"She has been ordered not to harm you." Jinn whispered, a gentle calm in his voice.

"A mistake on your part." She said to Jinn, eyes fastened on Kai.

Kai stepped forward, her expression remained neutral, but Jinn extended his hand to stop her.

"Your father's Second in Command, Lord Maon, survived the invasion. He's been hiding for years while leading an underground rebellion against your sister." Jinn explained, a bit of blood drawn from the tip of her blade dripped down his neck.

"Everyone died the night Niabi attacked," Salome huffed before standing to her feet, releasing her hold on him, but keeping her knife pointed at him. "I did too."

Jinn slowly rose from the floor and wiped the blood from his neck with his fingers. Somehow, even in the dark, he looked devastatingly handsome. Dressed in black fighting leathers, instead of royal robes, he looked dangerous, like an assassin.

"Now, he goes by Oden." Jinn hesitated before taking a step toward her and was met with a disapproving look. He retreated a few steps showing her his empty hands. "He sent me here to help you."

"And how did he know I would be here?"

"Oden thought there was a chance you might meet with your grandmother."

By the tone in his voice, she was inclined to believe him. "And what do you gain by helping this Oden? Helping me?"

"Our peoples were once strong allies. With Niabi on the throne, that allegiance has been shattered." Jinn's eyes darkened. "My sister, Anka, was betrothed to your eldest brother."

Salome rested a hand on her hip and tapped her foot. "My patience is running thin. What do you gain in helping me?"

"An alliance between our mighty houses. Peace between our people."

"Is your sister still in the market for a Northern prince?" Salome scoffed. "I don't think Crispin would be too keen on that idea."

"Anka died a few years ago," Jinn lowered his head and Salome regretted her spiteful words. "But there is another heir."

Salome saw the desire in his eyes, sending a shiver down her spine. "I am not interested," she furrowed her brows.

Jinn seemed surprised, as if rejection from a woman wasn't something that happened often, or ever. "You – You won't at least consider my proposal?"

"If that's a proposal, it's a piss poor one."

Kai took a heavy step forward, but Jinn waved her off, keeping her at bay. *An insult to her master*, Salome noted.

"Come to Sakurai with me," Jinn slid his hands in his pockets. "My people, we can protect you until the time comes to face your sister."

His voice was enticing, and it took Salome a second to catch her breath. "I am safe enough here."

"One man cannot protect you forever -"

"I didn't say anything about Adonijah protecting me," she cut him off. "I'm the one who had a knife to your throat. I'm the one who held your life in my hands."

"Then perhaps," he risked approaching her, his hands once again showing he held no weapons to harm her, "I can be the one standing by your side as you conquer our enemies." Jinn reached her and although her knife was still a threat to him, he cupped her chin and gently brushed his thumb along her jawline.

She hated to admit it, but her heart began to race just from his delicate touch. "You need to leave."

Jinn's eyes were filled with disappointment, but he withdrew his hand. His gaze drifted from her fiery eyes to her full lips. "Is that what you want?"

Salome pointed to the door with her dagger. "Get out."

Jinn bowed his head. "Consider my offer. The Eastern armies for your hand in marriage."

Salome sucked in a breath. Jinn was serious about their houses being joined. Political allies. Strong ones at that. And she needed his army if she was going to defeat her sister in battle. As far as she knew, she and her brother still hadn't secured one. Maybe his proposal was worth considering. But he didn't need to know that. She kept her face neutral as she once again pointed to the door.

"Out. And take your pet with you."

Kai stomped by them and opened the door for them to leave, but he stopped and brushed his fingers against Salome's left hand. "I have extended my stay for two more days. If you change your mind."

"Don't hold your breath." Salome snatched her hand back and he slipped out, shutting the door behind him.

She exhaled a sigh of relief, having run on pure adrenaline since the moment his hand clasped over her mouth. She believed for a moment that someone was there to kill her, and it rattled her that she was right there for the taking. If it had been his knife that reached her throat instead of his hand...

She didn't want to think about it anymore and rushed to light her lamps. The curtains on either side of her open balcony whooshed and she felt someone's presence. She whipped around, ready for those assassins Jinn had warned her about, but it was Adonijah who had entered, dressed in all black, as if he were the night.

"I thought they would never leave," Adonijah puffed his chest out to crack his back.

"One of these days," she sheathed her dagger, "you're going to catch a knife to the chest sneaking around the way you do."

"With your aim, I've got time." Adonijah flashed a wicked grin.

Salome folded her arms over her chest. "What were you doing out there?"

"You think those two got into your room unnoticed?" His eyebrows lifted, as if he was insulted. "I've not survived as long as I have without embracing the darkness."

"Is it safe to assume you heard..."

"His attempt at a proposal was..."

"Adonijah," she warned.

"Painful. Truly, painful."

"Am I detecting a hint of jealousy?" Salome snatched an apple from the bowl of fruit left on the dining table and took a bite.

"More like secondhand embarrassment," Adonijah leaned against the wall lazily, crossing one ankle over the other. "Knocked on his ass and his proposal rejected. Bad day to be a prince."

Salome perched herself on the edge of the table, swinging her legs freely. "I recall knocking you on your ass, the first time we met."

The Hollow. It seemed like such a long time ago they had fought as enemies.

Adonijah shrugged. "And it was still less humiliating than his encounter with you tonight."

Salome rolled her eyes and took another bite from her apple. Once she swallowed the piece, she stared at her feet. "He's not that bad."

"Oh?" Adonijah seemed amused. "Do tell, Princess."

Salome furrowed her brow and shot him a vicious look. "You're a brute, you know that?"

"Aye," he pushed up from the wall and approached her. "And you like that I'm a brute."

"Is that so?"

"Aye." Adonijah stood in front of her and leaned forward to rest his hands on the table. Her legs were on either side of him, straddling his hips.

They stared at one another. She could feel her heartbeat quicken and noticed his breathing was raspy.

"Will you consider it?" Adonijah whispered, his brown eyes fixed on hers.

"Consider what?"

"His offer."

Salome knew the moment her body tensed up he sensed what was going through her mind. "Maybe I should consider it."

"Is that what you want?" Jinn had asked her the same question moments ago when she told him to leave. But from Adonijah's lips, the question carried pain.

Salome shrugged. "We need his army."

"Is that what you want?" Adonijah asked again.

"I don't think it matters what I want anymore."

Adonijah's hand scooped her face, his fingers tickling the back of her neck. "It matters to me." His gaze dragged from her eyes down to her lips. "What do you want?"

"It's stupid," she whispered, his hands hot against her skin.

"Tell me."

"I want a home," she admitted softly. "To finally find a place where I belong. A place where I can finally be at peace." A tear slipped down her cheek, and he thumbed it away.

"That's not stupid." Adonijah slowly shook his head, his free hand resting on her waist. "I understand."

Salome breathed him in. His tobacco and earthy scent filled her nostrils, which swept her away to a cozy cabin in the middle of winter. A fire roaring, a tea kettle whistling, his arms wrapped around her tightly as the snowflakes cascaded slowly to the ground.

"I would be a fool if I told you what to do," Adonijah's voice sliced through her thoughts, "but please don't marry him."

Salome's heart leapt to her throat. "Why not?"

"You're wild and strong and opinionated. And that tongue of yours always gets you into trouble." He leaned closer, his lips within inches of hers. "He can't handle you."

"And you can?" She arched an eyebrow, her eyes bouncing to his lips.

"Aye."

"You seem awfully sure of yourself."

Adonijah tightened his grip around her waist, pulling her toward him. "Aye," he whispered against her ear, and it sent shivers down her spine. "I am."

She closed her eyes, waiting for his lips that dragged from her cheek toward her lips.

"What do you want?" Adonijah asked one more time.

Salome turned her head slightly to meet his awaiting lips. *Him*. She wanted him. Her hands reached up and clasped the back of his neck as they kissed, pulling him closer.

Adonijah's lips were soft, his kiss passionate. His rugged appearance didn't match his gentleness. She bit his lower lip and he responded by slipping his tongue into her mouth. He cupped her face with one calloused hand and splayed the fingers of his other hand through her hair. She could feel the muscles in his arms tense, as if he was using every bit of strength he possessed to hold himself back.

"Adonijah..." Salome whispered his name, and he planted an open mouth kiss to her neck. Goosebumps stretched over every inch of her body.

"I've wanted to kiss you since the moment I realized who you were outside the Hidden Tavern." Adonijah muttered against her warm skin. "I find myself thinking about you every minute of every day. If only you knew the power you hold over me."

"I thought I was a pain in your ass?" Salome smiled against his kisses.

"Aye," Adonijah lifted her up from the table and she wrapped her legs around his waist. "But you're *my* pain in the ass."

Salome planted another kiss on his lips, her heart soaring inside her chest. She thought she heard something whistle toward them. A soft thud sounded, and she was falling out of his grasp. She opened her eyes and saw Adonijah grimacing. He melted to the floor, and she fought to keep him on his feet. Her eyes darted to the back of his leg and saw a black arrow sticking out of his hamstring.

Salome looked at the balcony where six Thrak had climbed over the banister. Armed head to toe in weaponry, she knew they had come for her.

Adonijah ripped the arrow out of his leg with a groan and wrapped the bloody wound with linen off the dining table.

Salome rose from her crouched position, standing between a wounded Adonijah and the enemy. Her eyes trailed right to left, from one Thrak to the next. She had never faced these many opponents at once. If she lived, she would have to apologize to Jinn for dismissing his warning. She flipped her knives out from their holsters on her lower back and thigh and circled them around her hands.

Adonijah struggled to his feet but took his place next to Salome. He drew his sword, squaring his shoulders to the Thrak and shook his head with a tsk. "Does no one use the door anymore?"

"You're coming with us." One of the Thrak cocked his head to the side, eyes on Salome, ignoring Adonijah.

Salome spat at the Thrak's feet. "I've killed your kind before, and I'll gladly kill the lot of you."

The Thrak commander cackled, flashing a mouth filled with crooked yellow teeth. "As fun as it would be to see you try, our queen ordered for you to be brought back to Gomorrah unspoiled."

"The only thing your queen is going to be getting is your head in a bag." Salome took a deep breath. With her gaze still fixed on the Thrak leader, she mentally sent out a cry for help, hoping her magic worked both ways. *"If anyone is listening, I need help."*

The Thrak commander bobbed his head and the warrior nearest her lunged at her. She blocked the incoming blow of his mace with her knives and swept his leg out from under him in a fluid motion, like a dance. Like a Qata Vishna. And as he fell to the floor, she swung her knives in opposite directions. One sliced his neck open and the second slashed a deep gash across his unprotected abdomen. He fell to the floor with a loud thud. With his blood splattered all over her face and clothes, she beckoned another demon to come meet his fate.

"Kill the man." The Thrak leader sneered, done with her taunting, "Maim the bitch."

Two charged Adonijah and two leapt toward Salome, leaving the Thrak leader to watch with a sinister grin across his scarred face. Even with an injured leg, Adonijah didn't miss a beat in fighting them with his longsword. Salome grabbed a chair and tossed it at one of the Thrak rushing at her, tripping him long enough for her to focus on one assailant at a time.

Even though she had only trained as a Qata Vishna for a couple of mornings, she was picking up on their techniques quickly and now realized how effective their movement was in defeating their enemies.

Before coming to the Isles of Myr, she had seen her enemies as her equals, if not her oppressors. But by learning the way of her mother's people, she now understood what it meant to be a woman who waged war. A woman who looked at her enemies as lessers. A woman who was an extension of her weapon. A woman men should fear. She would haunt their nightmares. She would invade their minds. She would destroy them bit by bit. She would rise from her ashes and her name would be whispered from trembling lips. Her face would be what terrorized them when they closed their eyes at night.

She was Salome. She had Northern and Myridian blood coursing through her veins. And she would no longer fear her lessers. She would be who they feared.

With five Thrak dead, and blood pooling all over Salome's chamber floor, their leader was still unimpressed.

"Your turn?" Salome cocked her head to the side flashing a malicious grin.

The Thrak leader laughed before he whistled. Eight more Thrak scaled the walls and slithered over the balcony banister.

"You were saying?" The Thrak commander taunted.

Salome glanced over at Adonijah. Blood was dripping down his wounded leg and his left forearm had a slash that would need stitches, if they survived.

Adonijah met her gaze and winked. A silent comfort. He had sworn an oath to protect her, to fight by her side. He had kept his promise and was willing to die fulfilling those words.

Salome hadn't thought much about death. She was never afraid of it, knowing whether in battle or in old age, she would leave this world for another. But standing shoulder-to-shoulder with Adonijah, having felt his lips on hers, his hands caressing her skin, she knew she wasn't ready to die. She wasn't ready to leave him.

"No matter what happens," Salome whispered so only Adonijah could hear her, "I will fight, live, and die by your side."

Whatever thoughts were flooding Adonijah's head, she wouldn't have the luxury of finding out because the second wave of Thrak launched their assault.

They braced themselves for eight rushing them at once, but before the warriors could reach them, two assassins dressed in black fighting leathers swung in from above the balcony and landed behind the Thrak commander.

Kai was already armed with two blades in her hands, holding one in front of her chest and the other over her head.

The Thrak leader growled and whipped around, drawing his longsword, but before he could unsheathe it completely, Kai flicked her blades and each one splayed into a seven-blade fan. She swiped the fans in opposite directions, decapitating the Thrak commander. His head bounced on the floor and Salome could have sworn the remaining eight Thrak flinched in unison.

Salome's eyes moved from Kai to Jinn. The light breeze blew loose strands of his jet-black hair across his face and the glimpse of danger she had seen in him earlier, was now full-blown fury. His golden-brown eyes blazed and if she had stared for any longer, she would have backed away, intimidated by the sight of him.

Jinn retrieved two slightly curved, thin blades from his back and held them at his sides.

After a moment of silence, as if the Thrak were trying to process what was happening, Jinn and Kai jumped toward the group, and joined the fight from the opposite side.

It was still four against eight, but they were far more skilled than the Thrak and made quick work of them. It was more of a bloodbath than a battle.

Realizing there was only one Thrak left, Salome stopped Adonijah from slitting his throat. "Wait! We need him alive."

"Alive?" Adonijah's knife was still against the Thrak's bobbing neck. His black eyes darted back and forth between them.

"To interrogate him," Jinn answered, holstering his tachi blades against his back. "We need to find out if there are more Thrak on the Isles. If they were here just for Salome or if there were others -"

"I got it," Adonijah cut him off and lowered his weapon.

Kai flicked her fans and they retracted into daggers. She fastened them into the belt and quickly bound and gagged the last Thrak.

Salome's gaze met Jinn's. The assassin was gone, and the prince stood before her. She was relieved, happy even, to see him, and by the look in his eyes, he knew it. "How did you know we were in trouble?"

Jinn ran fingers through his hair and shifted his feet. "I wish I could explain it to you without feeling like a fool," he took a deep breath, blushing in embarrassment. "I thought I heard you calling for help. I mean, I didn't hear you out loud, but in my head. Like you were in my thoughts."

Salome's eyes widened. It had worked. Her mental cry for help was answered by Jinn. He had heard her. But how was that possible? She thought she could only communicate with the dead. But she *had* spoken with someone mind-to-mind before. Damaris. As soon as she could, she would talk to her aunt. Maybe there was more to Salome's magic than she originally thought.

"I know it sounds completely insane." Jinn rubbed the nape of his neck when she didn't respond.

Salome reached out and rested her hand on his forearm, catching Adonijah's watchful eye. "Thank you."

"You're welcome." Jinn seemed taken aback by her gratitude. "You don't think I'm crazy?"

Adonijah grunted behind her, but she ignored it, keeping her gaze fixed on Jinn. "I don't think you're crazy. I should have heeded your warning."

"Where do we take this monstrosity?" Kai asked, kicking the Thrak as he sat on the floor. He hissed through his gag and Kai hissed back.

"We take him to the queen. She will want to know about Thrak running rampant on her lands." And maybe, Salome hoped, this would sway Nym into joining her cause, joining her war.

CHAPTER THIRTY

PASH

Pash did as his queen had instructed and readied the troops and an elite group of Shadows to travel to Gomorrah. Leoti, Ophir, and the Nameless Rider would be accompanying him and Thanos to claim the prince's kingdom. Pash thought it was odd the Nameless Rider insisted on bringing the villager from the Tree House Forest, but he wasn't interested enough to question or deny the Shadow's request.

Before the group left Northwind, Pash made his way to see Niabi in her chambers per her request. But as he rounded the corner of the longest corridor leading to her room, Pash was met by his father and uncle. And by the desperate look in his father's eyes, the commander knew he wanted something.

"Father," Pash sighed. "Uncle."

Gershom squared his shoulders to his son's. "Pash, your uncle informed me he is travelling south with you."

"He is."

Gershom's brow furrowed. "I see."

"Is there a problem?" Pash asked, though he wasn't really interested in his father's opinion.

"I assumed since you are still Commander of the Shadows that Ophir would head the search for the Hunter while you were away." Gershom folded his arms across his broad chest.

Pash pinched the bridge of his nose. "Again, you have assumed incorrectly. Ophir is needed with me."

"But -"

"The search for this Hunter of yours has cost too many Shadow lives," Pash interrupted his father. "The queen won't allow the Shadows to leave the city without her approval."

Gershom gnashed his teeth and balled up his fists. "So, that's it?"

"For now." Pash nodded.

Gershom took a step forward. "You are a commander in title only. I should have known you wouldn't come through," he hissed.

Pash shrugged. "I haven't the time for these games, Father. We can discuss this when I return."

"*If* you return," Gershom grumbled as Pash tried to pass by.

"Glad you have such confidence in me," Pash flashed a contemptuous smile. "Now, I have a meeting with the queen before our departure. Is there anything else?"

Gershom reluctantly stepped to one side of the hall and let his son pass. "Oh, Pash."

Pash turned with an exasperated sigh. "Yes?"

"Give my well wishes to Her Highness on her news." Gershom grinned when Pash wrinkled his brow in confusion. "I know something about her you don't? How delicious. I figured it was yours, but perhaps, I was wrong."

"What are you talking about?" Pash asked as he approached, an eyebrow arched.

Gershom clasped his hands behind his back and rocked on his heels. "Perhaps she never intended to tell you. It suits her cruel nature."

Before Pash realized he had done it, he smashed his forearm into his father's chest and nailed him to the wall. "Speak about her like that again and I'll..."

"You'll what?" Gershom rolled his eyes. "We both know you won't harm me. Your mother passed her weakness to you."

Pash unsheathed a knife from his belt and pressed it against Gershom's neck. "Do not speak of my mother."

Ophir's hand gripped Pash's shoulder. "Pash, don't."

His nostrils flared as he reluctantly lowered the knife, releasing Gershom from his grasp. "What do you know?"

Gershom straightened his clothes and laughed. "Our queen is expecting." Pash stood in stunned silence which provoked another hearty laugh from his father. "Look at him, Ophir, he really didn't know!"

Pash took off down the hall, no longer caring what his father said or did. The soldiers stationed on either side of Niabi's double doors opened them, so he wouldn't have to break stride. His eyes scanned the room quickly and spotted Niabi reclined in a lounge reading a book. He realized he hadn't seen her drink a glass of wine in a while. In fact, there were no wine bottles on her wet bar.

Niabi glanced up from her book and smiled at him. She looked relaxed and stressed all at once. "I assume you are ready for your..." She planted her feet on the floor, closing her book, and setting it to the side. "Pash? Are you alright?"

Pash marched toward her and knelt before her, gently grabbing ahold of her waist. "I – You – Are you?"

Niabi cupped his face, a spark of realization hit her. "I was waiting for the right moment to tell you."

A wave of emotions flooded him. Joy, fear, surprise. He wasn't sure if he wanted to cry, jump, or run. "So, it's true? You're...?"

Niabi bobbed her head.

He lowered the side of his face against her swollen belly and closed his eyes. She wrapped her arms around him and kissed the top of his head.

"Who told you?" she asked.

Pash pulled himself from her midsection and met her gaze. "My father."

Her eyes flashed in irritation, but she shook the hate from her face, and smiled down at him. "Then it is safe to assume most of the White Keep knows our news."

"I can't leave you," Pash kissed her hand. "Not now. Send someone else to Gomorrah. You need me now more than ever."

"Pash -"

"You will be in more danger than before, Niabi."

"You know as well as I do, the soldiers guarding me are for appearance only." Niabi caressed his cheek. "I am perfectly safe."

"I know you can take care of yourself but..." Pash couldn't finish the thought.

"If it makes you feel better," she picked up where he left off, "I also have Tala and Anaktu to watch out for me." She lifted his chin. "I promise, I'll be alright. We'll be here when you return."

Her smile melted him. She still looked like a queen but the glow of her carrying life inside of her stilled his heart. Somehow, she grew in beauty when he thought that was impossible.

"I thought you would be happy," she tilted her head to the side.

"I am." He exhaled a sad sigh, "I know how you feel about remarrying and I accept that, but will you let me be involved in raising our child or will I be forced to remain a secret?"

Niabi leaned down and gently kissed his lips. "I love you, Pash. And our child will not only know you, but love you, too."

“Please don’t make me leave you,” he rested his forehead against hers.

“You are the one I trust to lead my men to Gomorrah.” She kissed his lips again and this time, he felt her saying goodbye.

“Does Tala know?”

“Yes,” she nodded.

He and the Andrago might not like one another but there was one thing Pash knew for certain: Tala would lay down his life to protect Niabi.

“There is nothing to worry about,” she squeezed his hand.

“My father -”

Niabi lifted her scarred right palm for him to see. “He cannot kill me without forfeiting his own life. And we both know Gershom loves himself too much to test the blood magic.”

Pash kissed her belly and then kissed her, lingering for as long as she allowed. “I will return to you as soon as I can,” he whispered.

“We will be waiting.”

Chapter Thirty-One

Crispin

The battle raged around him. Blood, soot, and smoke filled Crispin's nostrils as he fought his way closer to Northwind's front gate. An army at his back, Crispin waved them forward to attack with everything they had. Blood that didn't belong to him was splattered across his metal armor and dirt stained his aching hands. As they pressed onward, cutting down enemy soldiers in their path, Crispin heard the laugh that haunted him. Crispin's head whipped to his left where Gershom the Bear stood.

Crispin remembered the Seer telling him his life would be forfeit if he faced Gershom. He should walk away. He should heed the Seer's warning but seeing the man who murdered his mother and his brothers standing less than twenty feet in front of him unleashed a level of hatred he didn't realize he harbored.

Crispin drew his sword and ran toward the warlord. Gershom smiled as Crispin leapt in the air, swinging his sword to slice off Gershom's head, but the Bear deflected the attack, caught the prince by the neck, and began to choke him. Crispin dropped his sword, trying to peel Gershom's massive hand from his throat as his feet dangled in the air like a small child. In a last-ditch effort to free himself, Crispin brought his forehead down, smashing into Gershom's face. The Bear released him and hissed.

As Crispin coughed and stumbled to get to his feet, Gershom kicked him square in his chest, stealing his breath. Lying on his back, Crispin gazed up at Gershom who flashed a sinister smile. Hands stained with blood, Gershom lifted his sword above his head, and with one final cackle brought the blade down, slicing into Crispin's chest.

Crispin shot up from his small cot drenched in sweat. His hand roamed his bare chest, grateful to find himself to be intact. From the sway of the ship, Crispin breathed a sigh of relief to be aboard the *Shadow of Death*. It had been several days since he had that nightmare. But this time, it felt real. He could smell Death. He could feel Gershom's blade rip through his flesh and crush his bones. He could hear the screams of those who loved him as his soul left is body.

Crispin hopped out of his bed, stepped to the wash basin, and splashed lukewarm water on his face. He dragged a soaked wash rag over the back of his neck and chest.

"It was just a dream," he muttered to himself, but when he caught his reflection in the small mirror above the basin, he flinched. He looked weathered. For the first time since he was a boy, he saw fear staring back at him.

A soft knock on his door drew his attention from his horrifying reflection. He didn't move. With his hands resting on either side of the wooden table where the wash basin sat, he waited to see if whoever was at his door would walk away. But a second knock echoed through his narrow sleeping quarters. Whoever was on the other side wasn't going anywhere.

Crispin raked a hand through his messy curls before opening the door just enough to see who was on the other side. Out of all the people he expected to see, he was surprised to see Rahab holding two tin mugs of steaming liquid. The scent of honey, whiskey, and herbs wafted up to his nose and instantly calmed his nerves.

"I thought you could use a drink," she whispered, as if she didn't want anyone to wake up and catch her outside his quarters that late. "And maybe some company?"

If it had been anyone else, he would have declined the drink and slammed the door in their face, but something in him couldn't react that way with her. For one, she might stab him. And two, when he met her gaze, he could tell she was also in need of someone to distract her from nightmares. He pushed the creaky door open as wide as it could go and motioned her in.

Rahab offered him one of the mugs and he gratefully took a sip, letting the warmth and burn of the liquor coat his throat. She sat beside him on his cot and for a few minutes they sipped their drinks in silence and stared directly ahead at the wood panel wall where his wash basin sat.

"I couldn't sleep either," Rahab broke the silence, fingers tapping against her cup.

Crispin stiffened. When he had nightmares in the Tree House Forest, he would sweat, scream, and groan until he shot up in a panic or someone woke him. It's a wonder the pirates hadn't pounded on the adjoining walls to get him to shut up for disturbing their sleep.

As if she could read his mind, Rahab said, "We all have them, you know. The nightmares. We're used to sounds in the night. No one will bother you or mention it tomorrow."

The tension he'd been holding in his shoulders loosened and he slumped forward, rubbing his hand over his forehead. "Did I wake you?"

Rahab shook her head. "I was already up." She took another gulp of her drink, and grinned. "I'm surprised you drank something I handed you."

"I figured poisoning was beneath your stab happy self." Crispin smirked; lips pressed against his mug. "It's actually pretty good. What is it?"

"Something Leeondris showed me." Rahab didn't meet his awaiting gaze. "He told me to drink one whenever I have a nightmare. It helps me sleep."

Crispin straightened, cracking his back. He watched her swirl her mug gently. "Do you have them often?" She glanced up at him. "The nightmares, not the drinks."

Rahab sighed and bobbed her head. "I thought I had them under control. But after seeing the Pirate King..." She chuckled softly, "I suppose I should stock up on honey and whiskey when we get to Northwind."

Her attempt at lightening the mood didn't go unnoticed. Crispin was thankful she'd come to his room. Her presence alone was a huge comfort, and he wasn't sure if he should be happy or worried by that. Master Balor's words kept replaying in his head. If he chose his people, his heirs would rule for an age. But if he chose Rahab...

"What do you dream of?" Her question snapped him free of Balor's words. His brown eyes latched onto hers.

"I dream of how I die." Crispin was surprised when she recoiled, and he stared at his feet to avoid her gaze. "There's a battle outside the gates of Northwind. The man who murdered my mother and brothers is there. I have a choice to fight him or let him go. I choose to fight him every time, and every time his sword plunges into my chest."

Rahab reached over and grabbed his hand. When she squeezed, he looked up at her. "If you find yourself on the battlefield and see that man..." The ache in her voice sent a surge of warmth through his chest. "Let him go."

"I could promise you I would, but I don't know if I could keep my word."

"Your heart is fading, Crispin of Northwind." Amunet, the High Priestess in Numbio, had warned him. *"Do not let the evil that has consumed your enemies, fill your heart. Let your hatred go."*

"My hatred is all I have."

"If you lose yourself," she said, *"then you have already been defeated."*

Crispin's fingers cupped the pendant Amunet had placed around his neck in the Golden Temple. *"As long as you wear this, I will be with you. May this be an everlasting reminder to follow your path and not wish for another's."*

Rahab's hand gently turned his chin to face her. When their eyes met, his heart skipped a beat. The stubborn, fierce, dagger-clutching pirate was gone and a woman with eyes filled with compassion and concern held his gaze. "Let him go, Crispin."

"I don't think I can," he whispered.

"Even if it costs you your life?"

"Could you walk away if you came face to face with Uri again?" Crispin asked, expecting her nostrils to flare in anger or her hand to fly across his face, but she sighed and lowered her hand from his cheek.

"If I die, nothing will change. If you die, your people will miss out on their king." Rahab shrugged, her bottom lip quivering. "You need to let him go so you can live. People need you, Crispin." She stood up and rushed to the door.

Crispin chased her, grabbed her forearm, and spun her around before she could leave. He pinned her against the wooden door, cupped her face in his hands, and thumbed hair out of her face. Tipping her face up to meet his gaze, he whispered, "You think your life is less valuable than mine? That people don't need you? That you wouldn't be missed?"

"You are a prince," Rahab said softly, her weight shifting under his stare. "I am a pirate. We know our lives are not equal."

"I don't even want to think about a life where you aren't in it." Crispin held her chin firmly in his fingers. "If you died, it would break me."

Rahab's eyes bounced from his eyes to his lips. She exhaled a shallow breath before lifting her mouth to his. Crispin kissed her back, tucking his fingers behind her neck. Her hands wandered all over his bare chest, rubbing against the ridges of his abs.

Kissing her felt forbidden; like he was about to ride into a storm that could rip him apart. But kissing her also felt right; like he was supposed to have done it a long time ago. He didn't know if he would be able to stop kissing, her now that he'd had a taste of her lips.

Rahab pushed him gently toward his cot. When the back of his knees hit the edge of his bed, he fell back, and she straddled him. She didn't relent from kissing him as his fingers raked through her shoulder-length hair and trailed down her shoulders, her arms, and landed on her round hips.

"Please," Rahab whispered against his lips, their foreheads touching, "let him go."

With her voice added to Harbona and Amunet's counsel, he was inclined to listen. And what terrified him, was if she asked him to give up his crown, he might do it for her.

He gently flipped her around, so she was lying on her back, and looked down into her hazel eyes. Wrapping his arms around her, their limbs tangled, her walls coming down, he nodded. "I promise."

Chapter Thirty-Two

Salome

It was nearly midnight when everyone gathered in the circular War Room. Eight high back, wooden chairs were evenly spaced in a circle in the two-story library, with the open archways facing the sea. The room was located at the top of the highest tower and had one way in and out.

Nym sat with her back to the sea, with Zara to her left, and Mika to her right. Although Zara protested that men should not be allowed into their War Room, Nym overruled her because of the special circumstances. Harbona, therefore, claimed the chair to Salome's right and Jinn took the seventh seat next to him. Adonijah and Cato stood slightly behind Salome's seat and Kai took her place by Jinn's side.

Salome wondered why the last chair to her Aunt Zara's left was unoccupied. She glanced to her left at Damaris who sat between her and Mika and caught the oracle staring at the bound Thrak. He was forced to his knees in the middle of their circle where the Myridian sigil was tiled on the floor.

"Who does that seat belong to?" Salome mentally asked Damaris.

The Oracle didn't take her eyes off the monstrosity before them. *"That seat will always be left empty. It was Bilhah's."*

Salome's eyes drifted back to the empty chair, and she was taken aback when she saw her mother sitting in it. Bilhah's back was straight, her head held high, her smile warm and soothing. When Salome blinked, the vision vanished.

Salome shook her head and tore her eyes from her mother's seat. *"I need to talk to you about my magic."*

"What is it you wish to know?"

"How can you hear me? I thought I could only commune with the dead."

Damaris turned her head slightly to Salome, meeting her niece's gaze. *"Your magic is more powerful than you realize."*

"How powerful?"

"Your gift is like a bridge, uniting you to another side. You can commune with the departed, yes, but you also connect with the living. As long as you reach out, you can communicate telepathically with anyone that shares a bond with you."

Salome shifted in her seat and her eyes zoomed around the room to ensure no one was watching them. *"Jinn said he heard me ask for help in his thoughts. But I didn't address him specifically. I just asked for whoever was listening to help me."*

Damaris dared a brief glance at Jinn across the room. He was whispering something in Kai's ear, oblivious to their eyes on him. *"You two must share a strong connection if he heard you without you reaching out to him."*

"Does that mean," Salome sucked in a breath. *"Does that mean I could talk to Crispin?"*

Damaris glanced around the room before asking, *"You would have to share a bond with him."*

" We share the same blood."

"I am the Oracle of Myr," Damaris explained. *"My magic is what connects us. Us sharing blood is not the determining factor. Crispin might be your blood, but without the right bond, he doesn't have the ability to hear your voice."*

Salome huffed in disappointment. *"What kind of bonds are there?"*

"Magic and marriage."

"Could I hear their thoughts? Like you hear mine?"

Damaris bobbed her head.

Salome glanced at the prince. *"But Jinn and I are nothing to each other. How could he possibly hear me?"*

"Perhaps our prince has magic he doesn't wish for anyone to know about."

Salome and Damaris shifted their focus back to Jinn, but this time, he noticed them staring.

Salome looked at Nym and Zara whispering back and forth. She still had time to find out if Jinn could really hear her or not. Damaris said her magic was like a bridge. She had to initiate contact. She mentally envisioned herself standing on one side of a cavern and Jinn on the other. A swinging rope bridge stretched from her side to his.

"Jinn?"

Jinn crinkled his brow and opened his mouth to say something.

"Don't."

The prince snapped his mouth shut. Keeping as neutral a face as possible, he mentally replied, *"How are you doing this?"*

"It works." Salome was just as amazed as he was.

Realization hit Jinn and his eyes widened. *"So, I did hear you ask for help. I'm not crazy."* Salome bobbed her head an inch to confirm. He scanned the room, and no one seemed to notice them. *"Can you do this with everyone?"*

"Only with someone I share a bond with."

"A bond?" He arched a curious brow. *"What kind of bond?"*

"Magic or marriage."

Jinn's shoulders tensed. They clearly weren't married so there was only one possible explanation. *"I don't -"*

"You don't have to tell me what your affinity is," Salome interrupted him, *"but don't think me to be an idiot."*

"I would never think that." Jinn flashed a wicked smile, tilting his head to the side. *"Especially now that I know you can literally read my thoughts."*

Salome rolled her eyes but before she could respond, Nym and Zara straightened to address the rest of the group.

"From the report I received about what happened in your chambers tonight," Nym's sight darted to Salome, "I am beyond grateful you are alive." Salome nodded and Nym's green eyes turned vicious as she focused on the Thrak crumpled before her. "Are there any more of your kind in the Isles of Myr?" Nym asked sternly with an air of disgust.

The Thrak's eyes shifted, not focusing on anyone in particular. He spat at Nym in a final act of defiance.

In a flash, Mika was on her feet, a dagger drawn and poking against the Thrak's throat. "My queen asked you a question."

"You think I fear your queen more than my own?" The Thrak's gravelly voice trembled. "I would rather spend the rest of my days locked in your darkest dungeon than return to Gomorrah."

"Unfortunately for you," Nym nodded her head at Mika, "we do not harbor enemy soldiers."

The Thrak began to protest but Mika sliced her blade across his neck. He hunched over gurgling, his blood spilling on the Myridian sigil. They silently watched him die before Nym continued.

"So," Nym gazed at Jinn. "It would seem your report this morning was well founded. You have my gratitude."

"That's what you were meeting with her about?" Salome asked through their bond, her eyes drifting over to the prince, though he didn't meet her gaze.

"Had the Myridians discovered our true motive for being here, it could have been seen as an overreach of Eastern power. I let your grandmother know why I was really here, and she agreed to allow me to stay a couple more days to keep an eye on you." Jinn raised a hand to his chest, bowing his head in respect toward Nym. "I am relieved the princess was not harmed."

Salome heard Adonijah mutter something under his breath behind her but couldn't make out the words. If she could mentally chastise him, she would.

"Which brings us to the next matter at hand." Nym tilted her head to the double doors behind Salome. "Bring them in."

Mika opened the doors and Rosalina and Seraphina marched inside shoulder-to-shoulder. They stepped over the Thrak's body, without a second glance, and bowed before the queen and the crown princess.

Salome was confused as to why her ladies in waiting had been called to this meeting. As she observed the twins, she realized they looked different. They weren't wearing the cerulean dresses the palace workers donned. They were wearing pieces of bronze armor and brown fighting leathers. They looked like they were...

"Tell me," Nym folded her hands in her lap. "How did fifteen Thrak get past not one, but two Qata Vishna?"

"Qata Vishna?" Salome blurted without thinking.

"You don't believe I would let my granddaughter roam our halls unprotected, do you?" Nym refocused on the twins, ignoring Adonijah's disgruntled huff. "So, tell us. Why were you not at your posts tonight?"

Rosalina and Seraphina exchanged a side-eyed glance.

Salome caught Cato swaying side to side. She slowly turned her head to watch him and noticed he looked worried and was about to say something. His eyes met hers, and in his panic-stricken face, she realized he was somehow involved with them not being at their posts. She closed her eyes and took a deep breath. He would owe her an explanation.

"It's my fault." All eyes were now on Salome. Even Rosalina and Seraphina dared a glance back at her.

"What's that?" Nym snorted.

"I didn't know they were a protection detail. I wanted time to myself and ordered them to leave me." Salome lied but managed to keep a straight face.

Nym's eyes narrowed. "Is that true, Rosalina?"

Of course, Nym would ask the twin that couldn't keep a straight face.

Rosalina cleared her throat, "Yes, my Queen. The princess gave us an order. We obeyed."

Salome was oddly proud of Rosalina for lying through her teeth but maintained her own neutral expression so not to give them away.

"Had I known they were Qata Vishna," Salome pressed, eyes fixed on her grandmother, "I would not have given them such an order. Perhaps, it is best I am kept in the loop from now on, if we are to avoid these mistakes."

Harbona coughed to cover a laugh. Nym smirked. She could see right through Salome's deception but did not challenge her. There was no proof Salome was lying, so the issue was a mute one.

"Perhaps," Nym settled in her seat, resting her shoulders against the wood, "you should have been informed." She eyed the twins, "This will *not* happen again. You are bound to my granddaughter until I release you or she breathes her last breath. Is that understood?"

Rosalina and Seraphina bowed. "My Queen."

"Unless someone has something they wish to discuss," Nym waved them out, "I believe we are finished here."

As everyone began filing out of the War Room, Salome stopped when her grandmother rose from her seat and sternly said, "Salome, a word."

Salome slouched back into her seat, gearing up for a tongue lashing. Harbona winked at her, drawing a smile from her lips. He ushered a reluctant Adonijah and distracted Cato out of the room.

Jinn sauntered toward her, hands in his pockets, still dressed in his black fighting leathers. His golden-brown eyes danced.

Salome couldn't help herself. *"Why are you looking at me like that?"*

"Can't I just look at you?" Jinn smirked as jet-black strands of hair fell over his forehead.

"Not like that." She crinkled her nose. In an effort not to draw attention to them, she examined her nails, kicking a leg over one of the armrests.

"How am I looking at you?" He seemed amused.

"Like you want something."

"Maybe I do."

Salome couldn't help but look up at him as he passed by. *"And what do you want?"*

"Shut the doors behind you, if you will, Prince Jinn." Nym's voice interrupted them. "My granddaughter and I would like some privacy."

"Sounds like you might be in trouble for that stunt you just pulled." Jinn's voice echoed in her head as he walked out of the room without a second glance in her direction.

"I'm always in some kind of trouble." Salome rolled her eyes.

"Don't let her bully you."

"Worried about me, Prince Jinn?"

She could hear his warm laugh ringing in her head, and she hated that she liked it. *"Worried for your grandmother. You are quite the handful."*

"I've heard that before, too."

"I think I'm going to enjoy this direct line of communication with you."

"Don't get used to it." Salome snorted a laugh as the doors closed behind them, enclosing her with her grandmother. *"Once I figure out how to use my magic properly, I won't be this accessible."*

"You'll miss me."

Salome huffed aloud before noticing Nym was watching her.

"Do you drink wine?" Nym asked, her hands clasped behind her back.

Salome nodded and her grandmother walked to one of the built-in bookcases. She tapped her foot against the bottom of the shelf and the wall turned around revealing a wet bar. Nym grabbed a bottle of local wine and two glasses. She silently filled them and brought one over to Salome. Nym settled in one of the seats next to Salome. For several minutes they said nothing.

"You do remind me of Niabi." Nym broke the silence. Salome lowered her glass, her attention fixed on the queen. "But you also remind me so much of Bilhah. She pulled stunts like that all the time. Covering for her sisters, the servants. And she knew I knew she was lying."

Salome opened her mouth to protest but Nym held up a hand and she snapped her mouth shut.

"And just like your mother, I can't prove you are lying." Nym smiled, kicking her legs over the armrest like Salome, "I just don't want you thinking you pulled the wool over my eyes. I might be old, but I'm just as sharp as I was when I was your age."

Salome let out a much-needed laugh. "You're not mad?"

Nym shook her head with a wide grin. "I'm not mad. But Zara will be." The queen rolled her eyes and sighed. "I'll be hearing about this for at least a week."

Salome took another sip of red wine and inhaled the salty sea air that wafted through the room.

"Tell me, Granddaughter," Nym swirled the liquid in her glass. "Is it the prince or the sell-sword that has captured your heart?"

Salome coughed, choking on the wine that burned down her throat. "What are you talking about?" Her cheeks flushed, but she could easily blame that on the alcohol.

"They're both handsome, strong, tall, and the way they look at you," Nym slapped a freckled hand to her cheek and smirked. "Oh, what I would give for a man to look at me, the way both of them, look at you."

"I thought Myridians didn't like men." Salome said, hoping to redirect the conversation.

Nym chuckled, her mind clearly replaying a fond memory. "It's true. Some Myridian women hate men."

"You aren't one of them?"

Nym shook her head. "When I was around your age, I had many suitors. I was to be the next queen, so of course, I would be of interest. But there were two men in particular that captured my attention."

"How did you choose?" Salome asked, and when her grandmother met her gaze, she knew she had given herself away.

Nym smiled, "I got to know them both over the course of several months. And when it came time for me to choose a husband, I said a prayer, and went to sleep. When I woke up the next morning, the one that I thought of first, was who I married."

Salome's brows shot up. She didn't know what to say, so she took another sip of wine, finishing her glass. "And it worked?"

"I was happy," Nym nodded. "We had three beautiful daughters and enjoyed each other's company. He was my best friend. There are some in Myr who saw my love for him as a weakness. Zara included. But he brought me joy. And when he passed, I felt lost. Without my crown and my people to care for, I might have been lost completely."

"But you said men of power could not be trusted."

"My husband had no power, no title." Nym polished off her glass of wine and set it on the armrest of her chair. She squared up top her granddaughter. "He was never a threat to me."

"Do you ever wonder what would have happened, if you chose the other man?" Salome's eyes dropped to the floor. "Do you wonder if you made the wrong choice?"

"Why waste time thinking that way?" Nym tsked and rose to her feet. "I followed my instincts. I followed my heart. And I have lived a good life."

"No regrets?"

"Just one." Nym patted Salome's face. "Have you considered my offer?"

Salome rested her hand over her grandmother's. "I would love nothing more than to stay here with you."

Nym's eyes were filled with sadness, "But?"

Salome couldn't say once she killed her sister she would return, so she said, "I will come back to you when I can." A promise she hoped to keep.

Nym placed her forehead against Salome's and whispered, "You will always have a home here, Granddaughter."

Salome wrapped her arms around Nym, and tears streamed down her cheeks. She didn't know what the future held for her. She didn't know what this war would look like, if she would be victorious, or if she would lose everything, including her own life. But to know that she had a place she could call home, meant more than anything to her.

Nym pulled back and looked into Salome's teary eyes. "I'm sorry I wasn't able to provide a home for you before."

"As deep as the sea," Salome whispered the Myridian motto her mother had taught her.

Nym smiled warmly, cupping Salome's face in her withering hands. "As deep as the sea."

Salome marched down the hallway leading back to her chambers. But instead of walking into her room, she burst into the quarters Harbona, Adonijah, and Cato shared.

Cato nearly jumped out of his skin when she stormed in, her eyes filled with fury. She slammed the Stormcrag against the wall, holding him firmly in place with her forearm, and pointed a finger in his face.

"What did you do?" she growled through gritted teeth.

Adonijah hopped to his feet and made his way toward her, but she held a hand up to stop his advance.

"Cato." Salome's nostrils flared. "What did you do?"

Cato's eyes shifted to Adonijah who shrugged. "I'm sorry, I had no idea they would get in trouble."

"I lied to the queen to cover for you," Salome snorted. "I better get some answers and quickly."

"I swore I wouldn't say anything," Cato cast another pleading look Adonijah's way.

"Don't look at him." Salome lightly smacked Cato's cheek. "Look at me. What is going on?"

Cato relented, "At the Festival of Forbidden Fruit, I met a girl. We talked all night long. Then I realized I had seen her before. She was one of your ladies-in-waiting."

"What are you saying?" Adonijah's eyebrow arched.

Cato took a deep breath. "She wasn't at her post because she was with me. In bed."

Salome's jaw dropped. Adonijah rubbed a hand to the back of his neck and Harbona chuckled, not invested enough to put his pipe down and join them inside from the balcony.

"Who is *she*?" Salome asked as calmly as she could.

"I've already told you too much," Cato whimpered, "She'll kill me."

Salome furrowed her brow. "Who are you more afraid of? Me or her?"

"I feel like this is a trick question," Cato squinted.

Adonijah's hand rested on Salome's lower back, and he whispered in her ear, "I think I can help."

Salome side-eyed him but nodded in approval. She eased her grip on Cato's clothes. His eyes shot back and forth between Adonijah and Salome.

"I hate to tell you this, Cato," Adonijah thumbed at his stubbled jaw, "but I kissed Seraphina at the Festival of the Fallen -"

"That's not possible, she was with..." Cato slapped a hand over his mouth.

"The man-hating twin?" Salome laughed, releasing her hold on Cato. "My money would have been on Rosalina."

"I suppose Seraphina isn't as cold as I thought." Adonijah crossed his arms over his chest.

Cato rubbed small circles around his temple. "She's going to kill me," he mumbled.

"She will do nothing of the sort." Salome patted him on the back. "She owes me big time for saving her ass. That doesn't explain why Rosalina wasn't at her post though."

Cato grimaced. "We might have told Rosalina you wanted her to get you some tea before bed, so we could be alone."

Salome wasn't sure if she found this entire situation amusing or irritating. Dealing with Cato felt exactly like how she dealt with Crispin, and it left a soft spot in her heart for the Stormcrag.

"Are you upset with me?" Cato asked, not wanting to meet Salome's gaze.

Salome pushed a fist against his shoulder and laughed. "I was never angry. I just wanted you to think I was, so you'd tell me the truth."

"If that was you pretending to be angry," Cato huffed, wiping invisible dirt off his clothes, "I don't want to see the real thing."

Chapter Thirty-Three

Zophar

Three days after Sheik Ibrahim's men rescued them, Zophar and the Numbio began the rest of their journey north to Oakenshire, with food, water, and what remained of their horses to carry the supplies. They decided to heed Ibrahim's warning and avoided the main roads and headed east toward the Bone Mountains.

Rayma's uncharacteristic silence didn't go unnoticed by Zophar as he tugged Freya and Midnight along the narrow path. He had seen and dealt with this before. When Zophar, Crispin, and Salome escaped Northwind, Salome barely spoke for three months. He wasn't sure how to help her grieve – all he could do was let her know when she was ready to talk, he would be there.

Zophar slowed his pace until he was walking next to Rayma. He whispered, "Is something bothering you, Healer?"

"Leave me alone," she didn't look at him.

The bite in Rayma's voice didn't discourage or intimidate him. If he survived the teenage years with Salome, he could survive anything.

"Whenever you do want someone to talk to, I'll be there to listen." Zophar pressed onward, ignoring Rayma crossing her arms over her chest, and met up with Heru leading their company. Heru, too, seemed to be in a foul mood and if Zophar was a betting man, he'd wager it had something to do with the stubborn healer.

"No sign of the Thrak or the Krazaks." Heru stared at the tree filled Bone Mountains they were approaching.

"You don't sound pleased," Zophar said.

Heru shook his head, running a hand over the nape of his neck. "Forgive me, Zophar. I've had a lot on my mind lately."

"Any of those thoughts about our healer?"

If Heru was offended by Zophar's bold question he didn't show it. The prince shrugged, keeping his eyes on the horizon. "I thought one day she would be my wife – my queen, but... I was a fool to think so. To want her."

"The lady does not return your affections?" Zophar asked, stomping down the narrow, gravelly path.

"The *lady* had other intentions." Heru let loose a wounded breath. "She was sent to kill me."

"She's an assassin?" Zophar found that hard to believe, but Rayma gutting Bantu with Pyke's crystal dagger flashed in his mind. "You know she was sent to kill you and you let her live?"

"She confessed her master's plan. I already sent word to my father about Lord Memucan's treason." Heru pushed a branch out of his way. "We need a healer, and she is the best in Numbio. I told her once the war is over, she will not be allowed home."

"I'm sorry," Zophar scratched his beard. "Perhaps, her unprovoked confession proves she does have genuine feelings for you. It would have been easy for her to have assassinated you by now."

"How can I trust her?" Heru's nostrils flared, and his eyes watered. "No matter what her reasons were, she plotted against the crown. She's lucky to still be breathing."

Zophar felt an urge to defend the healer. He didn't know what her reasons were, but he couldn't help but see similarities between Rayma and Salome. Perhaps, she was a cold-blooded assassin masquerading as a healer, but something deep inside of him wouldn't accept that.

Before Zophar could speak on the topic further, Heru stopped dead in his tracks when a loud bird-like whistle sounded ahead. It was their scout. A low whistle signaled Krazaks. A loud whistle meant they had spotted Thraks headed in their direction.

Heru swiftly waved his hand in a circular motion and flashed a sign, ordering his troops to prepare for battle. Without a second's hesitation, the Numbio warriors unsheathed their weapons, pulled their horses deep into the woods, and hid in the darkness of the trees, waiting for the company of Thrak to walk into their trap.

Zophar drew his axe from his belt and scanned the trees and saw where Rayma was hiding. The only reason he spied her was because the crystal dagger she clutched to her chest reflected the sun's light. If he saw it, it might alert the Thrak to their whereabouts. But it was too late to warn her. Heavy footsteps and low grunts tumbled down the path toward them.

Zophar counted thirty of them, more creature than human. He had seen the Thrak once before, a long time ago, and the image of their sharpened teeth, black eyes, and pointy ears never left his nightmares. He would have preferred to fight the Krazaks. At least the Mountain Men wouldn't resort to eating the flesh clean off their bones.

As long as the Numbio held their position and didn't draw the attention of the monstrous slaves of Gomorrah, there would be no bloodshed. Heru made sure his warriors understood before they left Jannat Sin, they wouldn't initiate any fighting. But if attacked, the Numbio would take no prisoners and leave no witnesses.

Because the Thrak had broad shoulders, they marched down the trail one by one, passing the Numbio, none the wiser. Zophar held his breath as the last of the Thrak appeared around the wooded bend. The biggest and most scarred looking of the bunch was at the rear and when he stopped, Zophar clutched the handle of his battle axe tightly. The Thrak sniffed the air like a wild and hungry animal hunting for his next meal. He stood there for a minute before taking another step toward the line of Thrak in front of hi m.

Zophar exhaled the breath he had been holding since they started stomping through but winced when he saw the last Thrak cover his face from the reflection of Rayma's dagger.

Damn. Zophar's gaze bounced from the brute to Rayma across the pathway. She must have realized what was happening and tried to hide her dagger underneath her, but it was too late. The Thrak growled and with that one sound the band of thirty monsters armed themselves for battle.

The Thrak turned toward the trees and fanned out to find whoever was lurking in the shadow of the pines. Heru slammed his sword rhythmically against the wooden shield the people in Jannat Sin had given them to replace the ones they had lost in the Caverns of the Undead. A call to arms, a call to battle. The Numbio echoed their prince's battle cry, thudding their weapons against their shields. A ritual to intimidate their enemy and for a brief moment, Zophar noticed the Thrak looked rattled. The Thrak were surrounded, and they didn't know who or how many there were that would come for their necks.

Heru shouted and the Numbio freed themselves from their hiding places, attacking the cannibals. The sound of clashing swords, angry grunts, and thudding bodies filled the normally quiet and empty path. The Thrak were wild in their attack, but the Numbio fought as a unit. They fought as one body that knew exactly what each and every limb was doing. It was structured, it was confident, and it was effective.

Zophar felt alive, like he could battle enemies all day long and not tire of it. He was born and bred for war and felt most comfortable on a battlefield facing monsters of all shapes and sizes. He sliced his way through the Thrak, not a scratch on him, but smeared with the blood of the fallen.

When the last Thrak was defeated, Heru let out a pained groan. Zophar turned around to see a large, fur-clad man standing behind Heru with a knife to his throat.

"Drop your weapons." A female Stormcrag warrior stepped up next to Heru, flipping a dagger around her hand absent-mindedly. "Or your leader gets his throat slit."

"We mean you no harm," Zophar slowly bent to lay his axe on the gravelly ground. "You're Stormcrag, right? We are your friends."

The woman wiped strands of purple hair out of her face and hissed, "Stormcrags don't have the luxury of friends."

"Please," Rayma stepped forward, tears in her eyes as her gaze bounced from the woman to Heru. "Please, we will lower our weapons. Don't hurt him."

A sinister grin flashed across the female Stormcrag's face as she waved a hand in the air, making a spectacle of showing the Numbio they were now surrounded. There were archers with nocked arrows pointed down at them from the tops of the pine trees.

"As long as you don't do anything stupid," the woman scratched at her chest covered in tattoos, "no one needs to get hurt."

"Oifa." The enormous man holding a knife against Heru's throat drew her attention. "They're Southerners. Torrin will want to see them."

Oifa rolled her eyes and clenched her teeth. "Then we take them to the Tears of the Gods." She sheathed her dagger and turned on her heel, starting back up the path. "And no funny business, or I'll let my archers use you for target practice."

All Zophar could hope for as the Stormcrags blindfolded them was that the Mountain Men wouldn't lead them up the mountain to just push them over the side.

— • —

Chapter Thirty-Four

Nym

Nym shut the doors to her chambers quickly before anyone passing through the halls could see her come undone. She felt like her throat was closing in on itself. She rushed for the decanter of wine and poured herself a glass, washing it down, coating her dry mouth. Setting the empty glass down on the table, her hand flew up to her chest. Her heart was beating rapidly, and beads of sweat bubbled near her hairline.

Breathe. Just breathe.

These attacks started after Niabi was taken from her. It was worse than losing a granddaughter. She felt like she had failed her. She *had* failed her. And now, she was failing to convince Salome to reconsider launching an attack on her sister. By the time she discovered Niabi's plot to kill her father and usurp the throne, it was too late to save Bilhah and the rest of her grandchildren. Niabi had been willing to send Bilhah's body back to the Isles for a proper Myridian burial, but she refused to meet with her grandmother face to face. The day Niabi sailed from Myridian shores was the last time they had seen one another. If Nym could go back to that day, she would have fought to keep Niabi, even if it meant war with the North.

It was her one regret.

Her ears perked up when she thought she heard someone else in the room. Their rapid breathing gave them away.

"Does your unexpected visit mean my time has come, Marina?" Nym already knew who was watching her from the shadows of her bedroom.

Marina slowly stepped into the light. "How did you know it was me?"

"You and Niabi were inseparable." Nym filled her glass with another serving of wine, sat in her favorite velvet chair, and extended her arm, bidding her granddaughter to sit across from her. "The question was never *if* you would do her bidding but *when*. Tell me, how do you intend to kill me?"

Marina refused to look her grandmother in the eye. "She wants your heart," she whispered.

"I did not ask what she wanted, child," Nym sipped her drink. "I asked how you planned to murder me."

Marina sheepishly pulled a small vile from her cloak. "It will not cause you any pain. I promise."

"Is that supposed to bring me comfort?" Nym was clearly unimpressed. She set the glass down and turned to her vanity. She pulled the pins keeping her hair in place, picked up her comb and began to brush through her tresses.

"I...I..."

"I. I." Nym tsked as she stuttered. "If you intend to kill me, Marina, you might as well have the audacity to speak your peace."

"I did not want you to suffer, Grandmother."

"Poison is a coward's weapon, so it suits you."

Marina slammed her fist on the side table. "I am not a coward!"

"Slamming your fist like that only proves how childish and naïve you are, Marina." Nym finished brushing her hair and began to braid it. "If you intend to take my life, then do so as a warrior. But if you cannot do that, be gone from my sight."

"If I disobey her, my life will be forfeit." Marina fought back tears that welled in her eyes.

"Do you expect my pity?"

"I am not the only Myridian in her service." Marina cleared her throat. "If not by my hand, then it will be by someone else's, and they will not be as merciful."

Over Nym's lifetime, there had been many attempts to take her life. Each assassin's eyes were filled with hatred and contempt, but she did not see that in Marina's eyes. She saw true remorse. She saw fear.

Marina was right about one thing. If not tonight, Niabi would send another and another and another until Nym was dead. Better peacefully than mercilessly.

Her thoughts shot to Salome. She would miss the feisty Mainlander. But knowing Salome, she would add Nym to the list of names she would avenge.

Nym extended her hand, "Be quick about it."

Marina shakily handed her the vile. Nym poured it in with what remained of her wine.

"Tell Niabi I am sorry for sending her back to her father. She is a Myridian, and I failed her." Nym lifted the glass to her lips and downed the liquid before she could change her mind. "And Marina."

"Yes, Grandmother?" Tears streamed down Marina's cheeks.

"As deep as the sea." Nym recited the Myridian motto.

"As deep as the sea." Marina echoed it, wiping her nose with her sleeve. She held her grandmother's hand tightly in hers. "Grandmother?"

Nym closed her eyes. She was finally free of her guilt.

CHAPTER THIRTY-FIVE

NIABI

With or without Vilora present, Niabi practiced using her fire magic daily. In a short amount of time, she noticed the blackness inching up her arm had stopped spreading. She also noticed her fire wielding skills were improving quickly – as if the power had been dormant underneath her skin for years, hoping, waiting for the day it could awaken.

Playing with small dancing flames in her palm gradually turned into juggling balls of fire which evolved into shooting spurts of fire from her fingers like flying daggers. She incorporated fire into her sword and knife training and relished the fact she now had a new earth-shattering ability her enemies didn't know anything about.

As her belly swelled with new life, her newfound power blossomed into a dark peacefulness that enveloped her soul. The confidence of knowing she once again held the element of surprise. The news of her pregnancy was no longer a secret but this – her fire, her magic – was hers.

"Good," Vilora's voice sliced through the queen's tranquility. A slow clap followed the witch's crooked grin. "You have mastered the flame quicker than I expected."

Niabi detected a hint of jealousy from her aunt's dry lips but chose to ignore it. She stood up straight from her deep lunge, satisfied with the burnt wood and trail of ashes which littered her private training courtyard.

"I was always a fast learner," Niabi flashed the old woman a smile.

Being a fast learner was a truth her father hated. No matter what the task, Niabi always mastered it faster than her brother, Lykos. Her father's son and new heir couldn't measure up to her and it infuriated Issachar. After years of hoping and failing to earn his approval, Niabi knew her father would never be proud of her accomplishments. But what Issachar didn't know about were the late-night sessions and hours Niabi spent teaching Lykos in private.

"I'll never be as good as you," Lykos said during one of their late-night tutoring sessions.

"You're right," Niabi poked him in the ribs with her quill. "You'll never be as good as me. You'll have to be better."

"Why do you care?" He crinkled his nose, slamming the Tome of Northern Military Tactics closed and folding his gangly arms over his chest.

Niabi flipped the book back open and pointed at the page they were studying. "One day you'll be king -"

"It should be you."

Niabi grabbed her younger brother's hand and smiled at him. "It won't ever be me."

"You seem troubled, my Queen," Vilora said, drawing Niabi back to the present.

Niabi shook her head, motioning her Iron Guard, Anaktu, forward. He extended her floor-length coat and draped it over her shoulders. "Not troubled at all. Are you ready?"

Vilora nodded and joined Niabi at her side, with Anaktu following a step behind. As they marched inside the White Keep and turned the corner to follow the length of the hall to Niabi's chambers, the guards posted outside her room bowed and opened the double doors as the two women and the Nephilim swept inside. Tala was already waiting for them with Ziggy seated in a chair, wringing her hands together.

Niabi shrugged her heavy fur coat off, tossed it on a nearby chaise lounge, and sat in the chair opposite the redheaded escort. "Do you have anything useful for me today, Ziggy of Borg?"

Ziggy brushed red curls from her pale, freckled face. "I've been seeing more of Lord Gershom these last few weeks -"

"Do you have information for me or not?" Niabi cut her off with an irritated groan. Ziggy hesitated and Niabi narrowed her eyes. "Remember what I told you in the dungeons, girl. If I find you are keeping secrets, I will let my Shadows keep you as a pet."

Ziggy seemed to snap out of whatever fog she was in and shook her head. "Lord Gershom had an unexpected visitor one evening. I don't know anything about him. I didn't even see him. They talked and then I was told to leave."

"And what was so special about this visitor?" Tala clasped his hands behind his back, circling around from behind Ziggy to Niabi's side. "There must be some reason you found this to be important enough to tell Her Majesty."

Her blue eyes shifted from the Andrago back to the queen. "The man said he was from Numbio. That he had to escape before his king could execute him for treason."

Niabi and Tala exchanged a satisfied grin. "You're sure the man was from Numbio?" Niabi asked.

Ziggy bobbed her head quickly, sweat beading at her hairline. "Yes, my Queen. That is all I know."

"Keep your eyes and ears open," Niabi waved her hand, dismissing the redhead. "Let us know if you hear anything else about this man from Numbio."

Ziggy curtsied before being ushered out of the room and sent on her way.

"You think the man from Numbio is Lord Memucan?" Tala asked the moment the doors closed.

Niabi reclined in her chair, picking at her fingernails with one of her twin daggers. "I would bet my crown it's him. And he's in Northwind. If we can find out where he is, we could get the damning proof of Gershom's treason."

"I can dispatch plain clothed soldiers to scout around the city for him," Tala offered but Niabi shook her head.

"Have one of the new recruits, one Gershom hasn't seen before, stand guard at his chambers." Niabi flashed a deliciously wicked smile. "If Memucan shows his face, we will know about it."

Tala brought his hand to his chest. "It will be done, my Queen."

A knock on the door echoed through the room and had everyone's attention.

"Were we expecting someone else to give a report today?" Niabi asked flippantly, looking bored with the prospect of more royal business.

With a hand on the hilt of his sword, Tala crossed to the door and let a Shadow in tattered black robes inside. Niabi stood slowly, anger raging in her eyes at his disheveled appearance. She knew all of her Shadows and this elite warrior went by the name of Thrice. The other Shadows had given him the nickname when he supposedly sliced three rebels in half with one swoop of his sword. By just looking at him, Niabi knew the expedition to capture the Enchantress of the Swamp had failed. How badly it failed was what she now wanted to know.

"Thrice," Niabi gritted her teeth. "What happened?"

"We found the Enchantress but..." Thrice's throat was dry, as if he hadn't had a drop of water in days. Niabi poured him a cup of water from the glass decanter that replaced her wine and handed it to him. Once he had downed the liquid, he cleared his throat and started over. "We found the Enchantress, but she wasn't alone. She used her magic to summon tree roots that dragged the Shadows into the earth and swallowed them whole.

We set the swamp on fire and shot her with an arrow when another magic wielder appeared and extinguished the flames with water."

"Water magic?" Vilora gasped and Niabi didn't know if she was surprised or angered by another magic wielder.

"The other Shadows?" Niabi asked, eyes fixed on Thrice's muddy brown ones. "Did any of them make it?"

Thrice cradled his cracked mask and shook his head. "I'm the only one left."

That was what Niabi didn't want to hear. She had sent some of her best Shadows to capture Odelia and the Enchantress still managed to decimate them. And what was worse, the Enchantress wasn't alone. Whoever the water wielder was, Niabi would now have to deal with them, too.

The queen rested her hand on Thrice's shoulder. "Clean up, eat, and get some rest. We'll talk more tomorrow." Thrice bowed, crossed an arm over his chest in salute, turned on his heel, and left the queen's chambers.

Niabi felt the rage burning from the soles of her feet all the way up to her chest. Her breathing deepened and a lump rose to her throat at the thought of losing men she sparred and trained with. An easy mission. It was supposed to be an easy mission. But the Enchantress was prepared. She brought another magic wielder in to help her.

"Did you know about this water wielder?" Niabi's eyes flashed to meet Vilora's bewildered gaze.

The witch shook her head, plopping down on the chaise lounge where Niabi had thrown her fur cloak. "You think a fire wielder such as me would forget about a water wielder?" Vilora's tone had a bite to it and Niabi was inclined to remind her who she was speaking to but then her aunt said, "If there is a water wielder, we will have to kill them before they can become a real threat."

Tala tilted his head in confusion. "How can a water wielder pose more of a threat than the Enchantress of the Swamp?"

"What extinguishes fire?" Vilora kicked her sandals off her feet and lifted her dirty toes to rest on top of the white linen chaise. "Water. Water can render flame useless."

Niabi flicked her wrist and held a dancing flame in the palm of her left hand. She let the fire wiggle around her fingers before aiming her fingers at the unlit fireplace and sparking it to life.

"What else are you capable of doing?" Tala asked, lifting his head to look at her. "Obviously you can start a fire," he motioned to the crackling fireplace, "but are you powerful enough…"

"To burn cities to the ground?" Vilora finished the question he was too fearful to ask. She grinned. "If she wants to burn a city to the ground, she can."

Niabi shot her aunt a vicious look. "I have no intention of burning any city to the ground. But if my brother and sister think they know everything they need to defeat me, they will be surprised to learn I've got a few more tricks up my sleeve." She rolled her fingers one by one with a tight-lipped smile.

Tala stood; determination etched in his bronze face. "Tomorrow, we will begin the search for Memucan and the water wielder. Neither will pose you any threat as long as I still live and breathe."

Niabi reclined in her chair and rested her hand on her belly. She knew if Tala made a promise, he would keep it. As long as he was hunting her enemies down, they wouldn't step one foot inside the White Keep. And if by some miracle, they made it to her doorstep, then they would be hers for the taking, and she loved playing with her food before devouring it.

"Then we have nothing to worry about," Niabi smiled.

Chapter Thirty-Six

Salome

Sweat bubbled around Salome's forehead and her sheets were soaked in sweat. She tried desperately to wake up from the nightmares but couldn't. Gripping the blankets and gritting her teeth, she was forced to watch the memory play out.

She saw her brother, Lykos, standing on one of the White Keep's many balconies overlooking the Ignacia Sea. His hands were wrapped around an Immortal woman. Her platinum blonde hair, grey eyes, pointy ears, and white robe, reminded her of Harbona, except she had the Immortal glow.

"Harbona had a vision," Lykos stroked his fingers through the woman's straight, hip long hair. "Niabi is coming."

She scoffed, crinkling her nose. "You trust the word of an exiled Seer? There is a reason the Eldaar banished him."

"Harbona has loyally served the North for generations." Lykos tilted her chin up. "Why would I not believe him?"

"If Northwind is attacked," she sucked in a breath, "I will not leave without you."

"I have a duty to protect my people."

"You really expect me to leave you here?" She grabbed his hands and shook her head. "I am your wife, Lykos."

"And as your husband," Lykos rested his hand on her swollen belly. "I want you and our little one to be safe."

"And if your sister doesn't come?"

"Then you will return to me." He kissed her lips gently.

"By then there will be no questioning my condition," she rubbed her hands in a circular motion around her belly. "Your father will -"

Lykos cupped her face in his calloused hands. "You will be my queen and our child will be my heir. If my father disowns me, so be it. I made my choice the moment I saw you dock in our harbor years ago."

There were tears in her grey eyes. "Are you sure you will not come with me?" She held his hand tightly.

"I am needed here." Lykos cleared his throat, fighting back tears of his own. "I wouldn't be much of a king if I ran at the first sign of trouble."

"I will miss you."

"I will see you again, I promise." He brought her hands to his lips and kissed them.

"If he is a boy," she placed his hand on her belly, "I want to name him Dunlor after your grandfather. He was a great friend to my people."

"And if we have a girl?" His eyes danced in hopeful delight.

"I have not thought of a name yet."

"I like Keeva."

She crinkled her nose in disgust, "Where did you hear that name?"

Lykos grinned sheepishly, "I saw our daughter in a dream and that was her name."

"Let us hope he is a boy," she teased. She wrapped her arms around Lykos and rested her face against his chest. "You are frightened."

"I would be a fool if I wasn't."

"You still wear it," she slipped her hand in his shirt and brought a gold medallion necklace out.

"Of course." Lykos took it off and placed it in her hand. "Give this to our child if I -"

"Do not say it," she covered his lips. "Please. I could not bear to hear those words." A tear slipped down her cheek.

He forced her fingers to enclose the necklace she had given him on their wedding day. "Then take it for safekeeping. I would hate to lose it."

"Come back to me," she wrapped her arms around his neck, fighting back tears. "Promise, you will come back to me."

"I promise."

Salome heard someone scream Harbona's name. She smelled the fire that burned through her city the night they fled. Darkness enveloped her. She couldn't breathe from the ash and soot filling her lungs.

Her mind shot to a city with a palace made entirely of gold. Immortals in golden armor with white feathered wings flying above a glittering city. Lykos' wife's grey eyes flashed before her and held her gaze, refusing to release her.

"Lykos!" Salome screamed. Her eyes shot open to find Harbona sitting on her bed, holding her by the shoulders. She shivered, cold from the sweat dripping down her back. "Harbona?"

"What did you see?" Harbona narrowed his eyes, his hands still gripping her shoulders.

Salome's tears flowed down her cheeks. "I saw my brother with an Immortal woman."

"Is that all?"

She shook her head. "I saw a golden palace and Immortals with golden armor and white feathered wings. There was a battle. I saw ships and explosions," Salome blinked rapidly, wiping away wet hair sticking to her forehead. "Harbona, I heard someone calling for y ou."

"What else did you see?"

"The Immortal woman. My brother called her his wife." Salome watched him for a reaction, but he remained neutral. "Harbona, there's a child." Harbona's eyes widened. "You didn't know?" Harbona slowly shook his head, lips in a tight line. "What does it mean?" Salome asked.

"You have seen the past." Harbona relaxed his grip on her and rubbed his face. It was still early in the morning, the sun had yet to rise above the horizon. And if Harbona was in her room trying to wake her from the nightmare, she must have woken others. "You have also seen something that has been hidden from my sight."

"How is that possible?"

"A shield."

"You mean magic?" Salome brought her knees to her chest.

Harbona nodded. "This was not an ordinary vision, Salome. This was a message. Lykos wants me to go to her."

"Who is she?"

"Lavena." Harbona smiled but it was followed with what Salome could only identify as dread. "I will have to go."

"Go?" Salome sat up straighter. "Go where?"

"Caelestis."

Salome's mouth dropped. "I thought you were banished."

Harbona reached his hand out. "There is something I need to show you."

Salome looked at his hand wearily. The last time she grabbed his hand, she was rocketed through his past and it left her exhausted and in pain.

As if he could read her thoughts, he said, "Please."

Salome took a deep breath before resting her hand in his palm. She felt her mind sprinting to whatever memory Harbona wanted her to see. She closed her eyes to keep from becoming nauseous but that only made it worse. When she felt the motion stop, she opened her eyes. She was standing in a brightly lit throne room; everything from the floors to the two thrones were made of gold.

"How do you plead, Harbona?"

Salome looked up and saw a man and woman sitting stoically in their golden thrones on a dais ten feet in front of her. They had Harbona's features, but their cold grey eyes made her shiver.

"How do you plead, Harbona?" They asked again in unison. Their voices echoing through the extravagant throne room.

"If by aiding the mortals in an attempt to overthrow their enemy I am considered guilty," she heard Harbona's voice but didn't see him. She realized she was seeing his past through his eyes and his perspective like the previous time she touched him. *"Then I am guilty."*

"Then you leave us no choice, Harbona." The couple said again simultaneously. As if one did not exist without the other. "For attempting to assassinate the brother of the King of Adalore, we find you guilty, and hereby banish you from Caelestis."

Harbona's body convulsed, and he screamed in excruciating pain. His hand flew up to his right eye and covered it.

"You are no longer one of us," the couple continued. "You are no longer allowed to live amongst our kind. You are no longer allowed to have the Glow of Immortality. You are no longer heir to the Eldaar. You are alone."

Harbona's pain ceased, and he slowly stood, facing the Eldaar again.

"We hope your actions were worth your damnation."

Harbona nodded his head. "When faced with a decision to do what is right or do nothing, I will always do what is right. Even if that means I must stand alone."

"You are no son of ours." The man waved a pale hand in the air. "You are no son of the Eldaar."

"Maybe one day you will see, I did what you should have done."

"Should you return to our shores," the woman's grey eyes darted to Harbona's, "your life may be forfeit."

"Then it is forfeit." Harbona bowed and the vision faded.

When Salome blinked, she was no longer in Caelestis, she was in her room with Harbona. "You gave up everything." Salome had so many questions but the first one that flew out of her mouth was, "You are the heir of Caelestis?"

Harbona breathed in deeply. "Was."

"You can't go back there." Salome shook her head in protest. "Your own parents banished you."

"They followed the law of our ancestors." Harbona didn't seem bothered. "In my youth, I was what you would describe as overzealous."

"What was your crime?"

"I had a vision that Phlias would kill his brother, Greygor, for the crown. I told my parents, but they said it was not our place to interfere with the lives of mortals." Harbona sighed, rubbing a hand behind his neck. "I disagreed. I took a small company with me and attempted to assassinate Phlias as he slept. But I failed. And Greygor deemed an Immortal trying to kill his brother as an act of war."

"But Phlias did kill Greygor."

Harbona nodded solemnly. "My parents struck a deal with Greygor for my return. After my banishment, Phlias killed his brother, took the crown, and oppressed Adalorians for seven years. I wandered Adalore during those years until the Almighty gave me a vision of Malachi. The one who would save us from Phlias' tyranny."

"What aren't you telling me?" Salome cocked her head to the side.

"I knew one day I would return to Caelestis to face the Eldaar again." Harbona reached for Salome's hands but stopped short, realizing it could trigger her powers. "Lykos is the only one who could have sent you that vision. There's a reason and I am the only one who can find out what it is."

"Harbona -"

"Listen to me carefully." Harbona interrupted her and whispered his instructions. "Prince Jinn will be leaving for the Mainland, and you, Adonijah, and Cato must be on that ship. The Thrak will be keeping a watchful eye on the ships docking in Port Daelon, so you must not return there. Do not go to Sakurai either. You must have the ship dock where the Bone Mountains and the sea meet. Travel on foot through the mountains, Cato will be your guide. Get to Oakenshire. There, we will meet our allies."

"You will meet us in Oakenshire?"

"The Almighty willing, I will." He was telling her what she wanted to hear.

"The truth." She narrowed her eyes.

"If the Eldaar does not have my head for stepping foot on Immortal ground," Harbona rasped, "I will be in Oakenshire."

"Please don't go."

"I must. If Lykos does have an heir, we need to know."

"You don't think they would want to claim Northwind, do you?"

"I do not know. We have many questions that need answers." Harbona stood. "Make sure to follow my instructions."

Salome jumped out of her bed and fought the urge to wrap her arms around him and hug him. He stood stoically; hands clasped behind his back.

"What if this is the last time we ever see one another?" Tears welled in Salome's eyes; a lump forming in her throat.

Harbona tilted his head and returned her sad smile, "Then it has been my honor serving you and your family."

A thunderous knock echoed through her chambers before the doors flew open. Adonijah stepped inside, and by the look on his face, Salome knew something terrible had happened.

"What is it?" her voice cracked.

Adonijah's fingers twitched at his sides. "It's the queen."

Salome's heart shattered before he could tell her what happened to her grandmother. "Did she suffer?"

Adonijah's eyes were filled with sorrow. "They caught Marina trying to stowaway on a ship headed for Port Daelon. She admitted to poisoning your grandmother."

Salome stepped toward him, wrapping her arms around herself. "What aren't you telling me?"

"Marina carved out the queen's heart." Adonijah winced when he saw Salome's eyes widen in horror. "She said it was your sister's order."

"Where's Mika?" Salome's nostrils flared and she strutted to the dresser where her fighting leathers were laid out and threw them on over her clothes.

"In the Inner Depths with your aunts." Adonijah stepped to the side of the door to allow Salome a clear path.

Salome holstered her weapons, then whipped around to look at Harbona once more, knowing he wasn't going to stick around for her grandmother's funeral or a potential trial. "I will see you in Oakenshire."

Harbona rested his palm over his heart. "Princess."

Salome's gaze met Adonijah's, and she knew he had as many questions as she did, but she motioned for him to follow her.

When they had rounded the corner Adonijah asked, "Where is he going?"

"Caelestis."

"But -"

"I know." She cut him off, knowing if she dwelled on Harbona's fate, she would melt into a puddle of tears. "He gave us instructions to sail back to the Mainland. We are to travel through the Bone Mountains to get to Oakenshire."

"With Cato as our guide?" He kept his voice low so no one would overhear them.

Salome nodded. She noticed Adonijah had a slight limp from the arrow wound to his thigh, but she didn't mention it. He wouldn't like her gushing over his injuries.

"Will your Aunt Zara grant us passage?"

Salome grimaced. She knew Adonijah was not going to like the next part. "Harbona told us we need to ask Jinn for safe passage."

If Adonijah was angry, he didn't show it. He kept a neutral face and nodded in obedience. "Alright."

Salome stopped and after he took a few more steps, he realized she wasn't by his side, and he turned around to look at her.

"Is something wrong?" Adonijah tilted his head to the side.

"Alright?" Salome rested her hands on her hips. "You don't have anything else to say about us traveling with Jinn?"

"If Harbona said that's what we need to do, then we do it."

Salome looked around as if Adonijah was invisible. "I'm sorry, do you know where I can find Adonijah? Clearly, he's missing."

Adonijah took a step toward her and clenched his fists before composing himself. "Do I like Jinn? No. Do I trust him? No. Do I trust Harbona? Aye. So, if Harbona says that's what we need to do, then we do it."

"So, it does bother you?"

"How can I not be bothered when he looks at you the way he does?" Adonijah narrowed his eyes, but every bit of anger and irritation vanished when he met her gaze. He lifted his hand and stroked his fingers down her cheek. "This isn't about what I like," he said softly. "This is about keeping you safe. I could have lost you to the Thrak last night. And now your grandmother..." He pulled her into his chest and wrapped his arms around her. He kissed the top of her head and whispered, "No matter what happens. I will fight, live, and die by your side."

They were the same words she had sworn to him when they stood shoulder to shoulder against the Thrak. She had never made such a pledge to anyone before and she knew now, how much it meant to him.

Salome kissed his neck and allowed herself a moment to cry in the safety of his arms. Tears she knew she didn't have time for. Nym would not want her crying over her death. She would want Salome to rise like a queen. And she would. Once she let herself be vulnerable in Adonijah's arms for another minute or two.

When she pulled back from his chest, he thumbed the tears from her face. "Are you alright?"

Salome shook her head, sucking in a breath. "No, but I will be. I have to be."

She quickly wiped away any remaining tears from her cheeks, when she heard footsteps approaching from an adjoining hallway. Jinn and Kai walked around the corner and stopped.

Jinn's eyes bounced from Adonijah to Salome. He opened his mouth to say something, but she stopped him.

"We need to talk," she planted her thoughts in his head. *"Meet me in the Great Hall after sunset."*

"Will your bodyguard be with you?"

"No. But keep staring at me like that and I won't be able to keep him away."

Jinn bowed his head toward them and he and Kai kept walking down their hallway. *"I heard about the queen. I'm sorry."*

Salome wasn't sure how to respond, so she just said, *"Don't be late."*

She looked up at Adonijah who was frowning at them.

"You won't be allowed inside the Inner Depths." She continued down the corridor in the opposite direction of Jinn and Kai.

"I'll wait for you outside then."

"Just give Jinn a chance," Salome squeezed his forearm. "You gave Cato a chance and you two are ..."

"Careful now." He narrowed his eyes.

"Friends," she finished and smiled.

"Cato doesn't look at you like he's..." He snapped his mouth shut.

"Like he's what?" Salome challenged, as they arrived at the double bronze doors leading to the Inner Depths. She folded her arms across her chest, waiting for an answer.

Adonijah rolled his shoulders back and said, "Like he's wondering what's beneath your fighting leathers."

"I can think of someone else who looks at me that way."

Adonijah's eyes darkened, and his chest rose rapidly. "You should get in there."

Salome nodded, but as she turned toward the door, he grabbed her arm and spun her around. Her hands landed on his chest, and he kissed her.

"What was that for?" She smiled.

He pulled back and whispered, "I couldn't wait to kiss you again."

Salome squeezed his hands. "I'll see you soon."

Zara sat on the throne with a silver crown of pearls woven into her dark hair. It was the Queen's Crown.

Salome bowed upon entering the Inner Depths but before she could say a word, she heard the Five Virtues whispering to her.

"She has returned."

"We have been waiting for you."

"Do you think she knows yet?"

"Does she know her fate?"

"Who will she choose?"

Salome's eyes narrowed remembering Harbona and Damaris' advice of asking what the other side wanted from her. *"What do you want from me?"*

"She does not know."

"She does not want to know."

"She will choose me."

"Look at her, she is frightened."

"She is one of us, she will not fail."

"Rise, Cousin," Zara's melancholy voice sliced through Salome's exchange with the Five Virtues. Salome straightened, eyes darting from one Virtue statue to the next, but they had gone silent. "I take it you have heard."

Salome nodded, "What is to be done with Marina?"

"She is locked in the Tower Dungeon where she will remain until her trial." Mika wasn't in her red armor, she was in her red fighting leathers and by the dark circles underneath her eyes, it appeared she hadn't slept all night.

"There will be no trial," Zara said without looking at Mika.

Mika's and Damaris' mouths dropped, simultaneously.

"What?" Mika scoffed. "Anyone accused of a crime receives a trial."

"Marina confessed to her crimes. She is a murderer and a traitor." Zara pressed her back against the high back throne. "No trial will change her fate."

"Zara, that is not our way -"

"At dawn," Zara interrupted Damaris with a vicious glance, "Marina will face the executioner's blade."

"Mother, please reconsider."

"I don't have a choice, Mika!" Zara shouted, slamming her fist on the armrest of her chair. She closed her eyes and rubbed her forehead. "As soon as other kingdoms hear our mother, our queen, was assassinated in her room by her own flesh and blood..." Her voice cracked and she cleared her throat, fighting the tears in her bloodshot eyes. "I will not have them think we are weak or vulnerable. Marina confessed. Marina will die. That is my decision." Zara stood up, ending the discussion, and marched out of the room, Mika trailing her.

For once, Salome agreed with her aunt. Marina murdered Nym and carved out her heart on Niabi's orders. Marina could rot in the dungeons for the rest of her miserable days for all she cared.

Her attention returned to the Five Virtues. They were still silent. She reached out to them, but none answered.

Damaris clamped a hand on Salome's shoulder, startling her. "The Five Virtues. They've been speaking to you?"

Salome bobbed her head, eyes still bouncing from one statue to the next. "What do you think they want from me?"

Damaris tilted her head, "They are the guardians and protectors of the Red Maidens. Once a new one is named, they choose their Virtue."

"I'm not a Red Maiden, though." Salome turned her attention to the Oracle. "So, why are they talking to me?"

"Perhaps, one day, you might lead the Qata Vishna." Damaris shrugged. "Whatever their purpose, they mean you no harm."

"Which Virtue did Niabi choose?" Salome asked.

If Damaris was uncomfortable with the question or the mention of Niabi's name, she did not show it. She extended her arm to the statue on the right. "She chose Rebirth."

"The raven." Salome noted the bird perched on the Virtue's shoulder. "Makes sense."

"I suppose it does." Damaris agreed. "Mika chose Honor."

Salome glanced toward the bronze doors leading out of the Inner Depths. "Will Aunt Zara reconsider?"

Damaris sadly shook her head, eyes glued to the floor. "I'm afraid once Zara has made a decision, no one can sway her."

"What happened to Grandmother's..."

"Her heart?" Damaris' bottom lip quivered as she looped her arm through Salome's arm, guiding her out of the Inner Depths. "Before the Qata Vishna captured Marina, she stashed it somewhere, but refuses to tell us where it is. Marina was always a difficult child, but I never thought she was capable of murder."

Salome patted Damaris' forearm and stopped her before they reached the second set of bronze doors. "Harbona will be leaving today."

"Will you be going with him?"

"No," Salome shook her head. "But he has instructed me to leave in the next couple of days."

Damaris cupped her niece's face in her ringed fingers. "I hope you will return to our shores one day, when the time is right."

Salome smiled, but she didn't know if she would ever return. She had a feeling Death might be interested in meeting her sooner than anticipated.

Chapter Thirty-Seven

Niabi

Niabi never liked pirates. With King Uri and his filthy band of misfits standing before her throne with dirt riddled clothes and gold teeth, she liked them even less. Tala disarmed the seafarers before they entered into the queen's presence, their stash of weapons in a pile outside the enormous double doors.

Niabi sat on her White Throne, a glittering crown upon her raven locks fixed in an elaborate updo. Her emerald train stretched the length of the dais and rested upon the marble floor. With Anaktu and Tala on either side of her, and Vilora standing beside the Nephilim, she began the meeting.

Before she spoke, Uri stepped forward with a grin and lust filled eyes, "You're prettier than I imagined, Queen."

Niabi wrinkled her nose. "Perhaps your lack of courtly manners is due to being out at sea far too long."

Uri cackled, slapping a hand against his muscular thigh. "Oh, Your Highness has a sense of humor." He bared his teeth and Niabi wasn't quite sure if it was supposed to intimidate or entice her. It did neither.

"The Sovereign?" Niabi demanded. "Where is he?"

Uri stepped to the side and motioned for Neempo to be brought forward. His arms and feet were shackled, and the chains extended to an iron collar around his neck. He was in what appeared to be nightwear and still had his red wrap around his eyes.

"The Sovereign." Uri's chest puffed out in obvious pride. "Just as you asked, love."

"Show Her Majesty respect," Tala barked, his hand touching the hilt of his sword.

Uri gnashed his teeth and angrily met Tala's judgmental gaze. The Pirate King looked like he was going to say something vicious in return, but a shadowy hand slipped over his shoulder and the woman that slithered from behind him whispered something in his ear that caused him to relax. Niabi had not seen shadow magic before, though she had read about it in her recent study of magic wielders and their abilities. She learned that those with shadow magic had sold their souls to the Grim. Only an idiot would trust a shadow wielder.

"As you can see," Uri finally continued, "he is unspoiled as requested."

Niabi's attention fell on Neempo who stood quietly as he awaited his fate. For being in the company of these ruffians, he looked unharmed. She motioned for Tala to pay them for their services. Tala had two soldiers bring in a chest brimming with gold coins, and they set it in front of the grinning Pirate King.

"One million crowns, as agreed upon." Niabi meant it as a dismissal, but the Pirate King walked toward the dais and knelt on one knee at the foot of the steps leading to her throne. She stared at him with an arched eyebrow. "Is there something else you wish to say?"

Uri raised his head and met her gaze. "If you allow it, I offer our armada to you in the war against your siblings."

Niabi wanted to laugh, but she stifled it, keeping a neutral expression. "A generous offer, King Uri, but one I must decline. Northwind already has a mighty armada and will be ready for any potential attack, though I am certain one won't reach my shores."

"Then I request my crew be allowed to spend a week here in your fair city to rest before we set sail again."

Niabi preferred the pirates be on their way, but knowing their spending habits, and wanting to appease the Merchant and Night Districts, she acquiesced. "You and your crew are welcome to stay the week in Northwind."

Tala shifted his weight but remained silent as the Pirate King swept up to his full height and flashed a malicious grin that Niabi was sure he meant to look friendly.

"A thousand thanks, Majesty," he bowed his head before two of his men grabbed the chest. "Maybe our paths will cross again."

Niabi forced a tight-lip smile and nodded, relieved to see the misfits filing out of her throne room. The woman dressed in shadow whispered something in Neempo's ear before leaving.

"Unshackle him and leave us," Niabi stood and motioned for the guards and the members of her small council to leave her alone with the Sovereign. No one argued with her. A blind man shouldn't pose any danger.

Neempo rubbed his wrists and neck once the iron chains and collar were removed. His skin was raw and blistering red. He didn't move and didn't speak. He seemed resigned to his fate.

Niabi stood in front of him and asked, "Did they mistreat you?"

Neempo smiled warmly and shook his head. "No, they didn't mistreat me. Thank you for your concern."

"It is not my concern for you that makes me wonder of your treatment, Sovereign." Niabi clasped her hands behind her back. "I was curious to know if my orders had been obeyed."

The Sovereign didn't reply, but his smile remained.

"You must know why you're here." Niabi circled him, inspecting him head to toe.

"I suspect you desire my heart to try to resurrect your son," Neempo didn't flinch when she brushed her fingers on the nape of his neck. "But if I may offer you some advice, Your Highness, the Resurrection Spell..."

Niabi leaned close to his ear, her chest resting against his back, and whispered, "Has only worked once. I have heard that before."

"But have you also heard that the person who was resurrected was not the person their loved ones remembered?"

His question surprised her. "What do you mean?" She circled around to stand in front of him, arms folded over her chest.

"Over six hundred years ago, a witch named Hester, grieving the death of the man she loved, ripped out Sovereign Bocatan's heart. Hester drained all her power to bring him back to life using the Heart of the Righteous and it worked. But when he opened his eyes, they weren't the warm golden eyes she loved. They were tinted red and soulless. Gone was the man she had given her heart to, replaced by a monster who didn't remember who she w as."

Neempo stopped so abruptly, it rattled her. "What happened to him?"

Even with the red wrap covering his eyes, she could feel the grief they held. "He tried to strangle her, blaming her for his death in the first place. So, Hester did what she never thought she was capable of. She picked up the dagger he had given to her to protect herself and slit his throat."

Niabi shook her head and took a step back, refusing to allow one single tear to stream down her face. "How can I believe you? You could be saying this to trick me into sparing your life."

"You know in your heart I am telling you the truth, Your Majesty." Neempo spoke softly, as if he were speaking to a frightened child. "You are new to this world of magic and spells. I know your heart is in the right place when you wish to revive your son, but if you and the Old Witch of Endor succeed in resurrecting Prince Rollo, it won't be the son you lost. It will be a monster that will destroy you."

Images of Rollo flashed in her mind. Rollo taking his first steps. Rollo picking up a weapon for the first time. Rollo smiling, dancing, and riding through the city. She had failed him. She hadn't protected him.

"Enough!" she yelled. Her left hand was engulfed in flames.

"She hasn't taught you to control your fire magic, has she?" He asked, referring to Vilora. Niabi didn't respond. "If you don't control it, it will control you. I can help you if you'll let me."

Niabi gritted her teeth and willed the fire to extinguish. She called for the guards standing outside the doors and instructed them to take Neempo to his cell.

"I will prove you wrong, Sovereign," Niabi hissed as he was led away. "I will bring my son back."

"I hope for your sake, Your Highness, that you're strong enough to face the consequences."

When the doors closed behind them, Niabi let loose every bit of rage that was bubbling beneath her skin. She let loose a high-pitched scream and fire shot out of her hand, blasting against the wall, and leaving a burn mark.

As much as she hated to admit it, the Sovereign was right about one thing: she needed to learn to control the fire, before it consumed her.

Chapter Thirty-Eight

Crispin

Crispin's elbows rested against the black railing of the ship, eyes fixed on the white stone buildings of Northwind lit up by the full moon and lanterns scattered throughout the city. It was more beautiful than he remembered. Even at night, the city was humming with life. Music, laughter, and dancing filled the streets nearest the port because that's where the Night District was. Taverns, brothels, and inns picked this location for its quick and easy access to sailors from all over Adalore, as well as Her Majesty's soldiers, looking to lose money on booze, women, and gambling.

The crew had camouflaged their ship with different sails and hid anything that screamed pirate from view. Even their clothes had changed to give the appearance of traveling merchants bringing goods to sell and trade in the northern port. Haldane explained with a proud smile that this wasn't their first attempt at blending in to get supplies from large ports around Adalore. Crispin had to admire their cunning ways.

As they docked at the harbor, Crispin sucked in a breath, hoping their bold plan to rescue Neempo would be worth the risk of being recognized. With the hustle and bustle of the harbor and Night District activities, no one even noticed them.

The heavy wooden ramp was extended and landed with a loud thud. The hooded and cloaked Master Penn led her six Keepers off the ship, securing their position, waiting for Crispin, Rahab, and Corwin to join them.

Crispin hadn't been home in twelve years. Hadn't touched the white stones since he escaped his sister's wrath. Then, he was covered in blood and ash. Tonight, he was clothed in black, a hood over his curls to hide his wanted face, and his longsword swinging at his hip. From a forgotten child to a warrior prince.

He was the last to disembark, following Rahab and Corwin closely. He paused before his foot touched Northern soil. He could do this. It wasn't the homecoming he had imagined, but the one an exiled prince and wanted fugitive deserved.

Penn knew from meetings with Neempo, that Oden ran his underground rebellion, The Order, from the basement of his tavern, *The Whispering Fox*. They kept to the shadows on their trek to finding the bar, walking past drunk sailors and soldiers alike without anyone glancing their way.

Weaving through the Night District, they found *The Whispering Fox*, lit up and open for business. And from the looks of it, this tavern was the place to be to have the best time. Women clad in little clothing draped themselves over men with money to burn, whispering sweet nothings into their ears while robbing them blind. Liquor and ale were poured freely and frequently, and the gambling tables were filled with men willing to try their luck.

Crispin had Master Penn and her Keepers stay hidden in the shadows until he, Rahab, and Corwin could locate Oden. He didn't want to risk word reaching the wrong people about the arrival of warriors from The Sisters in Northwind.

The trio slipped inside the tavern, brushing past the crowd of smiling and dazed faces until Crispin spotted a door at the back of the tavern. It was the only other door they could see that wasn't the front door.

Rahab weaved through the bodies until she reached the door. Once she jiggled the knob and realized it was locked, she motioned for Corwin to get to it. He slid a tiny metal pick from his armband and made quick work of the lock. Making sure no one noticed them, the three of them slithered inside and gently closed the door behind them.

The torches fastened to the stone wall lit the wooden staircase that led to the basement. They tiptoed down the stairs, growing more nervous with each unexpected creak of the wood until they found what appeared to be an office with mismatched chairs arranged in a half circle.

He could hear Rahab breathing behind him and his mind flashed back to when she was lying on his chest, their fingers intertwined. Being tangled together felt like the most natural thing in the world to him. He had woken up before she did and he refused to move, fearing she would panic or pretend nothing happened when she realized she had spent the night in his room. But when her eyes fluttered open and she tilted her head to meet his gaze, she did the one thing he didn't expect. She smiled. Her smile warmed his heart, and he desperately wanted to kiss her, but before he could, she rolled on top of him and kissed him first.

"I told you I'd grow on you," Crispin murmured, his lips pressed against hers.

They spent the rest of the morning together until they had to prepare for their arrival.

Now, she was following him closely into the den of The Order's operations, and it made him nervous. He didn't want her to be in harm's way, but if he told her that, she would be more inclined to stab him than listen.

"Where is he?" Rahab walked around the windowless room before flipping through maps and papers chaotically strewn across Oden's desk.

"If you're looking for Oden," a voice boomed from another doorway they missed. "Then you've found him. But unfortunately for you, I'm not alone." He snapped his fingers and a large man with dark hair and a sword pointed at them, stomped down the stairs.

The trio stood still as Crispin put his hands in the air and turned to face Oden. The door the rebel leader had come through had been hidden behind a tapestry. As soon as Oden saw the prince, his face paled.

"We aren't here to hurt you -"

"It's you," Oden interrupted him, his eyes wide. "It's really you."

"Were you expecting us?" Crispin lowered his arms.

Oden took another step toward the prince and clasped his hands. "Nubis, it's him. Our prince has returned."

The giant man standing at the base of the steps sheathed his sword and watched as his leader extended a hand to Crispin.

"I hoped the rumors were true," Oden whispered, teary eyed. "I hoped I would see Bilhah's son again with my own eyes."

Crispin was used to being called the son of Issachar but being referred to as Bilhah's son threw him. "You know who I am?"

"Oh, yes." Oden rifled through the scattered papers on his desk and grabbed two wanted posters with his and Salome's faces. "Your parents were my dearest friends."

Rahab snatched Crispin's wanted poster and studied it with a smirk. She showed it to him and snorted, "Flattering."

"They managed to capture my good side." Crispin teased.

"It's face forward," Rahab's eyebrow arched.

"Exactly. My good side." He flashed her a smile that promised he'd be spending another night with her in his arms.

Her eyes darkened, and his heart nearly stopped beating when she gnawed at her bottom lip. Before he turned his focus back to Oden, he caught her folding the poster and stuffing it into her pocket. First excursion on land in days, and all he wanted to do was crawl back to his cot on the ship to be alone with her.

Oden cleared his throat, drawing the prince's attention. He still had Salome's wanted poster and Crispin reached for it. He hadn't seen his sister in weeks and missing her was an understatement.

"May I keep this?" Crispin asked, eyes still glued to his sister's face. Whoever described his sister to the artist managed to capture the quiet danger in her eyes and the impish smirk of her lips. Every night before he closed his eyes to sleep, he prayed for her and Zophar. Prayed that they would see each other again and soon. Prayed that they wouldn't forget him, even though he had been out of contact for a while.

"Please," Oden motioned for Crispin to pocket the drawing. "Take a seat. Make yourselves comfortable. I assure you, you are safe to speak freely down here. Nubis will guard the door."

"Master Penn and her Keepers are waiting outside. They should be here for this meeting," Crispin said as he claimed the wooden chair behind him. Rahab and Corwin plopped down in a seater built for two.

Oden nodded and Nubis marched upstairs to fetch them. Rahab nudged Corwin with her elbow, and he stood up and followed Oden's henchman.

Once the two men left, Oden smiled at Crispin. "You favor her."

"Who?"

"Your mother." Tears welled in Oden's eyes and Crispin wondered if there was more to the rebel leader's relationship with his mother that he didn't know about. Maybe didn't want to know.

"You knew her well?" Crispin regretted the question as soon as it spilled out of his mouth.

Oden nodded with a sad smile. "When your mother agreed to marry your father, he sent me to bring her to Northwind. We got to know one another on our journey, and she remained my closest friend until her..." he cleared his throat, not wishing to speak about Bilhah's death. "I swore that night, I would do everything I could to rid the White City of your sister. It's taken me twelve years, but our savior sits before me. Your mother would be so proud of you."

It was odd to think of this stranger knowing his mother better than he did, but he nodded in gratitude for his kind words. Before he could ask how Oden managed to elude his sister for twelve years, one of the walls opened revealing a secret passage. Nubis led Corwin, Master Penn, and her six Keepers into the basement.

"Led them through the back entrance," Nubis leaned against the wall at the base of the stairs. "No one noticed them."

"Good," Oden bobbed his head and bowed before Master Penn who seemed to be aware of his movements. She returned the greeting with a slight nod of acknowledgment. "Welcome to Northwind, Master Penn. I am surprised to see you here."

"Then I will assume you haven't heard," Penn ignored his pleasantries and got straight to the point.

"Heard what?"

"The Sovereign Neempo was captured by the Pirate King and brought here as Niabi's prisoner." Penn sat in a velvet high back chair, her six Keepers stationed around the room, ready for any possible altercation.

By the shocked expression on Oden's face, he had clearly not heard. "What could she possibly need the Sovereign for?"

"His heart." Penn stated.

"She's trying to resurrect her son," Crispin explained, "she needed the Heart of the Righteous to invoke the spell."

Oden pinched the bridge of his nose and exhaled a tired sigh. He reclaimed his seat and leaned back, rubbing his eyes. "There have been reports that her Aunt Vilora is the Old Witch of Endor and is now sitting on her small council."

"This we know," Penn's tight-lipped appearance would seem unfriendly to most, but Oden didn't seem to take offense to her harsh responses.

"Did you also know that Niabi seems to have inherited some of her aunt's power?" Oden asked, his fingers pressed together. "Fire magic."

Crispin's eyes nearly popped out of his head. "She has magic?"

"It would seem so," Oden motioned for Nubis to speak.

"The queen has been practicing with the witch for a couple of weeks. It seems the queen didn't know of her abilities until recently." Nubis shifted side to side, clearly uncomfortable with the attention he was getting. "But there has been chatter of the witch preparing for some kind of ritual. I didn't know what for, but I guess it's safe to assume it's for this resurrection spell."

Crispin's head was spinning. Niabi had fire magic? As if she weren't dangerous enough.

"We need to rescue the Sovereign before they carve out his heart," Rahab finally chimed in.

"We will do whatever you need us to do." Oden rose from his seat when the stairs creaked. Nubis unsheathed his sword and the six Keepers stationed around the room clutched their spears tightly. "Ah, Ziggy, we weren't expecting you tonight."

Ziggy stopped half-way down the steps and clutched her shawl tighter around her shoulders. "Is everything alright?" she flashed a hesitant smile.

Crispin rose to his feet and knew she recognized him when her pouty mouth fell open. "The prince. You found him?" Her blue eyes darted toward Oden who shook his head.

"He found us."

She bowed but Crispin motioned for her to stand back up. "Your name is Ziggy?"

Ziggy nodded, her eyes refusing to meet his gaze. "Yes, Your Highness."

Rahab stifled a giggle at Crispin being referred to as Your Highness.

"It's Crispin," he said with a smile.

Ziggy slowly looked up at him, "Crispin." It felt odd hearing his name roll off her tongue.

"Is there a reason for your late visit?" Oden asked, irritation clear in his tone.

Ziggy snapped out of her stunned stupor and rushed forward, sitting in the wooden chair that Crispin offered. The prince stood behind the two-seat lounge and rested his elbows on the cushion behind Rahab.

"It's about Lord Gershom." Ziggy glanced at the newcomers and waited for Oden to give her permission to speak before continuing. "He had an unexpected visitor the other night. He looked like he was from Numbio."

"From Numbio?" Crispin asked, his interest piqued. "Did you get his name?"

Ziggy nervously bobbed her head. "Gershom called him Memucan. I don't know who he is, but they mentioned something about a plan to overthrow Queen Niabi and the King of Numbio."

"Memucan is here?" Crispin straightened, his hand tickling the hilt of his sword. "Is he in the White Keep?"

"You know him?" Oden's brows furrowed.

"I met him in Numbio. He is King Osiris' advisor." Crispin saw the old man's weathered and wicked face flash before his eyes and he was itching to slit the traitor's throat. "Is he in the White Keep?" He repeated his question, directing it at Ziggy.

"No," she shook her head. "Gershom asked me to find him a room at one of the local inns. He wants Memucan to hide until he is ready to strike."

Crispin's eyes darted to Oden. "We need a plan to rescue Neempo. But first," he looked at Ziggy as she twisted the folds of her skirt with anxious fingers, "I need you to show me where Memucan is."

"Are you going to kill him?" Master Penn asked, her tone ripe with excitement.

"Once I get some answers from him, yes." Crispin didn't try to hide that his mission was to slit Memucan's throat from ear to ear. He had suspected the sandstorm was dark magic and there was only one person who hated Crispin enough to attempt risking discovery to bury him.

"What about Gershom?" Ziggy asked, her cheeks were flushed. "If Memucan ends up dead, he might suspect I had something to do with it."

The room stilled and Crispin reclined against the wall, deep in thought. This was an underground rebellion. Of course, they were spies. They put their lives on the line daily for information to further his ascent to the throne, for his sister's ultimate end.

But he couldn't allow Memucan to live. If he had a hand in the sandstorm, he had blood on his hands. And worse, if he was truly allied with Gershom, he betrayed his king and people. He had betrayed the alliance King Osiris had made with him. Memucan had to be dealt with. Quickly and quietly.

"Does he have soldiers watching over him?" Crispin asked, an idea forming in his mind.

"A handful of Gershom's personal guards are stationed outside the front door, strategically placed as to not draw too much attention." Ziggy seemed rattled so Crispin approached her and knelt in front of her.

"I know you're scared," Crispin grabbed her hand and squeezed it gently. "But I can't let him live. There are too many lives at stake."

"What about my life?" Ziggy's voice cracked.

"We can protect you," Crispin glanced over at Rahab, and she nodded, already knowing what he was going to ask her. "We can get you to safety."

Ziggy's face paled. "You want me to leave with you?"

"Leave?" Oden was surprised. "But you've finally come home. Are you not going to stay?"

"I came here for Neempo." Crispin rose to face Oden. "Once we rescue him, I will have other matters that require my immediate attention."

"More pressing than reclaiming your ancestors' throne?" Oden's smooth voice had more of a bite to it.

"I have given my word to help someone," Crispin stood his ground, sounding more like a king than a fugitive. "When I return, it won't include me slinking in the shadows. I'll have an army at my back and a crown to claim at my front. But if you and I are going to have dealings with one another," he took a breath, steadying his voice, "then you will need to follow my lead."

Oden's shoulders tensed and his mouth trembled, fire clearly raging inside him, as well. "I am here to serve, Prince."

Rahab rose from her seat, "Where's Memucan staying?"

Ziggy had tears in her eyes and Nubis moved to rest his massive hand on her petite shoulder. "You swear you can protect me?"

"Be aboard our ship by tomorrow night," Rahab bobbed her head to reassure the red-headed escort of Crispin's promise. "You'll be out of Gershom's reach when we set sail."

Nubis whispered something in Ziggy's ear that Crispin didn't catch, but whatever it was, seemed to settle her.

"Memucan is staying at *The Black Lotus*," Ziggy said. "I can take you there."

Crispin flashed her a reassuring smile before turning to Master Penn. "I'll leave the rescue planning to you and Oden. I'll be back as soon as I've finished with the Numbio."

Master Penn bowed her head a smidge before turning her attention to Oden. "I believe you owe the Sovereign a favor."

Chapter Thirty-Nine

Salome

Salome strolled into the Great Hall where the Festival of the Forbidden Fruit had been held. Without the floating lights, decorations, music, and mingling couples, it was just another ordinary room. It was still a beautiful space, but the magic of the other night was just that. Magic.

She heard Jinn's voice echo in the empty hall before she saw him.

"Rendezvousing where we first met," he cooed. "Sweet."

Salome turned in a full circle looking around the three-story room. The moonlight poured in through the round hole in the ceiling and made the space sparkle. She spotted him resting his elbows against the railing on the third-floor balcony: the exact spot they first met.

"You seem to have a flair for the dramatic." She climbed the rounding stairs to join him. "Was it really necessary for me to climb all the way up here?"

Jinn turned his back to recline lazily against the railing and shrugged. "When you said to meet you here, I figured you wanted to have a redo of the Festival of the Forbidden Fruit."

"Why, so you can make another bad first impression?" she snorted as she made it to the third floor. "I wanted to meet here because it's private and no one normally comes in here."

Jinn wiggled his eyebrows, "Cozy."

Salome rolled her eyes and stood in front of him, arms crossed over her chest.

"You know," Jinn straightened to his full height and stared down at Salome, "we could have had this private conversation in your chambers."

"Or we could have had this conversation mentally." She cocked her head to the side and smirked.

Jinn laughed and held his hands in the air, signifying his surrender. "What do you need to talk about?"

She scratched her lips, hating herself for loving the sound of his laugh. "Are you still leaving tomorrow night?"

Jinn crossed his arms, "Is this your way of saying you're going to miss me?"

Salome scrunched her nose. "Hardly." She glimpsed around the room to make sure they were still alone. "What would you say, if I asked for passage to the Mainland?"

Jinn's brows lifted, clearly surprised by her request. "You want to come with me?" His voice was soft, expectant.

A tinge of guilt surged through her heart. "Not all the way to Sakurai. Just to where the Bone Mountains and the sea meet. I have business there."

Jinn nodded with a tight-lipped smile. "Whatever you want or need that is within my power to give, is yours."

Salome reached for his hand and squeezed it. "Thank you."

Jinn's golden-brown eyes were glued to hers. "I suppose you haven't considered my proposal?"

Salome didn't want any potential eavesdroppers to hear, so she extended the mental bridge, and said, *"I need more time."*

"Are you afraid to say that aloud because you don't want anyone to hear us or because you don't want to admit to being attracted to me?" His eyes danced in mischievous delight.

Salome's eyes widened and her mouth shot open to deny it, but she snapped her lips closed, and continued their mental conversation. *"You flatter yourself."*

"At least, I'm honest with myself."

She rested her hands on her hips, *"And I'm not honest?"*

Jinn closed the gap between them and smiled down at her. *"Your eyes betray you."*

Salome refused to shrink back and stood her ground. *"What do you mean?"*

"You tell me not to look at you a certain way, but you forget I can see how you look at me, too." His fingers brushed against hers. *"I'm a patient man, Salome, not a stupid one. I know when a woman wants me."*

"Then perhaps, you should ask one of them to be your wife," she narrowed her eyes. *"I'm not looking at you any different than other men."*

"Liar." His gaze drifted to her lips.

Without realizing it, Salome closed her eyes and tilted her head up to him but stopped when she heard him softly chuckle. *"What?"*

"You leaned."

"So?" She snorted defensively.

"I told you, your eyes betray you, and now your body."

Salome took a step back from him, gritting her teeth, despising the itch in her hands to run the tips of her fingers along his perfectly chiseled jaw. *"You're delusional."*

Jinn shrugged, tucking his hands in his pockets. *"And you're in denial."*

"Since you're so determined for us to be honest. Why don't you tell me about your magic?" She knew it was a low blow, but she couldn't help but throw the secrecy of his power in his face. If he was going to accuse her of being dishonest and in denial, then she would gladly remind him that he was a hypocrite.

Jinn twirled one of her curls between his index finger and thumb. *"A secret for a secret."*

She was taken aback by his response. She didn't really think he would agree to tell her. And now, she was afraid of what he might want to know about her.

"Fine. But you go first. Tell me about your magic."

He stepped away from her. *"I think it's better if I show you."*

Salome nodded, but as hard as she tried to keep her expression neutral, anxiety was written all over her face.

"Don't be scared."

And then Jinn vanished.

Salome flinched. She stuck her hand out, but she didn't feel him. *"Where did you go?"*

"I'm right here."

She whipped around to see him leaning against the wall, one ankle crossed over the other, hands in his pockets.

"You're a Cloaker?"

"Does that frighten you?" He cocked his head to the side. She could see the desperation for her to accept him flashing in his eyes.

"I'm not afraid of you." Salome meant it.

"Don't worry," Jinn pushed up and slowly walked toward her. "I don't sneak into your room at night to watch you sleep."

"I wasn't worried, but now I am." She smiled, stifling a laugh.

"That's the first real smile I've gotten from you." Jinn swiped loose hair from her face and tucked it behind her ear. "You have a beautiful smile."

"A secret for a secret." Salome's gaze dropped. Looking him in the eye made her feel as if he could see right through her.

"Are you attracted to me?"

Why did he have to ask her that question? She couldn't lie to him. And even if she wanted to, she was positive her face had already given her away.

Salome sighed. *Yes."*

"Now was that so hard to admit?" Jinn whispered aloud against her ear sending a shiver down her spine.

For the first time in a long time, she was lost for words.

Jinn winked, *"Your secret is safe with me."*

His eyes flicked past Salome's shoulder and when she turned around to see who he was looking at, she saw Kai standing on the landing of the second floor. He nodded in understanding. "I'll expect you and your company at the docks tomorrow night," he said with a princely tone.

"Why the rush?" One of her eyebrows arched.

Jinn flashed a wicked smile and thumbed her chin. "Can't get enough of me, can you?"

Salome pursed her lips and cocked her head to the side. He laughed and it felt like a warm hug.

"Since this was supposed to be a private meeting," he said, "I best be off before your Qata Vishna bodyguards see us together."

He pecked a kiss on Salome's cheek as he passed her. He trotted down the stairs where Kai was waiting. As soon as they left, Seraphina and Rosalina walked in.

"Princess Salome?" Rosalina looked around until she spotted Salome descending the stairs.

"What is it?"

"It's Marina." Salome could hear Seraphina's gulp from the second floor.

"What about Marina?" Salome rushed down the last set of steps.

"She escaped," Seraphina continued, "and Mika took her place."

Salome stopped dead in her tracks. "What do you mean Mika took her place?"

"From what Queen Zara said, Mika helped Marina escape and in accordance with our laws," Rosalina quickly explained, "a life may be given in place of another's, so long as they accept the consequences."

Salome's heart leapt to her throat. "They're going to execute Mika in Marina's place?"

The twins exchanged a quick glance and Salome knew what that look meant.

Chapter Forty

Crispin

As promised, Ziggy led Crispin and Rahab *to The Black Lotus,* the three-story inn where Memucan was staying. The red-head spy's intel checked out when they saw a handful of Gershom's personal guards scattered around the front entrance attempting to blend in with the patrons of the narrow white cobblestone streets. Crispin knew exactly who was on duty by the simple fact that they were the only ones not drinking or chatting up the working women.

"How many are there?" Rahab asked, crouched behind him. They were a block away from *The Black Lotus* and Crispin was peeking around the corner of a bakery that was closed for the evening.

"I counted five." Crispin whispered and turned his attention to Ziggy who was standing a few feet behind Rahab, her arms hugging her torso. "Ziggy." Her frightened eyes darted to meet his. "What room is he in?"

Ziggy brushed the tight curls from her face. "He's on the third floor. Room six."

Crispin nodded. "Thank you, Ziggy. We'll take it from here if you want to go home." She seemed relieved he was letting her go, but he could sense a reluctance too.

"I know it was difficult for you to bring us here, but you've done your job." Crispin shot her a reassuring smile. "Now, it's time for us to do ours."

Ziggy bobbed her head, a silent thank you for not judging her for being fearful, and she stalked back into the dark alleys of Northwind. His eyes rested on Rahab, but she wasn't looking at him. Her gaze was fixed on the sloped roof of *The Black Lotus*.

"We have two options," she started, and Crispin noted her tone was that of a First Mate and not the woman who had curled up to him the night before. "Either we pick the guards off one by one and go in the front door or," her eyes twinkled when they met his, "we go up."

Crispin glanced around the corner again, spying the two guards at the front entrance and all the people walking in and out of the inns, brothels, and taverns on this street, and he shook his head. Too many witnesses. Messy. He looked up at the copper shingle rooftop and turned to face Rahab.

"Not as high as The Sisters," he flashed a grin. "You up for it?"

Her smile was wicked when she said, "Race you to the top."

Crispin didn't know why he let Rahab beat him to the top of *The Black Lotus*, but when she shot him a look over her shoulder, he stopped where he stood. The moonlight hit her icy blue tresses giving her the appearance of an assassin goddess. The unobstructed view of the starry sky above them, twinkling around her seated frame, stole his breath.

"What?" she asked, stretching her legs in front of her.

Crispin slowly approached her on soft feet, not wanting to alert anyone in the rooms below them of their presence. "Are you just as lethal on dry land as you are on the sea?"

She wiggled her eyebrows, "You concerned about me?"

He sat beside her, watching the people in the streets start to stumble their way back to their rented rooms or apartments as the taverns closed a few hours before dawn. "Have you done anything like this before?"

"Sit on a rooftop waiting to assassinate a foreign dignitary? Not recently," she chuckled.

"I meant," he cleared his throat, "have you killed a man before?"

Rahab sighed, bringing one of her knees to her chest, resting her chin on top. "My first kill was at sixteen. Shortly after recovering and joining the *Shadow of Death* crew, our ship was attacked by a rival captain with a vendetta against Haldane." She shrugged, the lights in the city flickering off one by one. "I didn't even know how to wield a weapon. I'd only had a few lessons with Leeondris before Rourke's crew tried to kill us and take our loot.

"Leeondris gave me one of his knives and told me to stay in my room until he came back. Before he made it back, one of Rourke's men kicked in my door. I could see it in his eyes. He was going to kill me but only after he had his fun. I had a choice. I could kill him, or he could kill me. So, I allowed him to get close enough, letting him think I was too afraid to fight back, and as soon as his sticky fingers snatched my wrist and pulled me close, I plunged the dagger deep into his heart. I watched the life leave his eyes and I swore that day, no one would touch me without my permission again."

Crispin soaked in every word she spoke, and a fire raged deep within his soul. She had seen and experienced horrors and atrocities he couldn't even begin to imagine. He had lost his family. He had lost his home. But he had never feared being overpowered or harmed in unspeakable ways.

"What happened to Rourke?" It was all he could ask to steady the anger pulsating through his body.

Rahab flashed a sinister grin and purred, "We stuffed the survivors in burlap sacks, tied weights around their necks, and let them sink to the bottom of the Obsidian Sea."

"Good."

"And you?" She leaned back and placed her palms behind her head. "Have you killed before?"

Crispin bobbed his head as he reclined, looking up into the night sky and seeing Orion staring back at him. "I killed Shadows that invaded the Tree House Forest and Wagura in the Caverns of the Undead."

"You were in the Caverns of the Undead?" Her voice cracked. He couldn't tell if she was frightened or impressed. "What do they look like?"

"They are the most horrifying creatures I have ever laid eyes on." He wiped the invisible green Wagura blood from his hands, their pale bony figures flashing before his eyes. He hoped Zophar and Heru had led the Numbio out of there. Hoped they were well on their way to Oakenshire to meet up with Salome.

Crispin realized it was quiet and risked a glance over the lip of the roof to see if Gershom's guards were still outside the front door. To his frustration, they were. Now without having to mingle with the crowd, they took up their positions for the rest of the night. Two at the front door, two at the back door, and one that patrolled around the inn at a steady pace.

"Unless we guess which window is Memucan's, we're going to have to use one of the entrances." Crispin didn't want to risk drawing the guards' attention if they entered the wrong room and added screaming civilians to the mix. "We're going to have to take them out."

By the grin stretched across Rahab's face, it looked like she had been waiting for him to come to the same conclusion. "Let the games begin."

They were three stories up. Too high for them to jump and land without injury. But Rahab, being the cunning pirate she was, brought a few supplies buried in her leather satchel.

"You just carry rope with you?" Crispin asked as she tossed him a line.

"Came in handy tonight, didn't it?" Rahab tied her end of the rope around her waist and knotted it. "Alright, when the patrolman passes by the two guards in the back, you'll lower me and let me do the rest."

"Wait, wait, wait." He shook his head with a scowl. "You expect me to lower you down there?"

Rahab snatched the ruby dagger from her hip and nodded. "Headfirst."

"Rahab."

"Crispin." She cocked her head to the side, batting her eyes slowly.

Crispin pinched the bridge of his nose. She was unrelenting. If he didn't lower her, she was liable to tie the end of the rope she'd trusted him with around the chimney and lower herself. "After you kill them, do you want me to pull you up?"

"I'll untie myself for you to climb down." She laid on her belly, overlooking the two guards at the back door. "We'll deal with the other three together."

"And why am I not the one going first?" He knelt beside her after he knotted the rope around the chimney, and she flicked her eyes up at him.

She hesitated, "You weigh too much?"

"Is that a question?" Crispin let out a low chuckle.

"Truthfully," she grinned, speaking to him in a sweet voice meant for babies, "I wouldn't want you messing up that pretty face, Your Majesty."

Crispin wasn't sure if he wanted to push her off the roof or slam his lips against hers, so instead, he leaned back, braced his feet against the gutters, and nodded for her to go. "Go, before I push you off."

"Ah, you'd miss me too much."

"Using my lines?"

Rahab winked before sliding over the edge. He wanted to watch her, to make sure she was alright, but he let the rope gently slip through his fingers as he steadied her descent. He knew she had made it when he heard two quick slices, muffled groans, and two bodies thudding to the ground. When she untied herself, Crispin repelled down the side of the white stone inn until he reached her at the bottom. His eyes darted to the two guards with slits across their throats.

"That was quick." Crispin was both impressed and terrified. Rahab had made quick work of them, leaving little evidence of the assassins having been there.

She propped the guards against the wall and once she was done setting the scene, it looked as if they had fallen asleep from a long drunken night. "What did you expect me to do? Ask them if they wanted to grab a drink?"

Crispin put a finger to his lips, signaling her to be quiet. He heard footsteps approaching at a steady clip. The patrolman was coming. Backing against the end of the building, Crispin unsheathed the dagger Corwin had given him and waited. His heart was racing. The prince had killed in combat, but he had never lurked in the darkness waiting for unsuspecting prey. There was no room for hesitation. Any audible warning would tip off the two guards in the front and that risked Memucan slipping through his fingers. That was not an option.

Taking a deep breath, Crispin listened for the footsteps that grew louder as they neared. As soon as the soldier turned the corner, Crispin clamped a hand over his mouth, slit his throat, and dragged his body toward the other guards.

"Three down," she whispered. "Do we go for the other two? Or take our chances going for Memucan through the back door?"

Crispin's heart was lumped in his throat. The gravity of what he had done weighed on him, but they didn't have time for him to dwell on the blood staining his hands. He pointed at the back door. "Let's worry about the other two guards later."

For once, Rahab didn't argue with him. She faced the door and turned the knob. Luckily it was unlocked, and they slipped inside. There was a long hallway that spanned from the back door to the front door. As quietly as possible, they crept down the corridor until they reached an unattended front desk. The clerk had stepped away making it simple to reach the staircase. They climbed the spiral staircase until they landed on the top floor.

"Room six," Crispin muttered, his eyes darting door to door. Memucan's room was at the end of the hall.

Knives drawn; the duo tip-toed to the Numbio's door. Rahab borrowed Corwin's lock pick since he was told to stay with Master Penn and keep his eyes and ears open on Crispin's behalf. Crispin could have sworn Rahab picked the lock faster than Corwin had at *The Whispering Fox*.

She nodded and Crispin quietly turned the brass knob, opening the door. Slithering inside the dark room, Crispin saw Memucan asleep in the opulent four post bed. The moonlight poured into the best room the inn had to offer and spotlighted the withering advisor wrapped in satin sheets. Crispin put the tip of his dagger against Memucan's throat and watched his eyes flicker open.

"You." Memucan hissed, the flash of fear in his face was gone and malice replaced it. "I had hoped you died in that sandstorm."

"Sorry to disappoint," Crispin crinkled his nose and poked the knife into Memucan's neck, drawing blood. "I have a few questions and you're going to answer them."

"And if I don't?" Memucan asked with a wicked smirk. "Are you going to kill me?"

Crispin was planning to kill him whether he answered his questions or not, but he said, "Maybe I'll just send you back to Numbio for Osiris to deal with you."

A spark lit in Memucan's face, but Crispin wasn't sure what the old man was thinking. "Ask your questions, *Prince*." The way he said prince was like he'd smelled something rotten, and it didn't sit well with Crispin.

"You sent that sandstorm," Crispin accused rather than asked, "with black magic."

Memucan flashed a sinister grin. "A simple incantation."

"Your people lost their lives -"

"Spare me your self-righteous speech," Memucan spat with a snake like hiss. "Their lives mean nothing to me."

That caught Crispin off-guard. "Then why rule them?"

Memucan let out a low chuckle, "I don't intend to rule them. I intend to enslave them. Osiris, Heru... they are weak. Control. Power. Fear. That's what makes a true king. With Gershom reigning in the North and me reigning in the South, we could make all of Adalore bend to our will."

"Was I your intended target? Or was it Heru?" Crispin had to know if his friend was still in danger.

"Oh, don't worry," Memucan bared his teeth, "if the prince managed to survive the Wagura, my servant will finish the job."

"Your servant?"

"You're too late. Heru's death is already set."

Crispin heard a low whistle from the other side of the bedroom door and knew Rahab was warning him of the guards' activity. He didn't have much time before he'd have to clear out of the inn.

"You think you can kill me?" Memucan slowly rose from lying on his back to a seated position, Crispin's hand tightened on the hilt of his blade, holding it against his throat. "You do not have what it takes to be a man wielding great power. You are nothing. You are no one. You will never be -"

Crispin slid the blade across Memucan's throat like a hot knife through butter. He didn't need to hear another word ooze from his crusty lips. Rahab rapped on the door before entering.

"We have to go," she quietly shut it behind her. "They must have found their friends and I heard footsteps coming up the stairs."

Crispin opened the window and motioned for Rahab to slip out. As he was about to follow her, he noticed a black book sitting on Memucan's nightstand. He grabbed it, tucked it under his arm, and ducked out the window.

As Crispin and Rahab made their way down the dark alleyways of the Night District, the alarm of the soldiers who found Memucan's body resounded behind them. Crispin couldn't help the smile of satisfaction that stretched across his face. One enemy was dead, but he knew there were plenty left to face.

Chapter Forty-One

Salome

Salome wished Harbona hadn't left. She needed his guidance on how to save Mika. Rubbing a finger over her drying lips, Salome silently paced around her chambers, deep in thought. Adonijah and Cato had offered several suggestions but none of them would work. And if they were caught, they'd be tossed into the dungeons alongside Mika.

"Could you appeal to your Aunt Zara?" Adonijah was leaning against the wall.

Salome shook her head. "Damaris has been with Zara all night begging for Mika's life to be spared."

"She would execute her daughter for a crime she didn't commit?" Cato had become a stress eater and had eaten both his dinner and Salome's.

"Mika took Marina's place. Meaning Mika accepted Marina's punishment." Salome ran fingers through her hair. "It's legal according to Myridian law."

"Surely, Queen Zara could make an exception," Cato insisted, picking at his teeth with his fork. "She could show mercy, grant her a pardon?"

"Zara was just crowned queen after her mother's assassination," Adonijah chimed in. "She can't afford to look weak in her people's eyes, even to spare her daughter."

"It's too bad Mika can't just fly out of here." Cato huffed, throwing his utensil on his empty plate. He scratched his stomach and pointed at the last remaining wedge of cheese. "Is anyone going to eat that?"

"What did you just say?" Salome turned around to face him, excitement strumming through her body.

Cato's eyes widened; his mouth was filled with cheese. "I asked if anyone was going to eat this."

"No," she waved her hand dismissively. "Before that. What did you say about flying?"

Cato swallowed. "I said it's too bad Mika can't fly out of here."

"That's it!" Salome clapped her hands. "Cato, you're a genius!"

Cato and Adonijah exchanged a look before Cato whispered, slightly terrified, "Can you fly?"

"No," she planted her hands on her hips, her mind racing, "but there is a way we can get Mika out of the Isles of Myr unseen."

Adonijah stepped into the light, arms crossed over his chest. Intrigued, he asked, "How do you propose we do that?"

"I can ask Jinn to get his ship ready to sail tonight, instead of tomorrow. If we can get Mika aboard, she will be safe and on her way to the Mainland."

Adonijah's nostrils flared when Salome mentioned Jinn's name. "Let's say he agrees," he sighed in irritation. "How are we supposed to get her out of that tower," he pointed toward the Tower Dungeon on the opposite side of the Scarlett Citadel, "and past all the Qata Vishna unnoticed?"

"What if you ask Jinn and someone overhears you talking about helping Mika escape?" Cato brought up a valid point. They were thinking about committing an act of treason. "What if Jinn doesn't agree to help and he tells the queen?"

"Jinn wouldn't betray us." Salome countered, surprised at how she defended him.

"Forgive us," Adonijah's tone was icy, "if we do not agree."

She kicked her foot aimlessly in front of her, eyes glued to the floor. She could feel Adonijah's frigid glare.

"You might not trust him, but I do." She held up a hand before either of them could protest. "And no one would overhear us -"

"But anyone could -"

She cut Cato off, "They wouldn't overhear us because Jinn and I can communicate with just thoughts."

"Excuse me?" Cato tilted his head, mouth agape.

"My magic is more than communicating with the dead and having visions of the past." She took a deep breath and met Adonijah's line of sight. "I can have a conversation mind-to-mind with people I share a bond with."

Adonijah seemed to catch on immediately by the frown that creased his brow. Cato needed some clarification.

"Could you talk to me that way?" Cato asked, waving a hand around his head. "With our minds?"

"No," she shook her head, rubbing the nape of her neck. "We need to share a bond of either magic or marriage to mentally speak to one another. Damaris said it's like extending a bridge to connect me to someone else."

"So, Damaris knows?" Adonijah said with a hint of bitterness.

Salome bobbed her head, wrapping her arms around herself. "I can talk to her mentally, too."

"You share this bond with Jinn and Damaris?" Adonijah looked like he could spit fire and Salome's instinct was to shrink back but she forced herself to stay put.

"Yes. Through our magic."

"Jinn has magic?" Cato nearly shouted in excitement. "Wait, does he talk to trees too?"

"I don't talk to tre..." Salome took a deep breath and stroked her palms across her eyes. "Jinn is a cloaker."

"So, he has cool magic." Cato seemed giddy. Impressed would be an understatement.

"I have cool magic," Salome snorted, furrowing her brows.

"Of course, you do." Cato bobbed his head and winked. "How else would we know what the trees have to say?" he snickered.

"You're as irritating as Crispin."

As soon as she mentioned her brother, she felt a lump in her throat. She tried to use the mental bond with him. She had called out to him several times that afternoon, but he never answered. Damaris asked before if he had magical abilities, but as far as she knew, he didn't. If he could see her now, he would be the first person to crack jokes like Cato. Crispin and Cato were probably long-lost brothers. The pranking, the jokes, the constant snacking. She was looking forward to the day they met.

Salome realized by how Cato was staring at her, she had been lost in thought. She plastered a smile on her face, so they wouldn't be able to tell something was bothering her.

"So, are we in agreement?" Salome's gaze drifted from Cato to Adonijah. "We ask Jinn to use his magic to get Mika out of the Tower Dungeon and onto his ship?"

Adonijah shoved his hands into his pockets, refusing to make eye contact. He bobbed his head silently. That was the most enthusiasm she was going to get from him, so she didn't press her luck by arguing.

Cato shrugged his shoulders. "You're in charge. If you say that's the plan, then that's the plan."

"Then I'll reach out to him."

"You do that." Adonijah marched past her to sit on the balcony, lit his pipe, and kicked his feet up on the iron railing.

It was apparent he was furious, but Salome would deal with one problem at a time. Whether he liked it or not, they needed Jinn's help. She plopped onto one of the pillow-infested couches and crossed her legs to get comfortable. With Cato snacking loudly in the room, she closed her eyes to focus.

"I need to ask for a favor." Salome reached out to Jinn.

"Anything."

Her heart was racing. This was going to be one big favor and she was prepared for him to tell her no. *"Before I tell you what it is, I want you to know that if we are caught, we could be tossed into Zara's dungeons."*

Jinn hummed a laugh. *"Sounds like fun. What are we doing?"*

"Could your ship be ready to sail tonight if need be?"

"It's possible, yes. But I fail to see how that could land us in any trouble."

Salome took a deep breath. There was no going back. *"Your magic. Could you cloak more than one person?"*

"How many people are we talking about?"

"You, me," she paused, *"and Mika."*

Salome braced herself when he didn't immediately respond. *"Now, I see how this could land us in Zara's dungeons."*

"You don't have to do this -"

"And let you have all the fun smuggling a fugitive?" He interrupted with a warm chuckle. *"Not a chance."*

"You'll help me get her out?"

"Why do you sound so surprised?" Jinn's voice was silky and danced around her head. *"I already told you, whatever you want or need that is within my power to give, is yours."*

"I guess I owe you a favor now."

"Spending time with you is all I want."

Salome couldn't help the smile that inched across her face.

"Wow," he purred. *"Two smiles in one day. Must mean you don't hate me."*

She arched an eyebrow, *"How did you know I smiled?"*

"I could sense it."

"More like a lucky guess," she snorted.

"Don't need luck."

Salome could sense him grinning and it made her heart skip a beat.

"Meet me in an hour in the Paraiso Gardens," Jinn instructed. *"I'll leave my watchdog, if you leave yours."*

Salome could picture those golden-brown eyes of his dancing in delight, wiggling his jet-black eyebrows. She refused to give him the satisfaction of sensing her smile, so she cleared her throat and remained tight lipped.

"He's not my watchdog. And if you think he's going to let me wander around that late without back up, you're not as smart as you think you are."

Jinn laughed softly. *"It was worth a shot."*

When Salome opened her eyes, her gaze met Cato's. He was perched in a chair directly across from her, clutching his legs to his chest, watching her intensely.

Salome scrunched her nose. "Can I help you?"

"So, you did it? You did the mind talking thing?" Cato motioned around his head.

"Yes," she smirked, "I did the mind thing." She stood up and glanced toward the balcony. Adonijah hadn't moved. "Was he watching me?"

Cato shook his head. "He didn't seem too interested."

"He's upset with me." Salome rubbed her palms up and down her face.

"Can you blame him?" Cato rested his feet on the floor and snatched some dates from a bowl on the table next to him. "He likes you, you know."

She nodded and cracked her neck. "I should go talk to him."

Cato tossed a date in his mouth. "If you need me, don't. I'll be stepping out for a bit."

"Well, aren't you smitten?" Salome caught the date he threw up in the air and popped it in her mouth.

"Hey!" Cato shook his head trying not to grin. "I guess she's not as scary as I thought she would be."

"Oh, Seraphina is scary. Don't let her fool you."

Cato's eyes widened. He scratched his short cropped, white hair nervously.

"Then again, all women are scary." Salome leaned over and planted a kiss on his forehead. "Have fun."

"Don't kill each other," he called after her.

"I make no promises." She winked.

Adonijah was quietly smoking his pipe. His legs were still stretched out, heels linked to the balcony railing. Salome leaned against the archway, crossing her arms across her chest.

"Is it alright if I join you?"

Adonijah motioned to the seat opposite him, and she sunk into the lounge chair. "All set?" he asked without looking over at her.

She bobbed her head, "We're supposed to meet him in the Paraiso Gardens in one hour."

"Alright," he exhaled a ring of smoke and watched it float away.

The warm ocean breeze wafted Salome's hair in front of her face. She peeled it back and noticed he still hadn't looked at her. "Out with it."

"Out with what?" His gaze was glued on the ships docked in the harbor.

"You're angry." She didn't tip-toe around the issue. "Is this about asking Jinn for his help?"

Adonijah retracted his feet and planted them firmly on the floor. He rested his elbows on his knees and met Salome's awaiting gaze. "Do you trust me?"

"Yes," she smiled, "I do."

"Then why keep your magic, this bond between you and him, a secret from me?"

Salome looked deep into his eyes and wished she could read what was running through his mind. If the pained expression was any indication of what he was feeling, he was not angry. He was wounded. And that was worse.

"I was still trying to figure everything out."

Adonijah rubbed his hands together and shook his head. "That's not what I asked, Salome."

She sighed and straightened her legs. "If I had told you the second I realized I could talk to Jinn with my thoughts, would you have been alright with that?"

Adonijah wiped his brow, gnawing at his bottom lip.

"I didn't tell you because I thought you would be so angry you would discourage me from using my magic anymore."

He ran his fingers through his hair and clicked his tongue. "You like him."

Not a question. An accusation.

"He's not a bad person."

"Please don't act like you don't know what I'm talking about." Adonijah hopped up from his seat and rested his elbows on the railing. "Do you like him?" he whispered, not looking at her.

She joined him at the railing but couldn't look him in the eye. "I would be lying if I told you I didn't like him."

Adonijah nodded. "At least you admitted it."

Salome reached for his arm, "Adonijah -"

He pulled his forearm away before she could grab him. Squaring his shoulders to her, he asked, "So, where does that leave us?"

She mirrored his body position and stroked her fingers down his face. "I care for you, Adonijah. I would die for you if it came down to it." She rested her hand on his chest. "But a war is coming. A war where I will be forced to make difficult decisions for the good of my family, my people, and my allies. You asked if I was considering his proposal. Yes, I am. I can't win a war without an army."

"Crispin could gather an army."

"And if he doesn't?"

Adonijah placed his hand on top of hers and she swore she could feel his heart breaking underneath her fingertips. "We can find another way."

Salome shook her head, "I am being realistic. I might not act like most princesses, but when it comes down to it, it's about power. I have the power to ensure we have a chance at defeating Niabi."

"Would that make you happy?" he whispered, and she felt her own heart shatter.

"What?"

"Offering yourself up to him, so he funds a war to reclaim your home? A home you won't be able to live once you marry him, because you will be expected to dwell in Sakurai. A home where your brother and his descendants will rule, and your name will be forgotten over time." Adonijah caressed her cheek, swiping flyaway hair from her face. "Would that make you happy?"

"You don't get it."

"Why?" he snorted as she stepped away from him. "Because I'm not a prince?"

"You don't have to carry the burden I do," she whipped around, eyes filled with fury. "People are going to die. With the Eastern army, maybe some of those lives can be saved. I can't bear to think about the dead stretched across the battlefield. To have their deaths haunting me for the rest of my life."

"War is ugly, Salome," he rooted his hands on his hips, trying his best to restrain himself from shouting. "No matter what you do, if Death has called them, she will take them."

"I have to try. If I don't, I don't think I could live with myself."

Adonijah froze in place. He looked like he'd been slapped across the face. "It sounds like you've already made your decision."

Tears pricked at her eyes. "That's not fair," she rasped.

Adonijah swept her up in his arms, wiping the tears that slid down her cheeks with his thumbs. He tilted her chin up and she met his gaze. "I want you, Salome. All of you. But I can't share you with him."

"I care for you," she said as his hand caressed her face. "I wish I could say I've made a decision on what to do, but until this war is over, I don't have the luxury of burning bridges."

Adonijah cupped her jaw. "No matter what happens. I will fight, live, and die by your side."

"No matter what happens," she inhaled to keep from sobbing in his arms. "I will fight, live, and die by your side."

Chapter Forty-Two

Harbona

As *The Golden Rose* approached the glittering harbor of Caelestis, Harbona breathed in the sight of his city, his once home, with a sad smile. It had been over a thousand years since his banishment, and the sweet hillside breeze filled him with the peace and warmth Caelestis was known for. Though it was technically no longer his home, being back made him feel whole.

Diron, the captain of the ship, stood by Harbona's side with his arms folded over his chest. "Should we be expecting the Ethereals to greet us or the Bellators?"

Harbona had nearly a week to mull over that question and he still wasn't sure which sect of Immortals would be at the dock when they arrived. Ideally, his own sect, the Ethereals would be there to accompany him from the ship. But if his parents, the Eldaar, had any say in the matter, the Bellators would be there instead.

While the scholarly and graceful Ethereals were known for their platinum blonde hair, grey eyes, fair skin, pointy ears, and tall, lean physiques, the Bellators were the opposite. They were gold armor wearing warriors with muscular bronze bodies, golden eyes, dark hair, and birdlike, white feathered wings that made them lethal in battle.

Harbona didn't know if any of the Bellators he knew before his banishment would still be active or retired, but if he were honest, he wouldn't be happy to see them first.

"Let us hope," Harbona flashed his friend the best smile he could muster, "the Eldaar do not know their banished son is coming home."

Diron pulled a spyglass out of his breast pocket and pointed it at the harbor. He hummed before extending it to Harbona.

To Harbona's surprise, the flying warriors were not standing at the wharf, but two Ethereals and three hippogriffs were. It had been such a long time since he'd been home that he'd almost forgotten that was how the Ethereals traveled. The Bellators had their wings, but the Ethereals had their beasts. Harbona loved flying atop the majestic creatures whose front halves resembled an eagle and back halves were horse-like. When he was young, Harbona would sneak out of his room to avoid studying the ancient texts of the Eldaar and would go for a late-night flight instead.

"It would appear that the Almighty is smiling down on us today, Diron." Harbona passed the spyglass back to the seafarer. He breathed a little easier knowing he wasn't going to be dragged from the ship in chains to be thrown at the Eldaar's feet.

As the crew prepared to tether *The Golden Rose* in the marina, Diron extended a hand to Harbona. "We will be docked in Caelestis to conduct some business for a few days. If you need me, let me know."

"Thank you, my friend," Harbona hugged the tan captain before he disembarked.

As soon as his feet touched Immortal ground, Harbona was filled with a joy he never expected to feel again. Though it hadn't been his home in years, he felt a power, a brightness, surge through his body. He felt the weight, worries, and grime of the last one thousand years walking mortal land wash away. He looked down at his hands and saw the Immortal glow he had lost when he sailed away was restored.

"I do not understand," Harbona muttered, thinking his aura had been stripped forever after being exiled. He caught a glimpse of his reflection in the water and all signs of him having aged on the Mainland were wiped away. He still bore the banishment mark around his right eye, but he looked like he was once again in his late twenties, exactly how he looked one thousand years ago. "What is happening to me?"

"Harbona," one of the Ethereals extended him a melodic greeting. "We have been instructed to escort you."

Harbona had so many questions, but he pushed them to the back of his mind, and obediently followed them to the hippogriffs. The one in the center was reserved for him and he was glorious. The Seer gently stroked the creature's bird-like neck before it cocked its head to the side and eyed him. The hippogriff bowed its head and lowered its horse-like body to the ground, granting Harbona permission to mount him. Harbona swung one leg over to the opposite side and sat in the leather saddle strapped to the flying beast.

"What is his name?" Harbona asked the Ethereals.

"Zandaar," one answered with an airy pleasantness. "Do you remember how to fly?"

Harbona smiled. "I believe I do. To the sky, Zandaar." With the command, Zandaar shot into the sky. As they teetered into a glide across the city, Harbona laughed, feeling like no time had truly passed since his last flight.

Zandaar seemed to understand his new rider hadn't been home in a millennium, so the hippogriff soared around Caelestis to give him a tour. The rolling green hillside was pocketed with stone villas. Throughout the city were canals and aqueducts, and the golden brick pathways twisted from one side of the kingdom to the other in serpentine fashion.

Set up on the highest hill was The Holies, a palace constructed entirely of gold. It was where the Eldaar dwelled. Where Harbona had been born and had spent his entire life before... He shook the thoughts of his past free and circled away from the impressive palace.

The Holies not only housed the royal family, but also the Tree of Eternity. When an Immortal was ready to cross over into the Next Life, the Eldaar would open the portal hidden in the tree for them to pass through. Harbona had looked forward to one day experiencing crossing over, but being banished, he wasn't sure that was possible anymore. Perhaps, when he took his last breath, he would join the mortals he loved so much and be buried in the ground to rot and decay.

On the other side of the kingdom, on the second highest hill, sat the grandest villa in Caelestis with a waterfall cascading behind the estate. Harbona knew whose home he had been beckoned to, and though he was relieved he wasn't going to The Holies, he wasn't so sure his reception would be any warmer here.

When they landed, the two Ethereals walked inside the gorgeous stone villa that boasted a new terracotta roof. Led through marble arches and breezeways to a lavish sitting room with views of the lush gardens, Harbona was left to wait for his host to make an appearance.

The Seer waited a few minutes before light footsteps slipped inside the room and stopped. He turned around slowly and when their eyes met, Harbona bowed his head. "It has been a long time, Lavena."

Lavena didn't say anything for several minutes. Her piercing grey eyes refused to release him from her glare. Her hip long, platinum blonde hair wasn't loose like it had been during her romance with Lykos of Northwind, but it was now fashioned in a braided crown.

"How did you break through my shield?" she asked, her hands clasped in front of her.

"I did not break through your shield." Harbona took a deep breath, the memories of his three-thousand-year life, growing up with Lavena, flashed through his mind at warp speed, and he had to quiet them before continuing. "Do you remember Princess Salome of Northwind?"

Lavena barely nodded her head in acknowledgement. "Of course, I remember Lykos' sister. What of her?"

"She is the Hunter." Harbona kept a fixed gaze on Lavena, hoping to get a read on her, but after three thousand years, she had become an expert on keeping a neutral face. "Lykos sent her a vision of the past – a vision about you. And a child."

"Have you come for my child, Harbona?" Lavena's voice used to have a sing-song quality, but now, it was icy.

"I have only come to talk." Harbona raised his hands in silent submission. "Does the child know about their father?"

"Why would I hide Lykos from his child?"

"May I see the child?" Harbona braced himself for a furious refusal, but Lavena glided toward him, and motioned for him to follow her into the gardens.

Quietly, the two Ethereals walked side-by-side through the garden, overflowing with thousands of budding roses, hydrangeas, lilies, and ghost caladium – all white to match the Ethereal essence. Harbona could hear the rushing of the waterfall on the far side of the garden, but they headed away from it.

When Lavena stopped, Harbona glanced at a golden fountain where a twelve-year-old girl knelt, wiggling her fingers through the cool water. She flicked her eyes up from the water and met his curious gaze. He felt as if a bolt of lightning zinged through his chest.

She had Lavena's grey eyes and tall, lean body. Her hair was straight like her mother's, but it was dark brown like Lykos'. Her olive skin, round ears, and smile were also gifts from her late father. Harbona teared up, grateful for the small glimpse of the friend he lost twelve years ago.

"Her name is Keeva," Lavena said softly, her lips slightly upturned. It was as close to a full-blown smile that Harbona was going to see from her.

"Hello, Keeva," Harbona turned his focus back to Lykos' daughter. "I am -"

"I know who you are, Harbona," Keeva interrupted him, and her warm aura washed all his worries and sorrows away. "Welcome home."

"You know who I am?" He exchanged a quick look with Lavena, who was once again stone-faced.

"I told mother you would be coming to visit me." Keeva turned her head to the side but didn't stop playing with the fountain water as she squinted at him. "You looked older in my vision, but I suppose by coming home, the Eldaar restored your aura like I asked them to."

"Is she a ...?" Harbona whispered, so only Lavena could hear him.

Lavena bobbed her head. "The first Seer born to our people since... you."

"And my parents know?" Harbona continued to speak in a hushed tone, as if Keeva didn't know what she was.

"The Eldaar know of her sight." Lavena looked at Harbona. "How else do you think you were allowed to step one foot on our shores and be restored to your former self?"

"She told them I was coming?"

"The Eldaar listen to Keeva. She is a Demi, half-Ethereal and half-mortal. She is rare, but even more so, because she is also a Seer." Lavena let a crack in her armor show, whether she could help it or not, Harbona didn't know. "The Eldaar see her as a sacred being, but she is just a girl, Harbona. And I will fight to give her as normal a life as I can. That's what Lykos would have wanted."

Harbona fought the urge to reach over and grab Lavena's hand to give her an encouraging squeeze. That was a mortal comfort. Ethereals wouldn't take kindly to being touched in that manner and most Bellators would certainly draw their weapons considering it to be a challenge.

Harbona approached Keeva who stood and started to make her way toward him. Before he got close, Harbona heard a flutter, and two loud thuds that shook the ground. He whipped around and saw two Bellators standing on either side of Lavena. She hadn't even blinked when the warriors landed and didn't look surprised by their sudden presence.

"Is it just me, Abba, or has Harbona gotten uglier since the last time we saw him?" The taller of the two muscular Bellators flashed Harbona a crooked grin.

Abba wiped his shaggy, dark hair out of his face, revealing the scars that stretched from his forehead, down the side of his face ending at his neck, barely missing his right eye. "Harbona has always been ugly, Kayven."

Kayven was the first to move toward Harbona. Half of his shoulder-length hair was pulled away from his bronze face, but rebellious strands hovered over his golden eyes. As soon as Kayven reached Harbona, he wrapped his enormous arms around the Seer, and it felt like he was being hugged by a bear.

"Welcome home, Harbona," Kayven whispered.

Harbona smiled with tears in his eyes, "It is good to see you, my friend."

Though Abba wasn't a hugger by nature, he returned Harbona's embrace when he made his way over to him. The scars Abba bore were from the night they attempted to assassinate Phlias – an everlasting reminder of their failure. But at least Harbona was able to keep them from being banished as well. Better him, than all of them.

"How did you know I was here?" Harbona asked, taking a step back from the brothers and fiercest commanders to ever lead the Bellators.

"I told them." Keeva's sweet voice sliced through the circle of testosterone, and Kayven scooped her up in his arms, planting a kiss on her cheek. "Hello, Uncle Kayven."

"Uncle?" Harbona arched a brow in playfulness.

Kayven shrugged. "When a toddler calls you Uncle Kayven, you become Uncle Kayven."

Lavena stepped forward, still wary of Harbona in their midst. "Why are you here, Harbona?"

"The war, of course," Keeva answered before Harbona had a chance.

"War?" Lavena's voice wavered and she narrowed her eyes as she stared at Harbona.

"Crispin and Salome are gathering forces to challenge Niabi for the White Throne," Harbona got straight to the point. "I am not here for aid. Salome had a vision that you and Lykos had a child."

Lavena folded her delicate arms over her chest. "And your precious mortals are worried Keeva will try to stake her claim to her father's throne? How typical of you to look out for the kingdoms and crowns of the mortals, instead of your own people."

"I did not come here to fight, Lavena," Harbona huffed, rubbing a hand over his forehead. "For being so against helping the mortals, you seem to have forgotten that you married one."

"Leave Lykos out of this," Lavena snapped, gritting her teeth.

"I had to see for myself if some piece of Lykos still lived," Harbona looked down at Keeva who took his hand in hers. "You have his smile."

"They will be excited to see you," Keeva said and Harbona tilted his head to the side. "Mother's shield must have prevented you from seeing them."

"Who?" Harbona asked, confused.

"I think the youngling is referring to us."

Harbona turned back toward the fountain and saw Odelia wearing white Ethereal robes, her arm in a sling. Reaper sat faithfully by her side while a younger version of Odelia stood next to her.

"Odelia?" Harbona had never seen Odelia outside of her swamp and his eyebrows shot up in alarm. "The Enchanted Swamp?"

"Shadows came for me," Odelia explained, though she didn't come any closer to them. "Makeda saved me, and the swamp."

Harbona's gaze drifted to Makeda. Other than her grey eyes, she was the spitting image of the Enchantress.

"Harbona," Odelia motioned a hand toward her daughter, "This is Makeda. Makeda, this is Harbona. Your father."

Harbona and Makeda's eyes widened when they heard the last bit of the introduction. The Seer knew Odelia had to be telling the truth. Only one with Ethereal blood had grey eyes, which would make Makeda not only his daughter, but...

"She's a Demi." Lavena stepped forward, a softness in her voice.

Odelia bobbed her head. "And a water wielder."

Harbona took a step forward, eyes fixed on the daughter he never knew existed. His heart was beating fast and hard in his chest, and he wasn't exactly sure what to say. She was a grown woman, and as of that moment, he knew only two things about her. Her name and her magical prowess.

"Makeda, I -"

Makeda's eyes welled with tears. She shook her head before he could say anything else, as if hearing him say her name was too much for her to handle. Snatching her arm from her mother's, and without saying a single word, she retreated into the garden.

"Why did you not tell me we have a daughter?" Harbona viciously spat the question at Odelia. She squinted, slamming her hands on her hips in response.

"And when was I supposed to tell you, Harbona?" She hissed, her accent thicker when she was angry. "You left before I even knew I was pregnant, and I saw you for the first time in almost twenty-five years a few weeks ago. So, please," she waved her uninjured arm wildly in the air, "tell me when would have been a good time to let you know about Makeda?"

Harbona's cheeks flushed in embarrassment. "I am ... You are right, Odelia. I am sorry."

Odelia's gaze softened and she sighed. "You will have to give her some time. She has been wanting to know who her father is all her life and didn't know she would be meeting you today."

A silence fell on the group, but after a few moments, Kayven slapped a hand on Harbona's shoulder. "So, tell us more about this war you've gotten yourself into."

Chapter Forty-Three

Salome

Salome and Adonijah followed the path through the Paraiso Gardens until they reached a bronze fountain. Her gaze trailed from the perfectly sculpted hedges up to the twinkling stars in the night sky. There were lights strung through the tree branches to illuminate their path, and the smell of jasmine hung in the air, bringing a much-needed smile to her face. The Paraiso Gardens was understandably a wonder of their world and a magical place. She could sit there all night, soaking in the floral scents and peaceful sounds, but that's not why she was there.

Adonijah's fingers tapped the hilt of his longsword hanging at his side. His eyes were alert, darting from one area of the quiet garden to the other. "I don't like this, Salome."

"He'll be here." Though she wondered if maybe he was already there, cloaked, and watching them for his enjoyment. She extended the bridge to Jinn. *"Where are you?"*

"For not being your watchdog," Jinn cooed, and she knew he was hidden nearby, *"he is awfully protective of you. Is it reserved just for me or is he like this with anyone who looks at you?"*

Salome snorted, folding her arms over her chest. "Show yourself." Jinn and Kai appeared out of thin air and were lounging on the other side of the fountain. Kai looked as menacing as the night they first met. She picked at her nails with one of her many knives, barely acknowledging Salome and Adonijah staring at them.

Salome's eyes floated to Jinn and felt a sudden warmth flood her. Her lips parted, but she had nothing to say. If the Prince of Darkness ever took mortal form, he would look exactly like Jinn. She was suddenly aware of how quickly her heart was beating, how her fingers ached with the need to run them through his dark hair.

The prince let out a low, warm chuckle. He uncrossed his ankles and stood from his reclined position. "Forgive the precautions, but we wanted to be sure you came alone."

Adonijah growled, inching closer to speak his mind, but Salome gently grabbed his arm, keeping him by her side. "You've had your fun." Salome narrowed her eyes, although her heart nearly dropped out of her chest when Jinn smiled at her. "We should get going."

"My ship is prepared to launch as soon as I give the order." Jinn approached with a lazy swagger. "I'll cloak us and get us past the guards, but we will need a distraction." He turned his focus to Adonijah. "That's where you and Kai come in."

Adonijah's brows furrowed, and he stepped forward, putting himself between Salome and Jinn. "You think I'm going to let her out of my sight?"

Jinn shrugged, unbothered by Adonijah's stance. "By all means, take her yourself. Let me know how that goes without my magic."

Salome tugged at Adonijah's arm. "I'll be fine. Go with Kai."

Adonijah's shoulders tensed as he turned to face her. "And if this is a trap?" he whispered.

"It's a risk I am willing to take to get Mika out." Salome nodded her head; she had made her decision. Her eyes darted across the small plaza until they settled on Jinn. "Let's go."

Cloaked, Salome and Jinn waited by the hedges surrounding the tower Mika was being held in. The tower dungeon was not what Salome had expected. It wasn't dark or ominous in appearance, it was merely an extension of the Scarlett Citadel in shape and color. The bronze door was guarded by two Qata Vishna stationed on either side. It was only a two-story tower, so Salome wasn't sure why the Myridians referred to it as Tower Dungeon. It was more like a cylindrical house.

Waiting for the distraction that would spur the guards to leave their posts, Salome and Jinn crouched close to one another. She could feel his steady breathing against the side of her neck. She hadn't been this close to the prince before and found her mind and body dueling. Wanting to put a foot or two of separation between them, but at the same time, wanting to feel his arms wrapped around her. No one would even know with them being cloaked. She shook her head, pinching the bridge of her nose.

She could feel his eyes on her. Not wanting to meet his gaze and give her thoughts away, she mentally shot to him, *"Thank you. I know this was probably a difficult decision. "*

"It was simple."

"Really?"

"You needed me," he smiled at her. *"I will always be there to help you."*

Salome shook her head again, *"I find it hard to believe you don't already have a wife."* She could have slapped herself for being so careless. Her cheeks reddened, and she felt his fingers trail up her jawline, gently forcing her to look at him.

"If I said I wanted to kiss you," he ran the tip of his thumb across her lips, *"would you let me?"*

Salome couldn't help the shiver that ran down her spine when his warm skin touched hers. *"Well,"* she managed, *"you can't* say *it."*

His laugh heated every inch of her body. *"An unfortunate technicality. I might not be able to shout it from the tallest tower, but I've thought about kissing you since I first saw you."*

"Yes, I know, I could see it in your eyes at the Festival of Forbidden Fruit," Salome rolled her eyes in an attempt to release the tension of her rapidly beating heart.

Jinn shook his head slowly, eyes fixed on hers. *"I saw you in the halls once before, when you first arrived to the Isles of Myr."*

Realization hit Salome, nearly robbing her of breath. She *had* seen Jinn in the halls on her way to meet with Zara for the first time. She thought he was one of the most handsome men she had ever laid her eyes on. And now, they were so close she was sure he could feel her longing for him.

"So, you see," he continued, interlocking his fingers with hers, *"you've been on my mind for a while now."* He leaned in to kiss her.

Salome desperately wanted to feel Jinn's lips on hers, and feel his hands grab ahold of her waist, pulling her against his muscular body, but in the corner of her eye she spotted movement. She placed her hand on his chest, *"Jinn."*

He pulled back, raking a hand through his hair, *"Sorry, I -"*

"Look," Salome pointed a finger toward the bronze door. *"They're leaving."*

The two Qata Vishna sprinted from their posts, weapons drawn. Salome watched them and saw smoke rising from the gardens behind them.

"Looks like our distraction worked." Jinn grabbed her hand and tugged her forward. *"Come on."*

Salome wriggled her hand free, *"They set something on fire?"* Her nostrils flared and he raised his hands to calm her down.

"Kai is an expert when it comes to fires. I promise nothing will be damaged."

Salome had no choice but to trust him. They wouldn't have much time to get Mika out before the Qata Vishna returned. She nodded and he focused on the door. He dropped to one knee before he fingered a skinny metal pick out of his sleeve and stuck it inside the lock.

"You pick locks, too?" Salome leaned against the stone walls; arms crossed over her chest. "If I didn't know you were a prince, I'd peg you for a common thief."

Jinn smirked. "I'm flattered." The door unlocked and he pushed it open. "Once you head up those steps," he whispered, "you'll be released from my cloaking. I'll stay here and keep an eye out for the guards."

Salome bobbed her head and sprinted up the stairs, taking them two by two. She reached another bronze door leading to Mika's one room cell. She opened the door and was surprised to see Mika's cell looked more like a lush guest room than a prison. Cushioned furniture, a small fireplace, a bookshelf, an unused bed, and a table with an untouched dinner plate rounded out the room.

Mika's back faced Salome as she entered the room. Her arms were wrapped around her torso as she silently stared out the only window. It wasn't big enough for someone to escape, just large enough for someone to see a sliver of the outside world.

Salome opened her mouth, but snapped it shut when Mika said, "I know what you're going to ask, but I don't know where Marina is. And if I did know, I wouldn't tell you."

"Why, Mika?" Salome rubbed a finger across her forehead. "She murdered our grandmother."

"I went to see Marina after our meeting with my mother. She told me she never wanted to hurt anyone, but if Niabi wasn't obeyed, she would've been killed instead."

"And you believed her?"

"Marina is a lot of things," Mika turned around to look Salome in the eye, "but she is not a liar."

"She's a coward," Salome snorted. "Your mother can't execute you in her place."

Mika nodded, and accepted Salome's tone graciously. "Our laws are clear. A life for a life."

"No," Salome shook her head. "I won't accept that. You are the Red Maiden. You are the heir to the Bronze Throne. You will not be executed."

"It was my choice to switch places with Marina."

"But -"

"Could you watch Crispin die?"

"I could watch Niabi die."

"Despite the person Marina is, and what she has done," Mika sighed, "I can't watch her take her last breath. She is still my sister."

Salome approached her and whispered, "There's a ship leaving for the Mainland tonight. I am going to help you escape."

Mika shook her head, "Salome -"

"I can't watch you die. Not in Marina's place. Not like this." Salome fought back tears. "It's not fair."

Mika grabbed her cousin's hands and squeezed gently. "I will not run. I took Marina's place, and I am willing to accept the consequences. But there is something I will ask of you."

Salome was fighting to keep tears from pouring down her cheeks. "Anything."

"Make sure Utara isn't there to watch." Mika's neutral expression turned into one of sadness at the mention of her ten-year-old daughter. "I couldn't bear for that to be her last memory of me."

Salome nodded. "I swear, from now until I draw my last breath, I will look after her."

Mika hugged her tightly. She took a step back, slipped a pin out of her hair, and clipped it in Salome's curls. "This is given to every Qata Vishna once she has completed training. You are now one of us."

"Please reconsider," Salome's bottom lip quivered. "I can get you out of here. I can help you."

She kissed Salome's forehead, "Make sure Utara knows how much I love her."

Jinn whistled up the stairs signaling their time was nearly up. "I thought we would be fighting side-by-side on the battlefield."

Mika smiled and escorted Salome to the door. "Perhaps we will, in the next life. Goodbye, Cousin." She closed the door and Salome was forced to retreat down the stairs to an awaiting Jinn.

She didn't break stride to wait for him to lock the door. Her breathing was rigid, and her eyes were burning from all the tears she was still holding back until she could reach the privacy of her bedchambers. Mika had made her choice, and Salome would have to accept it.

When she rounded the corner, she realized a second too late, that she hadn't waited for Jinn to cloak her. The two Qata Vishna who had abandoned their posts at the tower stared at her. They exchanged a quick glance before turning their focus back to the princess.

"I..." Salome's throat immediately went dry and any excuse she could think of to explain why she was walking the grounds this late, didn't come to mind.

"There you are. I've been looking for you." Jinn slipped his arm around her waist and slammed his lips against hers. Electricity shot through her body and her knees buckled. She expected him to be smug about finally putting his lips against hers, but she found a gentle longing and an apology before he pulled away. Their foreheads were pressed together, their breathing heavy, and she was ready to ram herself against him once more when one of the Qata Vishna cleared her throat.

Jinn whipped his head toward the guards and acted surprised to see them. "Oh, I see we aren't alone anymore, darling." He kissed Salome's temple, sending another wave of electricity down her spine. "I trust you will keep seeing the princess and myself to yourselves."

The Qata Vishna guards once again exchanged a quiet look, but both nodded their heads in agreement. One said, "If you are looking for a private garden, then try the Rose Garden."

Jinn flashed a charming smile at them, resting his hand on Salome's lower back, ushering her forward. "Thank you both for your discretion. The princess and I appreciate it."

As soon as the Qata Vishna were on the other side of the hedge and back at their posts, Jinn withdrew his hand from her back and shoved both of his hands into his pockets.

"Sorry about -"

Salome waved her hand in the air, "It's alright. It was good thinking on your part. I shouldn't have stormed off without you."

"What happened with..." Jinn wisely didn't say Mika's name.

"She refused to come. She made her choice." Salome wrapped her hands around her body as they silently made their way back into the Scarlett Citadel.

Once they stood outside her chambers, she turned to face him. "I hope I haven't caused you too much trouble tonight." Her eyes darted to the floor to avoid meeting his gaze. The taste of his kiss lingered on her lips, and the ghost of his touch warmed her skin. She craved him, and if she kept looking at him, she was afraid he would see it written all over her face.

Jinn's fingers tenderly lifted her chin, forcing her to make eye contact with him. "Earlier, when I said I was sorry for kissing you -"

She glanced up and down the hall making sure they were still alone. "I already told you, it's alright."

Jinn pressed a finger to her mouth. "I'm not sorry I kissed you. I'm just sorry that was our first kiss." He took another step toward her; her back pinned against the wall.

Before she could respond, a palace worker appeared at the end of the hallway and made her way toward them. Salome wasn't sure how she would explain what they were doing, but the woman walked by them without a word or a curtsey.

"I cloaked us the moment we stepped inside the palace," Jinn whispered. Salome met his gaze. "If I said I wanted to kiss you," Jinn repeated his question from earlier, "would you let me?"

Salome slammed her mouth against his, giving into desire. One hand cupped her face, the other gripped her thigh. She hopped up, wrapping her legs around his torso, and he pinned her against the wall, matching her passion.

It was an odd feeling to be in the middle of the hallway kissing. Ordinarily, anyone could walk by and see them, but with Jinn's magic, they were in a world of their own. They could do whatever they wanted, and no one would ever know. The magnitude of his power struck her, and she craved more of him.

Jinn had been right before. Together, uniting their houses, they could do a lot of good for their people. Their power would be unmatched. The other kingdoms in Adalore would think twice before striking or scheming against them.

Jinn murmured against her mouth, "You're thinking too much."

Salome pushed him away, her hands gripping his shirt so tight her knuckles were white. "You heard what I was thinking?" She hadn't extended the bridge to him.

Jinn shook his head. "I didn't hear your thoughts, but I can tell when you're thinking too much. Your body tenses."

Salome loosened her grip on him, feeling her cheeks brighten in embarrassment. "Sorry."

"Out of curiosity," Jinn kissed her neck, "what were you thinking about?"

Salome smirked and raked her hands through his hair, "I have to keep some thoughts to myself, Jinn."

"A secret for a secret," he whispered in her ear.

"You first," Salome opened their mental bond. Secrets were just for them, and no prying ears would learn them.

"Sometimes at night, you reach out to me in your sleep. I feel you at peace and it helps me sleep."

Jinn's confession nearly brought Salome to her knees. She uncoiled her legs from his body, slipping back to the floor. She cupped his face in her hands and kissed him gently on the lips before admitting, *"Sometimes, I think about what life married to you would look like, and I find myself wanting to accept your proposal."*

He rested his forehead against hers and sighed.

Salome ran her fingers along his jawline. "Did I say something wrong?"

Jinn shook his head and kissed her forehead. His eyes met hers and his smile wasn't as wide as it normally was. "My army will fight for you with or without you accepting my proposal."

"What?" Salome's gaze bounced between his eyes quickly, searching for answers.

"I don't want you to accept my proposal to win a war against your sister." Jinn absentmindedly twisted locks of her curly hair between his thumb and index finger. "I would always wonder if you accepted my proposal for my army or because you loved me. And I would rather you choose me for me."

"Jinn..."

"I don't need an answer tonight." Jinn continued. "I don't even need an answer soon. Whatever, whoever, you choose. I want it to be for the right reasons, and not because you felt you had to put your people before yourself. There will be plenty of difficult decisions for you to make without me adding another to your plate."

"You really mean that?" Her hand trailed down from his chest to his hand gripping her waist and she squeezed it.

"My army is yours. My sword is yours. My life is yours." Jinn kissed her and she wished he didn't pull away. "You should get some rest. I have a ship to delay."

"Thank you." She caressed his face before he pressed his lips against her palm and took off down the hall.

Salome caught her breath before entering her room and stopped when she saw Adonijah on her balcony smoking his pipe. The guilt in the pit of her stomach was back. She knew she cared deeply for Adonijah, but she clearly had feelings for Jinn, too.

She closed the door behind her making enough noise for him to turn his head toward her. "Are you alright?"

"Mika refused to leave." Salome sank in the chair on the other side of the balcony with a thud.

"I know." Adonijah bobbed his head. "Kai said you left the tower without Mika."

Salome's heart skipped a beat. Had he seen her kissing Jinn? "You two were watching us?"

"Kai had eyes on you." Adonijah planted his feet on the floor, squaring his body toward her. "I made sure the Qata Vishna didn't spot us. Once you left, we left."

"Thank you for helping, Adonijah." Salome rubbed the back of her neck. "I just wish she would have..." She inhaled deeply before standing up. "It's been a long day."

Adonijah rose from his seat and nodded. "If you need anything, I'm across the hall." He stepped toward her and wrapped his arms around her. "I'm sorry about Mika."

Salome embraced him, burying her face in the crease of his neck. She wondered if he could smell Jinn on her. She wasn't in a relationship with either man, yet she felt guilty for spending time with one knowing they both had feelings for her.

If Zophar were there, he would have crossed his giant arms across his broad, hairy chest and shook his head mumbling something about not letting either man distract her from what she needed to do. She missed him. Missed his impish blue eyes. Missed his gruff voice. Missed his boorish snoring.

She pulled out of Adonijah's hold and cleared her throat. "I'll see you tomorrow."

"Aye." He took that as her dismissing him for the night and left her room without another word.

Feelings or not, she hadn't come this far to lose herself to a man. She was on this journey for one reason, and that was to defeat her sister. She needed to remain focused, or she might not make it to the battlefield.

Chapter Forty-Four

Crispin

"When I become king, the first thing I'm going to do is change these uniforms." Crispin marched into Oden's office and waved his arms around in childish protest. "How do her soldiers wear this all day long?"

Nubis chuckled, seated in his simple wooden chair, muscular arms crossed over his broad chest. "You get used to it."

"How am I expected to fight in this?" Crispin fidgeted in the black armor. "I'll be glad when I can take this off." He rubbed the nape of his neck and plopped into Ziggy's high-back chair. "I remember when the guards wore navy and white uniforms with the White Wolf sigil on their chests. It seems like anything that reminded her of our father, she's gotten rid of."

"Then you're going to love how she's decorated the White Keep." Nubis chuckled when Crispin's eyes widened.

"She wouldn't."

Nubis shrugged. "Of course, I never saw it before the renovations, but there's a lot of black and white now. Oden gripes about it from time to time. Said your mother was the one to bring the White Keep to life when she arrived to marry your father."

"He seems to have known my mother well." Crispin shifted uncomfortably in his seat. "Do you know if they ever...?"

"I loved your mother with my entire heart and would have gladly given my life in her place," Oden's voice sliced into the underground headquarters with a sharpness that took Crispin by surprise. "But she was faithful to her marriage vows. We never had a relationship of any kind, other than friendship."

"You make it sound as if she didn't want to be with my father at all." Crispin folded his arms over his chest with a scowl.

Oden sat on the edge of his desk facing Crispin and pulled a pendant from under his shirt, holding it in his palm for the prince to see. "This was the last gift she ever gave me before your sister..." He cleared his throat and squeezed the emerald gemstone with teary eyes. "I used to tell Bilhah that her eyes reminded me of emeralds."

Hearing a different side of his mother's life made his heart ache. "She loved you?"

"We knew we could never be together," Oden slipped the necklace underneath his shirt, "but that never stopped me from loving her with all that I am. I wasn't even here when your sister attacked. The king had sent me to the Isles of Myr to meet with Queen Nym. If I had been here, I would have gotten your mother and siblings out of the city."

Crispin was having difficulty breathing. He tried to loosen the heavy pieces of metal weighing him down just to catch a breath.

"I know this isn't something a son wants to hear about his mother," Oden continued, as if he had been waiting for the right moment to confess. "She wasn't happy with Issachar, but she loved you children more than anything in this world."

"You never married?" Crispin asked, his tone edgier than he had intended.

Oden shook his head. "It wouldn't have been fair to another woman to live in your mother's shadow." He stepped toward Crispin and knelt before him. "I swore I would avenge her death. But now, I see I survived all those years ago, so I could serve you now. I swear by my life or by my death, I will help you take back your ancestors' throne."

Crispin rested a hand on Oden's shoulder and nodded. "I only hope to be worthy of such an oath."

Rahab, Penn, and Ziggy entered from the adjoining room. Penn somehow looked like the black armor was tailored for her specifically. She wore the heavy metal pieces as if they were as light as a feather.

Crispin's eyes drifted from Penn to Rahab and nearly choked when he saw her. Not in armor like Nubis, Penn, and himself, but in a dress similar to what Ziggy would wear on one of her late-night rendezvous with Gershom. Rahab planted her hands on her hips and snarled at him.

"Enjoying the view?" Rahab's head tilted to the side; any sign of amusement drained from her face.

Crispin shook his head and stammered, "I... I, uh. I didn't know you were... I didn't realize you were...I didn't expect you to be in a dress..."

"Yikes," Penn tucked the black helmet Nubis handed her under her arm. "I'm blind and even I could see that was the worst experience of your life."

Ziggy chuckled when Crispin blushed. "Nubis couldn't find another set of armor to steal -"

"Borrow." Nubis cut in.

"Nubis couldn't find another set of armor to *borrow*," she flashed Nubis a smile with the amendment. "So, I leant her one of my dresses. Doesn't she look stunning?"

Rahab huffed indignantly. With her waist cinched as tiny as it could go without breaking a rib, and her cleavage on display, Rahab would definitely catch a few wandering eyes tonight. If they needed a distraction, she was their ticket.

"You look beautiful," Crispin offered, trying to hide the flush in his cheeks.

Rahab shifted her weight, tugging at her ear. "As long as I get to slit a few throats, I suppose this will be worth the hassle."

Crispin could have stared at her for hours and not gotten bored, but they had a rescue mission ahead of them that needed his full attention. He turned toward the rest of the group. "Everyone knows their assignment?" Nods from around the room returned in response. "Good. From Nubis' report, the ritual will be happening sometime tonight. With any luck, we'll break into the prison and free Neempo before they come for him."

"And if we don't get there in time?" Rahab asked.

"We don't leave without him." Crispin said, and Penn nodded her head in agreement. "If we run into my sister," the word sister left him with a bitter taste in his mouth, "then everyone is to run as fast as they can. Do not engage her, leave her to me."

"Are you forgetting she has fire magic?" Nubis leaned closer to Ziggy who looked petrified.

"No," Crispin shook his head. "I'm aware of her magic, but if our plan fails, even if that means you leave me behind, get out. She wants me. Not any of you."

"Like hell I'll leave you in there to face her by yourself!" Rahab spat each word and Crispin was taken aback by her reaction.

"You'll have to," he replied as gently and sternly as he could without spurring them to fist fight. "Get Neempo out. If I'm left behind, then you find my sister, Salome. She'll come for me."

"Crispin -"

"Let's go," Crispin interrupted Rahab and motioned for the group to start leaving out the secret entrance. Once Oden, Ziggy, Nubis, and Penn left, Crispin turned to face an enraged Rahab.

"I don't know why you're trying to play the martyr," Rahab fumed, stomping toward him, "but I won't be following any orders that include leaving you behind."

"I don't want anyone getting hurt," Crispin stood his ground, fighting the urge to look down her low-cut gown. "What do you think will happen if she gets her hands on one of you? She'll torture you until you give me up or die. I won't have you or anyone else going through that to protect me."

"But if she captures you..." Rahab sucked in a breath and Crispin realized she was trying to keep tears from rolling down her cheeks.

"You care." Crispin met her watery gaze and smiled.

"If by care, you mean I don't want you to die, then yes, I care." She pointed an accusatory finger at him, but before she could open her mouth to argue further, he cupped her face in his hands and pressed his lips against hers.

"I love you, too," he whispered.

"Then you understand why I can't, why I won't, leave you behind." She raked her fingers through his hair.

Crispin kissed her one more time, before he motioned toward the door. "Then let's hope tonight will be easy."

Oden and Master Penn's six Keepers stayed outside the White Keep, patrolling the streets. Once the others rescued Neempo, they would have backup in escorting him to the *Shadow of Death.*

Ziggy took Rahab through the private entrance Gershom had her use when they would meet. Crispin worried the two guards wouldn't allow a newcomer to pass, but as soon as they saw Ziggy, they motioned the women forward without a second glance.

Crispin and Penn followed Nubis into the soldiers' barracks without a problem. No one questioned them, and it didn't seem like anyone cared as they stomped from one end of the stone building to the other, which was attached to a long hall that led down to the dungeons.

Trying to monitor and regulate his breathing underneath the stifling helmet, Crispin muttered a prayer, and hoped they would make it in time to free Neempo before his sister found out.

As they approached, the guard sitting at the entrance of the dungeons looked up from his desk. "What brings you down here, Nubis?" He checked his paperwork and shook his head. "You aren't scheduled down here tonight."

"I was told to bring the new recruits down for a tour." Nubis lied so effortlessly, Crispin almost forgot why they were there.

The guard narrowed his eyes, "This late?"

Nubis shrugged his massive shoulders, looking bored. "Look, if you want to send us on our way, I'd be glad. I was hoping to get down to the Night District for a drink. But Captain Glenn insisted I bring them down here. Something about putting them into the rotation this week."

At the mention of Captain Glenn, the soldier froze. "Oh, Captain Glenn sent you then."

"That's what I said, Kane," Nubis huffed, and Crispin stifled a laugh. "Now, are you going to let us pass, so I can get this tour over with? If I'm lucky, I'll still be able to make it to the Night District for some fun."

Kane motioned the three of them through and grabbed the giant soldier by the arm. When Nubis cast a judgmental glare down at him, he released him from his grasp. Kane whispered, "You won't tell Captain Glenn of the delay, right? I must have just misplaced the paperwork."

Nubis hesitated before nodding his head. "Sure, Kane."

Once they had gone down a few rickety flights of stairs, Nubis tapped Crispin on top of his helmet, and a clanging rang in his ears. "You can take the helmets off now. No one is stationed all the way down here."

Crispin ripped the helmet from his head, grateful to be rid of it, and took the deepest breath of air he could, only to start coughing. "What is that smell?" Crispin said between chokes.

"What did you expect a dungeon to smell like?" Nubis arched an eyebrow. "Roses?"

Penn chuckled and Nubis cracked the thinnest smile. "You've got a good sense of humor, Nubis."

"He's not that funny," Crispin rolled his eyes.

"According to the manifest," Nubis marched down the damp, sewer smelling hallway, ignoring the whimpers of prisoners behind the solid wooden doors, "he should be in this cell." Nubis pulled a pick out of his hair and went to work on the lock. As soon as it clicked, he swung the door open only to find the cell empty.

"We're too late." Crispin closed his eyes and tilted his head toward the low ceiling.

"They took him a little while ago," a soft voice echoed.

They turned around, looking for who spoke, but found no one.

"Who's there?" Penn asked in a militaristic voice.

A light tapping noise drew their attention to the cell next to Neempo's. "Your friend told me you would come looking for him. Said to tell you they're taking him to the Eastern Courtyard."

"Thank you for your assistance," Penn shucked the helmet back over her head, ready to stomp back down the hall.

"I am one with nothing to offer..." the man's voice trailed off and Penn stopped dead in her tracks.

She turned on her heel and replied, "But I am one with everything to give."

"What is going on?" Crispin looked back and forth between Penn and the prisoner's cell.

"Nubis, open it." Penn ignored Crispin's question and pointed at the wooden door, "He is coming with us."

"What?" Nubis protested. "We don't know anything about this man."

"Only the Sovereign could have told him that phrase," Penn explained. "It's a code. Whoever knows it is protected by The Sisters. This man is coming with us."

Nubis looked at Crispin for direction. The prince nodded for the Stormcrag to set the prisoner free. As quickly as Nubis had opened Neempo's door, he unlocked the second door.

A man not much older than Crispin stumbled out. By his frame, Crispin could tell he was once bulky with muscle, but he was now whittled down to skin and bones. His dark skin and hazel eyes indicated he was originally from Numbio. But how he ended up this far from his home, and in the White Keep's dungeon, was a story for another time.

"Do you need help walking?" Nubis asked as the young man limped, favoring his right leg.

"If it wouldn't be too much trouble," he rasped, as if he hadn't had a drink of water in a while.

"How are we going to get him past the guards in the barracks?" Crispin asked as Nubis wrapped the weary prisoner's arm over his shoulder.

"The same way we would have gotten Neempo out," Nubis puckered his lips toward a second hallway that led into darkness. "None of the guards venture down here. If they did, they'd know there's a grate that leads to the sewers. That's our way back to the city."

Crispin nodded in understanding. "And to get inside the White Keep?"

Penn slammed her palm against Crispin's chest, halting their trek. "You ask, as if you will be going on your own, Prince Crispin."

"You need to get this man to the *Shadow of Death* -"

"I came for the Sovereign." Penn's voice dripped with venom. "I will not leave without him."

"You decided to bring this man along with us," Crispin pointed out as respectfully as he could without riling the Master of Keepers to the point of dueling. "You are now responsible to see that he is safely delivered to the ship."

Before Penn could argue, they heard whispers headed in their direction.

"Soldiers," Penn whispered and began listening intently again. "One sounds like the guard who let us pass, and the man he's talking to is very angry."

"Damn," Nubis growled. "Kane must have alerted Captain Glenn."

"Is this Captain Glenn going to be a problem?" Penn asked, her hand on the hilt of her sword.

"Let's just say, I won't be showing my face around here anymore." Nubis shook his head, still supporting the exhausted and sickly-looking prisoner. "Oden isn't going to like this at all."

"There's just two?" Crispin asked Penn who was still listening.

Penn bobbed her head. "Yes."

"Then you two get him to the ship." Crispin instructed, not taking no for an answer. "I'll handle these two."

"What about the Sovereign?" Penn asked, a hint of alarm in her voice.

"I'll find him and meet you at the docks." The sound of voices grew louder, and Crispin waved the three of them to keep going. "Go."

Nubis nodded and practically carried the prisoner down the tunnel, Penn close in tow. Crispin reluctantly slammed his helmet back over his head and marched toward Captain Glenn and Kane. With his back firmly against the wall that cornered the hallway the two soldiers were walking down, Crispin decided to try to get out of the dungeons without spilling blood. As the two men neared him, Crispin stepped out from his hiding spot, and bumped into a burly, scarred man who he could only assume was Captain Glenn.

"Watch where you're going, soldier!" Captain Glenn bellowed, brushing the imaginary dirt from his pristine uniform.

Crispin straightened and saluted the superior officer. "Apologies, Captain.

Captain Glenn narrowed his eyes at Crispin, not being able to get a good look at him with the helmet hiding most of his face. "What are you doing down here? What's your name?"

"My name is Graves, sir." Crispin lied.

"What are you doing down here, *Graves*?" The captain repeated the name, as if he believed it to be made up.

"I was supposed to be on a tour of the dungeons, but I got sick from the smell and had to stop." Crispin hoped the captain believed that part of the story because it was partially true. "I was separated from the others and got lost."

"Where's Nubis?" Kane interjected, questioning Crispin as if he were a prisoner.

"I'll ask the questions, Kane," Captain Glenn snorted, and Kane took a sheepish step back. "Where's Nubis?"

"I told you, Captain, I got lost. I don't know where Nubis is, sir." Crispin had sweat dripping down his back, tickling his spine. He'd give this another minute before he'd have to slit their throats and find Neempo.

The captain looked Crispin up and down, clearly contemplating if he believed the tale he was being told. "Kane." Kane stepped forward like a dutiful lap dog and bowed his head in anticipation. "Take Graves and lock him up until we can find Nubis and the other guard on this so-called tour."

"Yes, Captain," Kane took a step toward Crispin with a wicked grin.

"I'm afraid that isn't going to work for me," Crispin unsheathed his sword and in the same breath, sliced his blade across Kane's chest. Turning his focus to the middle-aged captain, Crispin pointed the longsword at him. "Let me pass and you won't end up like him."

"I will see you hang for this!" The captain snarled and reached for his sword.

Ordinarily, Crispin would duel the captain for honor's sake, but tonight wasn't about being honorable. Before Captain Glenn could unsheathe his weapon, Crispin stabbed him in his chest. As quickly as he could, the prince stuffed both bodies into Neempo's empty cell and closed the door. Now, he needed to infiltrate the White Keep and find

Neempo before someone stumbled upon the bodies. It sounded simple, but then again, the night hadn't been going as smoothly as he had expected. Hopefully, Rahab and Ziggy were having better luck on their end.

Chapter Forty-Five

Rahab

"So far so good," Ziggy whispered to Rahab as they strolled through the glistening white halls of the White Keep. It was well past midnight and most people in the castle were tucked in their beds snoring the night away.

"How many more rooms do we have to check?" Rahab tugged and pulled at her corset until Ziggy smacked her hand away. The pirate gritted her teeth, ready to curse at the redhead.

"If you mess with your dress, someone is bound to notice." Ziggy kept her eyes forward, looking for anyone lurking in the halls, ignoring Rahab's menacing glare.

"So?" Rahab snorted.

"So," Ziggy met her irritated gaze, "experienced girls don't fidget the way you do. You'll give us away before I have a chance to lie our way out."

Rahab stiffened. Ziggy had a point. As badly as she wanted to continue scratching at the bone crushing corset, Rahab nodded her head in agreement. "Fine. I'll leave it alone. But I can't promise I won't rip this thing to shreds the second we reach the ship."

"Don't be too hasty." Ziggy flashed the pirate a playful smile and Rahab could have sworn the perky girl's freckles danced across the bridge of her nose. "I think Prince Crispin might want a chance to see you in it again."

Rahab couldn't stifle the laugh that escaped her lips. "You assume too much, Red."

"Red?" Ziggy's eyes softened. "I like it."

"You aren't scared of me, are you?" Rahab asked, as they poked their heads into another empty guest room; checking to see if Neempo was in one of the chambers, instead of a prison cell. The search was becoming tedious and for all they knew, he might already be dead.

Ziggy whipped around in surprise. "Of course, I'm scared of you. You live a dangerous life and from the way you talk, you've killed plenty of people."

Rahab didn't know what to say, but thankfully, Ziggy continued. "I don't mean to be offensive."

"No offense taken." Rahab shrugged. "I know what I am."

"To be fair," Ziggy whispered as they closed the last door on that floor. "I'm scared of everything and everyone. I just pretend not to be."

"But you're a ..." Rahab didn't want to say *spy* aloud, but Ziggy nodded, knowing what she was thinking.

"I've never had a chance to make my own choices." Ziggy shrugged. "Maybe one day, that'll change. Maybe one day, I won't have nightmares of having my throat slit. Maybe one day, I'll be free."

Rahab looked up and down the empty, quiet hallway. She met Ziggy's blue eyes and said, "You should go."

"Go?" Ziggy tilted her head to the side in confusion. "Go where?"

"Get to the ship." Rahab insisted in a hushed voice. "We've finished checking these rooms and there's no sign of Neempo. Get aboard the ship and you can finally sail to freedom."

"I can't leave you here," Ziggy protested but Rahab put a hand up to silence her.

"I'll meet up with Crispin, Penn, and Nubis. We won't be too far behind you."

"You love him, don't you?" Ziggy smiled, and her face lit up like the sparkling night sky.

Rahab motioned for her to go back the way they had come. "Go on, Red. I'll catch up." She couldn't hide her grin when Ziggy mentioned Crispin.

"Thank you." Ziggy hugged Rahab and for once, the pirate didn't push someone away for touching her. In fact, she wrapped her arms around the redhead, returning the embrace.

As Ziggy disappeared around the corner, Rahab felt a swelling in her chest. She'd never had a female friend before. Maybe, she could be friends with the Westerner. She rolled her eyes at the thought. Crispin was going to make fun of her. A pirate of Pulau in love with the Prince of Northwind and declaring friendship with a prostitute from Borg.

"Mainlanders," she muttered.

Chapter Forty-Six

Crispin

Crispin was surprised that after years of being away, he still remembered how to get around the White Keep. Spending his days wandering the castle and getting into trouble wasn't entirely a 'waste of his time' like his mother loved to point out. Nubis was right about the renovations; there was a lot of black and white throughout the keep, but thankfully the changes were mostly cosmetic and not structural. He made his way to the Eastern Courtyard where the Numbio prisoner claimed soldiers had taken the Sovereign.

Tired of being weighed down by the black armor, Crispin ditched the heavy pieces, opting for the black fighting leathers underneath. He also left the shield behind in the dungeon, but kept the crossbow strapped to his back. He hadn't been taught to fight with all that armor, and if he was going to have a chance at succeeding, he would need his mobility.

As he approached the end of the hall, he peeked around the corner, and saw soldiers guarding the entrance to the Eastern Courtyard. He rolled his eyes, resting the back of his head against the wall. Nothing was going according to plan, and the last thing he wanted to do was scale the side of the castle up to the roof in the dark. But that's what he was going to have to do to get a bird's eye view of the courtyard and avoid those guards.

Crispin slipped out one of the windows across from him and slithered up the side of the stone façade. Gripping divots and broken grooves in the wall, he made his way up to the slopped roof. He laid flat on his belly and crawled to the other side of the awning to look down into the courtyard.

Crispin saw Neempo strapped to a thick wooden pole in the middle of the two-story courtyard. Though the Sovereign had been stripped of his red eye wrap and shirt, he didn't look scared, as if he still had faith in being rescued from his cruel fate.

Before the prince could move closer, a weathered hag glided up the wooden steps that led to Neempo's stake. The moonlight streamed in and highlighted her white hair. From description alone, Crispin knew she must be the witch the members of the Order had told him about.

"It is time, Neempo." The witch nearly sang in glee.

"You don't have to do this, Vilora," Neempo remained calm. "You can let me go and all will be forgiven."

Vilora cackled and shook her head. "Righteous of heart until the very end." She leaned in close to Neempo and said, "Queen Niabi thanks you for your sacrifice."

Neempo screamed when Vilora dug her claw-like fingernails into his chest – she was going to rip his heart out with her bare hands. Crispin knew then he wouldn't make it down to the courtyard in time to save the Sovereign.

"If a rescue fails, you must do what needs to be done." Neempo's instructions echoed in his mind, and he finally understood what the Sovereign had been trying to tell him in his office before he was taken by the Pirate King.

Crispin couldn't rescue Neempo, but he could save him from being tortured to death. He nocked an arrow in the crossbow Nubis gave him. Aiming at first for the witch he repositioned his shot for the Sovereign. Even though his breath was labored, and his heart was pounding wildly inside his chest, Crispin let the arrow fly.

Neempo grunted when Crispin's mercy shot pierced his chest, right above Vilora's bloody hand. After a moment of hissed breathing, Neempo's head slumped toward his wounded body.

Crispin dragged his index finger from his forehead down to his chest. He failed to rescue the Sovereign and he felt the burden of his shortcoming perch on his shoulders.

Vilora whipped around, searching for who had killed the Sovereign. The witch snarled when her hateful gaze met his. She opened her mouth and spat fire at him. To avoid the inferno, Crispin slid off the roof, grabbed ahold of the lip of the shingles and flung himself on the second floor that was still open to the courtyard. He sprinted, luckily avoiding the blasts of fire and explosions against the stones. But as he neared the staircase to escape deeper inside the White Keep, a dark figure appeared.

Crispin stopped dead in his tracks. For a split second, he thought he was staring at his mother; her long raven black hair, green eyes, olive skin – but he realized too late it wasn't Bilhah. It was Niabi. Armed with a dagger in her right hand and dancing flames in her left.

"Hello, Crispin." Niabi's voice even sounded like their mother's, and it toyed with his mind.

Crispin drew his sword but was tossed against the wall when a blast from Vilora sent him flying.

"No!" Niabi shouted at the witch, though her eyes were still fixed on him. "He's mine."

Stumbling to his feet as a ball of fire soared toward him, Crispin wished he hadn't discarded the shield that came with his armor. Dodging the incoming fire attack his sister launched, he knew if he didn't find cover, she would succeed in burning him to ash. Bolting away from her, he turned the corner, and ducked behind a column hoping to outrun his sister. But Niabi was quick, ferocious, and unrelenting in her assault.

"You stole from me, little brother." Niabi said calmly, and the wicked chill behind her eyes pierced his soul. "And now you must pay the price."

Rushed footsteps echoed up the second staircase to his left and he was both relieved and terrified to see Rahab pop up. He waved for Rahab to retreat.

"Get out of here!" Crispin warned, but the pirate raced for him instead, determined to help him escape.

Rahab barely managed to reach Crispin before another burst of flame sizzled against the column they were hiding behind.

Niabi let loose a dark and dangerous laugh. "A friend of yours, Crispin?"

"Leave her out of this, Niabi." Crispin shouted; his arms still wrapped tightly around Rahab. "This is between you and me."

"Don't worry," Niabi's voice grew louder as she approached. "You can die together."

They wouldn't make it to the staircase Rahab had come up, and the other set of stairs was blocked by Niabi. She would strike them down with fire if they attempted to escape either direction. There was a window directly in front of them, but being hundreds of feet above the city streets, they would be lucky to die without feeling the excruciating pain of impact first. They were pinned and Crispin was out of options. He would have to face Niabi head on.

Crispin slowly slithered around the column, putting himself between the women. "Why don't you fight me without your magic?" Crispin hissed. "Unless you think you can't beat me in hand-to-hand combat."

A second dagger ejected from Niabi's left sleeve and the flames kissed it. "You want to fight, Crispin?" She flashed a crazed smile. "Show me what you've got."

Crispin clutched the hilt of his longsword tightly as he sprinted toward Niabi. He swung his sword, but she blocked the blow with her right dagger, and sliced at his chest with the blazing weapon in her left. He winced as the hot blade cut through his fighting leathers drawing blood.

Niabi clicked her tongue. "And here I thought this would be a challenge."

She dropped down, swept his legs out from under him, and laughed as Crispin crashed to the floor. The queen approached him as he unsheathed a small dagger in his boot, a trick Salome had insisted would one day save his life and launched it at her chest. Niabi bent backward, avoiding the knife. It was the distraction he needed to get on his feet and sprint back to Rahab.

When he reached her, he wrapped his arms around her torso, and tackled her out of the window behind her. Together they plunged toward the cobblestone streets hundreds of feet below. With the pirate tucked against his chest, he stared at the window they had jumped through and saw Niabi's face. Her hair blew in the light breeze, and he once again saw his mother's face. Would her face really be the last thing he saw before he died?

Rahab didn't scream, nor did she lift her face from his chest to see their fate. She clung to him, trusting him to the very end. But as they neared the city streets, spiraling to their deaths, a blast of air caught them, propelling them upward, before resting them gently on the cobblestones.

Crispin released Rahab from his grasp, and when she opened her eyes, she found herself laying on top of him. Alive. They were alive and sprawled in the street. Rahab glanced up at the White Keep and shuddered at the distance.

She punched his arm. "Don't ever do that to me again!"

Crispin nodded with a weak smile and pulled her to him, planting a kiss against her forehead. "There's no way we should have survived that fall." He pushed up from the ground and helped Rahab to her feet.

"This way, my Prince." A hooded Oden whispered from the darkness of an alley across the street. Obediently, Crispin and Rahab slinked after him. "Where is the Sovereign?"

"He..." Crispin rubbed a dirty hand through his sweaty hair and sighed. "He didn't make it."

Oden didn't turn around to acknowledge his friend's death or that Crispin had failed in rescuing Neempo. He pressed forward to complete the mission of helping them escape Northwind.

"Did you see anything strange?" Crispin asked in a low voice.

Weaving through the labyrinth of the Night District, now closed for business until the next night, Oden only stopped to answer the question once he felt no one would overhear them. "I saw you two falling from the White Keep, if that's what you're asking."

"We shouldn't have survived that fall," Crispin said, "and you were the only one around."

Oden sighed. "No one knows of my magic. Not even the members of the Order."

"You're an Air Manipulator?" Rahab nearly squealed and Oden nodded in confirmation.

"Me saving you; my magic – it needs to stay amongst us," Oden said sternly, his eyebrows knitted together.

"Why?" Crispin pressed as they started down the path again. "Why keep your magic a secret?"

"I haven't lasted this long as an enemy of the crown by speaking of such matters in the middle of the street." Oden whipped around, fire in his eyes. "Magic comes at a price, Prince. And with your sister keeping the company and council of that witch, she is looking to drain magic wielders to harness their power for herself."

"Come with us," Rahab offered as they reached the docks.

"I am needed here." Oden declined, his gaze shifting from her to Crispin. "You will need allies in the city when you return for your crown. Until we meet again, my Prince." He extended his hand and Crispin shook it with gratitude.

"I will return." Crispin said more for himself to hear than anything else.

Oden smiled and bowed his head. "Of this, I have no doubt." The rebel turned on his heel and disappeared into the Night District.

When Oden was out of their sight, Crispin and Rahab made their way to the disguised *Shadow of Death* and hastily boarded the ship as the crew prepared for departure. Haldane greeted them with a curt nod and kept ordering his men to get them out of the harbor before anyone could stop them.

Looking around the deck, Crispin mentally took note to make sure everyone had made it before their launch. Nubis and Corwin were gabbing about their knife collections. Rafi was shimming up to the crow's nest while Ondrej spotted him from below. Phex was giddily showing Ziggy his latest invention. And Rahab was informing Captain Haldane of their failure in procuring the Sovereign. Finally, Crispin spotted Master Penn, the prisoner they had freed from the White Keep dungeons, and her six Keepers huddled together for a drink, and his stomach sank.

He approached Penn, but before he could open his mouth to explain what happened she said, "Did he suffer?"

"How did you -?"

"Your footsteps are heavy, Prince Crispin." Penn stood from her crouched position and offered him a tin mug of what smelled like spiced rum. "Only a man with a burdened heart walks that way."

Crispin accepted the mug and took a sip, letting the rum burn on the way down. "I'm sorry."

"Did he suffer?" Penn asked again softly.

"Not long." Crispin tapped on his mug.

"Thank you for doing what needed to be done." Penn patted him on the shoulder and turned back to her Keepers.

"But I failed," his voice was strained.

Penn shook her head. "The Sovereign might not have survived, but you protected him from suffering a fate worse than death. You did not fail. You did what was asked of you."

"Are we ready to cast off?" Haldane asked Crispin, his arms clasped behind his back.

Crispin glanced up at the White Keep, now crawling with soldiers, smoke rising from the Eastern Courtyard. Despite what Master Penn said, Crispin knew he had failed. He failed to rescue Neempo, and he failed to defeat Niabi. The next time he looked upon the White Keep, he would come out the victor or he would die fighting.

"Crispin?" Rahab's voice brought him back to the present. "Are we ready to cast off?" She repeated Haldane's question and the prince nodded.

"Ready."

Chapter Forty-Seven

Niabi

In a fit of rage, Niabi blasted and burned every inch of the Eastern Courtyard. Smoke wafted up to the sky where streaks of purple, pink, orange, and yellow light glowed from the dawn. She had Crispin cornered and he still slipped through her fingers. He killed the Sovereign, robbing her of her one chance to resurrect Rollo. He would pay. She would make sure of it.

"Are you done?" Vilora's raspy voice grated Niabi's nerves.

The queen looked at her aunt and snarled, "I must speak with the Pirate King."

"For what?" Vilora's question was bordering on insubordinate, but Niabi stomped past her.

Tala burst through the doors of the courtyard, his hair wasn't braided, and he wasn't wearing his armor. He looked like he had heard the explosions, rolled out of bed, and sprinted there. "Niabi? What's going on? Are you hurt?"

She stared at him and hissed, "My brother paid me a little visit."

"What?" Tala's eyes popped open, now fully awake. "Your brother was here?"

"He's gone." Niabi swung the doors open and marched inside the White Keep, beelining for the throne room, Tala and Vilora hot on her heels.

"Gone? As in dead?" Tala asked, his gaze shot to the dirty-faced witch beside him.

"He must be," Vilora said, "he jumped out the window to escape our queen's attack."

Niabi turned around, eyes full of hate. "Crispin is alive! And once the Pirate King gets here, I'll make sure he hunts my brother down and brings him back to me in chains."

"He couldn't have survived that fall," Tala offered, but she interrupted him.

"They have an Air Manipulator." Niabi started her trek to the throne room, not caring if Tala and Vilora were following her. "Right before he and that woman hit the ground, a burst of air saved them. If I hadn't seen it with my own eyes, I wouldn't have believed it."

"An Air Manipulator?" Vilora said in a low, curious voice. "A powerful ally indeed."

Once they reached the throne room she found, Anaktu waiting for her. "Get me the Pirate King. Now!" The Nephilim bowed and thundered from the room.

Niabi sank into her throne and gripped the armrests to calm down and regain her composure before the Pirate King arrived. Crispin's face flashed in her mind, and she grimaced. He looked like a young version of their father, and it made her hate him even more.

She stewed in anger until Uri and his shadow wielder appeared before her.

"Queen," a swift bow from Uri was all Niabi allowed before launching into negotiations.

"How fast is your fleet?" Niabi asked, aware her words were laced with irritation, but she was in a hurry.

Uri flashed a proud smile and pounded a fist to his chest, "The fastest in Pulau."

"I am prepared to offer you double what I paid for the Sovereign, if you capture my brother and return him to me." She got right to it, and by the arch of his eyebrow, he was intrigued.

"Your brother was here?" Uri asked, rubbing his scarred jawline, and exchanging a brief glance with the shadow wielder.

"I don't have time for questions," Niabi shot up from her throne with a vicious growl. "He was headed for the harbor. Hunt him down and bring him to me *alive*. Is that something you can handle, or shall I send someone else?"

Uri raised his hands in surrender, "We can catch him. But what if I wanted another form of payment?"

Tala stepped forward to put the pirate in his place, but Niabi caught him by the forearm. "What is it you want?"

"A partnership." His dark eyes danced in sinister delight. "Unite our kingdoms in marriage. The King of the Seas and the Queen of the Mainland, bound together, we will be unstop -"

"Let me stop you right there," Niabi held up a hand to silence him. "I have no intention of marrying you or uniting our kingdoms. I have offered you a payday unlike anything you, or those filthy pirate scum you call a crew, have seen in your greedy, thieving lives. Take my offer or leave it. You are not the only ship to dispatch."

Uri took a moment to recover from the tongue lashing before nodding. "Double the pay?"

"That's what I said." Every moment she wasted talking to the pirate was another mile her brother gained in escaping her.

Uri whispered something to the blind shadow wielder. He glanced up at Niabi and smiled. "What shall we do with the rest of the ship's crew once we find him?"

Niabi waved a dismissive hand. "Do whatever you want with them. My price is for my brother."

"Then you have a deal. Your brother is as good as yours, Queen." Uri bowed again before strutting out of the throne room, his petite companion following him closely.

"Alive," she reiterated, "and unharmed."

Uri threw his hand up and glanced over his shoulder at the queen. "Yes, yes. Alive and unharmed."

With that, they disappeared and Niabi plopped down onto her throne. Her hand rested on her belly as fatigue set in. Soon, she would have her brother kneeling before her in this very throne room. Soon, she would slice her knife across his throat, making him pay the price for snatching a second chance with Rollo from her grasp. Soon. Just not soon enough.

Chapter Forty-Eight

Salome

Determined to keep her promise, Salome made sure Utara wasn't anywhere near the executioner's block to watch her mother take her last breath. She had dragged the girl through the Rose Garden until they found a bench tucked underneath an archway of roses.

Utara rubbed her eyes, from lack of sleep or from crying all night, Salome wasn't sure and didn't ask. With the sweet aroma of thousands of roses surrounding them, Salome wrapped her arms around Utara to keep her warm as the morning light broke across the horizon.

Salome closed her eyes, resting her chin on top of Utara's head. Mika was scheduled to be executed at dawn, so she reached for Damaris' mind, knowing the Oracle would be in the arena watching Mika's final moments.

"Damaris," she begged for her to answer, hoping to get a glimpse into what was happening. *"Damaris, please."*

Damaris answered her call, not with thoughts, but with sight. Being the Oracle of Myr, she gave insight into the past and present, and through her eyes, Salome could see what was happening.

Mika held her head high as she emerged from the mouth of the tunnel that led into the depths of the arena. She walked by the Qata Vishna who lined the path to the executioner's block. This arena was where Mika had fought, trained, and bled, and where she would take her last breath. Stripped of her red armor and standing in a loose white shirt and navy pants, Mika nodded her head, giving a silent order for her warriors to stand down. She glanced up to the royal box where her mother, the newly christened queen, and her Aunt Damaris sat.

Zara was pale, and the bags underneath her green eyes were visible from where Mika stood over forty feet away.

Damaris's face was stained with the dried tears she had cried all night. She grabbed Zara's wrist and pleaded for Mika's life once more. "Spare her, Zara."

Zara straightened in her chair and lifted her chin higher. "Mika made her choice. She knows our laws. A life for a life."

"But -"

"My first act as queen cannot be to forgive our mother's assassination. To show mercy would make me look weak."

"Mercy can also show great strength, sister." Damaris knelt before Zara's feet. "Spare Mika. Send the Qata Vishna to find Marina."

"A life for a life." Zara's throat bobbed; eyes glossed over with tears.

Mika closed her eyes. A peace washed over her as she listened to the crash of the waves against the cliffs and felt the light morning breeze dance around her. She could smell the sweet aromatics of the vineyards and the mixture of spices sizzling in the markets.

Surrounded by her sisters in bond and blood, the Qata Vishna crisscrossed their curved blades across their chests, paying their last respects to their Red Maiden.

Mika opened her eyes and met Damaris's teary gaze with a smile. She glanced at her mother who now had tears streaming down her face. Mika bowed her head. A silent goodbye. She knelt before the executioner's block and rested her neck against the wood stained red with blood.

The executioner heaved the scythe above her head. A sad smile tugged at Mika's lips as she whispered, "As deep as the sea." The blade sliced through the air, thudding loudly against the block.

The Qata Vishna slashed their two blades against each other as they whipped them to their sides. The sound echoed through the arena. Their Red Maiden had fallen.

Tears slipped down Salome's cheeks as she stroked Utara's braided black hair.

"She's gone, isn't she?" Utara whispered, biting her bottom lip, trying not to cry.

Salome tightened her arms around Utara's chest. "I'm sorry."

Utara's body trembled and Salome heard her softly sobbing. "I thought... I thought maybe..."

Salome buried her face in Utara's hair and together they cried until the noonday sun warmed their skin. Salome understood more than most what it felt like to lose a mother. Having to grow up missing her smile, her scent, her voice. She promised Mika she would look after Utara, and she would keep her word. No matter what it cost, she would survive the war, and she would come back for Utara.

"Princess Salome?"

Salome recognized Seraphina's voice, but instead of the icy bite it normally carried, it was solemn, almost broken. She peeled herself from Utara and met the twin's glossy gaze. It was odd to see Seraphina standing alone, her twin nowhere in sight.

"The queen has requested your presence in the Inner Depths."

Realizing Utara had fallen asleep in her arms, Salome lifted the girl to carry her back to her room, but Seraphina stepped forward, blocking her path.

"Please," Seraphina looked down at the child and whispered, "let me."

Salome didn't have the mental strength at the time to note Seraphina's rare usage of the word please. She just nodded, kissed Utara's forehead, and passed her into Seraphina's extended arms.

Grabbing Seraphina's shoulder before she could turn and walk away, Salome cupped the twin's face in her hands. Silently, they stared into each other's watery eyes, until Seraphina bowed her head and vanished into the palace.

Salome knew she was needed, but she took a moment to have a few uninterrupted breaths to settle her frayed nerves. Every time she closed her eyes, she saw the scythe slice through the air toward Mika's neck. The image of seeing her life end, took Salome's breath away. She'd not seen an execution before and she wasn't sure she could stomach another one, even if it was for someone she despised.

Death was close. Salome could sense her presence. Sometimes Salome felt as if Death tailed her day and night, waiting. Biding her time, taking those she loved, until she was ready to snatch Salome's soul too.

"I am not ready," Salome said, somehow knowing Death was listening. *"I have unfinished business."*

She turned on her heel and marched through the halls until she reached the double bronze doors that led to the Inner Depths. The guards opened the doors without her needing to break stride and she marched into the throne room. She expected to find Zara sitting on her throne, but instead, the new queen was crumpled on the floor, staring at her reflection in the small, rectangular pool in the middle of the room.

Her aunt was disheveled. The kohl around her eyes was smudged, and her hair wasn't fashioned in the intricate braids she fancied. Salome's heart shattered at the sight of this woman of great power on her knees, sobbing into the pool.

"It was Mika's last request that these be given to you," Zara didn't look up, but motioned to the table on her right, where Mika's red armor sat.

Mika's ghost. Her identity, her purpose, her passion, displayed on the table and being offered to Salome. She shrunk back a step.

"I don't understand," Salome's voice cracked as her gaze met Zara's bloodshot eyes. "That belongs to the Red Maiden."

"The Qata Vishna will need a commander." Zara reluctantly pushed herself up from the ground. "The Red Maiden must have royal Myridian blood. Mika is dead." The words smacked Salome across the face, awakening a fresh batch of tears. "Even if we found Marina, she is no warrior. And Utara is too young."

"But you -"

"My fighting days are long gone," Zara interrupted her.

Her aunt glanced down at her hands and Salome noticed them shaking. She hadn't noticed before, but when she thought about it, every time they were in the same room, Zara had her hands clasped in her lap.

"I can no longer grip a weapon." Zara admitted. "It has to be you. Mika knew it too. That's why she wanted you to have the armor." Zara stared deep into Salome's eyes. "If we are to go to war with the North, you will need to lead the Qata Vishna."

"War with the North?" Salome was surprised. "You are going to help me?"

"I have already ordered the Qata Vishna to prepare for war." Zara nodded her head and walked toward the table where her daughter's armor laid, she patted the breastplate gently.

"We will need time to ready our ships, but know the Qata Vishna, your people, your kin; we are with you."

Salome closed the distance between them. "Why?" she whispered.

"Bilhah. Nym. Mika." Zara tilted her head and Salome saw fire flickering behind those anguished green eyes. "Niabi will answer for their deaths. She will answer for all the blood she has spilled."

Salome slid a finger across Mika's helmet. "What do I need to do?"

"You are intuitive, just like your mother." Zara squared her shoulders to her niece. "If I could grant you the title of Red Maiden, I would, but I can't. No queen can. You must earn it."

Salome nodded. She assumed there would be some sort of task, some duel, that needed to be exacted for the Qata Vishna to see and accept her as their new Red Maiden.

"I have heard of your plans to leave with Prince Jinn tonight." Zara's eyes narrowed.

"I have business on the Mainland, before I reach Oakenshire." Salome offered, "Harbona's instructions."

Zara bobbed her head once Harbona's name was mentioned. She wouldn't question the orders of the Seer. "Can you delay your departure a day or two?"

"Yes." She was sure Jinn would accommodate her if she asked.

"Then you will need to rest tonight. Because tomorrow at dawn, you will face the Trial of Blood and Ash."

"I will not fail you." Salome said.

Zara clasped her hand and whispered, "You are my kin. You are Myridian royalty. You are a Qata Vishna. Failure is not in your blood."

— • —

Chapter Forty-Nine

Adonijah

After Salome met with her Aunt Zara, she was on edge. Adonijah assumed it had something to do with Mika's execution, but she refused to answer any of his questions, saying she needed everyone to be together, so she only had to explain once. When she said "everyone" he didn't realize she meant Jinn and Kai, as well.

Kai stood in front of the doors to Salome's chambers like a dutiful watchdog. Seraphina and Rosalina sat on the plush, white sofa. Seraphina pretended Cato didn't exist, even though he looked at her like she was the moon to his sun. Cato sat in the chair next to Adonijah, while Jinn took up the armchair directly across from him.

Adonijah could sense Jinn's eyes on him. If a stare off was what the prince wanted, that was exactly what he was going to get from him. Jinn smirked, as if to say he wasn't intimidated by Adonijah. And Adonijah exhaled a puff of smoke from his pipe in the Easterner's direction, not impressed.

Seraphina cleared her throat, drawing their attention. She shook her head with an icy glare as if to say, *"Knock it off, before I throw you both off the balcony."*

The men settled in their chairs and out of fear, or respect, for Seraphina, kept their dirty looks to themselves.

Salome walked into the lounge from her bedroom wringing her hands. She looked pale; like she had been crying for the last hour and was mustering up the courage to face them. She sat on the second couch facing the twins; Adonijah and Cato to one side, and Jinn and Kai on the other. She rubbed her hands up and down her thighs and cleared her throat.

"I figured having everyone together would make this easier on me."

Adonijah cocked his head to the side. "What are you talking about?"

Salome sighed deeply. "I met with my Aunt Zara today. She told me that Mika left me her armor, with the intent I become the next Red Maiden."

The room was quieter than a graveyard. Adonijah's eyes flew to the twins and noticed they had stiffened.

"You say that like it's a bad thing." Cato glanced around at everyone in the room and saw their hunched shoulders and tight-lipped grimaces. "Am I missing something?"

"In order to be the Red Maiden," Salome calmly explained to Cato, who always seemed to be the last to understand, "I will have to face the Trial of Blood and Ash."

Cato swallowed a grape whole and his body twitched. "Well, that sounds like... fun?"

Seraphina scoffed and shook her head. Cato seemed excited she even acknowledged him in public and smiled.

"The trail is at dawn." Salome announced, drawing all eyes, once again.

Jinn sat up straighter in his seat. "That soon?"

Salome looked at the prince, her fingers absent-mindedly tapping the armrests of her chair. "I know you were due to sail tonight -"

"The ship sails when I say it does." Jinn waved his hand in the air. "We leave when you are ready." He smiled at Salome and Adonijah wanted to rip his arms off.

"Thank you," Salome mustered a smile, but it didn't stretch far.

Adonijah crossed his arms over his chest. "What does this trial entail?"

"I'm not really sure," Salome admitted, her eyes shooting to the twins who exchanged a look. "Do I want to know?"

Rosalina nodded her head and Seraphina said, "There's an islet about twenty yards off the coast of Antrope. The candidate for Red Maiden is rowed out there and left to fight the Cornigera."

Cato squirmed in his seat, "What is a Cornigera?"

"It sleeps deep in the sea," Seraphina continued, her eyes filled with fear, "but when someone steps foot on the islet, it awakens and comes to ... eat."

"Is it...?" Salome didn't finish her question.

"Terrifying?" Rosalina filled in the blank and nodded, like she could see the creature in her mind.

"What does it look like?" Cato asked after a brief silence amongst the group.

Seraphina made eye contact with Cato for the first time that evening. She had tears welling up in her hazel eyes. "It has the body of an enormous cat, four legs with razor sharp claws. Its spikes run the length of its spine, starting from its oblong head to its whip for a tail. It is so thin; you can see its ribs from Antrope's shores. It has gills and scales and tiny eyes where a nose should be. But the most frightening thing about it, and the most dangerous, are its rows of jagged teeth. It can open its mouth wide enough to bite a Qata Vishna's head clean off."

While everyone in the room was focused on Seraphina's description of the Cornigera, Adonijah watched Salome. Although, she tried to keep a neutral expression, he knew she was terrified, and it pained him.

"You don't have to do this," Adonijah offered, hoping she wouldn't go through with the fight.

"Zara promised me the Qata Vishna for the war, but only if they have a Red Maiden to lead them." Salome steadied her voice. "Mika is gone. Utara is far too young. Marina is on the run and Zara is the queen. I am the only one left." Her eyes darted to Adonijah, and she shrugged, "I don't have a choice."

"You have other options, Salome." Jinn chimed in and Adonijah saw red.

"Are you seriously bringing up your marriage proposal?" Adonijah growled across the room at Jinn, fists clenched.

Jinn leaned forward; hands clasped between his knees. "I meant she could try to send word to her brother about his progress. Or she could meet with some of the rebels in Northwind." He smirked, "But it's nice to know you are well-informed on my affairs."

"She is none of your concern." Adonijah was itching to fistfight him.

Jinn tilted his head to the side, recognizing the challenge, and willing to accept. "And yet, she has not declined my offer."

Adonijah jumped to his feet and Jinn pushed himself out of his seat, squaring up.

Seraphina hopped up and stood between them, hands stretched out, pressing into their chests. "Stop it. Both of you. How dare you two argue with her in the room? She has more to worry about than your feelings and fragile egos." She pushed them back a step and closed the distance between her and Salome. "You will beat the Cornigera," she knelt before Salome's seat. "You just need to sleep and to keep focused."

Salome was quiet and didn't respond. It was then, Adonijah noticed her eyes were glazed over. Seraphina waved her hand in Salome's face, but there was no indication she noticed. Rattled, she grabbed Salome by the shoulders and shook her. "Your Highness? Princess? Salome!" Salome's eyes fluttered and the glossiness was gone. "Are you ok?"

Salome bobbed her head and whispered, "I know what I need to do."

"Did you have another vision?" Adonijah knelt by her side, grabbing her hand.

"Mika showed me how to beat it."

"How?" Adonijah asked. If Mika had given her insight, that might be the difference between life or death for Salome. And he desperately wanted, needed her to live.

She shook her head. "She told me not to say anything. Bad luck," she shrugged with a forced smile.

Adonijah traced his thumb down her jawline. He was grateful she had missed his encounter with Jinn. Seraphina was right, for once. Salome had more to worry about right now than him. Or Jinn. Adonijah narrowed his eyes as the prince approached Salome.

"If you need anything, let me know." Jinn squeezed her hand.

Seraphina's nostrils flared and she shooed them out. "If there is nothing else, Rosalina and I need to help the princess get ready for bed."

"You don't need to do that," Salome protested softly. "You are Qata Vishna -"

"We are sworn to serve you, to protect you," Rosalina interjected, still pale from Mika's execution. "We will continue to serve you until you die."

"That's not -"

"Please," Rosalina begged Salome once more, her bottom lip quivered. "It was our queen's last command. Our Red Maiden's last assignment. We are to serve until your grandmother releases us or you breathe your last. Please -"

Salome rushed to the couch Rosalina was sitting on and wrapped her arms around her. "It's alright," Salome brushed her fingers through the twin's hair. "I gratefully accept your service."

Seraphina's prickly disposition returned, and she motioned for everyone to leave the room. Adonijah reluctantly left, even though all he wanted to do was wrap his arms around Salome and make sure she was safe. To hold her as she slept and kiss her the moment she woke up. But with Seraphina and Rosalina determined not to leave Salome unattended, any hope for a private moment with the princess was gone.

Cato discreetly squeezed Seraphina's hand by the door right before she slammed it in his face. The Stormcrag turned around with a wide grin. "She likes me." He practically danced across the hallway and into the suite they shared, but before Adonijah could stride in after him, Jinn reappeared, leaning against the wall.

"What do you want?" Adonijah closed the door, so Cato wouldn't overhear them.

"I know you don't like me," Jinn started and Adonijah scoffed.

"An understatement, but please," he motioned for the Easterner to keep talking, "continue."

"I'm not going anywhere." Jinn slipped his hands in his pockets. "You care for Salome. I do, too."

"You only care about her because she's the Hunter." Adonijah snorted and Jinn straightened.

"She's the Hunter?" the prince whispered.

Adonijah rubbed a hand over his forehead. *Damn*. "Stay away from her."

"I already told you, I'm not going anywhere." Jinn tilted his head to the side. "I wanted to be upfront with you. You'll do what you want to do to win her heart. And I will do the same."

"You want to marry her for power." Adonijah's brow furrowed. "She deserves more than that."

"She's a princess," he took a powerful step toward Adonijah. "I am a prince. With our houses united once again, we can do a lot of good for our people."

"Salome isn't good with cages."

Jinn's eyes narrowed. "What is that supposed to mean?"

"She's going to lead armies into battle, and you want her to give up her homeland, her people, and her freedom, to be your prize." Adonijah shook his head in disgust and poked his index finger into Jinn's chest. "She doesn't belong behind stone walls."

"And she would be happy roaming Adalore with you for the rest of her life?" He flicked Adonijah's hand away. "When this war is won, she will have responsibilities you won't even begin to comprehend. Everything Salome does, will be for the benefit of her people."

"Crispin will be responsible for Northwind." Adonijah countered, his blood boiled each time Jinn said Salome's name.

"Crispin will be king, yes," Jinn agreed, "but Salome will be expected to be one of two things. She will either be asked to be an ambassador and travel to the Ten Kingdoms on her brother's behalf, or she will be married to strengthen relations with one of their allies. That is the life of a royal. I am no different."

"You are the heir to the Jade Throne; you can choose anyone to be your wife."

"If Crispin marries Salome to a foreign prince or lord, which he will most likely see as his only option as a new king to solidify alliances, who would you think he would commit her to?" Jinn ticked off his fingers. "There's me, of course. Heru, the heir of Numbio. A good man, but from what I've heard, already has his sights set on another. The Almighty forbid she is promised to that incestuous bastard, Thanos of Gomorrah. I'm sure Benaiah of Borg, that power hungry menace, would love if one of his sons married the Hunter.

And then there's the abusive Pirate King. So, you see, there aren't many good options available to her."

"You assume Crispin will be like the rest of the Adalorian kings, but you don't know him." Adonijah didn't know him either, but he refused to believe Crispin would offer his sister up on a silver platter just to make himself look like a powerful king.

"You don't know him either." Jinn flashed a wicked smile. "But maybe you're right. Maybe, Crispin won't be like other kings. Maybe, Salome will break with tradition and pick a sell-sword and roam Adalore on horseback. Power doesn't suit everyone." Jinn shrugged and patted Adonijah's shoulder as he walked by him.

"If it were up to me," Adonijah whipped around to look at him, "you'd be sailing back to Sakurai tonight."

Jinn stuffed his hands in his pockets. "Good thing, it's not up to you." Without waiting for Adonijah to respond, Jinn cloaked himself, and vanished, solidly ending their encounter.

Adonijah didn't care that Jinn tried to size him up and mark his territory. What bothered him was that most of what Jinn said was true. There was a possibility after the war, Salome wouldn't choose him. There was a possibility Crispin would ask or force her to marry a foreign dignitary and from the conversation he had with Salome before, she was prepared to do what was best for her people.

Her people.

They would trump him if it came down to it. Adonijah could spend the next weeks, months, or years fighting by Salome's side and still lose her heart.

Chapter Fifty

Salome

Dawn was a few hours away and Salome hadn't slept. The last thing she told her friends was that Mika showed her in a vision how to defeat the Cornigera. But that was a lie. She had a vision, but not one she could, or would share with them. She saw the Cornigera. It was everything Seraphina and Rosalina had described. Every time she closed her eyes she saw its scales, its red, oval eyes, and the jagged rows of seemingly endless teeth.

She didn't see how to kill the Cornigera.

She saw how the Cornigera killed her.

If her friends knew the truth, they wouldn't let her step one foot into the Trial of Blood and Ash. But she had to. She knew it deep in her bones.

Salome saw her death, but she wasn't going down without a fight.

Salome stood at the edge of Antrope, the isle where the Qata Vishna trained. There was a slight chill in the early morning air that made Salome cling to her cloak. Or maybe, she trembled because her fate was to be determined on the islet that she was staring at.

An audience had gathered and lined up and down the pebble beach, including Zara, Damaris, Salome's friends, and most of the high-ranking warriors of the Qata Vishna. *An audience to watch her die.* She shook her head, refusing to let that thought take root in her mind.

"Your Highness?" One of the Qata Vishna in a rowboat called out to her, "Are you ready?"

Salome nodded and shrugged off her cloak. She turned and handed it to Adonijah who hadn't said much all morning. She threw her arms around his neck and squeezed.

"No matter what happens..." She wanted to say I will fight, live, and die by your side, but instead she finished with, "...don't interfere."

Before he could respond, she jumped in the boat and was being rowed the short distance to the islet. As soon as Salome stepped foot on the tiny landmass, the Qata Vishna took off for shore.

Her eyes darted around the treeless islet that was less than an acre in size. It was nothing more than a flat, rocky piece of land with nowhere for her to hide. Nothing to pick up and throw in a pinch to buy herself extra time. She felt naked and alone. Images of her dying flashed in her mind. She blinked the negative thoughts free before the water started to bubble behind her.

Salome turned around and braced herself, planting her feet to the ground like Mika had taught her. She grabbed the two curved swords Mika had left her from their holsters on her back and held them at her sides. Her breathing quickened, and she focused on calming down, lest she get the jitters, and make a stupid mistake that could cost her, her life.

Slowly pawing out of the sea, the Cornigera's red eyes and sharp claws were the first things she noticed. She greatly underestimated how enormous the beast was; with his head at least twelve feet above the ground and teeth the length of daggers, Salome knew this would be the most challenging fight of her entire life. *And quite possibly the last.*

All she could do was wait as the creature rose from the watery depths with every intention of ripping her to shreds and swallowing her whole. She narrowed her eyes and held her ground as the monster shook the water from his body like a dog.

Inhale. Exhale. Inhale. Exhale.

Salome stood as still as a statue, watching the creature stalk toward her. His hungry, bloodthirsty gaze was fixed on her, sizing her up. Baring his teeth, Salome suspected the Cornigera didn't see her as much of a threat. A mistake on his part.

The beast circled her, hissing, and puffing hot breath against her skin. She side-eyed the creature; remembering everything Zophar had taught her about defeating a much larger opponent.

"Patience," Zophar had said. *"Let your enemy come to you. And when he underestimates you, use his strengths against him."*

The Cornigera completed his circle around her and stood a few feet in front of her. Their eyes met. It looked like he was smirking, if the beast could even manage that with all those razor-sharp fangs.

He hissed.

She hissed back.

Making sure to keep light on her feet, she knew she would never be able to overpower the beast with brute strength, but she could adapt, and Almighty willing, she would learn how to use the creature's strengths against it.

The Cornigera stood on his back two legs and howled, sending a shiver down her spine. His front paws thudded to the ground, shaking the area between him and Salome. The creature leapt toward her. She side-stepped and deflected his claws with her blades. The beast yelped as blue liquid oozed from his front right leg. She had drawn first blood.

Fire flashed in the beast's eyes. His tail whistled through the air and sliced into her side like a whip, leaving a red lash. She bit back a scream and regained her footing, bracing herself for another attack.

Salome lowered her body, hunching her back to make herself appear like a smaller target. Without warning, the Cornigera sprinted toward her, knocking her off her feet. Before he could slash her face with his claws, she tumbled out of the way, slicing his chest with her blades.

The monster furiously scratched and clawed her swords out of her hands. As the weapons flew in opposite directions and out of her reach, he trampled her, knocking the wind out of her. He turned on his heel and made his way back to run over her again, but she scrambled to her feet, and sprinted to snatch one of Mika's blades.

Salome hit the ground hard, smacking her forehead against the rocky terrain. Before she could touch her face to check for blood, she was dragged backwards. She looked at her left leg; his tail was wrapped around her ankle.

She unsheathed the wolf dagger from her thigh and in a desperate last attempt to escape his grasp, she turned, and sliced through his tail, freeing herself. The beast roared; anger, pain, and revenge were heard in his cries.

Salome pushed up to her feet, but her left knee was throbbing. As quickly as she could, she hobbled to grab ahold of one of the twin curved blades. She could hear the creature chasing her and pure adrenaline propelled her to the sword.

In a flash, the Cornigera was on top of her, his teeth digging into her right forearm which she used to shield her face from his attack. Her scream was piercing, and she heard murmurs and gasps from the shoreline where the crowd was watching.

Salome's blood was splattered all over her bronze fighting leathers. She took the curved blade clutched in her left hand and stabbed the inside of his mouth, forcing him to release his hold on her. To buy herself a moment to breathe, she stuck her fingers into the creature's red eyes, but before she could blind him, he retreated, stomping over her battered body.

Salome laid on the cold, rocky ground, with her eyes closed. She was beaten, exhausted, and was starting to lose consciousness from the blow to her head. Blood was flowing like a river from her mangled arm, and the sting from the saltwater breeze kissing her wounds was almost unbearable. As she started to fade and give into the darkness, she heard Jinn's voice, felt his hands on her skin, his lips on hers.

"Wake up, Salome," Jinn pleaded in a whisper, blowing air into her lungs. "You need to wake up."

"Jinn?" Salome called out through her thoughts, too tired to speak.

"You need to get up." Jinn replied mentally. *"If you don't, that beast will kill you and I can't watch you die."*

Salome's eyes fluttered open. She didn't see the prince anywhere, but she could feel his warm hands cupping her face. *"Jinn?"*

"I cloaked myself," he explained quickly. *"If the Myridians catch me interfering they will disqualify you."*

Salome rubbed the knot developing on her forehead when she spotted the beast. He was about thirty feet away, recovering from his wounds. The curved blade she embedded in his cheek now laid at his feet. Blue blood oozed down his pale scales. As soon as the wounded Cornigera caught sight of her, his red eyes flared in rejuvenated anger.

"Finish this, Salome," Jinn begged, squeezing her hands. He kissed her lips and rested his forehead against hers. *"Survive. I need you."*

"You need to go before it's too late." Salome didn't want to risk reaching out for him, fearful that someone might notice, and suspect Jinn helped her. *"Go. Please."*

She didn't feel Jinn anymore and hoped he listened and swam back to shore. She struggled to her feet. Her right arm was shredded, and she couldn't grip a weapon. Her left knee was already swollen to twice its normal size. Cuts, sprains, and forming bruises were littered all over her aching body. Blood trickled down to her feet, staining her clothes r ed.

Shaking the ground with each thundering step he took, the Cornigera sprinted toward her.

Jinn had saved her twice now, but if she didn't kill the beast charging for her in the next few seconds, she knew she wasn't going to survive. Her death flashed before her eyes again and she shoved the image away.

"I am not ready," she told Death once more when she felt her presence circling. *"I am not ready to meet you."*

Salome held her ivory, wolf dagger in her left hand tightly. Her last weapon. She stood her ground like the fearsome soldier Zophar trained her to be. Running, jumping, kicking, and leaping were off the table, meaning she only had one option left. Let the creature attack her.

With ten feet between them, the beast leapt into the air, teeth bared, claws out. This was it. The moment she would either live or die. It was her or the Cornigera. She heard gasps and cries echo from the shore, but she refused to take one last look. If she took her eyes off the monster, she would most certainly die.

Salome threw her bloodied right arm up to block the creature's jagged teeth from biting her face. As he landed on top of her, she fell to the ground with it, thrusting her dagger into its bony chest. The creature let out a bloodcurdling screech and Salome screamed as her back smashed onto the rocks.

For a moment, Salome just laid there, drenched with the Cornigera's blue blood. Her body ached; her right arm was too bloody to determine if it was ripped open from the creature's teeth or if it was severely broken. The dead beast wilted on top of her; his weight crushing and preventing air from reaching her lungs. She began to panic when she realized she was suffocating.

Jinn's last words echoed in her mind. *"Survive. I need you."*

Salome thought about her brother. She thought about Zophar, Adonijah, Jinn, and the friends and family she had found along her journey. And one thing was certain: this wasn't how she would leave this life; crushed and suffocated by a sea demon when there were people who needed her to live, needed her to survive.

Broken and bloody, Salome mustered the last bit of strength and tenacity she had to slip out from underneath the beast's carcass.

As soon as she was free, she shot to her swollen knees and sucked in the deepest breath she could, filling her lungs with the salty, sea air. She opened her bloodshot eyes and saw the line of Qata Vishna along the shore crisscrossing their curved swords against their chests. They were saluting her.

Salome forced herself to her feet. She no longer had her curved swords handy, but she crisscrossed her arms over her chest, paying them respect as their new Red Maiden.

The rowboat made it to the islet in a flash. Adonijah jumped out and ran to her, sweeping her battered body in his arms. He clutched her tightly to his chest, drawing a wince from her lips.

Adonijah planted a kiss on her dirty, sweaty forehead. "You did it," he whispered against her temple. "You did it."

That was the last thing she heard Adonijah say before she closed her eyes and drifted into darkness. But before she lost consciousness, she reached out to Jinn.

"Thank you. You saved me."

"You saved yourself." She felt a warmth flood her. *"Rest, Red Maiden. Rest."*

Chapter Fifty-One

Harbona

Several days had passed and Makeda seemed to have made it her mission to avoid Harbona at all costs. When he knocked on her bedroom door, she wasn't there. At dinner, she was nowhere to be found. Even strolling through the gardens reaped no reward. If he didn't know any better, he would have guessed Makeda's magical affinity was cloaking, not water wielding.

Odelia told him to give their daughter space, to let her come to him when she was ready to talk, but now that he had a daughter, he wanted to spend as much time with her as possible. He wanted to get to know her and make up for lost time.

Kayven and Abba refused to let Harbona sulk another day, and insisted he show them what mortal fighting tactics he picked up from his one thousand years on the Mainland. Harbona had been involved in more wars, than he cared to remember, and though he was reluctant to join them in the sparring ring, once they started, he was glad they dragged him there.

"So," Kayven wiped sweat from his forehead as they walked back inside Lavena's villa, "do you think your mortals can win this war?"

Harbona sipped from his glass of water and poured his friends a cup, which they gladly accepted. "I believe they can. They have the Hunter on their side."

"Ah, yes," Kayven chuckled, "the all-powerful Hunter. Mortals are delightful in their devotion to a myth."

"The Hunters are not a myth," Harbona shook his head. "I have fought side-by-side with most of the Hunters. They are remarkable beings."

"You really do care for them," Abba said, as he plopped down on the couch.

Harbona smiled, crinkling the sides of his eyes, "They are resilient creatures."

"And dangerous," Lavena's voice sliced through the room like an icy chill. Her grey eyes slid over to Abba, who had his boots kicked up on her marble table in front of the couch, and he immediately planted his feet on the floor.

"Why do you hate them?" Harbona asked, defensive.

"The hearts of mortals are easily swayed." Lavena paced the round room, hands clasped in front of her. "Their allegiance can be bought and sold to the highest bidder. For being called human, they lack humanity. They rule based on fear and they do not know when to show mercy."

"But Lykos was different?" Harbona regretted the question as soon as it left his tongue. Lykos wasn't like his father, Issachar. He was honorable, righteous, noble, kind, and brave: he was everything a king should be and was never given a chance.

Lavena's gaze nearly burned a hole in Harbona's heart. "The truth is, being with Lykos changed my mind about mortals. I began to see what he saw in them. Their capacity to love, grow, adapt, and hope. I knew he would be a great king, if not the greatest king the Mainland had ever seen. And I was willing to give up everything to be by his side: my home, my people, even my immortality."

She stood in front of Harbona, her eyes filled with tears, a rare and unsettling sight. "You asked why I hate mortals? I do not hate them, I pity them. Despite all the good they are capable of, they choose evil. They choose the way of the sword, instead of diplomacy. They choose to seek revenge, instead of pursuing justice. They fill themselves with hatred and wonder why their world burns." Her icy tone was now a rasped whisper. "And they choose to kill good men, so evil men may rule. They strip wives of their husbands and deny children their fathers – all for the sake of wearing a crown stained with the blood of the innocent."

"The good ones are worth fighting side-by-side with. The good ones are worth dying for," Harbona didn't care that it wasn't Ethereal in nature, he reached out and grasped one of Lavena's hands. Her pained gaze met his, but she didn't retract her hand. "Lykos knew before Niabi arrived that Death had called for him. He did not try to run or hide. He stayed to fight for his people and to protect those he loved. Lykos lived bravely and died with a clear conscience. That is the man you loved. And he is not the only good one lef t."

"What do you want from me?" Lavena asked, her eyes and voice softening.

"Nothing." Harbona smiled weakly. "But Lykos would want you to remember how much he loved you."

A tear slipped down Lavena's pale cheek. Kayven came up behind her and wrapped his arms around her, resting his chin on top of her head. "I am starting to forget what he looked like. If it were not for Keeva, I would have lost him completely."

Harbona lifted his hands to rest against Lavena's temples. "May I?"

Lavena nodded and closed her eyes.

Harbona planted fresh images of Lykos in her mind. As a Seer, he had crystal clear memories and was more than happy to share them with Lavena. When she opened her watery eyes, she smiled as if relieved.

"Thank you for giving him back to me." Lavena whispered. Kayven tightened his embrace around her, and she raised her hands to squeeze his forearms.

Someone cleared their throat by the arched entryway in the hall and the four Immortals turned to see Makeda standing in the opening. She shifted her weight from one foot to the other and twisted one of her braids.

"I'm sorry for interrupting."

Harbona took a step toward her, glad to see her standing there. "There is nothing to apologize for, Makeda."

Makeda's grey eyes shifted from the floor and met Harbona's longing gaze. "I thought maybe we could take a walk. If you're up to it, that is. I'm sure you're very busy -"

"I would love to," Harbona smiled.

Makeda led him through the garden until they came to the hillside cliff where the river disappeared over the edge. They sat on a granite bench and said nothing for several minutes. Harbona allowed her to take the lead. He didn't want to push her to talk. If this was all he would get from her today, it was more than enough. It was a start.

"She never told me who you were," Makeda spat the words out before she could change her mind. "I suppose I should have figured out the Ethereal part based on my grey eyes."

"I know this must be strange for you," Harbona offered.

"It shouldn't be though," Makeda shook her head, twiddling her thumbs in her lap. "I always knew you existed; you didn't know anything about me. This is probably weird for you."

"I left your mother all those years ago without any warning and it was not fair to her. I was a coward. I realized how strong my love for her was and did not think I was worthy of her." Harbona stared toward the horizon, taking in the sweeping views of Caelestis. "I was banished from my home and branded for everyone to know it. Here, I was the heir; the next Eldaar. On the Mainland, I have nothing to offer. I left to avoid the inevitable: the moment your mother realized she was better off without me." Harbona turned to look at Makeda who had tears streaming down her face. "Believe me, Makeda, if I had known about you, I never would have abandoned you."

"Mother never thought you were unworthy of her love." Makeda slid her hand toward Harbona's and hesitated before resting her palm on top of his hand. "If you could only see yourself through her eyes, through my eyes, you would never doubt how loved you are."

"I wish I could go back in time and be the father you deserved."

"If it's alright with you," Makeda exhaled a nervous breath. "I would really like it if we could get to know each other now. Maybe, it's not too late for us to be a family."

"You do not hate me?" Harbona released some of the tension in his shoulders.

"How could I hate you?" Makeda asked, wide-eyed. "I've waited my entire life to meet you."

He smiled. "So, are you really a Water Wielder?"

She bobbed her head with a chuckle. "And a good one, too."

"Well, of course you are a good one." Harbona puffed out his chest. "You are my daughter after all."

She laughed and stood up, motioning to the river. "Would you like to see what I can do?"

Harbona took her extended hand and nodded. "I would love that."

Chapter Fifty-Two

Salome

Salome's eyes fluttered open, and she stared up at the familiar wood beamed ceiling in her bedroom. Relief flooded her. She survived. But as quickly as relief rushed through her, so did pain. Salome lifted her right arm slowly and saw it was covered in cloth bandages. There was no telling what damage hid beneath all the layers of white wrappings, and honestly, she wasn't in a hurry to find out. Those scars would most likely be the ugliest ones yet.

A groan escaped her lips as she pushed herself up to a seated position. Wanting to get a better look at her appearance in the mirror, she attempted to swing her legs off the side of her bed, but gasped when she heard a voice behind her.

"You're awake."

She turned around and winced from the swift movement. Adonijah was resting beside her. His hair was disheveled and there were dark bags underneath his bloodshot eyes. *Had he been there all night?*

"Always sneaking," Salome shook her head and rubbed her chest, still calming down from the early morning scare.

"It's not sneaking, if I've been by your side the entire time." Adonijah cradled the back of his head in his hands, stretching his legs out.

She hadn't seen him like this before. No leather or weapons adorned his muscular body. No riding boots smeared with dirt. No hood to hide his face or pipe between his lips. Adonijah laid there in a loose white shirt that was untucked from his pants and unbuttoned at the top. She spied a glimpse of his toned chest and averted her gaze with a sharp inhale.

"How long have I been out?" Salome ran fingers through her tangled curls, brutally aware of what horrific shape she must be in.

"Four days."

Salome's eyes popped wide open. "Four days?" Panic flooded her. "The ship?"

Adonijah sat up, reached for her left, uninjured hand, and gently squeezed. "Breathe, Salome. Everything is fine." His gaze met hers. "Jinn hasn't left. He's kept his word about waiting until you are ready to travel."

Heat flushed Salome's face hearing Adonijah mention Jinn's name without a hint of anger or jealousy. Her mind was racing. *Did Jinn say anything about helping her? Did he come to see her while she was unconscious? Was he cloaked and watching them right now?*

She shook the chaotic thoughts free. Jinn told her once before that he never sneaked into her room to watch her sleep and she desperately wanted, needed, to believe that was true.

Adonijah shifted his weight and brought Salome back to him. "You've been with me the entire time?"

"Where else would I be?" He tilted his head to the side, lifting her hand to his mouth and kissing it. He rubbed small circles with his thumb over the back of her hand.

Salome nearly melted when his lips touched her skin. Lips. Her thoughts shot back to the moment on the islet, when she felt Jinn's lips press against hers. How she wished she had the strength to kiss him back. She thought of his powerful arms holding her as she bled, and all she could think about was hoping he had gotten to safety. If she had died fighting the Cornigera, she didn't want Jinn anywhere nearby.

"Are you alright?" Adonijah asked, once again returning her to the present.

She shook her head a little too quickly to look innocent. "How bad a shape am I in?"

Adonijah's eyes roamed her head to toe before he said, "The Myridian Healer was able to salve and stitch most of your cuts. You sprained your left knee. But the worst of it was your right arm."

Salome's eyes darted from Adonijah's attentive gaze down to her bandaged forearm. "Is it broken?"

Adonijah shook his head. "No, but it'll scar."

"Will I be able to hold a weapon again?" She whispered the question, picturing Zara's shaking hands.

Adonijah slipped out of the bed and walked around to her side. He knelt in front of her, her thighs on either side of his body. Cupping her face in his hands, he gently forced her to look him in the eye.

"You are the only woman I know who could defeat the Cornigera, be unconscious for four days, learn you're going to have a scarred arm, and only be concerned if you're going to be able to wield a weapon again." His smile warmed her belly. "You'll be back to your stab happy self soon enough, Princess."

Salome's gaze slid from his eyes to his lips, and he graciously obliged by leaning closer, and kissing her. He was careful of where he placed his hands, but his kiss was anything but gentle. It was filled with passion, concern, fear, hope.

She twisted her fingers through Adonijah's hair, pulling him closer to her, even though there wasn't much space separating them. She wanted to feel him. Wanted to be wrapped in his embrace. Wanted to feel the weight of him over her. After a brush with Death, she wanted Adonijah to know how much she cared for him. How much she wanted him in her life; needed him in her life.

As if he could read her thoughts, he tucked his arms under her thighs and lifted her off the bed. She wrapped her legs around his torso, only to wince in pain from her swollen knee.

Adonijah pulled his face from hers and whispered, "Are you alright?"

Salome smashed her mouth against his. She wasn't going to let their moment pass again. Her hands roamed down his neck to his chest, and she sucked in a sharp breath. She knew he was muscular but running the tips of her fingers across his chest, ignited a hunger in her.

Adonijah leaned into her touch and spun them around, so he was sitting on the bed, and she was straddling him. He pried his mouth away and rested his forehead against hers. Planting an open mouth kiss to her neck, she shivered, goosebumps rippled through her body.

"I thought I was going to lose you," Adonijah murmured into the crook of her neck.

"You can't get rid of me that easily," Salome whispered, running her fingers through his messy, dark hair.

Adonijah placed his hands on her waist and pulled back to meet her gaze. "I don't want to feel like that ever again." He squeezed her gently. "I thought I was going to watch you die and I just... Salome, I don't see myself living without you. I don't just want you; I need y ou."

Salome thumbed the stubble along his jawline. He had exposed his soul to her, and when she pictured the future, she saw him in it. But thinking that flooded her with panic.

Jinn's words on the islet rang through her head again, *"Survive. I need you."*

As hard as she tried to purge her mind of the prince, she couldn't rid herself of his smile, his laugh, his warmth, or his powerful presence.

"Did I upset you?" Adonijah's raspy voice sliced through her, and guilt gripped her heart. "I'm sorry -"

Salome placed a finger against his lips to silence him. "I thought I was going to die three days ago. I thought about you, about us." She kissed him again, but they both knew their encounter was over.

"But the war." Adonijah nodded his head, easily piecing together what she was worried about. He tucked pieces of her wild hair behind her ear. "No matter what happens, I will fight, live, and die by your side."

"You deserve more -"

Adonijah kissed her, not allowing her to finish. "Seeing you fight that Cornigera made me realize you're right. You're making hard choices on behalf of your people. I might not like you putting yourself in harm's way, or thinking that what you want doesn't matter, but I understand it. And as much as I want you to say that you are mine and I am yours, I can wait."

Salome wrapped her arms around his neck and hugged him tight. She realized she was falling in love with Adonijah, even though she wanted him, a part of her still wanted Jinn.

Salome knelt in the Inner Depths once more before joining her company aboard Jinn's ship. She was well enough to travel and as reluctant as she was to leave the first place she had ever truly felt at home, she knew her journey was pulling her elsewhere.

Damaris and Zara waited silently for her to answer. It was an important decision, and she was focused on making the right one. But concentrating was a monumental task that morning because the Five Virtues were loud in her mind, trying to sway her in their favor. Quieting her thoughts and drowning out their voices, her eyes shot open when she made her choice.

Salome met Damaris' awaiting gaze. "I choose Strength."

Damaris smiled and dipped her index finger into the bronze bowl she held. It contained the blue blood taken from the Cornigera she had slain. The Oracle dragged her blue dipped finger straight down Salome's forehead until she reached her chin.

"May Strength be your protector," Damaris recited the prayer, "and may her eagle guide you on your path."

Zara nodded; pride radiated from her face as she motioned for Salome to rise. "You are our Red Maiden, and we will follow you into battle. As deep as the sea."

Salome crisscrossed her arms across her chest. "As deep as the sea."

Zara embraced her niece and whispered in her ear, "Your mother would be proud."

Salome wanted to believe that was true.

Sailing away from the Isles of Myr ripped through Salome's soul and she had to clutch the railing of the ship to keep her knees from buckling or from diving off the vessel and swimming back to her newfound comfort. Although Adonijah, Cato, Rosalina, and Seraphina had all tried to persuade her to go below deck and get some rest, she had refused to leave her spot until the Isles of Myr was no longer visible across the horizon. No one bothered her for hours as tears slipped down her cheeks.

Salome thought of Niabi sailing away, forced to return to Northwind where she wasn't wanted, respected, or loved, when she had found a home and her place amongst the Myridians. She thought of her mother sailing away, agreeing to marry a man she had never met, to ensure her kingdom had a strong ally in trade and battle. Neither of them saw their home again.

Jinn rested his elbows on the railing next to her, staring out across the sea. He didn't say a word, just remained present in case she needed him.

"Have you ever had the feeling when sailing away from your home, that you might not see it again?" Salome didn't turn to look at him but mirrored his stance by placing her elbows up on the wooden banister.

"Every time." Jinn folded his hands together. "Are you afraid?"

"You will have to be more specific."

"Are you afraid you won't see the Isles of Myr again?"

She sighed, hoping he didn't see how scared she really was. "I'm afraid I won't live to see it again."

Jinn reached for her hand and squeezed it gently. She turned her head far enough to catch a glimpse of his golden-brown eyes. "You *will* survive, do you hear me?"

"I want to believe that, but..."

"But what?"

Salome couldn't tell him that she felt Death following her, watching, and waiting for the right moment to claim her soul. She couldn't, wouldn't, tell any of them.

Salome leaned close enough to rest the side of her face against his shoulder. "Maybe when the war is over, I'll visit Sakurai, and you can show me around."

His eyes were fixed on hers. She knew he recognized she changed the subject, but he wasn't going to pester her for answers. He bobbed his head with a sensual grin, hair falling over his forehead perfectly, making him look even more irresistible than normal.

"It would be my honor."

Chapter Fifty-Three

Niabi

Niabi had seen a heart before, but it was odd to see her grandmother's heart tucked in a box of blue velvet like a newborn swaddled for a nap. Satisfied with Marina's recounting of events that led up to Nym's assassination, she closed the lid, and handed the treasure to their Aunt Vilora. Her wrinkled hands wrapped around the tiny chest with a sinister, yet triumphant, grin.

When Niabi sent orders to Marina to bring her Nym's heart, she felt a pang of guilt tug at her heart. Nym had done more for during her childhood than anyone else, but she had to remind herself that her grandmother failed her. Nym abandoned her to Issachar's abuse. Nym hadn't fought for her freedom like she swore she would when Niabi arrived in the Isles of Myr. Nym gave her up. The moment she left Myridian shores, she never spoke to her grandmother again.

At least, those were the reasons she justified having Nym assassinated. The Myridian Queen's heart for the Resurrection Spell. Her grandmother's sacrifice would pave the way for her son's second chance.

But that opportunity had been stolen from her, too. Crispin had robbed her of another life with her son. Rollo was gone for good, and now Neempo, too, was dead; his heart rendered useless to her. She was so angry, she could feel the flames itching underneath her skin, begging for her to let them loose. The one piece of advice the Sovereign had given her about learning to control her fire magic had genuinely impacted her. She kept the fire at bay, mentally quenching it. Keeping her magic hidden was no longer an option after the debacle with her brother, but as long as she remained in control, she would continue to be lethal and dangerous to anyone who crossed her.

"That will be all, Vilora." Niabi dismissed the witch who silently slipped out of Niabi's office with the box containing Nym's heart tucked underneath her arm.

As soon as the door closed behind their aunt, Marina crinkled her nose and said, "Well, she seems...gross."

Niabi clicked her tongue. "With that attitude you'll end up looking just like her."

"If I end up looking like that, I'll drown myself in the sea."

"Play nice." Niabi's smile didn't stretch far, but it was the best she could offer to her cousin, considering the only reason they were in one another's company again was due to Marina killing their grandmother. "I suppose Northwind will now be your permanent residence. You are welcome to stay here in the White Keep."

Marina looked bored, slumped in the armchair on the opposite side of Niabi's desk. She tore her eyes from inspecting her fingernails and met the queen's gaze. "Seeing as I assassinated the Queen of Myr for you, I would think a room in the White Keep would be the least you could offer."

"Mind your tongue or lose it," Niabi's nostrils flared, and she dispelled the tempting urge to smack Marina across her smug face.

"Apologies," Marina purred. "I didn't realize you were such a stickler on formalities these days."

"It's about respect." Niabi reclined in her chair, sipping from her glass of water. "Something you seem to know very little about."

Marina shrugged lazily. "I stopped caring about respecting my *elders,* a long time ago."

Niabi smirked at the familial dig. "I'm older than you by one year, you witch. That hardly qualifies me to be your elder."

Marina flashed a playful smile and it felt as if no time had passed, since the last time they'd seen one another. Though Marina didn't train as a Qata Vishna like Mika and Niabi, she and her younger cousin were always close. They would stay up late talking, steal late-night snacks from the kitchen, and would play pranks on the staff, not caring about the punishments Zara would hammer down on them if, and when, they were caught.

"I suppose congratulations are in order." Marina rested her chin in her hand.

"You will have to be more specific."

Marina's eyes floated from Niabi's cup of water to her now noticeable belly. "How far along are you?"

Niabi's hand rubbed circles around her bump though her eyes were glued to her cousin. "The healers said, I have a few months left."

"And the father?"

"Is none of your concern."

Marina laughed but her smile quickly faded. Her gaze fell to the floor before she asked, "Any news from the Isles of Myr?"

Niabi knew what she was actually asking – what was Mika's fate for taking her place? Reluctantly, Niabi said, "Mika was... executed."

Marina's lips twitched but any other emotion was buried. "I didn't think mother..." She cleared her throat. "I didn't think she would go through with an execution."

"Zara was always one to follow the law. Even if that meant having her heir executed for a crime she didn't commit."

Marina's brows knitted together in a frown as she sat up straight in her seat. "Mika didn't deserve to die like that. She should have died on the battlefield or at a ripe old age, as queen." She twiddled her fingers aimlessly, her voice was hoarse when she said, "Mika would have been a great queen."

Niabi shifted in her seat. She wasn't wrong about Mika making a great queen. Out of the three of them, Mika had always been the most responsible and the most honorable. No matter what trouble Niabi and Marina found themselves getting into, Mika would always rescue them or clean up their mess. She died the same way she lived, covering for Marina.

"If only life dealt fair hands to those who deserved them." Niabi would never voice it aloud, but when word reached her of Mika's fate, she sat in her room and cried until she didn't have any tears left to shed. Mika was never supposed to be caught up in their scheme. She was never supposed to get hurt. She was never supposed to die.

"What of the Qata Vishna?" Marina's question sliced through Niabi's thoughts, more curiosity than concern in her tone.

"It appears the Qata Vishna has a new Red Maiden." The words left a bitter taste in her mouth. In her mind, she was the rightful Red Maiden, but that, too, had been ripped from her when Nym put her on the ship back to Northwind.

"Who?" Marina's eyes widened.

"My sister."

Marina's nose crinkled in disgust. "Of course, mother would back her as the Red Maiden."

"What's the matter, Marina?" Niabi smirked, a low chuckle escaping her lips. "Did Salome rub you the wrong way?"

"Let's just say," Marina cracked her fingers one by one, "I won't shed one tear when she dies."

Niabi tilted her head to the side. What a curious thing for her cousin to say. "Let's find you a room."

"Or an entire wing," Marina linked her arm in Niabi's and nudged her with a hip. "Whatever is the biggest. You know I have expensive taste."

"I am well aware of your tastes, Marina," Niabi patted her cousin's arm with a laugh. "And I am sure we can find something suitable, even for you."

"It'll be just like old times."

Niabi would give anything to go back to a simpler time, a simpler life. But that wasn't the hand she had been dealt. She'd been given a losing hand and had still found herself on top, as Queen of the North. Even if it cost her what was left of her black heart, she would keep her crown, and would gladly slit her siblings' throats to ensure her reign. No one would steal from her again.

Chapter Fifty-Four

Salome

Sailing to where the Bone Mountains and the sea met was a smooth and uneventful journey, minus Adonijah's severe seasickness. He was beyond relieved to be back on dry land and nearly kissed the rocky beach the moment his feet thudded to the ground.

Salome had spent the two days aboard *The Jade Warrior* wondering if Jinn and Kai would be continuing to Sakurai once she and her companions had disembarked. But as Adonijah, Cato, Rosalina, Seraphina, and twelve Qata Vishna sent by Zara as a protection detail went ashore, Salome noticed the prince handing the captain a sealed envelope to be given to his father, King Kenji.

Jinn turned to guide his black stallion, Yuki, down the ramp at the fishing village's humble dock, when his eyes met hers.

Salome stroked Snow's mane. "I thought this was going to be goodbye."

"Why would you think that?" He tilted his head to the side and the light breeze blew strands of hair across his face.

"I assumed a busy prince like you would be needed elsewhere." She flashed a coy smile before tugging Snow down the ramp.

"And what exactly do you think a busy prince, such as me, does all day?" Jinn asked, following her. She could hear the teasing in his voice and decided to play along.

"Oh, you know, wave at your people as you ride by on your noble steed, send someone to fetch your slippers, or wink at fancy ladies of your father's court." Salome bit her lip to stifle her laughter.

Jinn's warm laugh rumbled behind her, and although she smiled, she didn't turn around for him to see the effect he had on her.

"I suppose I'll have to find some way to entertain myself, since I won't be waving or winking at my adoring public."

Salome faced him once Snow was on solid ground. "And what do you intend to do with your time, Prince Jinn?"

Jinn closed the gap between them, hiding them from view behind their horses. "I thought I would go for a hike through the Bone Mountains with you."

Salome's heart leapt and her eyes darted to his lips.

"Those eyes of yours betray you again," he whispered, brushing his fingers against hers.

"There's something you should know," Salome said.

"You can tell me anything."

"It's about my eyes."

"And how they betray you?" Jinn chuckled softly.

"My left eye isn't just a different color than the right one." Salome took a deep breath. She hadn't told him before because she was afraid the truth might frighten him. But the way he looked at her now made her want to tell him every secret she had. *"It's a mark. The Mark of Orion. I'm ..."*

"The Hunter?" Jinn offered when she froze.

"You know?" Her eyes shifted from him to the others prepping their horses for the journey. *"How?"*

Jinn hesitated. *"Adonijah told me."*

Fire raged in her eyes. Why would Adonijah tell him? Why was she so upset he had said anything at all? It wasn't supposed to be a secret. She felt Jinn's warm hand tilting her chin back to face him.

"Don't be upset. It's my fault he said anything at all."

"What are you talking about?"

"The night before you fought the Cornigera," Jinn raked his fingers through his hair, looking almost embarrassed, *"he and I talked."*

Her head was starting to pound. She rubbed her fingers in small circles around her temples. *"What did you two talk about?"*

By his sheepish smile, she already knew the answer. *"I told him that I had feelings for you."*

Snow stomped her hooves on the ground alerting Salome that someone was coming. She looked over Jinn's shoulder and saw Kai approaching, the last one off the ship. Salome cleared her throat, but he didn't turn around to look at Kai.

"Are you upset with me?" Jinn asked, eyes fixed on her.

"No."

"But?"

"I don't know what to do," her voice cracked as she looked around to make sure no one was close enough to eavesdrop.

"About what?" His silky voice drew her in, and she wished he'd cloak them, so she could feel his arms wrap around her.

"You. Him." Salome sucked in a breath before turning away from his gaze. "I don't know what to do."

Jinn shrugged, but she could tell he was just as interested in what she was thinking. "It's not something you have to worry about."

"How can I not worry about it?" Salome glanced at the group and caught Adonijah staring at them. "At some point someone is going to get hurt," she whispered, making sure she was completely hidden behind Snow.

"Hey," Jinn grabbed her hand. "Don't focus on us. You have more important things to worry about right now."

"My guardian, Zophar, would have said the same thing," she smirked.

"Well," Jinn smiled, "he sounds like a smart man."

Salome couldn't help the step she took to close the gap between them. She felt drawn to him, like a moth to a flame. When their eyes met, it made her heart leap, and she had an undeniable urge to kiss him, to let him love her, and be her partner in both life and death.

"If I said, I wanted to kiss you," Salome whispered, her lips inches from Jinn's, "would you let me?"

"Using my lines?" He leaned closer.

"It worked for you."

Jinn slipped his arm around her waist, pulling her against him. "If you let me, I would kiss you every day for the rest of my life."

"Is that a promise?" Her fingers trailed down his jawline, brushing over his lips.

"My life is yours," Jinn whispered.

Salome pressed her lips against his and felt him kiss her back. He smelled of cedar and springtime and held her with a confidence and ease that made her feel at home in his arms. *Home*. Maybe home wasn't a place; maybe home was a person.

Heavy and determined footsteps nearing them forced her to tear herself away from Jinn and put a foot of distance between them. Her cheeks flushed when she looked at him and saw the disappointment in his eyes. She was so concerned about hurting Jinn and Adonijah, that she was beginning to think she might be the one to end up crushed and alone.

"Are you ready?" Adonijah's voice sliced between Salome and Jinn, and he didn't try to hide his scowl. Even though she and Jinn were hidden behind their horses, she couldn't help but wonder if Adonijah had seen them kissing.

Kai stepped forward noticing Adonijah's hostile tone, but the prince cleared his throat, halting her approach. Jinn glanced at Salome and smiled. "I think we're ready for that hike now."

The Tayborne Mountains that stretched from the Black Forest through the northern borders of Northwind were rocky and covered in snow, most of the year. The Bone Mountains, however, were riddled with pine trees, creeks, and vegetation. The paths winding up and around the mountains were shaded and provided breathtaking views of Adalore and the Ignacia Sea. The caravan rode horseback most of the day until they reached an adequate clearing to make camp.

Cato was on edge, and Salome thought it was because he was back in the Bone Mountains, but he kept looking into the tree line as if he were expecting someone to pop out at any given moment.

"What is it?" Salome stood next to him.

"We should have run into some scouts by now," Cato didn't look at her but kept focused on the woods.

"You know these paths," Salome offered, "you've been leading us to avoid scouts."

"Yes, but..."

Salome's eyes shot to where he was looking but didn't see anything. "Cato?"

"We're in Krazak territory." He finally met her gaze, arms crossed over his chest. "If I haven't seen them, I'm afraid they've seen us."

Salome patted his shoulder. "I'm sure we're safe. Perhaps a good night's rest -"

"Let me press onward," Cato interrupted her with a fire bubbling in his gut. "I'll see if we're missing something, so we aren't surprised."

Salome knew there would be no arguing with him. He knew these mountains better than any of them, so she had to trust him. "Alright but be back by dawn. Do you need someone to go with you?"

"I should go alo -"

"I will go." Seraphina marched up to them, wearing her bronze armor, with weapons strapped to her back, ready for an adventure. "If that suits you, Your Highness."

"You want to go?" Salome asked, surprised.

"Really?" Cato echoed, his mouth agape.

Seraphina kept a neutral expression. "It is my duty to protect you," she said to Salome. "What if he tries to abandon us or alerts his people of our presence?"

Cato snorted, offended, "I would never -"

"Even so," Seraphina interrupted, sounding bored. "I wouldn't be doing my job, if you were left unsupervised."

Salome bit her bottom lip, stifling a laugh. "Go. But Seraphina." The Qata Vishna twin glanced at her. "Play nice." Seraphina bowed and vanished into the woods with a bug-eyed Cato.

"You sure about that?" Adonijah came up behind her, pipe lit, exhaling a puff of smoke above her head. "They might kill each other."

"They might," she chuckled. "Or they might realize they make a great team – and a cute couple." Adonijah smiled down at her and she smiled back. "What?"

He shook his head. "Nothing."

"That's not fair," she nudged him with her hip. "You can't look at me like that and say it's nothing."

"Fine," he cleared his throat. "When I first met you, I never expected you to be so..."

"Badass? Intimidating? Witty?" She offered with a grin.

"Likeable."

Salome crinkled her nose. "What did you expect me to be? A monster?"

"I don't know," he shrugged, extinguishing his pipe, and putting it back inside his jacket pocket. "Just not... you."

"And now you're stuck with me," she laughed.

"There are worse fates." Adonijah's eyes darted back to the woods where Cato and Seraphina had ventured. "May the Almighty help Cato, if he angers that woman."

Rosalina cleared her throat and they turned around to see her and Kai standing quietly. Salome found it funny that the two quietest warriors had bonded over the last couple of days. What havoc they could wreak if they wanted.

The Qata Vishna bowed her head, "Princess, we are setting up a perimeter around the camp for the night. I will take the first watch unless you have other orders."

Salome shook her head. "Do as you see fit, Rosalina. I trust your judgment."

Rosalina crossed her arms over her chest, saluting her. She and Kai walked to the other side of the camp and Adonijah shuddered.

"What?" Salome asked.

"Those two are dangerous."

"We're all dangerous."

"Women with weapons." Adonijah shook his head and grinned. "It's a wonder we men survive you."

Salome couldn't sleep that night. Cato and Seraphina hadn't returned, and she was starting to worry that something had happened to them. She sat up and scanned their camp. Twelve Qata Vishna warriors slept on the outskirts, weapons at the ready. She was kept at the center, if anyone attacked, they would have a hell of a time getting to her.

As quietly as she could, she stood up, grabbed her weapons, and walked over to the side of the camp where one of the Qata Vishna was taking her watch.

"Why don't you get some rest, Irena," Salome whispered, clutching her cloak tighter around her. "No reason we both should be up." Irena furrowed her brow, but Salome followed her suggestion with an order. "I will take the rest of the watch."

Reluctantly, the Myridian marched away to her sleeping area and laid down. Salome sat on the stump, bow in hand just in case, and kept her eyes and ears peeled for anyone headed their way. The sun would be rising soon, and she hoped Cato and Seraphina would return by then. Maybe Cato was right to be suspicious.

Thirty minutes passed without an issue, but then Salome heard the rustling of leaves, and the sound of footsteps. They were soft footsteps, but they were loud enough for her to pick up on. She squinted into the tree line and spotted a shadowy figure tiptoeing closer. She tightened her grip on her bow, slowly nocking an arrow. It wasn't Cato or Seraphina. The body was too bulky to be either of her friends. She needed to alert the others without arousing the suspicions of the encroaching figure.

"Jinn," she bridged their bond as calmly as she could. *"Someone is approaching. I don't think he's alone."*

Jinn tapped Kai who was lying a few feet away from him. With three quick hand signals, the Ryoko Naga was armed and ready.

Quickly, but quietly, the rest of the camp was alerted of a possible confrontation and armed themselves. Salome kept her eyes fixed on the moving figure, but when he stopped suddenly, she could sense his gaze on her. He knew he had been made and bellowed a battle cry that sounded like a howl, and to her horror, others echoed in response. By sound alone, Salome knew they were surrounded. The man unsheathed a longsword strapped to his back and charged toward her.

Salome heard dozens of warriors charging their camp and started launching arrows to pick them off as fast as she could before they could reach them. She downed three of them with precision, but the clashing of metal behind her meant they'd reached them.

She shot one more enemy warrior in the neck before she whipped the curved Myridian blades from the holsters on her back and braced herself for hand-to-hand combat. Despite it still being dark, Salome managed to spot their enemies' long braids, furs, and red and black paint smeared all over their bodies.

Krazaks.

One of the brutes jumped out of a tree, battle axe in hand, and sliced his weapon down toward her as he landed on the ground with a giant thud. She deflected his attack with one of her blades and sliced across his midsection with the second. As he fell to the ground, she stabbed him in the neck, letting him bleed out at her feet.

She turned in time to see Kai and Rosalina back-to-back butchering any Krazak that got within a foot of them. Adonijah was right. They were dangerous.

As far as she knew, they hadn't lost anyone in their company. Mika wasn't exaggerating when she said the Qata Vishna were undefeated in battle. They were like dancing assassins. Every movement was graceful and deadly.

"Shield!" Irena yelled.

Salome watched Sabaa drop to the ground, flipping her rectangular shield to cover her back. Irena sprinted toward her, and as soon as her foot hit the shield, Sabaa propelled her up in the air. Flying toward an unsuspecting Krazak, Irena swiped both of her blades in opposite directions, claiming the enemy's head.

Damn. Mika would be beaming with pride.

As mesmerizing as the Qata Vishna were, something twitched in a tree above them, and caught Salome's attention. She spotted an archer perched on a tree branch, his arrow pointed at Jinn in the middle of their camp. The prince was fighting off two Krazaks and didn't look like he'd even broken a sweat.

Within seconds, she snatched her bow off the ground by the stump, nocked an arrow, and let it fly. It pierced the Krazak archer before he had a chance to release his shot.

What Salome didn't see in time, was a second archer hiding in the tree. She slid another bolt out of the quiver hanging from her hip, and dove to avoid his blow, but his arrow slashed her arm. She yelped and fell to her knees. He nocked another arrow; he was going to finish her off. If he had been a better shot, he would have killed her with the first arrow.

With adrenaline pumping through her veins, she launched the arrow nocked in her bow, and watched it slice through the air and pierce the archer's heart. The Krazak fell from the tree, landing on the ground with a heavy thud.

The battle continued to rage around her. The Krazaks were multiplying and coming in endless waves. Though they had slain dozens of Krazaks, it seemed like they were going to lose the battle based on numbers alone.

"Jinn," she whispered in his mind.

The prince stabbed a large Krazak in the chest and turned around to find her. Their eyes met and he paled instantly.

A giant hand grabbed ahold of her by her hair and jerked her head back, poking a knife against her throat. The Krazak behind her shouted, "Drop your weapons or I'll slit her throat!"

Jinn's eyes were filled with rage. If looks alone could kill, he would have massacred the entire lot of them.

"Jinn," she said calmly. *"It's ok."*

"I said, drop your weapons." The Krazak yanked her viciously and she winced, forcing Jinn to lay his tachi swords on the ground, with the others following suit. "Now, what have we got here," the Krazak hissed in Salome's ear. "Looks like trespassers to me."

"We're just passing through." Adonijah stepped forward, hands held at the level of his eyes to show he was unarmed. "We're traveling north and wanted to avoid running into the Thrak."

"Don't we all," the Krazak laughed, his grip on Salome's hair was unyielding.

Salome glanced around their camp and saw they had lost two Qata Vishna, Trin and Valha, and her heart ached. They were sent to protect her. Instead, they died fighting these vicious Mountain Men for no reason other than them being territorial.

Her eyes met Jinn's. She could see the wheels in his mind turning, thinking through any strategy that would work to free her and slaughter the remaining Krazaks. From her count, there were maybe twenty left. They'd killed at least twenty-five.

"Whatever you are thinking," Salome warned, *"don't do anything stupid. I'm rather fond of my neck."*

His gaze softened. *"I'm rather fond of your neck, too."*

"You are trespassing on Krazak territory," the Krazak leader's voice bellowed. "The penalty for crossing into the Bone Mountains is death." The light, morning breeze ruffled the Krazak's furs and Salome could feel his hot breath against the back of her head.

"Parlay," Salome's voice was strained.

The Krazak turned her around to face him. His long, thick, dark braid fell over the front of his chest, and the sides of his head were shaved. Though clean shaven, his face was splattered with red and black paint, and his arms were smeared with ash and clay. Tiny bones protruded through his ear lobes, and his fearsome brown eyes were glued to hers.

"What did you say?" he hissed, pulling the knife away from her throat.

"Parlay," Salome repeated, this time loud enough for everyone in the camp to hear. "I request a parlay."

"You want to meet with King Gerd?" The Krazak looked genuinely surprised.

"I trust you will honor my request.".

He lowered his knife, and the remaining Krazaks lowered their weapons. "Then you shall meet the king."

Before forcing Salome to travel to Fennor to meet King Gerd, the Krazaks allowed Rosalina to patch up her wound. Once she was bandaged, the Mountain Men led them down the twisting pathways to the City of Bones.

Adonijah and Harbona had warned her before of how cruel the Krazaks were and that they would rather slit throats than make deals.

Where were Cato and Seraphina?

If the Krazaks captured or killed them...

She shook the thought free. She couldn't dwell on that possibility.

The Krazak that had held a knife to her throat walked in front of her, glancing back at her occasionally to make sure she wasn't plotting an escape.

"What's your name?" She dared to ask.

"None of your business." He shot back with a snarl.

"You wouldn't do me the honor of knowing my captor's name?" Salome tried once more and to her surprise, he obliged.

"Rune. I am the Commander of the Krazak Militia."

"Rune," she repeated so she would remember it. "I wish I could say it's nice to meet you."

"Save your pleasantries for King Gerd," Rune huffed, shouldering his furs to keep him warm from the early morning chill.

Salome risked a glance behind her to see how her company was holding up. Adonijah was grumbling under his breath, Kai and Rosalina flashed dirty looks at any Krazak who dared look in their direction, and Jinn's eyes were already on her.

"Are you alright?" she asked.

"I'm more concerned about you," his eyes scanned the area she'd been shot.

"I've had worse." She turned her focus forward, her hands bound with rope like the others.

"So," his warmth flooded her mind and she felt like he was wrapping his arms around her. *"A parlay was a nice, unexpected touch."*

"Cato told me a lot about his people. I figured maybe the Krazaks and Stormcrags weren't entirely that different."

"What is the next phase of your plan?"

Salome had an idea but wasn't sure if it would work. Before she could explain her plan to Jinn, Rune announced they had arrived.

From the outside it looked like they were walking into a cave, but as they marched through the tunnel, it opened into a city carved inside the mountain itself. The peak was exposed to let sunlight inside, and Salome's mouth dropped. She never thought the City of Bones would look so beautiful.

Thousands of caves were carved into the rock where the Krazaks lived with their families. They had a market in the open area of the mountain base as well as training grounds, an arena, sheep and goat pens, blacksmiths, and tanners. Torches hung from the rocky walls and illuminated the city, so it didn't feel like they lived inside the mountain.

Furs, tapestries, curtains, rugs, and pillows filled the underground city with patterns and color that made it feel cozy and almost homey.

Salome watched some children kick a ball around with broad smiles as the caravan was led to the only freestanding building, other than the arena, which housed King Gerd and the Throne of Skulls.

Rune halted them. "Only three of you may meet with the king. The rest of you will remain outside."

Salome motioned for Adonijah and Jinn to come with her. They followed Rune inside the humble castle made of stone, but they didn't have to walk far before they reached King Gerd who was sitting on his throne made out of the skulls of his enemies.

Gerd was such a large man he made his throne look tiny. He had the same caramel skin tone that Cato did, but his black eyes were filled with lust and malice. His braid was longer than Rune's and hung to his hip. The sides of his head were also shaved, but he had a scraggly beard that rested on his broad, hairy chest. Salome noticed he didn't have a shirt on and spied tiny bones pierced in his nipples. Gerd sported dark pants, worn out boots, and gold rings on all his stubby fingers.

"Who do we have here?" Gerd's gravelly voice boomed in the small throne room. He reclined in his seat, his dirty hands gripping the armrests where two small skulls screamed back at Salome. "Which one of you is the leader?"

Salome stepped forward, fighting the urge to crinkle her nose at the foul smelling ruler. "I am."

Gerd scoffed. "You are a woman."

Salome ignored the disgust rolling off his tongue and said, "My company and I are travelling north. We wish to continue our journey."

The king wheezed out a laugh and shook his head. "You will never leave this mountain. Rune spared your lives; therefore, you will be our slaves. Truthfully, death would have been more merciful." Gerd slipped out of his throne like a serpent and slithered toward Salome. He sniffed her hair and flashed a lustful grin. "Especially, for someone as pretty as you."

"You refuse to let us go?" Salome held her ground, despite every inappropriate glance or touch from the king.

"Like I said," Gerd put his nose against Salome's ear and whispered, "you will *never* leave this mountain."

"Dagaal." Salome rasped, averting her eyes from the king's gaze, not wanting him to notice her two color eyes. Jinn told her the Krazaks would think her to be a witch and she didn't need to add to her list of problems.

"What did you just say?" Gerd hissed, taking a step back.

Did she detect fear in his voice?

"I invoke the right to a Dagaal." Salome said louder. Rune and the handful of Krazak warriors stationed around the room stilled. Their eyes darted to their king.

Gerd stood wide-eyed before a nervous chuckle escaped his lips. He waved a dismissive hand in the air. "You have no rights here. You cannot declare a Dagaal, unless you are a rival attempting to overthrow my rule."

"Then consider yourself challenged." Salome spat, and the Krazaks started whispering amongst themselves. "If we win, you release us to continue our journey."

"And if we win," Gerd's wicked smile beamed, "your companions will be our slaves and you," he twirled a lock of her hair between his scarred fingers, "will belong to me."

Before Adonijah or Jinn could protest, Salome nodded. "Agreed."

Gerd clapped his enormous hands together. "Choose your champion."

"I choose myself." Salome wasn't willing to issue a challenge and back away from a fight, even if she was injured.

Gerd sank into his throne and shook his head, a mocking look inching across his face. "You cannot be your own champion. You must choose one of your own to fight my champion. If no one will fight for you, then you forfeit." His smile sent an unwelcome chill up her spine.

Adonijah stepped forward, "I'm her champion."

Salome slowly turned to face him, her face pale, and her eyes wide. "Adonijah -"

"Done!" Gerd snapped his fingers and Rune approached the throne. "Gather the people. They will want to watch Orn, do what he does best."

Salome stood in front of Adonijah and whispered, "What are you thinking?"

Adonijah brushed hair out of her face and flashed a tight-lipped smile. "I am your best chance, and you know it."

"Adonijah -"

Adonijah bent forward and kissed her forehead. It felt too much like a goodbye kiss for Salome's liking. "I will fight, live, and die by your side, remember?"

Before she could say anything, Rune and two Krazak warriors grabbed Adonijah and escorted him out.

"Where are they taking him?" Salome faced Gerd with a rising rage.

"The arena, of course." For a man that seemed nervous about the mention of a Dagaal, he now seemed awfully confident. "Orn will make quick work of him. Don't worry. He won't suffer. Long."

Chapter Fifty-Five

Adonijah

Adonijah stood in the center of the arena where Rune and his men had escorted him. Carved into the mountain, half of the coliseum arches were open to the outside world, boasting some of the most spectacular views of the surrounding mountains. Thousands of Krazaks filled the roofless stadium, ready to see their champion spill the blood of another enemy on the dusty arena ground.

King Gerd ordered his soldiers to carry the Throne of Skulls from his castle to the coliseum and set it on a suspended wooden dais at the end of the arena grounds. With the mountainous view as his backdrop, Gerd raised a hand to silence the deafening crowd. "I have been challenged to a Dagaal. A mistake on our enemy's part." He laughed and the Krazaks echoed his cackle. "But we all know how this will end." He motioned to the Krazak who entered the arena. Our champion, Orn the Bone-Crusher!"

Orn was a seven-foot-tall behemoth of a man. Clay and red and black paint were smeared all over his body, making his broad shoulders and python size thighs seem even bigger. His muscular body was riddled with scars, but the one thing that instantly caught Adonijah's attention was the Bone-Crusher's braid.

Adonijah knew the Krazak warriors grew their braids longer for every battle won. Some of them had shoulder-length braids while others had braids that stretched below their waists. Orn was one of those Krazaks. The giant's braid was dark, thick, and ran the length of his spine, stopping at the back of his knees. Adonijah imagined it was quite possible that Orn had never cut his hair before.

Adonijah had to win, and quickly, because Orn certainly wasn't going into this Dagaal to lose. He would slit Adonijah from neck to navel if he got a clear opening. Strength wouldn't be Adonijah's friend today; he would have to play this smart.

Based on Orn's gait, Adonijah noticed three things. One, the giant favored his right side. Two, from the slightest limp most people wouldn't even notice, he was recovering from a recent leg injury. And three, his legs were so muscular, he could probably stomp someone to death.

The Krazak stood ten feet away from Adonijah, the king sitting behind him, with a devilish grin. The giant brute had the audacity to laugh when he looked at Adonijah. He should have been insulted, but he wouldn't give the Bone-Crusher the satisfaction. He would just kill him instead.

Adonijah caught a glimpse of Salome and the rest of their company sitting in the first row guarded by Krazak warriors. When his gaze met Salome's, he expected to see fear or worry in her eyes, but he didn't see either. He saw a pissed queen staring back at her champion.

No matter what, I will fight, live, and die by your side.

He repeated her promise in his mind. He would fight for her. He would live for a future with her. He would even die for her if it came down to it. But what he wouldn't do, was let Orn win this Dagaal.

Adonijah tuned out the cheers and taunts from the Krazaks and focused solely on the Mountain Man standing between him and freedom.

Rune stomped between them and gave them their choice of weapon. A longsword, a mace, an axe, or a pair of daggers. Orn snatched up the mace without a second thought. It had a long metal shaft and gave him the option to keep Adonijah at a distance. And the heavy, spoked head was perfect for bludgeoning. Not an ideal way to die.

Adonijah was most comfortable with a longsword, and it would normally be his weapon of choice, but knowing his strength would not match Orn's power, he chose the twin daggers. They were lightweight and fit in his palms as if they were forged just for him. He would have to use his speed if he stood any chance of winning.

"Krazaks!" King Gerd raised his fists in the air with a sinister grin. "Who is your champion?"

"Orn! Orn! Orn!" The people chanted, their fists pumping in the air.

"Let the Dagaal begin!"

Gerd nodded his head and Orn took off running, slamming his mace down on the ground, shifting the dirt. Adonijah leapt out of the way and got back up on his feet, clutching the hilts of his daggers tightly. Circling Orn, Adonijah waited for him to make another reckless lunge for him, then he would swipe at the giant's favored side. True to his prediction, Orn raised his weapon over his shoulder to swipe at Adonijah's head. He dodged the blow and sliced the giant's right side, drawing first blood.

Orn yelped, and backhanded Adonijah across the face, sending him tumbling to the ground. "I am going to tear your flesh from your body and wear your bones."

Adonijah had been threatened many times in his life, but this was the first time he felt fear surge through his body in years. Orn didn't mince words, and knowing the Krazak way of life, he knew the giant would proudly wear his bones like a necklace.

Jumping back to his feet, Adonijah parried with the Krazak, hoping to get him off balance to swipe at the back of his knees. If Adonijah could get him to the ground, he might be able to disarm him. But Orn was faster than Adonijah expected, and after letting his guard down before, the Krazak kept a safe watch over his right side.

Orn whipped the mace toward Adonijah's head. He leaned back to avoid the blow and the Krazak jumped at the opening. His gigantic foot landed a firm and heavy blow to Adonijah's chest, launching him into the air.

Adonijah's breath was snatched from him, and it took him a second to recover from the blow. He knew his ribs weren't broken, but another kick like that and he wouldn't be so lucky. Hearing Orn's mace slice through the air forced Adonijah to roll away, narrowly avoiding the shattering thud on the ground.

Adonijah's gaze met Salome's and it was as if everything slowed down around him. She had confidence in him, but as her eyes began to widen in fear, he realized a split second too late that Orn was going to land a solid blow. He scrambled to escape but the spikes of the Krazak's mace ripped across his right thigh, drawing blood.

Gritting his teeth, Adonijah swallowed a scream. The giant loomed over him. Desperate to get back on his feet, Adonijah kicked the Krazak's weapon free from his grasp with his uninjured leg. Now disarmed, Adonijah sliced Orn's arm, and the giant retreated to find his mace.

Adonijah dashed to his feet and ran as fast as his limping leg would allow, toward his opponent. As Orn bent down to pick up his weapon, Adonijah jumped on top of the Krazak's back and shoved one of his daggers into the warrior's chest.

Orn roared. He grabbed Adonijah by his hair and whipped him over his back, slamming him on the ground. A swift punch met Adonijah's wrist when he tried to block Orn's attack, and Adonijah felt his wrist pop from the impact. A second punch followed, and without being able to block it, it landed squarely across his jaw.

Adonijah could taste the blood oozing from his mouth. His eyes watered, blurring his vision. He sensed a third punch coming his way. Gripping his second dagger, he stabbed it into the arm Orn used to pin him to the ground.

Orn released him, but Adonijah quickly realized both of his daggers were now embedded in the giant's chest and bicep. With no weapons to fight with, Adonijah realized defeating his opponent wasn't going to be easy.

As Orn was distracted by the knives protruding from his body, Adonijah caught sight of the long braid dangling behind the Krazak's knees. It wouldn't be a clean death, but without weapons, it was the last chance he had to walk out of that arena alive. Without a second thought to convince himself otherwise, Adonijah dove for the braid and as quickly as he could, wrapped it around Orn's neck several times. He jumped on the giant's back, this time keeping his head out of his reach, and pulled the braid as tightly as he could, strangling the Krazak.

Orn abandoned the daggers in his chest and arm, panicking as he tried to pry the braid from his throat. Adonijah heard him gurgling and gasping for air, but he wasn't going to loosen his noose until he was dead. The giant fell to his knees, desperately trying to claw Adonijah from his back, but failed. The arena of bloodthirsty Krazaks fell silent as they watched their champion die a slow and agonizing death.

Adonijah had never strangled anyone before. He made sure all his killings were swift and clean. But as he felt the Krazak take his last breath and the life leave his body, he felt a heaviness creep into his heart, a weight on his shoulders he had never experienced before.

Slowly lowering Orn to the ground face first, Adonijah checked for a pulse, but there wasn't one. The Krazak was dead. The Dagaal had been won. But the joy and relief of victory didn't flood him.

His eyes darted to Salome. Adonijah wasn't sure what he expected to see in her eyes, but satisfaction wasn't it. She rose from her seat slowly, her gaze now fixed on King Gerd, who was seated behind Adonijah.

Turning just in time to see the Krazak king angrily snap his fingers, Adonijah was suddenly encircled by six archers. He didn't have any strength left to fight the soldiers, and when he saw spears pointed at Salome, something inside of him wanted to snap, but he stilled, when he heard her voice.

“My champion won the Dagaal,” she snarled, fire raging in her eyes. "You will honor your word and release us.”

Gerd lurched to his feet, slamming his fists against his chest, "You will never leave these mountains!"

Rune stepped to his king's side and whispered something in his ear. Whatever words he used were clearly not the right ones. Gerd unsheathed his sword and held the tip of it against Rune's chest.

"You would seek to undermine me, old friend?" Gerd hissed like a serpent.

Rune spoke loudly enough for all the Krazaks to hear, "You dishonor our people with your refusal to honor the Dagaal. Our ancestors would rip that wicked tongue out of your deceitful mouth if they were alive."

"Well, they're dead." Gerd smirked, his fingers dancing on the hilt of his blade. "So, tell them, King Gerd sends his regards."

Before Gerd could run his commander through with his sword, the sound of a war horn echoed. It sent a chill up Adonijah's spine and goosebumps covered his dirty skin. The Krazaks stilled, as if they were in disbelief of who announced their arrival.

Archers covered in blue ink tattoos, furs, and hair dyed in shades of blue, purple, and white, popped up around the top of the arena. Their arrows nocked in their bows, ready to strike anyone that moved an inch without their approval. The thunder of marching soldiers grew louder as hundreds of Stormcrags stomped into the arena, weapons in their hands, ready for battle.

The man who led the rival Mountain Men clan was well over six feet tall and had ancient runes tattooed all over his bald head. To his right stood a ferocious woman with lavender hair with beads and trinkets strewn throughout her locks. Her neck and upper chest were covered in rune tattoos, and she had the same caramel skin that Cato did.

And that's when Adonijah saw them. Cato and Seraphina stood to the Stormcrag leader's left with hunger in their eyes. Not for food, but for blood. Cato snarled and gritted his teeth, looking like a warrior, and not the scared, skinny boy who had been chained and headed to the Gomorrian gallows.

Unless Adonijah's weary eyes were deceiving him, he swore he saw Numbio warriors gathered with the Stormcrags; their prince and a Westerner leading them.

Chapter Fifty-Six

Salome

Zophar.

Zophar was in the City of Bones with an army. Tears welled in Salome's eyes at the sight of him but when their gaze met, she felt as if someone had stabbed her straight through her heart. Those impish blue eyes of his didn't dance like she thought they would. They carried pain. *What horrors had he seen these past few weeks?*

Looking through the masses for her brother, she failed to find him. Her eyes darted back to Zophar and a tear slipped down his cheek. Her heart stopped. She wanted to jump over the stone barrier and drop the eight feet to the arena ground to run to him. She needed to see her brother. Needed to know he was safe. Needed to know that tear racing down Zophar's rosy cheek wasn't in memory of someone they both loved deeply but would never see again.

"What are you doing here, Torrin?" Gerd's serpentine voice sliced through her thoughts.

"We have come for our friends," Torrin, the Stormcrag leader, stepped forward, smirking. "And from what I see, they won the Dagaal, meaning you are no longer the rightful ruler of the City of Bones."

Gerd growled through gritted teeth, lowering his sword from Rune's chest, and pointing it at the rival tribesman. "Take your kind and leave my city, before I order my warriors to cut you down and wear your bones."

Torrin's laugh boomed throughout the arena. "I don't think your people will be as dishonorable as you."

"Krazaks!" Gerd shouted. "Kill them all." But not one Krazak moved. Gerd looked around the arena and snarled. No one obeyed his command. No one even looked frightened of him anymore. "I said, kill them!"

"Your champion lost the Dagaal," Rune said again, stepping up to the former king. "You are no longer our leader."

Gerd whipped his sword over his head to strike Rune down, but his body was peppered with arrows.

Salome thought the Stormcrag archers had killed the king, but none of them had loosed an arrow. Her eyes darted to Adonijah in the center of the arena and saw the arrows had been launched by the six soldiers surrounding him.

Rune stepped over Gerd's body and marched toward Salome. When he got within ten feet of her, he lowered his head in respect. "Your champion won the Dagaal, and therefore, we acknowledge you as our new leader. My sword," he lifted his weapon in outstretched hands to Salome, "is yours."

Salome wasn't sure what to say. She didn't want to be their leader, she just wanted to continue her journey north. She looked over at Zophar who seemed just as surprised. But before she could say anything, the Krazaks in the arena bowed their heads, acknowledging the beginning of her reign.

Once the arena had been cleared, and Adonijah had been taken to the medical cavern, the leaders from every group assembled in the castle.

Salome and Jinn entered the dining room where a circular table and eight chairs were. Her eyes found the red-bearded Zophar immediately. They walked toward one another until they stood inches from each other, tears streaming down her cheeks. She had thought about what she would do when she saw her guardian again and pictured herself running into his outstretched arms. Then he would say something about how much he missed her and how he couldn't wait to see her beat Crispin in a sparring match again.

But she didn't run into his arms. Zophar didn't say a word for a full minute as they breathed one another in. He looked as if he had aged years in a matter of weeks.

Salome reached for his scarred and calloused hand, wrapping her pinky around his index finger. "Zophar?" she breathed, a rasp in her throat. It was just his name, but the Westerner knew she was asking about her brother.

"I'm sorry," Zophar whispered as his bottom lip quivered.

Salome took a step back, her knees buckling. She felt Jinn wrap an arm around her waist to keep her from crumbling to the floor. Words failed her. She extended the mental bridge to Crispin, begging him to hear her, to answer her. But she was met with silence; a door that was locked and would remain unanswered. He couldn't be dead. He couldn't be gone.

The man she had seen Zophar standing next to when the Stormcrags entered the arena stepped forward. He placed a hand on his heart and said, "Your brother was lost in the River of Lost Souls, but there is still a chance he survived -"

"Who are you?" Salome interrupted him, her words coming out far sharper than she intended.

"I am Prince Heru." He smiled as widely as he dared. "Your brother was my friend."

Jinn helped Salome to a seat and knelt in front of her. He squeezed her hand, but her eyes were distant. "Salome?"

Salome's gaze settled on his face, and she saw the pain in her eyes reflected in his. "My brother is gone?"

Zophar stood in front of her, arms clasped behind his back. "I have failed you. I have failed your brother, and I have failed your family," his voice cracked. "I will accept whatever punishment you deem worthy, Princess."

Salome's voice cracked, "It's not your fault."

Jinn rubbed small circles in her palm, begging her to let him in. She extended the bridge to him, *"Crispin can't be dead."*

"Heru said there was a chance he survived. We can send some soldiers to -"

"And where would I send them?" Salome stifled a cry. *"What if they bring back his body? Then it will be true, and I don't think... I can't lose him, too."*

Jinn wrapped his arms around her, and she cried into his shoulder. The room was silent and allowed her the moment to grieve in peace. She pulled out of Jinn's embrace and wiped her tears. She would cry herself to sleep that night, but first, there was a room filled with leaders from all over Adalore who needed her to be strong.

Torrin, the leader of the Stormcrags, stepped forward when Salome glanced at him. He crossed a fist over his chest and bowed his bald head. "Your loss is a great one, but if you will permit me an audience, I believe we can help one another."

"You don't have to do this." Jinn cloaked them. She knew the second they vanished from sight because the other leaders, Zophar included, panicked. *"You are allowed to grieve and meet with the Stormcrag tomorrow."*

Salome glanced at Jinn, grateful and humbled he cared enough about her to show everyone else the magic he tried to keep a secret. *"Tonight, I will grieve."* She grabbed his hand and squeezed tightly, not wanting to release him. *"Today, I will carry on."*

Jinn bobbed his head, relinquishing his magical barrier over them, and sat in the seat next to hers. Kai immediately took her place behind her prince's chair, eyes scanning the others, looking for a reason to pull out her knives and poke a few holes into their flesh.

"Are we not going to talk about what just happened?" Torrin's eyes narrowed as he stared at the prince.

Jinn shrugged lazily, "I'm a Cloaker. The end."

Salome could tell by the Stormcrag leader's flared nostrils he felt he had been disrespected, but she didn't need them brawling in the small room. She motioned for Torrin to sit in the seat behind him. "I believe there are more important matters to discuss than Prince Jinn's magic."

Torrin reluctantly sank into a wooden chair across from Salome with Cato and the lavender haired woman named, Oifa, behind him. If Salome thought Kai was intense, Oifa put the Ryoko Naga to shame. There was nothing soft about the warrior, and if Oifa had her way, she would have ripped every Krazak within grabbing distance to shreds.

Heru, the Prince of Numbio, sat to Zophar's left. The healer, introduced as Rayma, stood behind him. Salome spied a crystal dagger hanging from the healer's hip and thought it odd to see someone sworn to save life with a weapon on their person. Whatever the Numbio had seen on their journey through the Sand Lands had impacted them.

Although Zophar protested, Salome insisted the Westerner sit to her direct left. Her Master of War would always have an honored place by her side. The twin Qata Vishna stood behind her and Salome knew Seraphina and Rosalina were just as eager to strike someone down.

There was one leader left that Salome asked to join their inner circle, to the great irritation of the Stormcrags. Rune quickly took his seat next to Jinn with a fierce and devilish looking bowman, Hanzo, taking up watch behind him.

Salome thought she heard Oifa and Hanzo muttering ancient curses against each other's tribes before the meeting had been called to order. Once all the introductions had been made, Salome took a deep breath and began.

"I suppose first thing's first," she exhaled sharply, eyes scanning one leader to the next. "Although my champion won the Dagaal, I have no intention of staying in the City of Bones and ruling the Krazaks."

"Then allow me," Torrin puffed out his hairy chest, "to volunteer."

"Shove that thought back up your ass, Torrin," Rune shot viciously, a clear history between them was beginning to take form in her mind. "The Krazaks will not be ruled by the likes of you."

Torrin bared his teeth like a seething animal. "Do you not see her *eyes*, Rune?" The Stormcrag pointed a stubby finger in Salome's direction. "Do you not remember the prophecy?"

Rune waved his hand in the air, dismissing the religious fanatic. "You have spent too many years up in the Tears of the Gods. You are no longer of sound mind."

"Prophecy does not lie -"

"What prophecy?" Salome asked, confused by their tit for tat conversation. "I thought your people would think me to be a witch for having two different color eyes."

Rune's gaze met hers and he looked into her eyes, as if it was the first time, he truly observed her. "None of us would fear you to be a witch. It's an unfounded rumor and superstition about our people." His eyes shot to Torrin's dirty face. "But *they* are firm believers that a woman with two different colored eyes would come to unite our tribes once and for all, ending the war between brothers."

"Brothers?" Salome asked.

"The Krazaks and Stormcrags are the descendants of King Phlias' soldiers who were exiled for serving the usurper. There were two brothers who led Phlias' armies and when neither would relinquish their rank or claim to lead the exiles, they broke into two tribes." Rune explained quickly, despite Torrin's judgmental looks flashed his way every now and then, as if he could tell the story better. "For a thousand years, we have been at war with one another, fighting over control of the City of Bones. For three hundred years, the Krazaks have lived in this mountain. We have built this kingdom with the blood, sweat, and broken bones of our people." Rune's even-tempered voice started to rise, as if anger was starting to overtake him. "And we will *not* bend the knee to a Stormcrag king. Not now, not ever."

"But you would willingly bend the knee to this outsider from the North?" Torrin snorted, referring to Salome's new reign over the Krazaks.

"You know our laws, Torrin." Rune crossed one leg over the other, not wasting his energy meeting Torrin's gaze. "She declared a Dagaal, saying she was challenging our king. Her champion won. We Krazaks may be a lot of things, most of them cruel and wicked, but what we aren't, and never will be, is dishonorable."

"You wish to speak of honor, but your kind have given Stormcrag men, women, and younglings to the Thrak for generations," Oifa spat at Rune's feet. "You know nothing of honor, only self-preservation."

"And *your* kind has never sacrificed a Krazak before?" Hanzo, Rune's bowman, snarled back. "Both Krazak and Stormcrag blood has been spilled for as long as we can remember, so don't blame us when you are guilty of the same sin."

Oifa launched herself at the Krazak archer. Though she was armed with knives and an axe at her hip, she chose to scratch at his face like a mountain lion protecting her cubs. Hanzo pushed her off him, nocked an arrow, and pointed it at her face. She flashed a vicious grin, daring him to let his arrow loose.

"Enough," Salome barked, and Hanzo lowered his weapon, already listening to his new leader's voice. "There is too much history for this to be resolved in one afternoon."

"So, you just expect us to -"

"Live amongst one another until we figure it out?" Salome interrupted Torrin as if she were separating children from brawling in the street over a toy. "That's exactly what I expect."

"As you wish," Rune folded his arms over his chest, flipping his braid behind him.

Not to be shone up, Torrin mirrored the Krazak's body language, stroking his beard separated in two sections, and nodded. "As you wish."

Salome turned her attention to Zophar and Heru. It was difficult to look at them and not think of her brother failing to return to her. She sucked in a breath, stifling the tears, and swallowing the lump in her throat. She would cry all night long, but not now, not here.

"How did you find yourself in the company of the Stormcrags?" she asked.

Zophar wiggled in his seat; he was never comfortable sitting at a table of leaders when he was better at following orders. "As we were traveling north, we were ambushed by a horde of Thrak. They fought hard and claimed six of our men."

Salome noticed Rayma, the Numbio healer, tense up when Zophar said they had lost six men. Their eyes met, and Salome could sense the animosity she harbored in her heart. She wasn't sure if it was directed at her specifically or the Numbio's involvement in general.

"We defeated the Thrak, but Torrin's men captured us, and took us to their city," Heru picked up on the story. "When we explained who we were and where we were going, Torrin invited us to rest and resupply with his people before continuing north."

"When we were returning from scouting, we saw the Krazaks surround the camp," Cato explained how he and Seraphina fit into the saga. "We wanted to warn you, but we knew we wouldn't be able to get past their ranks in time. I thought it best to find the Stormcrags and tell them of your capture. That's when we met Zophar and realized we were all on the same side."

The puzzle Salome was trying to piece together was complete. She understood how the Stormcrags knew she was in trouble and why Zophar was with them. She knew her business between the Stormcrags and Krazaks was far from over, but at least she knew with her as a buffer between the tribes, there shouldn't be any violence. But she wanted to make sure it was stated plainly in case someone tried to make an excuse for bloodshed.

"Until we figure out what to do next, I don't want any bloodshed or violence between the Stormcrags and Krazaks." Salome's eyes darted between Oifa and Hanzo instead of Torrin and Rune. She knew the latter would obey her words, but she had to ensure the hot-headed warriors standing behind them would understand.

They both reluctantly nodded in agreement. They would comply. For now. Salome would have to figure out how to bring these two tribes together or there would eventually be another war.

"Unless there's something else..." Salome began to rise from her seat when Rayma spoke.

"We were told that you had the Hunter. Is that the case or was that just a ploy to trick the Numbio into fighting your battles?" Rayma's tone was less than cordial and Salome was ready to rip her tongue from her mouth.

Salome might have accepted someone speaking down to her when she was a nobody in the Tree House Forest, but she would be damned if she was spoken to in that manner, with the titles that now followed her name.

Heru jumped to his feet and whipped around to face Rayma. The prince attempted to hide his rage but failed miserably when he snarled at the healer. Normally, a servant of any crown would cower and fumble over an apology for the looseness of their tongue, but Rayma didn't back down. She didn't tremble in fear, nor did she offer an apology. She planted her hands on her hips and her nostrils flared.

Salome knew a standoff when she saw one, but there was something else going on besides a defiant healer and her prince. They must be in a relationship or had been at one point in time.

She just instructed the Mountain Men not to squabble and fight, so she had to squash the tension between her and the healer immediately. They followed her brother into the desert, ready to fight along his side for him to reclaim their family's throne. Crispin trusted them, so she would as well.

"My brother was not one for tricks." Salome's voice cracked when she said *was* and not *is*. Eyes from all around the room shot to her and no one uttered a sound. "My brother was an honorable man, and he was honest to a fault." Salome's eyes were focused on Rayma. "Crispin told you that we have the Hunter, and we do."

Zophar's shoulders tensed. He flashed her a warning look, but she wasn't afraid of the title anymore. There was no turning back, and if people were going to march into battle under her banner as her allies, they deserved to know the whole truth.

"I am the Hunter." Salome said boldly and relished the shock in Rayma's face upon her declaration. "I bear the mark of the Hunter," she pointed to her left eye, "and I will do what all Hunters are expected to do: avenge innocent blood."

"You are the Hunter?" Heru squared his shoulders to Salome's and the awe in his face nearly knocked her off her feet.

Salome nodded, holding her chin higher than before. "I am."

Heru placed a hand over his heart. "I swore to march with your brother and now, I swear the same oath to you. The Numbio will fight with you."

Jinn stood. "The East will fight with you."

Torrin and Rune eyed each other before rising.

"The Stormcrags will fight with you."

"The Krazaks will fight with you."

One by one, everyone in the room pledged their allegiance. Salome was humbled by the four mighty men who swore fealty to her, backing her claim. Whether Crispin was still alive, or Death had swept him into her cold embrace, there was no turning back now. Salome would face her sister with an army that could, and would, rival Niabi's.

"Her name is Salome. Daughter of the White Wolf of Northwind and the Sea Monster of the Myr. Princess of Northwind. Red Maiden of the Qata Vishna. The Hunter of prophecies foretold. Long may she reign." Seraphina presented Salome's titles boldly and proudly.

She was Salome and she would not fail.

Chapter Fifty-Seven

Crispin

Crispin tossed and turned throughout the night as they sailed west toward The Sisters. Sleep eluded him for the two days since they left Northwind. Neempo's pained face kept flashing in his mind. Every time he closed his eyes, he saw the witch's fingers digging into the Sovereign's chest. He heard his screams until Crispin's arrow pierced him, stealing Neempo's breath, but also ending his suffering.

But it wasn't just Crispin's failure to save Neempo that tormented him. There was an eerie presence that whispered in the darkness of his narrow cabin. At first, he couldn't decipher what the strange, shrilly voice was saying, but tonight, it was clear.

"Open the book. We can make you powerful. Open the book. We can make you powerful."

Crispin elbowed himself up from his cot and planted his feet on the creaky wooden floorboards. He scratched at his chest, the necklace Amunet had given him seemed to be weighing him down, as if it, too, detected the evil lurking in his room.

"Open the book?" Crispin rubbed his bloodshot eyes and threw on a loose white shirt. "Open the book?" He muttered trying to figure out what book he was supposed to open when realization hit him.

Sinking to his knees, he pulled out the leather satchel containing his few belongings from underneath his cot. Rummaging through the folds of the bag, he found the small, black book he had lifted from Memucan's nightstand at *The Black Lotus*. When his fingers grazed the binding of the ancient book, the presence he sensed before seemed to want to touch him back. The pendant started to glow around his neck and Crispin lurched back from the book. The necklace had never reacted that way before and he knew whatever power the book possessed wasn't good. He needed to get rid of it.

Careful not to touch the book again, he wrapped it in a hand towel and beelined for the door. He nearly sprinted to the ship's railing to toss the wicked book overboard when a voice startled him.

"Where did you get that?" The prisoner from the White Keep dungeon approached, his eyes glued to the book wrapped in Crispin's towel.

"You know what this is?" Crispin arched an eyebrow, and he hesitated to throw it overboard.

"That is the Book of Noot. It's filled with black magic."

Crispin stared at his hands, thankful he took the time to wrap the book and avoid direct contact with his skin. "I'm going to throw this overboard, unless you know something I don't....?" Crispin realized he didn't know the man's name. "What's your name?"

His gaze met Crispin's curious and frightened face. "My name is Inaros. I spent the last three years of my life in prison because I stole that book from my master."

"Your master was Lord Memucan?" Crispin didn't know who he had expected the man to be, but that wasn't it.

"You know the master?" Inaros' shoulders tensed hearing Memucan's name. "How did you steal this from him and escape?" Inaros asked in a low voice, not wanting anyone to overhear.

"Memucan is dead." Crispin said in a satisfied, matter of fact way. "I killed him."

"And you took the book?"

Crispin nodded. With every second that passed, he wanted desperately to be rid of the book once and for all. "I didn't know what it was, but it was at his bedside table the night I ..."

Inaros bobbed his head in understanding. "You took a man's life and that must weigh heavily upon you, but believe me when I tell you, not even the Almighty One himself will mar your soul for his death."

"Thanks, but I wasn't concerned about that." Crispin held the book over the edge and took a deep breath. He could sense the book screaming at him, commanding him to open it. Promising him power, promising him what he desired most, promising him victory over all his enemies. Crispin was ashamed to admit it, but he was tempted to keep the Book of Noot and open it to see if it was telling him the truth.

"Do it," Inaros cut into Crispin's thoughts. "Cast it into the water."

Before he could think it over or allow the tempting whispers to change his mind, Crispin let the Book of Noot splash into the seas below.

"It is done." Inaros exhaled a sigh of relief and seemed to stand taller if that were possible. Maybe Crispin was just imagining it.

"How did you end up in the White Keep dungeons? Why not a prison in Numbio?" Crispin asked, leaning against the black wooden railing.

When they freed Inaros, he had a scraggly beard and wild unkempt hair. But once they put Northwind behind them, Inaros was given the opportunity to bathe and clean himself up. Now clean-shaven, with short black curls, he reminded Crispin of someone he had met before.

"Memucan picked me and my sister off the streets and gave us a home after our parents died. Seeing my sister's aptitude for herbs and potions, he sent her to the finest healing school in Numbio, and took me under his wing, educating me in history, politics, economics, and diplomacy. But as I began mastering those subjects, he tried to teach me from that little black book. He said if I wanted to be powerful and follow in his footsteps, I would need to master the fifth subject: magic." Inaros shifted from one foot to the other. "Once I realized the magic he was talking about wasn't light magic like our ancestors wielded, but dark, evil magic, I stole the book, and tried to get my sister to escape with me. But..."

Crispin's eyes widened and he straightened. "Is your sister Rayma?"

It was Inaros' turn to look surprised. "You know Rayma?"

"If the prince managed to survive the Wagura, my servant will finish the job."

Memucan's words floated in his mind as Inaros' story settled. The last piece of the puzzle was finally put in place: Rayma was Memucan's servant. She was the one who was supposed to kill Heru.

"If she hasn't already, I think your sister is supposed to kill Prince Heru." The words spilled out before Crispin had a chance to process them.

"She wouldn't do that," Inaros said nervously.

"Let's hope you know your sister better than Memucan." Crispin glanced at the Mainland in the distance, hoping and praying Heru, Zophar, and the rest of the Numbio survived the Caverns of the Undead.

Before Inaros could say anything else, a giant, blazing ball of fire lit up the night sky and headed straight for them. Crispin grabbed Inaros' arm and dragged him away before the catapulted object grazed the hull of the ship. Crispin's eyes shot back up into the starry night and saw two more spheres of flames soaring toward them.

“We’re under attack!” Crispin yelled, stumbling to ring the bell to wake up the crew. “We’re under attack!” The two fireballs splashed into the sea directly behind them, splashing water across the quarterdeck.

“There’s a fleet behind us,” Inaros watched the ships cut through the waves at an alarming speed.

Crispin knew without looking who was pursuing them. “It’s the Pirate King.”

Chapter Fifty-Eight

Niabi

Niabi's eyes flew open the second she heard the scratching of a boot against the stone railing of her balcony. Someone was attempting to sneak into her bedchambers by way of her private office. The queen slipped out from underneath her satin sheets, grabbed her twin daggers from under her pillow, and tip-toed to the door. She pressed her back against the wall and listened as someone made their way to her room.

The steps were light, meaning they belonged to a female assassin or a small male. Either this killer was so confident in their slaying ability they came alone, or they were stupid. Both suited Niabi just fine. She would slice whoever had come for her into pieces and scatter them in the Ignacia Sea.

The assassin's fingers twisted the doorknob and as quietly as possible, the assailant slipped inside the queen's bedroom. Niabi leapt toward the intruder, slicing her knives in fury. The masked assassin whipped around in time to block the surprise attack. The two traded spars, almost a mirror image of one another's movements.

The killer dropped to the floor, attempting to sweep Niabi's legs out from under her, but the queen easily hopped out of danger's way, knowing that move all too well, because she used it often in battle. Suspended in mid-air, Niabi landed a roundhouse kick to the intruder's chest, sending them soaring. Not wasting time for the assailant to catch their breath, Niabi pressed a knee into their breastbone and tucked a dagger against their throat.

"Guards!" She beckoned the clueless soldiers guarding the doors outside her room. They fumbled inside, wide eyed at the queen sitting atop an armed intruder, and they arrested the masked trespasser.

"Wait." Niabi stopped them from dragging the would-be assassin to the dungeons when she caught a glimpse of the assassin's knife. The pearl handle resembled one she had given to a friend as a Name Day gift years ago. Niabi reached a tentative hand up and ripped the mask off. The queen took a step back, shaking her head. "Marina?"

Marina met her cousin's gaze; her eyes raging with hatred.

"Why?" Niabi barely got the one-word question out. She never expected Marina to try to kill her. Hurt was an understatement. Devastated, crushed, shattered. Niabi was flooded with the pain of her cousin's betrayal and felt as if someone had taken one of her precious daggers and plunged it deep into her heart.

Marina spat at Niabi, muttering incoherent curses under her breath as the soldiers dragged her away.

"Take her to the Eastern Courtyard," Niabi ordered. "Have Tala and Vilora meet me there."

Pulling a blue, long-trained coat over her sleepwear, she glided through the empty, cold, white halls to the Eastern Courtyard. The corridor was shaking, and she braced a hand against a wall to steady herself. Only then did she realize the hallway wasn't moving, she was the one trembling. She backed up against the marble and slid down to the floor. Wrapping her arms around her knees, tucked as closely as she could get them without squashing her swollen belly, she cried. Niabi hated crying, but her soul was so wounded, she couldn't help it.

Marina was more than just a cousin to her. She was like her sister. She had picked up the pearl-hilted knife Marina intended to use to slit her throat off her bedroom floor and only realized she had it clutched in her hand when her fingers started to go numb. Niabi had that dagger designed and forged with Marina in mind. It was a Name Day gift that was supposed to remind Marina that even though she wasn't training to be a Qata Vishna, that deep inside, she was a warrior.

Plenty of assassins had tried their hand at taking Niabi out. All of them had failed and were sent to meet Death sooner than they had anticipated. But Marina...

Marina had to be dealt with.

The queen pushed herself up from the black and white tile floor and made her way outside. With torches lighting the crumbling Eastern Courtyard, Niabi could see that Tala, Vilora, Anaktu, and a handful of soldiers were gathered around the wooden platform Neempo had been strapped to before he died. Marina was tied to the stake, her head hanging, avoiding Niabi's glare.

She brushed Tala's extended hand away and walked up to Marina, stopping a few feet in front of her. "Who ordered you to assassinate me?"

Marina slowly raised her head and looked at her with a blank expression. The rage and hatred she had seen in her bedroom was gone. But whatever was racing through Marina's mind remained a mystery to her. "No one."

Niabi didn't believe her. "Who ordered -"

"No one!" Marina shouted, thrashing against the pole. Soldiers went to draw their weapons, but Niabi motioned for them to stand down. "No one ordered me to kill you. I wanted you dead."

She felt a lump in her throat. She wouldn't cry in front of all these people. She wouldn't allow it. "Why, Marina?" The queen took another step forward. "Why?"

"Because I could get close enough to kill you." Marina didn't try to fight the bonds anymore. She rested her head against the wooden pole and sighed. "Mika agreed to take my place, if I agreed to assassinate you when I had the chance."

"So, Mika sent you."

Marina let out a low chuckle and shook her head. "You really have no idea."

"No idea about what?" Niabi narrowed her eyes. Marina's grin sent an eerie shiver up her spine.

"We always knew one day, you would ask me to do something unspeakable," Marina whispered. "I didn't think it would be killing grandmother, but I did it with the end goal in mind."

"What are you talking about?" Niabi asked.

"Have you heard of a rebel group known as the Order?"

Niabi drew a breath. She had heard of the Order before and dismissed them as insignificant. Perhaps, she had been wrong to write them off as disgruntled peasants.

Marina's smile widened at Niabi's reaction. "By the look on your face, you have heard of us."

"Us?" Niabi lurched back as if she'd been stung.

"Mika and I were both part of the Order." Marina's voice grew louder so everyone in the courtyard could hear. "There are more of us than you realize. Magic wielders, royals, commoners. All banded together with one purpose: to see your reign end."

"How could you betray me, Marina?" Rage bubbled within Niabi and she could feel the itch of the magic groaning underneath her skin. "We are blood."

Marina shrugged, "Blood means nothing to you."

"Say what you want about me, Marina," Niabi hissed, inching closer. "But we are guilty of the same sin. We have blood-stained hands, deaths marring our souls."

"And if you don't take my life now," Marina didn't back down from Niabi's intense, wicked glare, "I swear I won't stop until I carve your heart from your chest."

"Then you will die a traitor's death."

"May you never find peace," Marina cursed her. "May you never find happiness. May you die a death worthy of your sins."

"You first." Niabi stepped off the wooden platform and the flames that had been begging to be unleashed, danced in her palm. "Goodbye, Marina." She rested her hand against the wood, and it ignited. Niabi turned on her heel and stomped away, heading toward the doors to enter the White Keep.

Niabi never looked back. Not when she smelled the charring of wood. Not when she felt the heat of the fire licking at her back. Not when Tala pleaded with her to reconsider. Not when Vilora nodded in proud approval. Not even when she heard Marina's screams.

Just before heading inside, she dropped the pearl hilted knife on the ground, swearing she would never step foot in the Eastern Courtyard again.

Chapter Fifty-Nine

Crispin

Haldane shouted orders at his crew, preparing them for battle. The captain explained that this hadn't been their first explosive encounter with another ship, and it wouldn't be their last. But to know it was the Pirate King assaulting them made Haldane even more excited about sinking the attacking ship.

"Phex!" Haldane barked, and the auburn-haired pirate strutted forward, arms filled with explosive trinkets.

"Captain?" Phex grinned like a beast who knew it was about to be unleashed.

"Light them up." Haldane ordered.

"With pleasure." Phex scrambled up the steps to the back of the quarterdeck. Throwing the explosives as far as he could toward the fast-approaching ships, Crispin thought Phex's inventions didn't work. They didn't come close enough to hit the Pirate King's ships.

"Did they not work?" Crispin came up behind the explosive's expert and leaned over the edge to get a better look at the bobbing bombs. Phex grabbed Crispin by the back of his shirt collar and pulled him away from the railing.

"I wouldn't do that if I were you." Phex shook his head. "Wouldn't want you falling to your death."

"I can swim," Crispin said, but Phex waved a dismissive hand in the air.

"Watch, Prince. Just watch."

Crispin looked at the oncoming ships. As they approached the floating spheres Phex had disposed of, they began exploding as soon as the ships made contact. Loud booms, pirates screaming, and splintering wood echoed in the night. Crispin patted a proud Phex on the back.

"Not bad, Phex." Crispin smiled at the sight of one of Uri's ships sinking. "Not bad at all."

"You haven't seen anything yet." Phex motioned for Crispin to follow him. "I'll need some help with the next one."

"Let's go."

Phex yelled for Corwin, Ondrej, and Rafi to come help him uncover a machine that had been sitting on the deck covered by a tarp. Crispin had wondered what was underneath since he first joined the crew, only to be told several times that he would find out when he needed to. It seemed today was that day. Once the wooden machine had been uncovered, Crispin still didn't know what he was staring at.

"What is it?" Crispin asked as more explosions sounded behind them.

"I call it *The Fist*." Phex was giddy, rubbing his hands together. "Alright, boys, you know what to do."

Crispin watched Corwin, Ondrej, and Rafi attach a few loose pieces into the main mechanism and pointed it toward the stern. Phex hopped into what appeared to be a seat, slapped some goggles on, and gave the others a thumbs up.

The pirates scattered. Corwin grabbed Crispin by the arm and pulled him away. "Keep your distance, unless you want to know how it feels to fly."

Crispin's eye was caught by Rahab on the other side of the ship, making sure Master Penn and her Keepers, Ziggy and Nubis, and Inaros were either armed or updated on battle strategies. She must have felt Crispin's gaze and turned to look at him. Gone was the woman he had kissed and held in his arms. The pirate, the Queen of the Obsidian Seas, was standing there, commanding her crew, readying for the possibility of their ship being boarded. She nodded her head in acknowledgment, before returning to the others.

"Ready!" Phex's scream ripped Crispin's eyes from Rahab and back to the explosives-crazed pirate. "Launch!"

Phex shifted some wooden gears which propelled similar looking spheres to the ones that floated in the water. Except these spheres were bigger and traveled a generous distance. Circling the gears as fast as he could, Phex kept launching different size balls at the Pirate King's fleet. Uri had started with seven ships, including *The Leviathan*, and thanks to Phex's floating minefield, he had lost two of the smaller ships.

Crispin watched in curiosity as the bombs smashed into the Pirate King's ships: the hulls, masts, quarterdecks, and bowsprits. Phex was grinning like a madman and didn't ease up on launching his one-man annihilation. No wonder the Pirate King wanted Phex to work for him.

Corwin elbowed Crispin in the ribs. "Glad he's on our side."

"He's a genius!" Crispin was amazed by the workings of Phex's dangerous mind. Another ship met a watery grave and Phex wasn't even close to finished.

Rafi rang the alarm in the crow's nest. Crispin looked up and the halfling was pointing to three ships in front of them. Rahab joined Crispin as they made their way to the front of the ship to get a better look.

Rahab pulled out her spyglass. "Westerners." She glanced at Crispin. "We can't fight both Uri and the Western Patrol."

Haldane joined them and let loose a string of profanities before realizing Master Penn was standing next to him. "Apologies, Master Penn, I didn't know you were standing there."

"Apologies are not necessary, Captain," Penn waved a hand in the air. "I agree with the sentiment."

"What's the plan?" Rahab looked from Crispin to Haldane.

"We surrender to the Westerners," Crispin said before Haldane had a chance to comment, knowing the pirate was more likely to try to fight everyone and go down with his ship. Despite the pirates' wide-eyed disapproval he continued, "Master Penn and I can vouch for your safety and ask to see King Benaiah. The Westerners won't risk a war knowing Salome is out there amassing an army."

"I don't like it," Haldane snorted. "We can take both the Westerners and the Pirate King."

"I don't like the idea any more than you do," Rahab folded her arms over her chest, wind whipping her blue locks around her face, "but maybe we should let Crispin and Master Penn take the lead on this one."

Master Penn nodded her head. "The Westerners make it a point to keep relations with The Sisters amicable. Prince Crispin and I will do what we need to do to ensure everyone's safety."

"Another one down!" Phex cried in delight, sinking the fourth ship Uri commanded. "You want some more, you bastards?"

Crispin leaned over the railing and saw the Pirate King retreating, salvaging what he had left of his fleet. Whether it was fear of Phex sinking another ship or the sight of the

Western Patrol in the distance, Crispin wouldn't know, but he was grateful they would live to see another day.

"Raise the white flag," Haldane ordered, and the words sounded weird coming out of his mouth.

Rafi shouted down from the crow's nest, "Sorry, Captain, I thought you said to raise the white flag."

"I did, you twit!" Haldane barked. "Raise the white flag!"

"Captain." Rafi did as he was ordered, confusion still in his shifty eyes.

"You better be right about this, lad," Haldane said.

Dawn breached the horizon as the lead Western Patrol ship crashed a wooden ramp down, connecting their ship with the *Shadow of Death*. Gathered on the deck, Crispin, and the rest of the crew, new and old, waited as a tall, broad-shouldered captain stomped from his ship to theirs. Two uniformed officers flanked the clean-shaven, redheaded commander. His eyes were the color of the sea and were just as dangerous.

With his arms clasped behind his back, the captain's eyes scanned the group left to right. His eyes stopped when he spotted Ziggy, but he continued until his gaze rested on Haldane. He smiled. "I am Captain Ivar, the commander of this fleet. We have been hunting the *Shadow of Death* for quite some time. King Benaiah will be pleased to know you will no longer be terrorizing the seas."

Haldane muttered under his breath, but Crispin stepped forward before the pirate could say something damaging. "Captain Ivar, I am Prince Crispin of Northwind. I would -"

"Why would the Prince of Northwind keep the company of criminals?" Ivar interrupted him with a calm, threatening tone.

"Would you say the same of me, Captain Ivar?" Penn stepped forward, her feet shoulder-width apart, flanked by her six Keepers.

If Captain Ivar was surprised by her presence, he didn't show it. "Master Penn," he bowed his head in respect. "Have these ruffians kidnapped you?"

"They are friends of The Sisters." Penn said, matching his menacing inflection. "And they will be treated as such."

"Master Penn," Ivar started but stopped when his eyes once again landed on Ziggy. "What is your name?"

"Ziggy," she replied as loudly as she dared.

"Ziggy," he repeated. "Were you taken by this crew?"

She shook her head, "No, they rescued me."

Ivar scoffed, "Rescued. That's not the term I would associate with their kind."

Crispin could sense Rahab's nostrils flaring like a raging bull and squeezed her hand. Their eyes met and she released the anger in her face.

"Captain Ivar," Crispin's focus bounced back to the Westerner. "Unless you want my sister, Princess Salome, to see your aggression toward us as an act of war, I would strongly encourage you to take all of us to meet with King Benaiah. I'm sure he will be inclined to speak with me."

"And me." Penn threw her weight around like a political pro.

Captain Ivar mulled over what they were saying. "Fine." He reluctantly agreed. "I will take all of you to Borg to see King Benaiah. He will determine your fate and I will still be rewarded for the capture of the ever-elusive *Shadow of Death*." His tight-lipped grin barely qualified as a smile. He motioned everyone to board his ship. "Consider yourselves guests of His Majesty until he says otherwise. But while you are passengers on my ship, you will abide by my rules, or I'll happily throw you in the brig. Understood?"

Affirmative grumbling was the closest Ivar was going to get to an enthusiastic response and he allowed it. "Welcome aboard The *Drakkar*."

Crispin didn't need to ask what the name meant. He had learned enough of the ancient Western language from Zophar to know it translated to *The Dragon*. Because of the stories Zophar shared, Crispin always dreamt of visiting Borg after he reclaimed his kingdom. But now, he would be going before the king accused of piracy. Maybe, Benaiah wouldn't be as cut-throat as he'd heard. But with his luck, he was in for a hell of a first meeting.

Rahab's hand slipped into his as *The Drakkar* set course for Borg. He dared a kiss to her forehead as they abandoned the *Shadow of Death* and made their way to the land of battle hungry warriors.

Chapter Sixty

Salome

Salome slipped inside Adonijah's room the next morning and found him lying in bed flat on his back. He was shirtless and his boots had been placed neatly at the foot of his bed. There were bandages wrapped around his torso, his right wrist, and the cuts on his face and leg were freshly salved. His eyes were closed, so she thought better than to wake him, especially since he had just fought a giant Krazak to the death for her.

For her.

That point had not gone unnoticed. He had fought in the Dagaal she had invoked. It was meant for her. She was prepared to fight it, too. But he volunteered to be her champion and she was angry with him. Angry that he would place himself in that position. Angry that he would risk his life to save hers. Angry. But she wasn't angry anymore. How could she be with him lying there injured?

If she were honest with herself, she might not have been able to defeat the giant he faced with the injuries she was still nursing. She was skilled, but Adonijah bore the brunt of several heavy-handed beatings and still got back on his feet. Had he not volunteered, they might all very well be dead or enslaved. She swallowed hard. She wanted to hug him. To thank him. But it would have to wait. She was going to let him rest.

Salome turned to leave when he asked, "Leaving so soon, Princess?" His eyes were still closed when she whipped around.

"I told you not to call me that," she tried to hide the smirk begging to stretch across her face.

"I suppose I just like riling you up." Adonijah smiled and turned his head to lock eyes with her.

Although he seemed pleased to see her, his bloodshot eyes screamed he needed rest desperately. She could always tell when he was in pain because the corners of his mouth would twitch.

"I should let you rest -"

"Stay with me." Adonijah cut her off with his gentle request.

Salome wanted to stay with him, like he had stayed with her when she was recovering in Myr, so she agreed with a nod. "How did you know it was me?" she sat on the edge of his bed.

Adonijah propped himself up on his elbows as she placed a second pillow behind his back. "I'm not sure how I knew, I just did."

Salome eyes scanned all the cuts, bruises, and bandages covering his lean, muscular body. She then became painfully aware that she was sitting very close to a man only wearing pants. She lifted her gaze from his bare chest to his chiseled jaw, his lips, his eyes... When their eyes met, he seemed to recognize she had been ogling, but he also didn't seem bothered.

"How are you feeling?" she tucked hair behind her shoulders, hoping he wouldn't call her out for staring.

"I feel about as good as I look." He said and she blushed. "So, not great." He motioned toward his bandages.

She released an awkward breath and relaxed her eyebrows. After a moment to compose herself, she asked him what she really wanted to know. "Why did you do it?"

"Do what?" He sat up with a quizzical look on his face.

"Why did you take my place in the Dagaal?" Her gaze swept to the floor, twiddling her fingers in her lap. "It should have been me in that arena."

Adonijah shrugged, flashing a half-smile, "You needed a champion."

"Look at you, Adonijah." She reached out and gently touched the cut along his jawline. "You shouldn't have volunteered. What if you had been...?"

Killed. She wanted to say killed, but she couldn't bring herself to utter the word. Didn't want to think of his lifeless body lying in the dirt of the arena.

Adonijah tipped her chin to look at him. "If I had to, I'd do it again."

"Why?"

He intertwined his fingers with hers and rested them against his chest. "You already know why, Salome."

"Your oath to protect me." She knew as soon as she said it, it was the wrong answer.

Adonijah brought her hand to his lips and kissed it. "My oath had nothing to do with my decision."

Salome brushed her free hand across his chest, and she felt his heartbeat quicken. Her eyes met his again. She leaned forward, touching his face, running her fingers through his loose, shoulder-length hair. His hands reached around her, the pads of his fingers stroking up and down her back.

"I owe you my life, Adonijah."

"All I want," he leaned closer, so their lips were inches from touching, "is your heart."

"You have it," she whispered.

Adonijah kissed her softly, before pulling her closer to him. He flipped her on her back, so she laid underneath him. One of his hands raked up her neck to the back of her head while the other rested on her hip. She cupped his face in her hands, kissing him, unwilling to let him go.

She craved his lips against hers. Shivered as his hands roamed freely over her skin. With every kiss and every moan, she saw their journey flash before her eyes. Their first encounter in The Hollow; the brawl at the Hidden Tavern; facing their fears in the Enchanted Swamp; fighting the Thrak, freeing the Stormcrags, and their fleeting, private moments together in the Isles of Myr. It had always been him tugging at her heart, whispering his love for her in every smile. Their paths had been destined to cross and she knew, wrapped in his embrace, his mouth pressed against her neck, that he would keep his promise to fight, live, and die by her side.

"Salome," he pulled back. "Salome, wait."

She opened her eyes, "What's wrong?"

He strummed his thumb up and down her jaw. "There's something I need to tell you. Something I should have told you a long time ago."

She propped herself up on her elbows. "What are you talking about?"

"I need to tell you who I really am."

"I know who you are, Adonijah."

His eyes drifted from hers. "I should have told you before, but I was afraid of what you might think of me. Honestly, I'm still afraid."

She kissed his lips once more. "You can tell me anything." She held his hand tightly, even though her stomach was in knots.

Adonijah took a deep breath. His eyes filled with a pain that made her ache. "Salome -"

"Your Highness," Zophar cleared his throat, standing in the entrance with a red tinge spreading across his pale cheeks.

Salome gently pushed Adonijah off her and stood up, trying to meet Zophar's gaze, but he purposely avoided making eye contact with her, knowing he interrupted a very intimate moment.

"You don't have to call me that, Zophar." Salome rested her hands on her hips, not knowing what exactly to do with her hands.

"It's important to use your title now that you command an army." Zophar scratched his face. "Torrin has requested all leaders gather for a meeting. It seems the Stormcrags captured a man claiming to have escaped a Northern camp."

"Northern camp?" Salome's eyes widened as she took a step forward. "There's a Northern camp nearby?"

Zophar held his hands up stopping her approach. His eyes finally meeting hers. "Before you go in there, you should know the man they captured said he knows you."

"Knows me?"

"I didn't get a good look at him," Zophar admitted, "but he has red hair."

"One of the villagers?" Salome's voice cracked; she felt her emotions bubble in her throat. "Take me to him."

Zophar bobbed his head and held the curtains blocking the entrance into Adonijah's cave open for Salome to leave. Adonijah hopped up and said, "I'm going with you."

"You should rest." Salome turned back to him.

"I'll be fine," Adonijah threw a shirt on and fastened his boots, not taking no for an answer. "If there's a Northern camp nearby, I want to know what we are dealing with."

Salome reluctantly nodded, knowing arguing with him would be futile. She found every step she took toward the assembly cavern was heavy and filled with dread. *Which villager had escaped? Were there more villagers that needed help? Was there even a Tree House Forest left for those they rescued to return to?*

Zophar strode inside first but Salome hesitated. Adonijah rested his hand on her lower back.

"You alright?" he whispered in her ear; his chest pressed against her back.

Salome inhaled deeply and rolled her shoulders back. She was the heir to the White Throne. She was the Hunter. She was the Red Maiden. She was the leader of armies and the bringer of rebellion. When she thought about who she used to be, she realized the girl from the Tree House Forest was long gone.

"I'm ready." Salome swooshed the curtains open and walked in with a regality that took some of the other leaders by surprise. All eyes were fixed on her, but her attention was glued to the man standing before them in tattered clothing, with matted red hair, and barely healed scars.

She rounded to her seat in the half circle of leaders and recognized the villager as the baker who once pestered her to teach him to hunt. The villager who declared his intentions of marrying her. And the one she continuously brushed off without a second thought. She nearly gasped at the disheveled sight of Jacobi. The once plump baker with rosy cheeks was thin, bruised, and had hollow cheeks. His wrists were bound with rope, and he swayed on his feet in exhaustion, but she kept her face neutral as she claimed the Throne of Skulls between Zophar and Torrin.

The Stormcrag leader leaned forward, the wooden chair hissing underneath his massive frame. "My warriors found you wandering the mountains. They said you escaped a military camp from Northwind."

Jacobi nodded weakly. "That's true." His eyes floated to Salome. "After you left, more Shadows came to the village." His bottom lip quivered, and Salome's stomach plummeted. "I am the only one left."

"Can you tell us who is in the camp?" The Stormcrag leader didn't care about Jacobi's sentimentality. "Who is their leader? Why are they this far south? How many men are in their company?"

"Prince Thanos of Gomorrah asked Queen Niabi for aid in claiming the Gomorrian throne from his mother." Jacobi explained what he knew, his lips were dry, and his voice was raspy.

"Someone, give him some water," Salome ordered. "Did no one care to help him earlier?"

Kai stepped forward with a sheepskin of water and Jacobi drowned himself in the cool drink.

"Thank you," Jacobi bobbed his head in gratitude.

Torrin huffed an irritated sigh, his fingers tapping the armrest of his chair. "How many soldiers march with them?"

"There are a few hundred soldiers and a company of elite Shadows."

"Which Shadows?" Adonijah straightened from leaning against the entrance threshold, but the villager didn't exert the energy to turn around to look at him.

"The Commander of Shadows leads their entire force."

"Pash? Gershom's son." Heru rubbed his chin, elbow resting on the armrest of his chair.

Jacobi nodded. "His Uncle Ophir rides with him and the one who burned our village to the ground. They call him the Nameless Rider."

Adonijah stiffened at the mention of the Nameless Rider, and it didn't go unnoticed by Salome.

"They have no interest in finding our city?" Rune the Krazak asked, with Hanzo standing behind him. The archer eyed Oifa as she picked her teeth clean with her long nails, grinning at Hanzo as he watched.

"I don't know," Jacobi rolled his shoulders. "All I know is they are preparing to attack Gomorrah within the week."

Heru shifted in his seat, stretching his legs out in front of him. "If we could capture some of their leaders, we could get valuable information about Northwind and their military strategies. Maybe even find a weakness in the White City's walls."

"This sounds too convenient for my liking," Jinn chimed in, lazily lounging in his chair.

"What do you mean?" The Stormcrag leader turned to look at him.

"Tell us," Jinn directed his question at Jacobi, resting his chin in his hand. "How did you manage to escape from the Northerners' camp?"

Jacobi cleared his throat. "When they fell asleep, I bit through my bindings and ran."

"You don't believe him." Salome glanced at him from across their half circle.

"How many people do you know of that have escaped an elite company of Shadows and lived to tell the tale?" Jinn's eyes shifted from the prisoner to her.

"Perhaps we send some scouts to gather information about the camp." Heru suggested.

"Agreed." Torrin nodded. Even sitting down, his biceps bulged, demanding attention. "We will have Cato lead a band of our finest scouts in the morning. We should know more in a couple days."

"I will send Hanzo with these scouts," Rune interjected with a haughty smile. "Just to make sure they are safe, of course."

"If *he* is going," Oifa stepped forward, not stooping to refer to the archer by name, "then I will, too."

Seeing a fight brewing, Salome said, "Hanzo *and* Oifa will accompany Cato. There will be no violence. You are there to protect our scouts if something goes wrong. Is that understood?" Hanzo and Oifa bowed their heads in agreement. "Then it is settled." Salome stood, ending their meeting.

"We never should have sent you away," Jacobi halted the leaders from leaving. His eyes were fixed on Salome. "We never should have sent you away," he whispered sadly.

Salome nodded, her eyes burning as she blinked. She turned to Zophar and said, "Make sure he gets something to eat."

As she turned to leave, Jacobi lunged on bended knee and grabbed her arm. Knives were drawn around the room, but Salome waved them down.

"I..." he whimpered. "I haven't stopped thinking about you. Hoping our paths would cross again. My feelings for you... they haven't changed."

Salome gently pulled her hand from his grasp. "Nor have mine."

She walked out of the room and didn't stop until she entered her private cave. She was shaking. Pouring herself a cup of water, she downed it in one gulp. Tears slipped down her cheeks. She hadn't allowed herself to think of the villagers or what might have happened to the Tree House Forest after they left. But seeing Jacobi, hearing of the devastation and destruction he managed to escape...

Arms wrapped around her from behind. She knew by the scent of cedar and springtime that it was Jinn. He didn't say anything, he just held her until she turned to face him, laying her head against his chest. Jinn stroked her hair and let her soak his shirt in tears. He kissed the top of her head and tightened his arms around her.

"I didn't let myself think about them," Salome's voice cracked. "I didn't want to know what had happened to them..."

Jinn pulled her from his chest and gently lifted her chin forcing her to meet his gaze. "It's not your fault."

"Then why do I feel guilty?" Her lip shook and he swiped her tears away with his thumbs.

"Because you are a good person. Your heart will always feel heavy when the lives of innocents are lost." Jinn took her hands in his and rested them against his chest. "It's cruel, Salome, but good people don't always win the battle. Good people don't always accomplish their goals. And sometimes, good people die before we think they should. You are leading an army to battle your sister. Not all of us are going to make it home when the dust settles. Hell," Jinn tilted his head to the side and dark strands of hair fell over his forehead, "there's a chance I won't even make it."

"Jinn," Salome shook her head furiously, fresh tears streaming down her face, "don't say that."

"I'll still follow you into the blood, ash, and fire of war and not regret it, even if it brings me face to face with Lady Death." Jinn rested his forehead against hers. "We could do everything right and it still not be enough to win, darling."

"Why are you saying these things?" Salome took a step back.

"I don't want you to be unprepared for the reality of war." Jinn said softly. "You have suffered loss. You have felt pain. You have experienced battle, but nothing prepares you for war." His hand slid down her arm, entwining their fingers. "My father and uncles fought against your sister when she first came to power. They were never the same. One of my uncles never made it home."

Salome cupped his face with her free hand, gently rubbing her thumb against his cheek. "You can walk away. I wouldn't fault you for thinking of your people."

"Where you go, I go."

"You are your father's heir. His only son." Salome tried to reason with him.

"And it seems you might be the last of Issachar's children who can avenge your family." Jinn countered.

Salome's thoughts shot to Crispin. Heru told her there was a chance he might have made it, but she also knew there was a possibility her brother was gone.

"A secret for a secret." She sent through their bond.

Jinn nodded. *"You first."*

Salome took a deep breath, maintaining eye contact with Jinn. *"I don't want the crown or the White Throne. If Crispin is gone... He was the one who was supposed to rule Northwind. Not me."*

Jinn squeezed her hand, straightening his shoulders. *"A year ago, I ran away from home because I didn't want to be king. That's when I met Oden and realized I could still be useful. When he asked me to go to the Isles of Myr to see if you might be there, I jumped at the chance."*

"And then you found me."

"And then I found you." Jinn smiled and said, "I understand you, Salome, more than you will ever know."

Salome rested her hands against his chest. "I need you to promise me something."

"What?"

“If things don’t go as planned, I want you to cloak yourself and get as far from Death as you can. Even if that means you leave me behind.”

Jinn shook his head, “I told you before, if it is within my power to give, I will, but that is something I cannot, will not, promise.”

“Why?” Salome furrowed her brow, frustration bubbling inside her. “Your people -“

“I love you,” Jinn’s confession stole the words from her mouth. “Sakurai stood before I was born, and it will remain even if I fall. But I will not abandon you, even if it costs me everything.”

“You love me?” It was all she managed to whisper.

Jinn leaned close, his lips hovering over hers. “With all that I am, I love you, Salome.”

“Jinn,” she pressed a hand to his chest. He retreated a step, raking a hand through his hair. “I do care for you, but...”

“You chose him.” Jinn shrugged with a sad smile. “I knew there was a chance you would.”

“I never meant to hurt you,” Salome wrapped her arms around herself. It hurt to look into his pained eyes, but she forced herself to maintain eye contact. She owed him that much.

Jinn stuffed his hands into his pockets and tilted his head to the side, clearing his throat. “I meant what I said before. About my armies being yours whether you accepted my proposal or not.”

“Jinn...”

“My sword will always be yours, Salome.” He bowed his head and turned to leave.

“Survive this war.” Her words stopped him, but he didn’t look back. “Whatever you have to do, survive.”

He walked out and she fought every urge to reach out to him. She had made her choice. But instead of wanting to be in the comfort and warmth of Adonijah’s embrace, she found she would rather be alone.

Chapter Sixty-One

Adonijah

Adonijah shook Jacobi awake, holding a finger up to his lips, instructing the villager to keep quiet. Adonijah whispered, "Could you find your way back to the Northern camp?"

Jacobi froze. "Why?"

"Can you find your way back or not?" Adonijah growled and Jacobi flinched. "I won't harm you. I just need to know if you can find your way back."

The redhead reluctantly nodded as he sat up. "I could probably find my way back. Or at least get close enough."

"I need you to take me there tonight."

Jacobi fell to his knees. "Please don't make me go back there. Please. I can't go back. He'll kill me."

Adonijah dropped to one knee to be at eye level with the whimpering prisoner. "I know you don't want to go back, but I need a guide. It's important that I make it there and quickly."

"Why do you want to go?" A fearful tear slipped down Jacobi's cheek. "I told you all I know. Your scouts will confirm it. I swear I told your leaders everything."

"The Nameless Rider – he killed my mother," Adonijah blurted before he had a chance to think it through. The tension in his shoulders vanished and he sat on the ground. "I've been trying to track him for years and I've never gotten this close before. This is my chance, Jacobi. Please." Adonijah met Jacobi's bloodshot eyes. "Will you help me?"

Jacobi puffed out a short, tired breath. "I betrayed them."

Adonijah tilted his head, unsure who he was talking about. "Who?"

"I was scared," Jacobi whispered, wiping a tear with his finger. "He said I could tell him what he wanted to know or I could die with them... I... I..."

Adonijah averted his gaze, not wanting to watch Jacobi suffer with his cowardice. "You can't bring them back. But now, you can try to do what is right."

Jacobi hesitated. "You can kill him?"

Adonijah bobbed his head and met Jacobi's eyes. "Aye."

"Then I will help you," Jacobi agreed.

The two men trekked down the mountains for several hours before hearing the clinking of metal, crackling campfires, and the chatter of guards gobbling their mush before heading to bed.

Ducking behind a cluster of boulders, Adonijah popped his head over to have a look at what he was dealing with. Hundreds of white tents were erected at the base of the mountain. Although there were a few guards patrolling, no one was truly expecting an attack. *Who would be foolish enough to attack the Northerners in their own camp?*

Jacobi shivered, his back pinned against the rocks, refusing to look.

"If something happens to me," Adonijah whispered, "then you go back up the mountain until you reach the City of Bones."

"You're not forcing me to go any further?" Jacobi seemed surprised.

Adonijah shook his head. "I only asked you to get me here. You're not a soldier; you have no place here." His eyes scanned the camp again. "If I don't come back in an hour, leave."

"And what do I tell them when I get back?"

Adonijah hadn't thought about him not coming back. In his mind, killing the Nameless Rider wouldn't take him long, and he would be on his way without anyone knowing he'd been there. Of course, there was a possibility he didn't walk out alive, but this was the closest he'd been to finding his mother's murderer. He could go back now, leave the Nameless Rider for another time, but his desire to protect Salome was overshadowed by his need for revenge. Before he met Salome, this had been his life's purpose. He would be lying if he said he didn't have this unquenchable thirst to spill his enemy's blood.

He took a deep breath. "Tell Salome, I'm sorry." Before Jacobi could reply, or he changed his mind, Adonijah skirted around the trees to get to the base.

Eyes darting both directions looking for a passing patrol, Adonijah only came out of hiding to cross into the Northern camp once he was in the clear. It was a wide-open space, no trees, or boulders to take cover behind. He had to be quick if he was going to get into the camp unnoticed. Nearly there, he quickened his soft-footed pace before the patrol could make another pass, but he stopped dead in his tracks when twelve Shadows emerged from outskirt tents and surrounded him.

The Nameless Rider's feet thudded against the ground as he pointed a long sword at Adonijah. "State your business, trespasser."

Adonijah suppressed the rage brewing inside his chest. There was no way he was going to make it out of this alive if he launched an assault. He kept a neutral face and flashed an impish smile. "Sorry. Must have gotten lost."

The Nameless Rider chuckled through gritted teeth. "I see you are going to make this difficult. I like difficult."

Ophir took a step toward Adonijah, an eyebrow arched. Adonijah recognized the old crone he fought in the tavern and saw the moment the Shadow remembered him, too. The bald soldier hissed, "You're that sell-sword from the Hidden Tavern." His eyes darted across the circle, "I saw him escape with the queen's sister."

"Turn around." A familiar voice ordered. "And remember you are surrounded. Don't do anything stupid."

Adonijah slowly turned around, hands at the level of his eyes, and flashed a wicked smile when Pash's eyes widened. "Hello, brother. It's been a long time."

"Brother?" Ophir rasped. "But that would make you..."

"Satara's son," Adonijah finished for him, though he didn't look his way.

Pash lowered his sword and approached his younger brother cautiously. "Is it really you, Adonijah?"

"Better looking than the last time you saw me."

Pash's pace quickened and Adonijah thought his brother was going to take a swing at him. But to his surprise, Pash wrapped his arms around him and whispered in his ear, "I thought you were dead."

"You'd miss me too much if I died." Adonijah tried to keep the conversation light, but he saw the pain in his older brother's eyes when he pulled back.

"Come with me," Pash threw his arm over Adonijah's shoulders. "We have a lot to talk about."

"Pash, he is our enemy -"

"No one is to lay one finger on my brother," Pash hissed, interrupting his uncle, and turning in a circle to meet every Shadow's gaze. "That's an order. Anyone who disobeys will lose their head."

"Wow," Adonijah folded his arms across his chest. "You've trained your dogs well." His eyes drifted to the Nameless Rider's one icy, blue eye. As much as he wanted to slit the Shadow's throat and watch him die in a pool of his own blood, that would have to wait. For now. The last time he was this close to the seven-foot monstrosity was when he was fleeing his mother's burning house.

Pash flashed him a warning look before leading him into the middle of the Northern camp. The commander ushered him inside a large white tent and made sure no one was snooping around to listen to their conversation.

"Wine?" Pash offered, pouring himself a glass from the lavish wet bar.

"Your life must be fancy if this is what roughing it in a military camp looks like." Adonijah sank into a leather chair and kicked his muddy boots up on an end table.

Pash snickered, "Is that why you risked coming to my camp? To mock my lifestyle?" He passed a glass to Adonijah and sat in the chair opposite him.

"Actually, I came to kill one of your men."

One of Pash's eyebrows arched in amusement. "You've got balls, Adonijah, I'll give you that."

"But?" Adonijah sipped his wine with a smirk.

"You know I can't let you do that." Pash rolled his shoulders and sat straighter in his seat.

"Pity."

"When I heard about your mother..." Pash strummed his fingers against his cup. "I went looking for you, but you were gone." He looked at Adonijah, "Where have you been all these years?"

Adonijah shrugged, "Here and there."

"Why didn't you come to Northwind?" Pash's voice cracked, and he cleared his throat, shifting his weight. "I would have helped you."

"We both know what would have happened if I sought you out and Gershom got his hands on me. He would have broken me and molded me into a monster of his own design." Adonijah hated thinking about his father, but over the seven years of being on his own, not a day went by that he didn't think about Pash. "I did miss you though."

Pash nodded in understanding. "I hate him, too, you know."

"Seems like we both have father issues." Adonijah scratched a finger across his forehead.

"You know I have to ask," Pash's tone sharpened. "Are you fighting for Salome?"

"And you know I won't tell you anything of value."

"Well, that answers that question." Pash shook his head with an irritated sigh. "Uncle Ophir is going to push for me to take you to Northwind in shackles. Especially if he sends word to our father -"

"That bald man is our uncle?" Adonijah snorted a laugh. "Seems more like a grumpy old man than a fearsome Shadow."

"Don't let his age fool you," Pash finished his wine and set his empty glass on the table next to him. "He'll gut you for looking at him the wrong way."

"Temper, temper," Adonijah clicked his tongue. His gaze met his brother's, and he could tell the wheels in Pash's mind were racing. "What is it?"

"Who were you here to kill?" Pash tilted his head to the side, "Me?"

"Why would I come here to kill you?" Adonijah was caught off guard by the question. Half-brothers they might be, but Pash had never wronged him. When Gershom would come to visit Adonijah, he would bring Pash along to "get to know his bastard brother." At first, they didn't like one another, but that changed when they realized they both hated their father.

"So, if not me, then who?" Pash furrowed his brow. "Did Salome send you to -"

"She doesn't know I'm here," Adonijah interrupted sharply. "She doesn't know who I really am."

"Interesting." Pash smirked, kicking one leg over the other. "You're in love with her."

"Sounds like we both have a thing for powerful women," Adonijah's eyes danced in delight and Pash barked out a laugh.

"How is it possible you even know about me and -"

"The Monster Queen?"

"Watch it, Adonijah," Pash warned in a big-brother tone.

Adonijah threw his hands up in surrender, "Apologies."

"So, how did you know about us?"

Adonijah met his brother's curious gaze and sighed. "Just because you didn't see me, doesn't mean I wasn't around. I've kept an eye on you since my mother..."

"Do you plan to return to your princess?" Pash asked, sparing him from talking about his mother's death.

"That was the plan." Adonijah nodded. "But my plans haven't been going as smoothly as I had hoped. If things had worked out, I would have killed my mother's murderer, and been on my way. Salome never would have known I was gone."

"And I wouldn't have known you were alive." Pash pinched the bridge of his nose and sighed. "You really won't tell me who you came to kill?"

"If I told you," Adonijah flashed a menacing grin, "would you let me kill him?"

Pash threw his head back and laughed. "Who knows what could happen if you conveniently escaped?"

Adonijah's smile disappeared. "The Nameless Rider."

Pash pursed his lips and rubbed the nape of his neck. "I'm not surprised. He's the worst."

"Then I'll be doing you a favor by killing him."

"As much as I hate him, I can't sanction his assassination." Pash shook his head, leaning forward so his hands dangled between his legs. "But I do have a proposition for you."

Adonijah looked bored. "What kind of proposition?"

"From what Ophir said, you were a bounty hunter before you teamed up with Salome on her ill-advised rebellion."

"Keep Salome out of this."

"Right," Pash rolled his eyes. "Is it true you were a bounty hunter?"

"Are you going to put me in shackles if I say yes?" Adonijah snorted a laugh.

"No," Pash's eyes were lasered on Adonijah. "What would you say, if I asked you to kill someone?"

"If it's not the Nameless Rider, I'm inclined to say no."

"Even if that person were our father?" Pash reclined in his seat, looking victorious, knowing Adonijah wanted Gershom dead just as much as he did.

Adonijah's eyes widened. "You want me to kill Gershom?"

"I want *us* to kill Gershom."

"Why?" Adonijah folded his arms over his chest. "So, you can claim your birthright?"

"I don't give a damn about his titles." He growled through gritted teeth.

"Then why?" Adonijah asked and included, "And if you don't tell me the truth, my answer will be no."

"I think he murdered my mother around the time he had your mother killed." Pash jumped up from his seat and refilled his wine glass. "I would have done it years ago, but he was still in Niabi's good graces."

"And now?" Adonijah slid out of his seat and joined his brother at the wet bar.

"She would dance on top of his corpse if she could." Pash faced his brother. "No one would bat an eye if Gershom was found dead. And I know Niabi wouldn't bother to investigate. We could kill him and not be sentenced to the gallows."

Adonijah would be lying if he denied being tempted by his offer. Killing their father with no repercussions was a bounty hunter's dream. But what about Salome?

"I don't think I could -"

"Here are your options." Pash placed a hand on Adonijah's shoulder. "Either you agree to help me kill our father, and I make sure you don't sit in the White Keep's dungeons for the rest of your life, or Ophir gets his way, and imprisons you in our camp as a rebel, until we head back to Northwind, where I'm sure our father will be most interested in seeing you."

"If I agree, you realize we are still on opposite sides of this war." Adonijah rolled his shoulders back, standing an inch taller than his brother. "Once the job is finished, you'll release me to return to Salome."

Pash smiled. "You have my word."

Adonijah nodded but held out his hand. "Your word would normally satisfy me, brother, but I'm afraid I will need more than that this time."

Pash retrieved the dagger from his hip and sliced the palm of his right hand. Adonijah let him slash his right palm and they shook on it. An agreement in blood. If one of them went back on their word, their life would be forfeited.

"Do me a favor," Pash smirked. "Don't cause any trouble while you're in my camp. I would hate to have to break you out and desert my command to save your ass."

"I'll do my best." Adonijah's heart was pumping quickly in his chest. The chance to kill the Nameless Rider *and* his father was finally within reach. Salome's face flashed in his mind and the guilt of leaving her soured his stomach. He swore to protect her. She chose him. Hopefully, once they found their way back to one another, he could explain, and she would understand why he had to leave. As much as he hated to admit it, even in his absence, Jinn would look out for her. She would be safe until he returned.

"So, when do we start?" Adonijah asked after his brother poured him another glass of wine.

"Once this business with Gomorrah has been settled, we will head back to Northwind."

"You two really are idiots, if you think you'll march into Northwind and kill your father."

Pash and Adonijah whipped toward the tent's entrance where Leoti stood with her arms crossed over her chest.

"Who is this?" Adonijah scanned Leoti head to toe and didn't see any weapons on her person. She wasn't a soldier, but she wasn't dressed like a priestess or servant either.

"This is none of your business, Leoti." Pash huffed. He grabbed her by her upper arm and dragged her further into the tent. "How long have you been listening?"

"How angry would you be, if I told you I was listening the entire time?" Leoti flashed a malicious grin.

"What do you want?" Pash closed his eyes and rubbed his fingers over his forehead.

"I want to join you." Leoti sank into the chair Pash had used and stared at Adonijah sitting in the opposite seat. "As much as you hate your father, I hate him more. He is responsible for my husband's death, and I will fight to my last breath to see him suffer."

Adonijah chuckled. "No disrespect to you, but what do you know about killing?"

"I know the taste of having the man I love die in my arms and being helpless to save him." Leoti met Adonijah's gaze and straightened in her seat. "I have been invisible in the White Keep for years. I know passages even the commander here doesn't know about. I am also a warg, and with my magic, I can make sure our path is clear for the journey ahead."

Pash dropped to one knee in front of Leoti. "This will be dangerous. My father is no fool. He is always prepared for someone to try to assassinate him. Your father -"

"Let's not pretend you care about what my father thinks." Leoti cut him off with a hiss. "You have two options," she used the same phrasing Pash did with Adonijah, "either you let me join you, or I go tell Ophir what you're planning and find a way to kill Gershom myself."

Adonijah barked out a laugh. "Oh, I like her."

Pash smirked. "It seems you have me neatly backed into a corner, Leoti."

"Am I in or not?" Leoti leaned closer until her face was inches from Pash's. She wasn't going to back down and the brothers couldn't afford loose ends.

"You're in." Adonijah took his pipe out of his jacket pocket and lit it, blowing a puff of smoke up toward the ceiling folds of the tent.

Pash nodded in agreement. He extended his hand to her, and she rested her hand in his, palm facing up. He quickly sliced across her right palm, and they shook on it. "Now, we just need to plan the perfect murder."

CHAPTER SIXTY-TWO

KAI

Kai hadn't trusted Adonijah the moment she laid eyes on him. Perhaps, it was because he was a rival for Salome's heart or because he was just as comfortable in the darkness as she was, but Adonijah was on her list of people to watch.

When she spotted Adonijah slip into Jacobi's cave, she waited for him to come back out. But when Adonijah and Jacobi emerged from the room and crept to the tunnels, she followed them. She didn't know what the sell-sword was planning, but if the villager was involved, she was determined to find out. Following them against the rocky outskirts of the City of Bones, they easily slipped past the guards who were neglecting their watch. A matter she would absolutely address once she dealt with Adonijah.

Kai knew when they left the city, she should have alerted Jinn, but there wasn't time and she decided it was more important to trail them. She pursued them in the shadows at a safe distance until she caught sight of the villager whimpering behind a cluster of boulders. Occasionally, he popped his head over the rocks, watching someone or something. The sell-sword was nowhere to be seen. She drew two knives from her belt and quietly approached Jacobi.

In a flash, she held a dagger to Jacobi's throat and whispered a warning in his ear. Peering over the boulders, she saw Adonijah standing in a clearing outside the Northern camp, surrounded, with his hands up in surrender.

She muttered a string of curses thinking she would now have to rescue him from being tortured or killed when she spied him turning to face the Commander of Shadows with a smirk.

"Hello, brother," Adonijah said, and it stopped Kai's heart from beating.

The brothers embraced and she watched them wander inside the camp. No shackles or restraints were clamped to Adonijah's body. He walked side by side with Niabi's most trusted sword and disappeared into what she assumed to be Pash's tent.

Another series of expletives poured out of her mouth and her attention refocused to the Shadows in the clearing. They would do a sweep of the area to make sure Adonijah had come alone, meaning she and the villager needed to leave. Now.

Kai gripped Jacobi's upper arm and dragged him away from the boulders. They had to move quickly and quietly, but with the clumsy, exhausted baker in tow, Kai knew it wasn't going to be easy.

She could hear the Shadows beginning their patrol and glared at Jacobi, hoping that would put a pep in his step. But it didn't. She practically carried him back up the mountainside and away from the potential danger of being captured. Once they were a good distance from the Northern camp, Kai let Jacobi take a breather, handing him her flask.

Breathlessly, he nodded his head in gratitude and slurped the contents. "Where are you taking me?"

Kai didn't like talking unless it was necessary, but she also knew this villager wouldn't stop pestering her until he received an answer. "Back."

"Back where?"

Kai rolled her eyes, mentally counting to five so she wouldn't lose her temper. "Back to the City of Bones."

His eyes widened. "Please, I didn't hurt anyone. I didn't want to leave -"

Kai lifted a hand to silence his blubbering. "What were you and Adonijah doing?"

"He asked me to lead him to the camp. He said he wanted to kill the Nameless Rider because he murdered his mother." Jacobi couldn't spit the words out fast enough.

Kai nodded, grabbed her flask from Jacobi, and motioned for him to stand up and follow her. She was right not to trust the sell-sword. But the hard part was going to be telling Salome that the man she loved wasn't her friend.

It was late in the afternoon by the time Kai and Jacobi made it back to the City of Bones and Jinn was waiting for her by the tunneled entrance. He didn't look angry, but he was far from pleased. Once his gaze found Jacobi slinking behind her, his face hardened.

"What is going on?" Jinn asked with a furrowed brow.

"Where is Princess Salome?" Kai asked, wiping the beads of sweat that bubbled around her hairline.

Jinn softened at the mention of Salome but then worry drowned his irritation. "What happened?"

"I think it would be best if I spoke to the princess first, Your Highness." Kai wasn't one to be emotional, but she knew what she was about to tell Salome would be devastating. "It's about Adonijah."

Jinn ordered two Krazak soldiers to put Jacobi in his room and guard him while he walked with Kai to Salome's cave. When they arrived, the curtains were drawn, but they could hear the princess inside.

"Is he...?" Jinn didn't finish with the word *dead*, but Kai knew where his question was leading.

"No," Kai shook her head, "but it would be better news."

Jinn looked like he wanted to go inside with Kai, but he took a few steps back, giving them space to talk. Kai took a deep breath before swooping inside Salome's room. She stood at the entrance and bowed her head.

"Kai?" Salome's face remained neutral, but Kai could see the fear in her eyes. The two of them had never spoken alone before; the princess was right to be leery.

"Princess Salome," Kai met her gaze, "there's something I would like to report."

Salome motioned for the Ryoko Naga to sit with her, so she did. Kai's back was straight and even sitting, she looked deadly.

"What is it, Kai?" Salome asked, offering her a drink which Kai politely declined.

"During my rounds late last night, I noticed Adonijah and the prisoner sneaking out of the city." Kai was going to rush through her story, uncomfortable she had to do this in the first place. "I followed them all the way to the Northern camp. When Adonijah was surrounded by Shadows, I thought I was going to have to rescue him but..."

There were tears welling in Salome's eyes and it honestly pained Kai to finish. "He addressed the Commander of Shadows as his brother and walked with him inside his tent."

Salome didn't say anything. She just stared deep into Kai's eyes, as if she was trying to determine if she was telling the truth.

"I'm sorry." Kai uttered words she hadn't used in years and found she meant them. She never trusted Adonijah, and she never liked him based on her loyalty to Jinn, but she had come to care for Salome as a friend, if she could be as bold to think of herself in that manner.

Salome still hadn't moved, had barely blinked. Tears hadn't streamed down her face, and it struck Kai as odd. Maybe Salome was in shock and her body completely shut down. The princess had been through a whirlwind of emotions in the past week. She had lost her grandmother and her cousin within a day of each other. She had been reunited with her guardian only to be told her brother might be dead. She had declared her love for a sell-sword who swore an oath to protect her, but he turned out to be someone she didn't know at all.

Kai stood to her feet. If she sat there any longer, she would feel like she was intruding. She bowed and made her way to the doorway when Salome finally spoke.

"If he's Pash's brother then that would make him..."

"Gershom's son." Kai cleared her throat, desperate for a drink, but her flask had been drained by that sickly baker.

Salome seemed to snap out of her stupor. She flashed Kai a sad smile and a tear slipped down her cheek. "Thank you," she whispered.

Kai bowed again, knowing she had been dismissed, and marched out. She inhaled a deep breath and Jinn's hands rested on her shoulders as soon as she cleared the cave.

"Are you alright?" Jinn asked and she nodded, straightening to her full height. "What about Salome?"

"She's no longer safe here. We will need to move her as soon as possible." Kai ignored his question. "Adonijah is Pash's brother."

Jinn flinched as if she'd struck him. "His brother?"

Kai nodded in confirmation. "One can only assume that he will divulge the princess' location and we will have a much bigger problem to deal with."

Jinn's gaze darted to the curtains wafting in Salome's doorway. "Tell the others. We will need to make the necessary preparations for our journey to Oakenshire."

Kai bowed and walked away to do as her prince commanded. She still felt an ache in her chest for delivering Salome yet another crushing report, but she knew the princess was strong. She would survive. She had to survive.

Chapter Sixty-Three

Salome

Even though Salome sat quietly in her room, her mind was racing, her soul was screaming, and her heart was breaking. *Adonijah was Gershom's son? How was that even possible?* She thought about the day before, when he said there was something he wanted to tell her. *Was he about to tell her he was Gershom's son?*

Salome soaked the memory of him in. She felt his arms around her, his lips on hers, his eyes filled with passion. She saw him fighting for her, standing by her side. He had sworn an oath to protect her, but he left. He had broken his word and in turn, he had shattered her already fractured heart.

If Zophar hadn't interrupted them, would he have told her about his father?

Would she have accepted him if she knew the truth?

Did it matter if the truth came from his lips or someone else's?

Gershom killed her mother. Gershom killed four of her brothers. Gershom was her sister's Second in Command, and he was Adonijah's father.

What had he expected her to say once he told her? Once she found out?

How could the man she loved be the son of the man she hated?

The man she loved. Loved. She loved him.

When Salome closed her eyes and pictured Adonijah's face, she didn't see the son of the man that murdered those she loved. She saw the man who swore to protect her. She saw the man who equaled her in both wit and skill. She saw the man who knew every truth about her and stayed because he wanted to. She saw the man she *loved*.

But she also saw the man who had ripped her heart apart, even though she was barely hanging on. She saw the man who had so many opportunities to tell her the truth and didn't. She saw the man she thought she knew, but realized she only knew what he wanted her to know.

Salome's head was pounding, and her chest felt like it was imploding. Tears she was sure were emptied from the last couple of nights of grieving for Crispin flowed down her cheeks. She felt like the walls of her cave were closing in on her and for a second, she forgot how to breathe.

She didn't know how it happened, or how long it took her, but she bolted from her room and sprinted past the guards at the tunnel entrance. She didn't stop running until she reached a small clearing in the pine trees. There was a slab of rock that looked like an ancient altar in the center, and she plopped down on it.

How long she wept, she didn't know. But when she heard the crunch of footsteps approaching, she snapped out of her grief, and swiped her knives from the holsters on her thigh and lower back. She hadn't armed herself with anything else before bolting from her room. Her curved Qata Vishna blades and her bow and arrows had been left behind and for a split second she regretted being so careless.

Zophar stepped into the clearing and stood with his hands buried deep in his pockets. "Are you alright?"

Salome shook her head. If there was one person she would allow to see her vulnerable and broken, it was him. "How many more people will I lose, before I just walk away?"

"War is ugly -"

"The war hasn't even begun," Salome interrupted, nostrils flared. "I don't think I can do this anymore, Zophar."

"And if you don't, who will?" he walked toward her and sat beside her on the slab. After a moment of silence, Zophar said, "I had a wife once. And two sons."

Salome's eyes widened. "I... I never knew that."

"No one did." Zophar shrugged with glossy eyes. "When I lost them, I thought there was nothing left for me to live for. I won't lie to you and say things got better because they didn't. Life got harder and my pain lingered. Although my grief and the pain of losing my wife and my sons has never gone away, I have grown stronger in dealing with my loss."

"I'm sorry, Zophar," Salome whispered, slipping her hand into his.

"Your grief will never end," Zophar swiped tears from her face, "but you will become stronger in walking without them."

Salome sucked in a breath, "Did you hear about...?"

Zophar nodded. "I know how much you cared for Adonijah."

She didn't want to talk about Adonijah anymore. "I don't want the crown," Salome spat before she could change her mind. "I don't want the White Throne. I don't want to rule Northwind. I don't want any of it."

"What do you want?" Zophar asked, without a trace of judgment for speaking her truth.

"Sometimes, I wish I was back in the Tree House Forest where things were simpler."

Zophar shook his head gently. "The Tree House Forest, although simple, was a façade. It was never meant to last forever."

"What do you think I should do?" Salome asked, needing his guidance. She hadn't felt so lost before. She was doing everything she had been asked to do and more, but she didn't feel like she was moving forward. She had suffered so many losses. Was it worth it? Was it worth losing everyone she loved and cared for to sit on a throne she didn't even want?

"Get down!" Zophar grabbed her shoulders and pushed her down to the ground, behind the stone altar. An arrow zipped by and then another. They were being attacked.

Salome muttered curses under her breath. Why had she been so reckless in storming out of the City of Bones not properly armed or protected?

"How many are there?" Salome asked, knowing every second they sat, they were probably being surrounded. It could be Shadows sent by Adonijah and his brother. It could be the Thrak still tracking her. It could be another foe she didn't even know about.

Zophar's eyes darted to hers. "I don't know. But if we're going to get you back to safety, we are going to need help. I don't know how to get reinforcements here in time."

"I do." Salome reached for Jinn and felt herself slam into his mind. *"Zophar and I are surrounded. I need your help."*

"Where are you?" He answered immediately.

"In the woods. We're taking cover behind an ancient altar."

Jinn's response was delayed. *"Rune knows where you are. We're coming. Hold on."*

Salome met Zophar's curious gaze; he was looking for an explanation.

"Short story," Salome risked a glance over the slab only to see an whizzing at her and ducked before it pierced her. "I have magic that allows me to communicate with other magic wielders with my mind."

"What?" Zophar choked on the word. "Have you always been able to do that?"

"No," she grabbed the hilts of her daggers tightly. "I promise to explain everything once we get out of here, but we can't sit here any longer. We have to move, or we might not be able to hold out for help."

"You were able to get help?"

"Jinn." She nodded quickly, her mind racing to formulate a plan of escape. They were a good ten feet from the tree line in front of them. They could hide in the forest, but those ten feet might as well have been a hundred feet. The archers had them pinned. "How do we get out of here?"

Zophar shook his head. "I'm afraid our best option is to wait for reinforcements."

But waiting for reinforcements wasn't going to help them, because crunching through the mulch of the woods, were thirty Thrak who appeared in the clearing. They were indeed surrounded and by the worst of her feared opponents.

The bulkiest Thrak stepped forward, sniffing the air with a grin that Salome wanted to peel off his disfigured face. "We've been looking for you for quite some time."

"Did you get my gift?" Salome cocked her head to the side, knowing she had ordered the heads of all the Thrak who had been sent to the Isles of Myr to fetch her, be delivered to Matildys, as a warning.

The Thrak snarled. "They were my brothers."

"And now, they're dead." Salome knew she was riling him up, but she was trying to buy herself some time for Jinn's reinforcements.

The Thrak didn't take the bait. "Bind and gag them both. Our queen will be excited to finally meet you."

Salome spat at the Thrak's feet. As two Thrak approached her with shackles, rope, and white cloth to gag them, Jinn uncloaked himself standing between her and the Thrak. He sliced off both of their heads in one swift movement.

Jinn held his tachi swords out to his sides, "Who's next?"

A roar came from behind the Thrak, and Rune led a group of Krazak warriors into the clearing, armed to the teeth. The sound of metal on metal clashed through the air as the battle for Salome ensued.

Kai sprinted for Salome, leaping over fallen Thrak, and grabbed her arm. The Ryoko Naga pulled Salome to her feet before the princess had a chance to join the fight. "We need to get you out of here."

"But -"

"I have my orders, Princess," Kai interrupted her, dragging her further toward the trees. She wasn't going to let Salome fight and it enraged her.

Salome glanced over her shoulder and saw Jinn slicing through any Thrak that came within three feet of him. Zophar swung his axe with fury and the eyes of a born warrior burned in his skull. Rune and his Krazaks were vicious and were evenly matched with the monstrous Thrak. They even seemed to be enjoying the bloodshed, which should have unnerved Salome, but didn't.

She wanted to fight, but knew Kai was right in getting her back to the City of Bones. She couldn't fight in every battle, and she needed to be smart. As she turned to face Kai, who still had a firm grip on her forearm, Salome spotted the glint of a couple of arrowheads pointed at Kai's back.

"No!" Salome whipped Kai around, her back taking the two arrows meant for the Easterner. She saw the horror flash in Kai's face as Salome sank to the ground. The pain that shot through her body was excruciating. Kai cried out for someone to help her.

Salome's face hit the ground as Kai unsheathed her daggers and prepared for the wave of Thrak headed their way. Salome glanced up at Jinn and saw him fighting his way to get to her. *Fear*. She saw fear in his eyes and right then, she knew he wasn't going to reach her in time.

Several Thrak surrounded Kai and she started cutting them down, refusing to let them take Salome. Zophar jumped into the mix and started slaying men left and right. Blood was splattered across his beard and the mighty Westerner was ready to add to the tally of enemies killed.

Another arrow sliced through the air, piercing Kai in her chest, and a second cut into her thigh. More Thrak appeared and Salome knew they were going to be overrun. Zophar tossed Kai toward the Krazaks where she would be defended, and perhaps saved by Rayma.

Salome extended the bridge to Jinn, feeling herself giving into the pain riddling her back. *"Get Kai out of here."*

"I'm not leaving you!" He shot back, his golden-brown eyes watering. She could hear the love, the fear, the struggle raging in his mind. *"Don't give up, do you hear me?"*

"They're going to take me."

"No, Salome -"

"I should have accepted your proposal when I had the chance."

Salome saw one of the Thrak hit Zophar over the head, knocking him unconscious. As the soldier threw Zophar over his shoulder, she felt massive hands sweep her off the ground and drape her across broad shoulders. The Thrak started running away from the battle with their prize, their mission complete.

"Salome!" Jinn screamed, before everything went black.

Acknowledgements

First and foremost, I want to thank God. Without Him, I would be lost and on a different path.

To my husband and best friend, Brad. Thank you for every bit of encouragement, support, and love you send my way. Without you, I would have given up on my dream years ago.

To my daughter, Remi, thank you for telling me how much you love me. You will never know how much that means to me.

To my son, Archer, thank you for your hugs throughout the day. They are my favorite interruptions.

To my daughter, Roux, thank you for bringing all the sass and smiles. It fueled me.

To my Mom and Dad, thank you for all your love and support. Mom, thank you for encouraging me to read and write from such an early age and for helping me edit my work! Dad, thank you for seeing my talent before I saw it myself.

To my sister, Logan, thank you for playing video games with me whenever I needed a break from work!

To my brother-in-law, Matt, thank you for your friendship, and for believing in my success before I published a single word.

To my friend, Mercedes. Thank you for your past ten years of friendship and for being the godmother to my three children. I love you, girl, and I'm so grateful for our talks.

To my book loving, writing sound board of a friend, Pier! You are an amazing friend, and I appreciate all your encouragement, support, and for being the best hype woman around!

To my author friends, Whitney Dean, Gabbie Delacourt, Jessica S. Taylor, and Brindi Quinn: THANK YOU for your support and encouragement! I appreciate you hyping me up and for listening to me vent and bounce ideas off of you!

To everyone reading this. I appreciate YOU! Thank you for your support and for reading (and hopefully loving) my work. It has been such a dream come true to put all the stories running wild in my head down on paper. I am so excited for you to follow my career and fall in love with the characters who take up all my free time.

Also By Morgan Gauthier

Fantasy:

Wolves of Adalore (2021)

The Red Maiden (2022)

The Raven and the Wolf (2023)

A Song of Shadow and Starlight (2023)

A Ballad of Beasts and Brothers (2024)

Contemporary Romance:

Aloha, Seattle (2021)

The Maine Attraction (2022)

Meet the Author

Morgan Gauthier lives in East Tennessee with her husband and best friend, Brad, and with their three children, Remi, Archer, and Roux (who are 5 years old and younger!). If five people wreaking havoc in the same house wasn't enough, Morgan also has three dogs, Potter, Skye, and Bubba, and one grumpy bird named Titus.

Her first book, *Wolves of Adalore*, was published in 2021 and is the first book in a YA Epic Fantasy Trilogy. The third book, *The Raven and the Wolf*, is due for publication in 2023.

Morgan also published *Aloha, Seattle* in November of 2021. It is her first Contemporary Romantic Comedy and she is planning on writing more in the genre.

If Morgan isn't writing or reading, she can be found binge watching Netflix shows, playing video games attempting to cook like Gordon Ramsay (not even close to his level), and practicing archery.

You can follow her on:

Instagram: @authormorgangauthier
Facebook: @authormorgangauthier
Goodreads/Amazon: Morgan Gauthier
Pinterest: @authormorgangauthier
TikTok: @authormorgangauthier

More N&E Books

Windsong by Stephanie E. Donohue

Life doesn't wait for tears to finish.

Eighteen-year-old Roxana Welhaven has lived her life by this motto. When her mother is diagnosed with terminal cancer, Roxana swallows her tears and vows to do whatever is necessary to save her.

Even if it means making a deal with a talking polar bear.

The bear offers to cure her mother, but only if Roxana lives with him for one year. When she agrees, the bear whisks Roxana through a portal to another world and gives her lavish accommodations in an enchanted castle. Although she's determined to serve her year and return home, the impatient and high-strung Roxana finds her heart drawn to the bear's tranquil nature. He's compassionate, clumsy and utterly adorable.

He's also a cursed man, trapped inside a bear's body.

True love won't be enough to break his enchantment. To save him, Roxana must embark on a treacherous quest to find his captor, a journey that will lead her east of the sun and west of the moon.

www.ingramcontent.com/pod-product-compliance
Lightning Source LLC
Chambersburg PA
CBHW020451310726
48979CB00016B/2602/J

* 9 7 8 1 9 5 8 6 7 3 4 4 7 *